Conzett Verlag

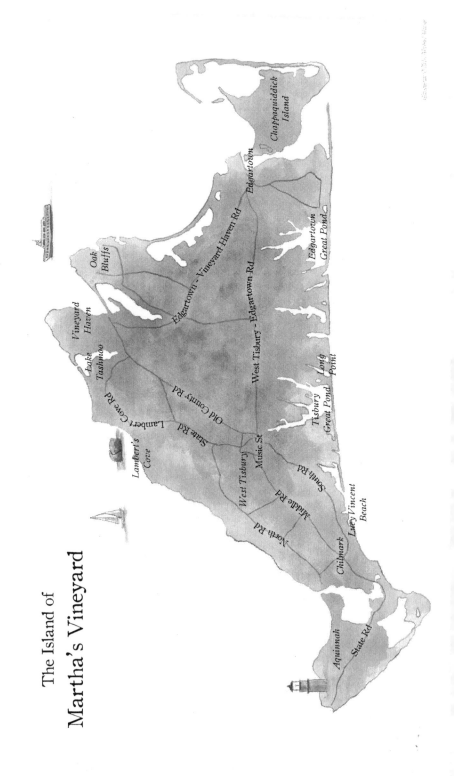

The Island of
Martha's Vineyard

Chappaquiddick Island

Edgartown

Edgartown Great Pond

Oak Bluffs

Edgartown - Vineyard Haven Rd

West Tisbury - Edgartown Rd

Vineyard Haven

Lake Tashmoo

Long Point

Tisbury Great Pond

Lambert's Cove Rd

Old County Rd

State Rd

Lambert's Cove

West Tisbury

Music St

South Rd

Middle Rd

Lucy Vincent Beach

North Rd

Chilmark

Aquinnah

State Rd

Split Rock

A Martha's Vineyard Novel

Holly Hodder Eger

Conzett Verlag
Zurich

First edition published in Zurich, Switzerland, by Conzett Verlag. Second and third editions published in the United States of America by Holly Hodder Eger.

ISBN 978-0-9978351-0-6

Printed in the United States of America.

Book design by Claudia Neuenschwander, Zurich.

Martha's Vineyard map illustration copyright © 2016 by Michael Musser.

Cover photo by Joe Mikos. Author photo by Jeanna Shepard.

A portion of the profits from the sale of this book will be donated to the Vineyard Conservation Society.

Grateful acknowledgment is made for the following:

Extracts from *When We Were Very Young* by A. A. Milne. Text copyright © The Trustees of the Pooh Properties WWWVY 1924, published by Egmont UK Ltd. Used with permission by Egmont and Penguin Random House.

My One And Only Love
Words by Robert Mellin
Music by Guy Wood
© 1952, 1953 (Renewed 1980, 1981) EMI Music Publishing Ltd. and Warock Corp. All rights for EMI Music Publishing Ltd. Controlled and administered by Colgems-EMI Music Inc. All rights reserved. International copyright secured. Used by permission. *Reprinted by permission of Hal Leonard Corporation.*

Golden Moments (James Taylor)
© 1976 Country Road Music
Used by permission. All rights reserved.

For my family

Disobedience

James James
Morrison Morrison
Weatherby George Dupree
Took great
Care of his Mother,
Though he was only three.
James James
Said to his Mother,
"Mother," he said, said he:
"You must never go down to the end of the town,
if you don't go down with me."

James James
Morrison's Mother
Put on a golden gown,
James James
Morrison's Mother
Drove to the end of the town.
James James
Morrison's Mother
Said to herself, said she:
"I can get right down to the end of the town
and be back in time for tea."

King John
Put up a notice,
"LOST or STOLEN or STRAYED!
JAMES JAMES
MORRISON'S MOTHER
SEEMS TO HAVE BEEN MISLAID.

LAST SEEN
WANDERING VAGUELY:
QUITE OF HER OWN ACCORD,
SHE TRIED TO GET DOWN TO THE END
OF THE TOWN—FORTY SHILLINGS
REWARD!"

James James
Morrison Morrison
(Commonly known as Jim)
Told his
Other relations
Not to go blaming him.
James James
Said to his Mother,
"Mother," he said, said he:
"You must never *go down to the end of the town*
without consulting me."

James James
Morrison's Mother
Hasn't been heard of since.
King John
Said he was sorry,
So did the Queen and Prince.
King John
(Somebody told me)
Said to a man he knew:
"If people go down to the end of the town, well,
what can anyone do?"

       —A. A. Milne

1

Sylvan Fell, Maryland, _USA!!!_

Chase was explaining something on the bridge in Paris, but she couldn't make out his words. She pushed him away and with one step dove over the stone side into the river below, barely making a splash. She started swimming, but she wasn't in the Seine because she kept getting tangled in seaweed. She swam underwater through a school of silver minnows toward a sunlit coral reef, violet and turquoise and teeming with rainbow and butterfly fish, and there was Aunt Faye in snorkeling gear, pointing. This must be the South China Sea, off the coast of Bali. Hundreds of seahorses floated by and she reached out to touch one, but now she was back in the fast-flowing Seine. Chase was calling down from the bridge, his arms outstretched, but she couldn't fight the current and got sucked under, and all at once she saw herself in the middle of the Atlantic Ocean, freezing cold, long hair streaming, hands grasping—

"Mommy, Mommy, Mommy …"

Annie pried her sleeping husband's elbow from its firm lock around her body and sat up. Her eyes slowly registered Meg in the dim light from the hall, rosy in her sleeper and dragging her blanket.

"I want to sleep with you, Mommy," her little girl said. "My new bed's too big."

Sunlight peeked through the new Sleeping Beauty curtains in Meg's room, and the long yellow school bus rumbled outside the window. The heavy front door thudded shut, causing the whole house to shake.

Annie opened her eyes, feeling warm and content in Meg's bed, until a voice in her brain reminded her that Aunt Faye was dead. She wondered if one day she might actually make it all the way downstairs before she had to remember. Breathing in the sweet vanilla of Meg's skin, she slid her arm out from under her, somehow managing to get down to the front walk in time to wave to her third-grader, Robbie, on the bus.

Gordon, her husband, was in the kitchen, handsome in his dark blue suit pants and striped silk tie. He was putting Robbie's cereal bowl in the dishwasher, which he'd just emptied. The counter was clear except for a lone mixing bowl whose place he didn't know yet. Slivers of silver glittered in his short-cropped hair in the May morning light.

"Good morning, gorgeous," Gordon said, kissing her and placing a hot cup of coffee in her hands.

"Nice outfit," Annie said, stroking his pressed white sleeve. She was alluding to the day before, when he had deliberately worn his button-down shirt backwards to show the girls, per the suggestion of their daughter Lily's kindergarten teacher, that little children weren't the only ones who sometimes got confused getting dressed. Nobody's perfect—everyone makes mistakes.

Annie watched her husband take a few long strides to open the back door and bring in the gallon-size glass bottles of fresh Maryland milk delivered in the wee hours of the morning.

"I'm meeting with Zhen at eight-thirty. She probably wants me to reprioritize Indonesia, now that their financial system is exploding," Gordon said. "Not sure I have the capacity, with all the stuff I have to fix for the Handover in Hong Kong. I knew 1997 was going to be a headache. Would you mind reading these reviews I wrote, before I pass them on to personnel?"

Whether or not she did mind, he placed three typewritten pages on the kitchen table.

"Can you hand me a pen?" she asked, sitting down, her eyes still a little bleary.

He looked at her.

"From the drawer?" Annie pointed. "Next to the sink?"

Gordon grinned and gently tossed over a red fine-point marker, the kind she'd used in her copy-editing days at her cousin Juliet's publishing house in Boston. With zeal, he began rearranging everything in the refrigerator to make room for the new glass bottles.

"Pretty great to have a milkman," Gordon said. "Nothing like this in Asia, that's for sure."

He was talking more to himself than to her, continuing his own version of their shared attempt to convince themselves they had made the right decision to move back to the States.

Making little marks on his papers, Annie asked herself for the umpteenth time why he couldn't get the hang of the semicolon, especially since she'd explained it to him ad nauseam, but caught herself before she said anything out loud. It probably wouldn't be helpful anyway.

"If I can get home early enough, maybe we can finish raking the backyard and plant some more flowers. And I'd like to move the azalea, which reminds me: I couldn't find your old gardening gloves in the boxes in the garage, so I got you a new pair. Not that you wore the old ones out." He kissed the top of her head.

Annie wrinkled her nose, pretending annoyance at his comment. He loved to dig up plants and move them around for no apparent reason, at least none as far as she could tell.

"Those gloves probably got lost in the move," Gordon said, winking at Lily.

Lily, who was five, was sitting in her little blue chair at her purple table, shading in a Disney coloring book. Like Annie, she was meticulous about coloring within the lines.

Still holding a bottle of milk, Gordon set his strong, square jaw the way he did and gazed out the window at the Bradshaws' yard next door, where the flowers were arranged by color. "Will you look at Gloria's garden? Spectacular."

"Sometimes when I get up with Meg at three in the morning," Annie said, feigning sarcasm, "I spy Gloria out there, raking like a whirling dervish in her short shorts just to stay ahead of you and the venerable Sylvan Fell Garden Club."

Annie wondered whether Gordon noticed that Gloria was, in fact, not so perfect, and bit her lower lip as she rewrote one of his sentences in her tiny cursive. Gloria could certainly be annoying, asking his opinion on all types of climbing roses for their shared fence and batting her eyelashes as if she didn't already know everything there was to know about roses and their particular gardening zone. *Zephirine Drouhin, Stormy Weather, Morning Magic* ...

Annie used to help her college boyfriend Chase St. Clair's mother, Piper, with her roses on Martha's Vineyard—watering, fertilizing, trimming—but didn't feel like getting involved in her husband's current discussion and had elected to keep quiet. Besides, Annie had a feeling Gloria already had her chosen varieties waiting in buckets in her garage.

Even if Gloria's garden *was* straight out of a magazine, her house wasn't, and her children always looked a mess. Not to mention she left dirty dishes in the sink overnight, as Annie saw for herself once when she'd walked her old dog back to her kitchen.

"I don't see why we should spend a lot of money on the garden when we're not even going to be here this summer," Annie said, sipping her coffee. "Well, I guess it will be nice for you, during the weeks." Gordon could spend his evenings endlessly moving plants around.

"I'll be able to bring you a fresh bouquet on the plane when I come up every Friday night."

"I'd like that, although I think they have flowers on Martha's Vineyard." Annie was starting to make so many corrections on his papers he wouldn't be able to read them all. One of them should probably start over.

"By the way," she said, "can you get those summer weekend flights finalized today? And … what d'you think? Should we put an ad in the *Vineyard Gazette* for a babysitter? Or just wait till we get there?" She straightened out her shoulders. "Jeez, my back aches today."

"You'd feel better if you stretched, Annie," Gordon said, a little bossy. "Yesterday you just *took off* on your jog."

Gordon had been a track star at Georgetown and had managed to fit in six marathons, in the United States and Asia, since they'd started having kids, and he was always careful to warm up. But if Annie took as much time as he did, something would inevitably come up and she'd never get out the door. He had no idea how many catastrophes—how many near-death experiences—she intercepted with the kids while he was out stretching and training; how many she intercepted every ordinary day, come to think of it.

This was her job now, after all, so it probably wouldn't do to complain.

Gordon didn't mind being left in charge occasionally, but Annie always worried about the disaster that might await her return. A few Saturdays ago, she'd come home from her first morning off since they'd moved here—she swam at the Sylvan Fell YMCA, then got her hair cut—only to find him building a Lego extravaganza with Robbie, oblivious to where the girls were: alone in the upstairs bathroom playing their own game of beauty parlor and taking turns chopping off each other's hair, the last of Meg's precious baby curls all over the floor.

Incredible, what damage those little paper scissors could do. Meg's bangs were only just now starting to stop spiking up straight.

Annie had hauled them back to her stylist (recommended by Gloria Bradshaw) to see if he could repair the damage, which cost a lot more than hiring a real babysitter would have in the first place. She was furious at Gordon but mostly at herself, for assuming he could handle all three of the kids at once.

When they'd had live-in help in Asia, Annie and Gordon could go out knowing not only that the kids would be safely looked after, but also that their glass-and-marble apartment would be clean and orderly upon their return. They had time to be a couple, not merely tag-team parenting partners, and went on real dates. It had been romantic. Sometimes, Gordon would even step outside the apartment, ring the doorbell, and pretend to be picking her up. Once, he presented her with lavender orchids tied with a ribbon when she answered the door.

Now, Gordon stopped moving long enough to study the open refrigerator, trying to figure out where in his reorganization to perch a bowl of strawberries so it wouldn't break.

"I wish I could take Meg for a long bike ride," Annie said, placing her edits in his briefcase. "But the roads are too narrow around here and everyone drives so fast. I can't wait for the Vineyard, can you? The bike paths, all that swimming."

She knew the bike paths by heart from college summers when she and her old boyfriend Chase used to ride everywhere, rolling from pavement to dirt roads to rocky trails, and doing what they dubbed their West Tisbury triathlon. The wind at their backs, they'd ride from his parents' house at the top of Indian Hill, over to Manaquayak Road and up to Ice House Pond, swim across, run back through the woods to their bikes, and race home like ten-year-olds. Chase always let her catch him on the steep part and win at the end.

Gordon pulled out one of the new glass bottles and replaced it with the strawberries.

"Maybe we should get a kayak," Annie continued. "We could paddle around Chilmark Pond, Squibnocket, Tisbury Great Pond."

"Or a canoe," Gordon said. "More stable."

"Kind of heavy for the Vineyard," Annie said. "Incidentally, I had that drowning dream again." She didn't mention the part about the bridge and Chase. "Aunt Faye was in it."

Ever since two months ago, when Annie had inherited Aunt Faye's Martha's Vineyard house, her old boyfriend seemed to pop up everywhere. She'd thought about Chase St. Clair more in the last few months than in the last fifteen years combined. She'd been too busy to think about him much, really, before this. Hadn't she?

Gordon reached in for a Tupperware container of leftover spaghetti and meatballs.

"Were you planning to eat this for lunch? Think it will be okay if I leave it on the counter for the morning?" He peered into the back of the refrigerator. "You always have weird dreams when we relocate, sweetheart, I don't know why you never remember. Moving is disorienting. Sometimes I wake up on business trips and don't even know what *country* I'm in."

He stood back, satisfied at last with his handiwork. "We should probably find a second-hand fridge for the basement, Annie, or else order less milk."

She admired his reorganization and wrapped her arms around his waist. "You should have been an engineer, Gordon. You're wasting your talents toiling in the developing world." Reaching up to kiss him, she traced her finger along his jaw. She loved the shape of his face.

He laughed, the corners of his warm brown eyes crinkling up in that inviting way. "I guess we might as well wait until we remodel the kitchen, and get a bigger fridge then."

Gordon closed the refrigerator and nodded toward the honey-do list stuck there with a "Bloom where you're planted" magnet. "I fixed the cellar window for you this morning, by the way. You can cross that one off." He charged up the back stairs two at a time to get his suit jacket.

"Don't forget to hug the little girls before you go," Annie

called after him. "Lily cried for five minutes yesterday because she didn't get to say goodbye."

Lily had finished with the coloring book and drawn a picture for Gordon, which she handed to Annie. It was a heart shaded in with strips of color in the order of the rainbow, and on the bottom it said "I LOVE YOU DADDY." The "L" and the first "D" were backwards, but otherwise the letters were perfect.

"Wow," Annie said. "How did you know how to write that?"

"Mrs. Balzac." Lily pronounced her teacher's name *Ballth-thwack*.

Mrs. Balzac was endlessly perky and, to herself, Annie sometimes referred to her as Mrs. Ball of Wax. But, well, yes. The teachers and schools here in Maryland *were* better than the ones they'd left in Asia, and it *was* smart of them to have moved.

"It's beautiful, Lily. Run and give it to Daddy."

Annie poured more coffee for herself, noticing a red cardinal studying her from a tree branch outside again. He had been here the past few days. She opened the window over the sink a crack and, holding her warm cup against her cheek, watched him puff up his chest and prepare to sing for her. Annie had grown up in New England, where northern cardinals are the archetypal songbirds, and in Asia she'd missed their sunny songs. She loved their warbling trills, the way their notes slurred as they swept upward. They sounded like summer.

It had been nice to see Aunt Faye in her dream, snorkeling. Faye had loved anything outdoors. For her seventieth birthday, she'd invited Annie to jump with her off the famous bridge on Martha's Vineyard where a scene in the movie *Jaws* had been filmed. So, on a hot, cloudless day, they'd ridden bikes from Edgartown along the Beach Road wearing bathing suits under their clothes, parked on the sandy shoulder, stripped down heedless of the cars passing by, and climbed onto the rickety wooden bridge.

"This is a crazy Vineyard ritual, isn't it?" Aunt Faye had grinned, patting the top of the sign that said "No Jumping or Diving from

Bridge." She had placed a slender foot on the first wooden railing and remarked over her shoulder, "Never let your life be dictated by someone else's arbitrary rules, Annie dear." Aunt Faye's skin, like her hair in those days before she quit coloring it, was the color of caramels and always seemed to have a slightly auburn glow.

Aunt Faye had climbed up the four railings by herself, holding Annie's hand for only a split second, to stand upright on the top. Annie had climbed up beside her and they'd admired the view of the water and the sailboats, holding hands. "Ready, steady ..." Aunt Faye called, until together they jumped off the bridge into the current below, rushing from Nantucket Sound into Lake Sengekontacket. People lining both sides of the inlet cheered. Faye and Annie couldn't stop laughing as they swam to shore and climbed out over the rocks, got back on their bikes, and rode back to Edgartown.

Annie studied a photo taken of her aunt on her eightieth birthday beaming, holding her new puppy on the back deck of the house Faye had, amazingly, bequeathed to Annie on Martha's Vineyard; Annie could see the hammock in the background hanging from the beetlebung trees. Aunt Faye's picture was in the center of the refrigerator door, surrounded by photos of Robbie, Lily, and Meg (sweating in the humidity) atop an elephant at the Singapore Zoo before they moved to Hong Kong last summer; with her parents (sitting up straight) on the Swan Boats in the Boston Public Garden; with Gordon's father and his third wife (posing awkwardly) in front of the California State Capitol in Sacramento; on a picnic with just the five of them (happy).

Last week, one of Lily's kindergarten friends had informed her, "Mrs. Tucker, your fridge-a-rator is *very* messy." But Annie liked it that way. It was a comforting contrast to the pressure she felt to keep her house so tidy.

Among the slew of photographs and magnets was an envelope addressed to Annie in *Sylvan Fell, Maryland, USA!!!* by her mother,

Adair, uncharacteristically emotive, showing her relief and enthusiasm that they had moved back "home."

Ironic that as soon as the Tuckers settled back in the United States, her parents disappeared to New Zealand to stay with her brother, Percy.

Gordon's honey-do list, on the refrigerator next to Adair's envelope, was like the one Aunt Faye used to keep for her first and second husbands, both putterers like Gordon. Annie was careful to write *Please* at the top and *Thank you!* at the bottom the way Aunt Faye had, so as not to come across as too much of a nag.

Annie hadn't actually known Gordon was a putterer, because this was the first house they had owned. In San Francisco and Asia they'd lived in rented apartments, and when something needed fixing, all Annie had to do was call the superintendent. Gordon told Annie recently that her to-do list was a lot more superficial than the one he kept running in his head. Hers was for easy tasks—*fix Robbie's window, adjust water heater*—while his tended to concern deeper structural issues of which she was apparently unaware, like designing a whole new kitchen.

All her life, Annie had loved to make lists. When she was growing up, she constantly kept one for her own self-improvement: *Do math homework first. Lose five pounds. Try harder on serve and volley.* No doubt she should create one now, although the thousands of things to work on could probably fall under one simple umbrella ambition: *Keep up.*

Gordon, now carrying Lily piggyback through the kitchen to the foyer, deposited her in the small TV room, originally designed as a parlor in which to greet guests, and opened the front door to gauge the temperature outside.

Annie put down her coffee and followed them.

"I think I'll install one of those indoor/outdoor thermometers," he remarked, pulling Annie toward him just as three-year-old Meg appeared at their feet, grinning and dragging her pink blanket. She was already sporting the sparkly dress-up tiara she'd taken to wearing lately.

"Good morning, princess," Gordon said, stepping back to scoop her up. "Daddy has to go to work now. You have a fun day and when I come home, I'll push you on the swing."

Meg sucked her thumb with her blanket and snuggled into his shoulder. Gordon hugged her until she let go and padded off to find her sister. He always waited for the other person to let go first.

The light was bright and yellow from the azaleas, just blooming, and the air brimmed with birdsong and the smell of fertile, wet earth. The majestic trees lining their street were in full green leaf, and the delicate cherry and dogwood trees blossomed pink and white. Annie had forgotten how exquisite spring mornings were on the East Coast. Energetic housewives marched briskly along the sidewalk, lifting their hand weights up and down.

"Let's see, where was I?"

Gordon wrapped his right arm around her and pulled her close in a quick two-step, humming a few bars of his favorite Frank Sinatra song. He bent down to give her a long kiss goodbye and, pressing her closer, managed to slide a hand through the folds of her robe to cup her bare breasts through her nightgown. Really quite astonishing, after so many years, especially considering she hadn't even brushed her teeth yet.

This two-step was all the dancing Gordon ever did. It was Chase who had been the dancer, and he and Annie had been known as quite the pair. "What d'you say we cut up this floor and show how it's done?" Chase would propose, taking her hand. People would stop to admire them, sometimes backing up in a wide circle to give them more space.

Chase and Annie had loved all kinds of dancing: salsa to the Caribbean steel drums that played sometimes on the Vineyard in Menemsha; swing dancing at the starlight party Skip St. Clair threw for his wife Piper's fiftieth on their lawn above Vineyard

Sound; rock and roll at college. Acknowledging Annie's irrepressible tendency to lead, Chase always kept his right hand, fingers splayed, pressed firmly against her back. "This way I won't step on your toes and you'll know when to twirl," he'd say. Dancing with him had been like dancing in a fairy tale: her feet scarcely touched the ground.

Gordon, on the other hand, invariably had a sore knee or pulled hamstring or some other running ailment that made him want to sit down as soon as possible whenever there was dancing.

Her husband's sexy goodbye usually made her tingle, but Annie felt self-conscious today, worried the marching housewives might see them and be shocked at this racy family who'd just moved in from Asia. Gordon adjusted himself, as he tended to do after even the quickest kiss, and picked up his briefcase.

Annie swung the girls up, one onto each hip, and stood in the wide doorway before the glassed-in porch that ran the length of their new, run-down Victorian.

She watched Gordon square his shoulders toward the driveway, focusing on his day ahead, and back out his car. Waving at them as he pulled down the street, he reached for his new car phone on the dashboard.

She wondered how he could stand to leave them.

2

On the Rebound

It was always interesting, after this cozy morning ritual, to see how long before the two girls would fight. Annie carried them back to the kitchen, turned *Sesame Street* on the little television she'd bought at a yard sale, and poured some cereal for each of them.

"She has more than me!" Lily whined, standing up in her chair to peer into Meg's bowl.

"I can't see Oscar!" Meg cried. "Lily's in the way. Get out of the way! Stupid butthead."

"You *baby*. Mommy, don't you think Meg is a B-A-B-Y?"

"Sit down in your chair, please, Lily."

A big 5 appeared on the screen, and Lily beamed. "That's *me*," she crowed. "Five five five FIVE!"

Meg held her cereal spoon suspended in midair. "I *hate* the letter five," she muttered to herself. "I *only* like the letter three-and-a-half."

Lily shook her head at her sister with despair, and Annie made a mental note to spend more time on Meg's counting and alphabet books and a little less time reading her fairy tales.

"Today is show-and-tell, Lily, and it's the letter E," Annie said brightly. "Did you decide to take Babar or your stuffed elephant from the Singapore Zoo?"

"Everybody is going to take elephants. I want to bring an *eraser*."

"Good idea," Annie said, getting one from the drawer of her neat kitchen desk and enjoying a stab of pleasure at her excellent organization. It had taken her a long time to unpack and arrange this kitchen.

As the girls ate their cereal, Annie climbed up to the third floor to start what she wryly referred to as her morning rounds, not exactly like the ones Louise, her college roommate the surgeon, was probably making at this minute at the New York City Hospital. The coffee had taken hold and her back didn't hurt anymore; it had to be the middle-of-the-night moves into Meg's room. "Musical beds," Gordon called it.

Or maybe it was because she was forever moving furniture around by herself to see how another configuration looked, because she wanted everything to look just right. Both her mother and the home-furnishing magazines she'd worked at had drilled into her that nothing should stand out in a room, everything should appear harmoniously "of a piece." Nothing should be noticed.

Annie was embarrassed at how many times she'd lugged the two heavy, Javanese-carved sofa tables across the whole downstairs only to lug them back again a few hours later. Not to mention how much time she'd wasted determining the best alignment of sofa pillows, or which Japanese silk *obi* table runner looked best where.

All she wanted was to see how their new house looked unpacked. But the fact was, with the old wallpaper, horrendous carpeting, and outdated bathrooms and kitchen in this place, she could only do so much. She knew she'd slipped into the pitfall of what expatriates in Asia refer to as "*amah* syndrome" and gotten too used to things being perfectly tidy, but she couldn't help it.

Gordon may love to move, but the chaos of unpacking—boxes, packing paper, piles of stuff everywhere—made Annie want to jump out of her skin. That's why she kept everything so neat: when it was messy, it reminded her of the pandemonium of moving in. She wanted to have everything put away so she could start her life.

Yet ... maybe it was a natural law that everything never *was* put away. Maybe, like children growing, all aspects of life were untidy, complicated works in progress, and her trying to keep everything orderly was simply an excuse to postpone starting.

She worked her way now around the central stairwell with a white plastic laundry basket, gathering up yesterday's dirty clothes and trash. Luckily, she was quick at making the beds, thanks to two college summers working at the Edgartown Inn on Martha's Vineyard as a chambermaid. Chase had manned the front desk, and at five o'clock they'd take off swimming in the ocean at Katama or Long Point. Afterwards, they'd stretch out sleek and long on the gold sand, tanned and blond from the salt water.

It was apparently impossible for her to think about Martha's Vineyard without also thinking about Chase St. Clair, and vice versa.

Annie put away toys as she went but bypassed, as usual, the large floor in Robbie's room, covered with a thousand pieces of Legos in various stages of construction. She and Gordon had an ongoing quarrel about whether Robbie should have to pick them up at night, with Annie maintaining he deserved uninterrupted, creative space. (What she wouldn't do for that herself!) She still regretted having to make him dismantle the elaborate city he'd been building when they'd had to pack up in such a hurry from Hong Kong.

Gordon complained she was setting a double standard, since she made the girls pick up their toys every night—most of which were baby dolls, Barbies, and an infinite number of pastel-colored accessories. (She had tried to get them to play with trucks, to no avail.) But the thing about Barbies, Annie tried to explain, was that you might as well pick them up because you started a new game each day anyhow. Part of the fun was that you constantly got to choose a brand-new identity: one day you could be teacher Barbie, the next day lawyer, the next day astronaut Barbie. It was actually satisfying to put everything away at night because you knew that tomorrow you got to be someone different. No interruptions or complicated combinations. Nothing like real life.

Robbie had stormed around for a few days after the Hong Kong movers packed up their apartment, but as soon as the Sylvan Fell movers unpacked them here he'd begun reconstructing his Lego city, block by block. He hadn't lost any pieces. Meanwhile the girls' Barbies, for some reason, lost a lot of shoes, and they had to settle for dressing them in mismatched high heels—not that they minded.

The children didn't seem to leave parts of themselves behind with every move. Oh, they lost bits here and there, perhaps. But Annie seemed to have misplaced big chunks.

What was that terrible dream about, and why did she keep having it? The current kept getting swifter, Chase's hands kept getting nearer, and she could never manage to keep her head up.

Each time they moved, she thought, putting some picture books back on a shelf, Gordon advanced a rung up the career ladder and she got sent back to the mailroom. Square one. And somewhere along the way, the real Annie, the Annie she thought of as *herself*, had been forgotten, buried at the bottom of a discarded packing box.

She carried her basket down to the basement and started the laundry.

They'd lived in Singapore for two years and Hong Kong a mere five months; the new drapes she'd fretted over had only just been installed when the Foundation informed Gordon he was needed in Washington immediately. It had been fun to live in Hong Kong a second time, on a bigger budget, its perpetual buzz particularly invigorating after rule-abiding Singapore. What was different in the mid-1990s, though, was the ambivalent disconnect between optimism on the part of Chinese locals and anxiety on the part of expats as everyone anticipated the Handover and independence from Britain. No one knew what to expect, and now Annie and Gordon wouldn't be there to find out.

All those pains of finding the best schools and teachers, the perfect places to shop—for nothing! She'd met a few women at the Hong Kong International School whom she thought might be her friends, but they hadn't even had time for a farewell lunch.

Gordon had received a few calls lately about a private-sector job in San Francisco, the only place she considered worth moving to again. (As if she had a say!) She missed the salubrious fog, her job at the magazine on Montgomery Street, the ubiquitous smell of coffee roasting, her interesting friends, and most of all, the children: Robbie's nursery-school friends were growing up and she was missing it.

Living there—especially when she was pregnant with Robbie and when, looking back, they didn't have much in the way of responsibilities—had been the most special time of her life. Gordon's, too. Annie often thought of one night, not long after they'd moved there, when they'd climbed back up Union Street to their tiny apartment after a romantic Italian dinner at a restaurant on Hyde and, just as they crossed Jones at the peak of the hill, heard the cable car crossing below, its bell clanging through the fog. Gordon had swung her into his arms and kissed her long and hard, smack dab in the middle of the street.

What would it be like to live in one place your whole married life—to be, say, her cousin Juliet, whose book group had begun as a mommy group twenty years ago? She would get invited to a lot of weddings, and be one of those people who could say she'd known the bride since she was a toddler.

Maybe it was a quirk of her particular personality, Annie thought, sorting clothes, that kept her feeling she was on the outside. Maybe it had nothing to do with moving. Chase had always been on the *inside*, acting like he owned the place, no matter where he was. At his family's property on Martha's Vineyard, you could see it when he'd throw a Frisbee, the way his arm swept across the lawn to embrace the whole of Vineyard Sound.

Annie herself had spent many summers on the Island, both as Aunt Faye's niece and as Chase St. Clair's girlfriend, and was probably entitled to feel more ownership than she did. Yet... she didn't. Come to think of it, there was no place where she felt she truly belonged.

Gordon was forever excited about what might lie around the next corner—or country, more like. (Or continent!) He was the opposite of Chase, who had grown up in Dover, Massachusetts, next to Annie's hometown of Wellesley, and used to say he had no intention of ever living beyond the Northeast. In college at Brown, he hadn't even wanted to take his junior spring semester abroad in France and did so only because his father practically pushed him onto the plane.

Gordon preferred living and working in countries to merely visiting them, and had a strange abhorrence of looking like a tourist: he was so self-conscious about fitting in that, when they explored someplace new, he refused to carry a map. Instead, he would memorize where they were going before they set out. And set out Gordon and Annie did: in all the places they had lived, before they owned their own house and he'd started puttering, they had explored someplace new every weekend.

Chase had returned from his semester abroad confidently speaking French with a Massachusetts accent.

Funny that Annie, and now her brother, Percy, were living such international lives. With the exception of one daring great-grandmother, there had been no adventurers in their family, at least not recently. In fact, the sum total of her parents' international travel, before this mysterious extended visit they were currently on in New Zealand, was when Annie was twelve and they'd toured "the British Isles," as they referred to them, and repeatedly exclaimed that everything reminded them of Vermont—which, now that Annie thought of it, probably made them feel more broad-minded than if they'd had only the villages and hills of

Massachusetts as points of comparison.

Now, Annie pulled the clean shirts and pants out of the dryer, smoothing them against her body so she wouldn't have to iron, and headed back up the cellar stairs with her basket.

Some of her college friends, according to her roommate Louise, thought she had married Gordon on the rebound from Chase. (She was, in a weird way, on the rebound now, from all this moving.) But so what if she had? Gordon had fallen in love with her, appreciated her, taken her on a picnic and proposed on one knee—he wanted to whisk her off to the exotic-sounding Far East because, he said, he didn't want to live a single day without her. He was five years older, very organized, ready to settle down. He had, quite literally, swept her off her feet and she, in turn, had fallen so in love that she used to want to climb right inside him.

Their little daughters were still watching *Sesame Street*.

Putting down her laundry basket in the dining room, Annie drew out a dust cloth and quickly ran it across the enormous Indonesian table they'd bought in Singapore. Even with the extra leaves tucked underneath, it was about three feet too long for the room because, along with the *lemari* stuffed in the corner stacked with their wedding dishes, it was designed for a high-ceilinged Asian house, not a suburban American one. She couldn't resist polishing it because it seemed to acquire a more lustrous sheen, the way a marriage was supposed to, every single day.

She and Gordon had commissioned the table in Singapore from a shop on Tanglin Road. Gordon, wearing Meg in a baby pack that day, had done a quick calculation to determine how long the table should be and how many chairs to order. His eyes had gazed ahead the way they did whenever he pondered something and he'd asked Annie, in a faraway voice, "How many children do you think each of our children will have? If we count spouses and grandchildren, do you think fourteen chairs is enough?" She had been so overcome at this thought, she could only nod in agreement. "Let's get a couple extra in case we have to squeeze around," Gordon told the shopkeeper. "Make it sixteen."

In the kitchen, Annie could still hear the call of the red cardinal. He had settled on the deck railing outside the back door, just as he had the past few mornings.

Taking Lily and Meg's dishes to the sink, Annie handed them both what was left of their toast. The girls went outside and broke the crusts into small bits the way she had shown them, and she added *Set up bird feeder* to Gordon's list. She turned off the television, switched on the new CD player, and started making a snack for Lily to take to kindergarten.

James Taylor's unmistakably reedy, vulnerable-sounding voice came on. But instead of one of the classic old albums from the 1970s, all of which reminded Annie of Aunt Faye and Chase and Martha's Vineyard, and which she had been buying at the record store lately as soon as they became reissued on compact disc, it was his new one, called *Hourglass*. Gordon had left it in her car with a note on the steering wheel. (He'd filled up the gas tank for her that day, too.)

Heard on the radio that JT wrote this while he was grieving his father and a close friend. Hope it helps. I love you more than you know.

The cardinal was still standing on the railing, waiting for them, when they left for school.

"This bird is the old lady you love, Mommy. The one who died," Meg said, blinking in the sunlight.

Annie studied the cardinal who, undeterred by their commotion, gazed back.

"Do you think so, Mommy?" Lily asked. "Is this bird Aunt Faye?"

"Aunt Faye is in Heaven," Annie said, locking the back door.

The cardinal darted up to the roof ledge and, not taking his eyes off them, launched into a supportive whistling call that sounded a lot like "*cheer, cheer, cheer.*"

3

Perfectly, Happily

The day took on a life of its own once Annie got out of the house, as it tended to do. Really, she was not cut out for domestic work: simply pulling out of the driveway was like downing a double shot of espresso. She should probably be polishing her résumé instead of that dining table, but—she glanced in the rearview mirror at her daughters, sublime even with their unfortunate haircuts, Lily's blond head now resting against Meg's dark one—how could she miss this?

They would most likely move again next year. Not much point in pursuing anything new.

Annie's mother, Adair, was constantly urging her to go back to work. But, as usual holding an opposite point of view, Aunt Faye had urged her to wait, and often reminded her that these years with young children would probably be her happiest, most magical, and most fleeting; that the years would pass more quickly than the days. Aunt Faye had lost her only child when he was still in college, and she often remarked that she was grateful she had savored the time she'd had with him ... and that if she'd known what was to come, she would have savored it even more.

Annie knew that if she stopped long enough to consider all this, she wouldn't be able to stand it.

The sky was the same blue as the ocean on a sunny day, and the bucolic road to the combined nursery school/kindergarten was bursting with color.

At this morning's drop-off, the thirty-something Mrs. Balzac greeted them. She was wearing a fuchsia spring coat, her blond hair brushed back under a matching headband. Unbuckling Lily from her car seat, she winked at Meg. "See *you* at school tomorrow!"

"See *you* at pickup time, Lily! I love you!" called Annie, trying to mimic the enthusiasm in Mrs. Balzac's voice.

"Okay," Lily said, yanking her little backpack from under Meg's legs. "But Mommy? Please can you remember not to be last in line again today?"

Annie had memorized the directions to their next stop, a lighting store Gloria Bradshaw had recommended—not because she was worried about looking like a tourist, but because she still had to focus on driving on the right, as opposed to the left, side of the road. The other day, coming home from the Acme with the back of the station wagon overflowing with groceries, the girls started fighting and Annie had turned a sharp left into the left lane, missing an oncoming car by inches. The driver of the car had honked and stared at her in such abject terror, as if she had just been released from the loony bin, that Annie needed to pull over to collect herself. Lily and Meg had stopped swatting each other and begun to cry.

Even with a manual transmission car, Annie had easily mastered driving on the left in both Singapore and Hong Kong, the two former British colonies they'd lived in. But she had first learned to drive in America, on the right! Why was it so difficult now to remember that she, as driver, needed, as Gordon so often reminded her, to hug the middle? "Just keep your left shoulder along the dividing line," he said. The problem was, there was not always a dividing line.

Driving had made Annie slightly nervous ever since her cousin Emmett, Aunt Faye's only child, had died in a car crash when he was twenty-one. Annie and her two cousins, Emmett and Juliet, had grown up together, in Wellesley and on Martha's Vineyard, thanks to Aunt Faye's remarkable generosity and her often-vocalized regret about not having a daughter. Annie's brother, Percy, had never been part of this cousin triumvirate because all he wanted to do was hang out at the country club and play golf.

In her will, Aunt Faye left everything she had to her three surviving heirs: her Martha's Vineyard house to Annie, her turn-of-the-century New England Colonial in Wellesley to Juliet, and some cash and stocks to Percy, who hadn't even bothered to fly back from New Zealand for the funeral—although his first wife, Kathleen, had taken a day off work, driven out from Harvard Square, and kept things running during the reception in the church hall, refilling wine glasses and platters of cucumber sandwiches.

Annie's cousin Juliet, executor of Aunt Faye's estate, already had her own Colonial on the other side of Route 9 and was preparing Faye's house to sell while also taking care of the three-year-old Labrador retriever she'd left behind. Annie should probably offer to help more, but it was a seven-hour drive up to Massachusetts, and she didn't exactly have a lot of her own help. She made a note to call Juliet, and also Kathleen, when she got home.

Juliet didn't love Martha's Vineyard the way Annie had, forever complaining about Cape traffic and being beholden to the ferry schedule. An island, to Juliet, was more trouble than it was worth, and as soon as she got married she'd begun spending summers in Kennebunk, Maine, where her husband, Lonny, had summered with his family.

Annie got a little lost finding the lighting store but eventually pulled up in front of it. In her mind she could hear Aunt Faye, who rarely compared her nieces, say, "Juliet simply doesn't *get* the Vineyard. But *you* do, my dear. *You* do."

Carrying Meg on one hip, Annie balanced the broken lamp on the other. A woman wearing a Baltimore Orioles cap was ahead of them in line. She had that familiar shade of dyed blond hair a lot of the women in Sylvan Fell had, cut in the same shoulder-length blunt style. Annie felt self-conscious and wondered if she was supposed to chop off and color her sandy-brown hair, rather than just keeping it the same as it had always been.

What was it with the baseball caps around here, anyhow? Was that some fad that had surfaced while they were abroad? Annie didn't like to judge, but they looked ridiculous.

It is simpler for Americans to move between countries than states, she thought, noticing that the young salesman and the woman in the baseball cap had the same Baltimore accent. People don't consider enough before they relocate. They don't realize how drastically different each state is, or that they will never truly fit into the local culture despite everyone pretty much looking the same and speaking English. That's, in fact, what makes it harder: you can't spot other displaced newcomers the way you can, say, a white American expat in Asia. And being able to spot each other, not to mention *be spotted*, is comforting. It helps you from feeling invisible.

"The problem here is that you don't even have the adventure aspect to compensate for the loneliness," Annie whispered to Meg, who nodded sympathetically.

Next to the store—the lamp would be ready in two weeks— was a fancy home-accessories shop, definitely out of their price range. But feeling disoriented and not wanting to turn right around, Annie decided to browse through the silver candlesticks and extraneous bric-a-brac. These were the kinds of furnishings her magazines in San Francisco and Shanghai had featured.

Her eyes fell on an almond-colored brocade pillow almost hidden by a medley of royal purple and burgundy shams and bolsters. *Perfectly, happily ever after* was stitched on it, in gold calligraphy. She visualized it on her and Gordon's bed and read the words aloud to Meg, who nodded approvingly.

It was expensive for a pillow, but she brought it over to the elderly man at the cash register. He stood, in a plaid jacket and striped bowtie, writing in an old-fashioned ledger with his right hand and typing on an adding machine with his left. He examined her up and down, and Annie wondered if maybe he thought she looked too frumpy to be in his shop.

"I was wondering who would buy this," he said, wrapping the pillow in tissue. "Don't abide the silly sentiment. Nothing is that simplistic, nothing lasts forever, and nothing sure as hell is perfect. Not marriages, not pillows." He handed her the bag. "Final sale."

Now, of course, they were late. Annie headed back toward Sylvan Fell to the Acme and, pushing Meg in the grocery cart, had to hurry up and down the aisles to make it back to Lily's school in time for pickup. She couldn't find her shopping list, couldn't remember all the ingredients for the Indonesian dish she was planning to make for dinner, couldn't find her way around the store either. She suddenly felt very tired. A cheerful, older woman in the frozen-food aisle looked like Aunt Faye, which was probably what caused her to well up with tears when the checkout lady asked how she was.

Sometimes, lately, Annie didn't always remember where she was living; she'd been surprised to see that woman in the lighting store wearing a Baltimore Orioles cap, because she seemed to have temporarily forgotten she was living in Maryland and almost thought she still lived in Boston. Or San Francisco. Or Shanghai or Singapore or Hong Kong. It was confusing, she thought, as she arrived back at nursery school. She couldn't get her bearings. Her attachment to all of these different people, cities, and places around the world made her feel so … crowded.

That night—after raking the yard, supervising homework and baths, and improvising a kind of curry for supper that tasted like Chinese meets Indonesian meets Maryland, pretty much as mixed-up as she felt—Annie was in bed with Robbie's third-grade required reading. One of her parenting books said that it helps communication, particularly with boys, if you try to keep up with what they're reading at school.

Enjoying the cool feel of the new sheets her mother had sent as a housewarming present, she was still ruminating about how she would manage the summer not knowing anyone, with Aunt Faye not there and Gordon only on weekends. She couldn't remember ever having been on Martha's Vineyard without Aunt Faye to anchor her. Or Chase.

Would Chase be there?

Were she and Gordon crazy to be doing this commuting thing? Her mother had written that she thought this plan was "unrealistic" and they should reconsider.

It wasn't as if she and Gordon *liked* to be separated: in future summers they assumed they would rent out the Vineyard house for July, enroll the kids in a day camp or something here in Sylvan Fell (assuming they still lived here), and spend August together on the Island like other families. Only this year, since they didn't know anyone to speak of in Maryland and the prospect of living in their new house on Middle Road was so alluring, they decided she and the kids would live up there both months and return in September to start the school year fresh.

After speaking with her now *ex*-sister-in-law, Kathleen, and her cousin Juliet on the phone this afternoon, Annie had a hunch that they, and maybe her mother, suspected she craved some peace and quiet away from Gordon. Obviously, no one brought up the possibility of her running into Chase; they probably assumed, reasonably, that she was over him by now (which, of course, she was). And it wasn't as if she and her husband weren't still madly in love. It was just that Gordon could get a little, well, *tiring*, and it was understandable that she might appreciate a weekly, predictable break from his perpetual motion. It could be nice. Restful.

Suddenly Gordon, still wearing his gardening clothes, bounded into the bedroom in that Road-Runner way he had, lugging one of his new tools, a particularly large one. He was like the Energizer bunny! She had become so inured to his projects she didn't even bother to look up when he foraged around, noisily, for an electric outlet. She heard a loud whirring noise. He had the window wide open and was trying to balance whatever this awkward round machine was on the sill.

"I'm going to sand this window frame so it will close better!" he shouted, knocking her out of her reverie. And then, "*Hello, Franklin!*" to Gloria Bradshaw's husband, who happened to be walking their dog down the middle of the street.

"It's nearly eleven, Gordon," Annie said calmly, knowing he couldn't hear. "The neighbors are going to think you're insane." She got up to wash her face. He yelled something else she couldn't hear over the sound of the sander and the running water. He turned off the machine precisely as she turned off the water, and shouted again so exuberantly she thought surely the whole town must have heard him.

"Tomorrow I'll put a weather strip along this window so it won't be so drafty in here!"

This old house was one big disaster. There was no way it would ever be finished! Would they never get to be a normal couple? People who invited friends over and watched television and got to read books all the way to the end?

"I called my father today!" Gordon was still shouting. "His birthday! He didn't even know we'd moved back to the US!"

Annie had forgotten to send a card. Oh, well. Not like he'd even once sent anything to them or the kids.

Was she supposed to have married Chase? (*His* family loved her! Hadn't Mrs. St. Clair continued sending birthday cards for a few years even after she'd married Gordon?) Or was she supposed to have married someone else altogether, whom she never got to meet?

Gordon clambered into bed beside her and started vigorously flossing, pausing only to fill in blocks of the crossword puzzle in the *Washington Post*. Annie tried to ignore the flossing. This summer, she would have to put up with it only on weekends.

"What's a seven-letter word for armor that begins with *p*, ends with *y*?"

Panoply, she thought to herself, hoping maybe if she didn't respond he'd leave her alone to read Robbie's book. Why did everyone feel they could interrupt her all the time?

"You know, Annie, I forgot to mention: your to-do list is getting pretty long with simple things you could fix yourself. You already know the difference between a slot-head and a Phillips-head screwdriver. Do you know what an Allen wrench is? What if I showed you how to fix that back door? Then you could also fix the back gate. Same principle."

Plodding around with a toolbox was just about the last thing she wanted to do. "That's okay," she murmured, her eyes on her book. "No rush."

"I'm just saying, if you did some of the simpler things, I'd have more time to fix these big problems, like the fact that all the windows in this house leak."

"Hmm."

He shrugged and resumed his flossing, and she turned the page.

During the beginning of her sophomore year at Brown, Annie had been dating a tall rower named Brent, or Brendan or, oh, what was his name? They had been at a party when Brandon—right, that was it—went to get them drinks and Chase had elbowed his way over to introduce himself because someone had mentioned she also went to the Vineyard. She was so struck by how handsome he was that for months after couldn't understand how she had not noticed him freshman year. Brandon, returning with the drinks, steered her across the room, and when she glanced back at Chase through the sea of people, he was holding one hand up to his ear with a pretend telephone, implying he would call her, and tugging at a dog's imaginary choke collar around his neck with the other.

This was how she felt sometimes with Gordon: that the leash was too tight.

She skipped to the end of the chapter.

"This is an odd one," Gordon mused, his flossing emitting a light spray over the puzzle. "What are the names of your fingers? Pinkie, ring, middle …"

She sighed and, putting down Robbie's book, shimmied over to look. She wiped his saliva off the newspaper with the back of her hand.

"Do you mind?"

He laughed, the corners of his eyes crinkling together in that way she loved so much, and jumped up to brush his teeth.

60-Down: Japanese mushrooms. They had had a romantic trip alone to Kyoto a couple of years ago when they lived in Singapore, thanks to their amah, Susheela; she ought to know this. *Shiitake*, that was it …

She filled in the answer and turned off the bedside lamp.

Gordon was beside her in a second, his soft, large hands framing her face, simultaneously gentle and strong, pulling her toward him. "Sorry about my saliva."

"Most people, you know, floss in the bathroom."

"They do? Then when do they get to do the puzzle?"

"It's disgusting," she said. "You get miniscule pieces of food all over the covers."

He laughed again. "Well, my mouth is all rinsed out now …" He kissed her.

He could be so irritating, but he did have the softest lips. And the way he touched her with his hands really was, well, incredibly romantic. The minute he tightened his upper arms, his forearms, she felt her bones dissolve and the little hairs stand up across the nape of her neck.

Gordon really had the most remarkable arms. In college, her roommate Louise used to comment on a boy's hair and ears, neither of which Annie particularly noticed. What she paid attention to, besides square jawlines, were arms.

Her body softened and molded into his.

A friend from Singapore told her recently that her husband never kissed her anymore while they had sex. Gordon kissed her practically the whole time. He enveloped her now, nuzzling his nose and lips into the fold of her neck the way she liked, and she surrendered as she always did, regardless of what she may just have been thinking or how tired she was. She could never resist the silk of his skin or his clean smell—not to mention, of course, she couldn't stand to disappoint him. He did, after all, work so hard to take care of them.

He slid his hands the length of her body, over her breasts, her belly, her hips. For someone always in a rush, he never hurried his lovemaking, and he had this knack of keeping it focused all on her. He lifted her cotton nightgown over her head and kissed her throat, his hands enjoying every inch of her.

"Annie," he murmured. "Are you sure you want to be on the Vineyard all summer?"

Afterwards, drawing her onto his chest, Gordon asked, "Did you get this pillow today? *Perfectly, happily ever after?*"

She nodded, nestling her head to its spot in the middle of his breastbone.

"Very true," he said. "Very true. Today at work I was talking about taxes to this guy who just got married, whether to file joint or separate, and we got into this whole discussion about sharing money, the mortgage, house stuff, cars. About what it means to live jointly."

Gordon had such a mellifluous timbre to his voice.

"And?"

"I just realized, as we were talking, that I love living jointly with you. I love sharing my life with you."

"Me too."

"And you know what I love to share best of all?" He grinned. "Our bed."

Annie laughed and kissed him, sleepy and content.

"I want to hold you in my arms like this forever," Gordon said, kissing her some more. "I wish I could peel open my skin and tuck you inside, safe and sound. You are my everything. You're the very best thing in my life."

What else was there in his life, besides their children? Or in hers, for that matter?

She kept her head on his chest until the beat of his heart slowed to the same pace of her own. Once she could no longer distinguish between the two, she fell fast asleep.

4

Crossing the Sound

⸻

Annie and Gordon decided they would move up to Martha's Vineyard for the summer on the Sunday after school ended, Father's Day.

As the Tuckers pulled down their street in the early morning, it didn't occur to Annie to look back at the house, and not until they were already on the highway did she realize she hadn't. She remembered the longing she used to feel when they had to leave their grand apartments in Asia. But those apartments weren't really theirs, and they wouldn't have been able to afford them if the Foundation hadn't paid the rent—which is why the Foundation got to tell them, whenever they pleased, when it was time to move.

They had bought this house in Sylvan Fell, it was their very own, and she wished she appreciated it more.

In the back seat, Lily was coloring a detailed picture of the family on their trip. The way she'd positioned their blue car and its five passengers so miniscule at the bottom of a long, winding road, reminded Annie of the board game Life she and her cousins Juliet and Emmett used to play.

"I like your drawing, Lily," Annie said. "It marks the beginning of our summer's journey."

It was only June fifteenth, not even officially summer yet, but there were some complications on the horizon with Gordon's Foundation projects in Indonesia, and no one knew what was going to happen with the Handover pending in Hong Kong, so he was anxious to get them safely moved in during what he thought might be a calm before the storm at work. Despite having a whole week's vacation, Gordon was already worried he wouldn't have enough time to fix whatever might need fixing in this cottage they'd just inherited in the town of Chilmark, Massachusetts, on the island of Martha's Vineyard—before he had to return to Washington to fix the rest of the world.

Martha's Vineyard would still be a bit cool, but it would also be less crowded. Maybe they'd feel like real summer people, rather than summer tourists, stocking up at the big A&P grocery store and at Shirley's Hardware before the Fourth of July rush.

As far as Annie knew, her own parents had never considered buying a vacation house—not only because they were perfectly content in Wellesley, but probably because they couldn't afford it. While Annie's father made a good-enough living as a lawyer, maintaining their house, country club, and golf fees was expensive. Not to mention that he and Adair used to drink a lot, which might have infringed upon the get-up-and-go required for setting up another household.

And, of course, her father's affair with Mrs. Pedrick, the married golfer—what was it with the men in her family and married golfers?—had taken him and Adair out of commission for a while. Breaking into another social scene may have seemed too daunting. She ought to ask her mother some time.

Meg was singing along with James Taylor on the CD, not really catching the words but keeping up with the tune.

"Hey, Meg," Gordon said. "After this, what do you say we put on the Chairman of the Board? Ol' Blue Eyes, Sinatra? He's more appropriate for New Jersey, anyway."

"Do we have to change it so soon?" Annie asked. "I love it. I'm just starting to get the meaning." It was the CD he'd given her, the one about mourning. She hadn't grieved anyone since her cousin Emmett had been killed, and, sitting in the front seat missing Aunt Faye, was marveling at how it could make your insides hurt as intensely as if someone had punched you.

Gordon shrugged. "I'm a bit sick of it already, but suit yourself."

After a while, they pulled into one of the giant rest stops along Route 95 to buy gas and use the restrooms.

"Let's not linger," Gordon said, unfastening the girls' car seats. "The ferry is at six-fifteen and we still have to get across the George Washington Bridge and the whole of Connecticut and Rhode Island. Could be traffic. Want me to buy some chips to go with the sandwiches you made for lunch?"

In the bathroom, while Annie was helping Lily scrub green marker off her hands, Meg wandered down to the end of the long bank of sinks. Annie glanced up in the mirror and saw her chatting with a woman dressed in a short skirt and knee-high black boots (in June!), her gigantic breasts spilling out of a tight white tank top. The woman was leaning forward, applying a bright red lipstick, and Annie could see her nipples right through the clinging fabric. She looked like a caricature, hair the lurid color of overripe mangos piled on top of her head.

Meg, her brown eyes wider than ever, stood transfixed.

"Cute kid," the woman said, huge hoop earrings swaying, her heavily made-up eyes meeting Annie's in the mirror.

Annie flew down the length of sinks and swung Meg onto her hip, then turned on her heel and snatched Lily's hand on the way out.

"Mommy! Why are you pulling so hard?"

"We can't be late for the boat. Just mind me and come along."

She snapped the girls back into their car seats.

"Took you long enough," Robbie snickered, with a touch of sarcasm they hadn't heard before.

Gordon handed her a cup of coffee and turned the ignition.

Annie was out of breath. "Ugh," she whispered. "There was a *prostitute* in the ladies room. At least, I think she was." She gestured for him to get going. "Let's get out of here."

"Huh? Is she chasing you or something?" Gordon asked, dead-pan.

"Ha, ha."

He kept glancing over his left shoulder as he steered carefully back onto the highway.

"What kind of pathetic man would find someone like that attractive?" Annie demanded, handing him back her cup so she could buckle her seat belt. "Is she some creep's idea of a Father's Day present? *So* gross." She was still panting. "Why aren't you saying anything?"

"How should I know? And since when do you care so much?"

"Once I saw a woman who was a dead ringer for that one in the bathroom," Annie continued, turning up the music in the back seat. "Summers when I was in high school, my father used to drive me to South Station early to get the bus to Woods Hole. It would only just be light out … I remember waiting two hours one time. 'You'll be fine, Miss Muffet,' he'd say, just so he could make his tee time. I thought the woman was waiting for the bus along Atlantic Avenue."

"The bus?"

"Yeah. I asked my dad why she was waiting there instead of inside the bus station, but he didn't answer. Changed the subject, dropped me off."

"Why did he call you Miss Muffet, anyway?"

Annie paused, trying to get her breath back to normal. "I think because he thought I could be, you know, a little supercilious. Sitting high on my tuffet, whatever that is, judging people below. Queen-like."

"You?" Gordon looked at her sideways, braking as a souped-up Trans Am cut in front of their car.

"I know what a tuffet is, Mommy," Robbie called from the back seat. "It's a fancy, poufy cushion."

"Sounds about right," Gordon said, grinning.

What Annie didn't tell Gordon, and had never told anyone, was that she'd forgotten her tennis racket that muggy morning in the front seat of the car and had rushed back lugging her suitcase to flag down her father—only to see his beige Buick pulled up next to the woman and her leaning through the rolled-down window, talking to him across Annie's racket.

In the back seat, Lily and Meg were discussing the woman's outfit.

"She looked like the Barbie Mommy didn't let us get," Lily remarked.

Meg nodded wistfully as she arranged her pink blankie around her thumb. "I loved her boots."

"They were *so* pretty," Lily agreed. "Did you see those white ribbons hanging from the top of them? I think you call it *frayed* … or *stringe* … I forget. Mommy, what's that string stuff on the top of those boots called?"

"You mean *fringe*?"

"That's it. Fringe."

"How do you know that word?"

"Mrs. Balzac wears those same boots sometimes," Lily said, starting in on a new picture, hopefully not of a prostitute. "She told me. I love them."

Meg nodded her head. "Me too."

"Mrs. *Balzac* wears boots like that? Oh, my goodness." Annie fanned herself with the MapQuest directions.

When Aunt Faye picked her up at the Vineyard Haven ferry that long-ago morning, Annie had asked her about the woman at South Station, and she had explained about prostitutes. Annie had been mortified, and from then on, growing up at St. Andrews Church, had automatically assumed that "Lead us not into temptation but deliver from us evil" meant, "Watch out for prostitutes."

In Asia, Annie sometimes worried Gordon might encounter one while traveling, when she was home with the children unable to defend her territory. An older expat woman had once advised her, "Give your husband sex every time he wants," because prostitutes were legal and cheap there. Gordon would never hire one—how much did they cost, anyway?—but it was infuriating that they might hustle him, the same way she was hustled at Asian markets to buy housewares and silk pashminas.

It was impossible to compete with someone who was invisible.

When Annie and Chase had visited Amsterdam after college during their summer-long Eurail trip, it was Annie who wanted to venture over to the smoky canals of De Wallen, the famous red-light district. They had gone about ten feet along the alley when they saw a despondent, pathetic-looking woman sitting on an upright chair in the window of a shop where a mannequin would ordinarily be, wearing an expression as dead as if she were. She sat smoking, spread-eagled, just like one of Toulouse-Lautrec's whores. Annie had stared and begun to cry, and Chase had tightened his arm and spun her in a sharp U-turn.

"Satisfied?" Chase had said, annoyed and with such little curiosity that for a second Annie wondered if he had been down this alley before. They retraced their steps to the tram, and he led her back to Leidseplein, the pretty neighborhood near the Museumplein where they'd spent the whole day looking at Van Goghs and Rembrandts. "This is your neck of the woods," he said.

What Annie hated most was the fact that the whole business was so clandestine, an inaccessible jurisdiction available only to men, a private club. It was cheating of the worst kind: sleazy, lazy, exploitative. Annie had always had more male friends than female and in general felt a man's view of the world wasn't terribly different from hers, except where prostitution was concerned. She didn't understand how men could be so shameless.

Annie had played tennis in high school and during her first two years at Brown, but eventually quit because she couldn't stand the ubiquitous line-call cheating, the intense frustration of not being able to prove her opponent was lying while simultaneously being too confrontation-averse to request an umpire. It was awful to have to call an opponent's ball "In!" when it bounced at her feet on the line for match point, but Annie did, and she couldn't stand people who didn't. She didn't care if she had a losing record. She would never cheat.

Gordon swerved, deftly avoiding a strip of tire tread that had fallen into the left lane.

He had gone ahead and changed the CD, and "My One and Only Love," the song they'd chosen for their wedding's first dance and the one Gordon liked to sing to her, came on. Annie wasn't a huge Sinatra fan, but thought this was the most romantic song she'd ever heard. Forcing herself to relax, she reached for Gordon's hand.

"Try to hold it from now on, okay, Meg?" Gordon called back. "Because if we miss the ferry, we'll have to spend the night in the parking lot."

"Sleep in the *parking lot*?" Robbie asked. "We should have left a little earlier, Daddy."

"I still don't know why you pulled my hand so hard in the bathroom, Mommy," Lily said.

Annie didn't say anything.

"Mommy?"

"I just didn't like that lady talking to Meg."

The sun was beating through the windows. Annie fiddled with the air conditioning.

"Let's play I spy," Robbie interjected, seeming to detect his mother needed some help changing the subject. "I spy, with my little eye … something silver."

"That tractor-trailer truck," Lily said, not bothering to look up. Annie glanced behind and noticed she was drawing, what else, a voluptuous woman wearing big earrings and fringey go-go boots.

Meg craned her neck, wanting to play too though not sure how, as a fire engine pulled onto the highway.

"I spy," she shouted, "with my little eye … a *hooker and ladder* truck!"

"Good grief," Annie gasped, tossing her hands up in surrender.

Gordon burst out laughing. The three kids thought this was hilarious, too, despite the fact that they had no idea what the joke was. It took a while, but Annie finally joined in—and before long, they'd crossed into New England.

By the time they got to Providence, traffic had slowed down.

"Not sure we can make it," Gordon said, reading the directions against the front of the steering wheel. "Says it's another ninety minutes. Rush hour. How long do you think it will take?"

Annie's hands felt clammy. "I don't know," she said. "I've never gone this direction before. I always came from Boston."

He started to drive faster, but there was an accident outside Fall River. Meg swiped one of Lily's new markers and colored her arms and legs orange while no one was looking; when Lily saw she'd ruined the marker, she hit her—at which point they both started crying. Robbie bonked them both on the tops of their heads with his book and told them to shut up.

"Can you call and change the reservation to a later ferry?" Gordon asked.

Annie retrieved her new cell phone from her purse and turned it on; she wasn't used to it yet. She examined the ferry ticket for the phone number, but the line was busy. "I guess I'll just keep calling," she said, and turned off the phone so as not to waste the battery.

She felt that familiar lump rise in her throat the way it did when she mismanaged time. Why hadn't they left earlier? Why did they have to live so far away—in such a godforsaken state as Maryland, for heaven's sake?

At last they sped under the CAPE COD AND THE ISLANDS highway sign, and it was as if the car itself heaved a huge sigh of relief. They crossed over the Cape Cod Canal on the steel rivets of the Bourne Bridge at five-forty.

Gordon had visited the Vineyard a few times over the years, of course, but it wasn't his "place." At least not yet. He could never get the hang of idiosyncratic nautical terms like "up-Island" and "down-Island," which traced back to the particular direction whaling captains chose to embark upon when leaving the Island: west was "up" because it was farther from zero degrees of longitude at the prime meridian in Greenwich, England, while east was "down."

Gordon was more comfortable with "east" and "west." He also didn't appreciate that there were no maps, or even street signs, for most of the dirt roads. Maybe he was too exacting to be a Vineyarder. Annie and Chase used to spend whole days deliberately getting lost on dirt roads and ancient ways, uncovering hidden, magical places. Gordon wasn't a meanderer.

It was impossible for Annie to imagine what Chase would be like now. He was someone else's husband, maybe someone's father. She'd heard he worked in New York City, so there was no way he would be here more than weekends. Well, a couple weeks at most, assuming he didn't spend his vacations doing something more marvelous such as, say, sailing the Yugoslav coast. He would be hanging out at Quansoo, his family's private beach, rather than driving all the way to Long Point, and his wife probably traveled with a cook, so it's not as if Annie would run into them at Cronig's Market. Even if he did go to Lambert's Cove, he would be on the private side—while she and the kids would be on the down-Island, town beach side.

Aunt Faye had never been one for private beaches.

"Why so quiet?" Gordon asked, taking his hand off the wheel to squeeze her knee.

Along Route 28, around the two rotaries they went, past the pristine golf course and the Sands of Time motel, where she and Chase stayed once when they'd missed the last boat. And there on the left, in all its glittering glory, was Vineyard Sound.

Gordon put down the car windows so they could smell the sea air and listen to the cries of the gulls, swarming around them in a kind of welcome. Everything sparkled, as if it had just been washed. Annie felt that familiar thrill of expectation and thought of the phrase "filled with gladness." When, in all of her travels, had she last felt so *glad*?

They could see the slow line of cars inching onto the ferry. It was exactly six o'clock.

"*Marr-a-lin*, eh?" asked the attendant, in a broad Massachusetts accent. "Don't cut it so close next time. Lane Two."

Soon they were in the belly of a big white boat called *The Islander* and Gordon was turning off the car, the kids bouncing in their seats. He swiveled toward her, the corners of his eyes crinkling up in a grin, to give her a high five and a kiss.

"I knew you'd get us here on time," Annie said, leaning her head on his shoulder and kissing his neck. "Thank you for being such an excellent driver. I never doubted for a second."

Eventually, they made their way up to the top deck of the ferry, and Annie felt the serenity she'd anticipated for months, since first learning she'd inherited Aunt Faye's house, radiate throughout her whole being. She could practically feel her Sylvan Fell aches and pains lifting from her body, see them floating away like jetsam.

"Can we explore the boat, Mommy?" Robbie asked, holding Lily's hand.

Annie nodded; she'd almost forgotten they were there.

She held Meg up against the railing. A faint silver-slipper moon was rising in the east, barely perceptible against the colorless sky.

"Look at these crazy seagulls, Meg, flying all around us! Close your eyes and breathe in the salt air, feel it on your face. There's no ocean near Sylvan Fell. Feel how clean everything is here."

The last few years she had seen so many seas, but the clear green of Vineyard Sound, even more than the rusty blue of San Francisco Bay, was to her the most beautiful.

"Don't hold me so tight," Meg squirmed.

But Annie shuddered and held her closer, remembering her dream. Maybe they should go inside to the lunch counter and see if Chase was sitting at one of the little round tables, eating a cup of clam chowder like he used to, three bags of oyster crackers crumbled on top.

Annie pointed out the misty contour of Martha's Vineyard across the water. The ferry sounded its long horn and they stayed at the rail, gazing toward the lonely Elizabeth Islands and the pale blinking flash of the West Chop Light and then, as they got closer, toward the wide sandy shore of Lambert's Cove.

5

Middle Road

Aunt Faye's house, known as a saltbox, had a long pitched roof that sloped down to the back.

"It looks like the particular kind of box the New Englanders used to store salt in during Colonial times," Annie began, as they drove up the driveway. "What's funny is the Americans came up with this design because they were trying to trick the British, who had made up a rule that all buildings two stories or higher had to pay more taxes. So the colonialists figured out how to make the back of the roof come down to the height of the first floor—"

Gordon turned off the car.

"Maybe tell us later, Mommy," Robbie said, leaning over the seat to unbuckle the girls. "Time to explore. Let's go!"

They began running up the side path in the twilight but Annie, so pleased to be back she could hardly breathe, stopped in her tracks. She was struck at how much smaller the house seemed. She never anticipated this being her first impression.

The gray shingles looked old and worn out. The window shutters drooped. Everything looked different from how she remembered.

Waiting for them on the railing of the pinewood deck was a red cardinal. It chirped a cheerful song of greeting, and it was the girls' turn to stop short.

Meg, grinning, nodded hello.

"Aunt Faye beat us here!" Lily exclaimed.

"That's the dumbest thing I ever heard," said Robbie. "Anyway, that bird can't be Aunt Faye. It's a male. Daddy said."

The inside of the house, thankfully, did not look as run-down as the exterior. Rather, it was comfortably worn in and smelled to Annie like cinnamon: like Aunt Faye, like her childhood. It seemed to greet them with open arms as if to say, "You finally got here! Welcome back!"

Aunt Faye liked to visit the Vineyard throughout the winter, and everything was just as she'd left it. She didn't know she was never coming back. Annie had spoken on the telephone with Caleb, the caretaker since Faye and Uncle Emmett had built the house in the 1950s, and knew he'd been over to check the heat and turn the water and electricity back on. She'd have to make a point of meeting him this week while Gordon was here.

Next to Aunt Faye's side of the bed, a bookmark from Bunch of Grapes, the bookstore in Vineyard Haven, peeked out of the middle of one of the biographies she liked to read, her glasses folded neatly atop. A stately tartan dog bed inscribed with the name "Tashmoo" appointed one corner of the bedroom. The *Boston Globe* book section from December 1, 1996, was on the counter under a *New Yorker* with a cartoon cover of a man presenting a roast turkey. Faye's short, lace-up walking boots were next to the door; her winter jacket hung in the closet.

Things looked as if she had run out for a moment to buy some milk at Cronig's.

Annie opened the refrigerator with some trepidation. The door still held a bottle of Heinz ketchup, a few homemade jams and mustards from the West Tisbury farmers' market, a small jug of Vermont maple syrup, six-packs of 7Up and Schweppes tonic water. She stared at the emptiness on the shelves for a while.

Gordon appeared next to her, carrying a duffel bag. He closed the refrigerator and wrapped his arms around her.

"It's harder than I thought," Annie whispered.

"I miss her too," Gordon said, stroking her back. "It's going to take some time to adjust." He held her quietly for a while. "But look at it this way. She's given you an amazing gift, and she'll be able to stay in your life forever in this house, in this place. She's here with all your old memories, plus all the new ones our family is going to make. ...." He swallowed. "For the rest of our lives."

The kids were outside playing, shouting happily on the big lawn in the dusky light. Gordon held her tighter.

"I so wish you would let yourself really cry it out, sweetheart. That's the best thing you could do."

This, from someone she had never once seen cry, not even when he first told her about the death of his own mother.

Luckily, the weather was cool for the end of June and too cloudy for the beach, because it took a couple of days to figure out what they needed to do to settle in. The morning after they arrived, Annie and Robbie drove the ten miles to the big Edgartown A&P to fill the station wagon with groceries and supplies. Unfortunately, she lost her composure in the checkout line once again because yet another elderly woman, from the back, looked so much like Aunt Faye.

The house was as carefully arranged as the inside of a sailboat, so putting things away in the narrow kitchen cupboards and storing stuff on the compact shelves in the basement was like assembling a puzzle: everything had to fit exactly, not an inch to spare. Robbie's Lego building came in handy.

Finding space for her and Gordon's stuff in the closet and drawers of the big bedroom was more difficult, because first she had to do something with Aunt Faye's clothes. Annie pulled out Faye's favorite purple sweater and a couple of her printed sundresses ("happy colors," Faye used to say), then couldn't stand it and simply folded them, along with everything else, into two boxes and brought them down to the cellar. She saved Faye's signature straw beach hat and a couple of sweatshirts, but would figure out someplace to donate the rest later.

The house had a front door, but since no one had ever gotten around to creating a path from it to the driveway, no one had ever bothered to open it, and because the key had gotten lost, it remained locked. This was ironic for the Vineyard, where no one usually locks anything. Aunt Faye used to say this inaccessible door simplified things and was also very lucky, because she believed the old wives' tale about always going out the same way you went in. She deemed it bad luck to mix up one's egresses.

Each day, Gordon got up before everyone else and completed a set of tasks that astounded Annie. How did he know what to do? She hadn't even created a list yet! *Oil hinges on the windows, replace fire-alarm batteries, set up outdoor deck furniture, remove skunk's nest, connect outdoor shower, fertilize lilies and hydrangeas.*

Annie admired his zest. She also appreciated how everything was in working order. But did he really need to tackle all these tasks at once? Couldn't they make time for the beach, or a bike ride? Gordon spent so much time setting up and getting ready, there was no time left to enjoy anything.

The house, so shipshape, was almost spare compared to Aunt Faye's Colonial in Wellesley—where her first husband, the portly Uncle Emmett, had been born ("gray and with a pipe in his mouth," Annie's mother used to say) in 1910 and lived his whole life. Annie used to find it hard to breathe in that house, so chock-full of generations' worth of his family's dusty, musty antiques and books, but old Uncle Emmett loved the past and loved teaching it, and wore it as comfortably as he did his three-button Shetland wool cardigans. After he died, Faye hadn't gotten around to clearing things out before Jared, a newly retired professor of photography at Columbia who sported a dashing, very un-Boston mustache, had moved in with his own paraphernalia.

No wonder Aunt Faye loved Middle Road so much—it must have been liberating for her to be so Spartan. She could be free here, whereas in Wellesley she must have felt she was drowning in a sea not only of other people's junk, but also of the past.

Two days later, Aunt Faye's caretaker, Caleb, and his wife, Jane, a Wampanoag from Gay Head, having allowed a polite amount of time before calling, appeared at the door.

They'd been shocked and sorry to hear of Faye's passing, Caleb said, and gave their condolences; she'd been a real favorite around here, an uncommonly kind person. Did Annie plan to keep them on? They lived up the road in Chilmark, and he tended to come only as needed in the summer, but was at her disposal. And he hated to have to mention it, but there was this matter regarding payment for the past few months' work, if it wasn't too much trouble.

Annie found her checkbook.

As Caleb and Jane turned their pickup truck around to leave, a woman younger than Annie with long auburn hair appeared on the far side of the lawn, sidestepping her way through the pink rhododendrons. In one arm she was carrying a toddler wearing a blue-and-gray checked dress; in the other was nestled a pie.

"My name is Heather," she said, placing the little girl on the grass. "And this is my daughter, Apple. We're your neighbors. Welcome back to the Vineyard, welcome to summer, welcome home. And I hope you like strawberry-rhubarb pie." Heather had a soothing, soft way of speaking that sounded like smiling. "This is your aunt's recipe, by the way. You might want to add some salt … I didn't put in as much as she said."

Lily and Meg peeked out from where they were playing under the round table on the deck to see Apple, a live doll. Robbie, in the wide hammock under the beetlebung trees, looked up from his book and rolled his eyes as if to say, "What? *Another* one?"

"I miss her every day," Heather said. "Still can't believe it. Faye was the most generous-hearted person I've known in all my life."

Annie thanked her, still not used to the fact that people she didn't even know were so upset. She had heard about Heather's husband, Nick, a nice guy who, according to Aunt Faye, had gotten mixed up with the wrong Island crowd and recently been sent to federal prison for dealing drugs. If she remembered correctly, he was learning to become a master tradesman in tiling.

Aunt Faye, a great lover of redemption stories, had told Annie that this would end up being the best thing that ever happened to Nick. She was always giving everyone the benefit of the doubt, even if they had been proven guilty. Poor Heather had been blind-sided and needed a job, so Faye had introduced her to practically all the summer people she knew. Annie was pretty sure she had lent her money, too, before ultimately helping her land a waitressing job at the Beach Plum Inn in Menemsha.

Heather told Annie how eternally grateful she was to Faye for her job, and hoped Annie would count on her to be a good neighbor. "I'm always around during the day and would be honored to help you any way I can. Please call if you need me to watch the kids."

Honored? Annie grinned. "Today I feel like Dorothy, definitely not in Kansas anymore. Where we live now in Maryland—at, er, our other house—our neighbors haven't been too friendly."

"They haven't? Well, it might just take a little time," Heather said, securing Apple back on her hip. "Nick and I grew up in Oak Bluffs. When you live on an island, you need to be able to rely on your neighbors and friends, as well as on your family."

Just then, Gordon pulled up on the gravel driveway, back from the lumberyard and the West Tisbury dump. He had been inspired to clean out the garage and cellar that morning.

"That was a little time-consuming," he announced. He was carrying several strips of wood across his arms, and a new bird feeder dangled off one hand. "So I just signed you up for trash pickup."

"This is my husband," Annie said, smiling. "The fix-it guy."

They chatted for a while, although Gordon was clearly anxious to start building whatever it was he had planned. Annie made Robbie get out of the hammock and introduced him and the girls formally to Apple and Heather, who reiterated her offer to babysit. They then disappeared the way they'd come.

"We already have three friends here, four counting Apple," Annie called to Gordon, as she made turkey sandwiches—one with mustard, one with mayonnaise, two with both, one without. He had hung the bird feeder outside the kitchen window, and was now building a large box to hold the deck cushions so they wouldn't have to haul them inside every time it rained. "I wonder whether I should put an ad up for a regular babysitter, a teenage girl. What do you think? Can we afford it?"

He mumbled something she couldn't make out because he was holding so many nails between his teeth.

She brought a bowl of fruit salad onto the deck. "You're spending the whole week fixing and building stuff."

He stood up and stretched his back, then bent down to kiss her lips. "It's fun. But I'm a little worried about the plumbing in this house. And remind me to show you how the fuses work, because I can tell that old box is going to be temperamental. Did you notice these door handles? They're as loose as the ones in Sylvan Fell."

"Everything is fine."

"At least your Uncle Emmett or Jared or someone left an excellent toolbox here."

"Aunt Faye used to fix stuff herself. Please don't worry so much, Gordon. The weather is supposed to be nicer tomorrow and we've bonded with the house enough, don't you think? There's a lot to see on Martha's Vineyard besides our field. I'd like to take the kids to the beach, to Long Point. And maybe we can drive up to Gay Head while you're here. *Aquinnah*, I mean."

Gordon finished hammering his nails, and the kids sat down around the table.

"Did you know this past spring the town voted to switch the name back to the original Wampanoag name? We're supposed to call it Aquinnah, not Gay Head anymore. I suppose it is a funny name, now that 'gay' isn't usually used to mean 'brightly colored' the way it was for the British settlers."

Annie had always loved reading Wampanoag legends, and went on for a while about how Aquinnah meant "land under the hill" and how the people of Noepe, their name for the Island, were related to the Algonquin, the Native Americans who helped the Pilgrims in their first Thanksgiving—until she realized no one was listening to a word she was saying.

A few nights later, after Robbie had beaten them at Monopoly again and they were going to bed, Gordon held her and said, "I love how light and carefree you are here, Annie. I really want you to have a good summer after all the work you've done settling us into Maryland. That's why I'm trying to fix everything up before I have to leave. So you can all be safe and sound."

She kissed him.

Then he surprised her by saying, "What do you say we get up early, before the kids wake up, go over to Lambert's Cove? Do you think we could ask Heather to be on call, and give Robbie her number? The kids will be okay for an hour. We can bring our new phones … hopefully we'll have cell coverage." He finished his flossing. "I remember we had a couple of pretty walks out there."

They had? She didn't remember ever having gone there with Gordon.

Annie went upstairs to run the plan by Robbie. He was in the middle of *The Blue Book of Fairy Tales*, finding it a little scary and reading with both the overhead and bedside-table lights on, and he'd put a flashlight next to his pillow. If the girls woke up before they returned, she told him, he could pour cereal and let them watch a video, and tell them that if they minded him, they could each have a jelly doughnut from Humphrey's.

Gordon climbed up the steep stairs, bowing his head under

the low ceiling. "If all is well when we come back from our walk," he said, "how about I pay you a dollar for minding each sister? Deal?"

Robbie's eyes lit up. "I'd rather have money than a doughnut any day."

"Dough for dough," Annie said, and Robbie grinned. "I'm going to run downstairs and phone Heather, make sure she'll be home in the morning. She said she wasn't working tonight."

It wasn't quite nine yet. Annie was a stickler about her mother's rule that people should call only between the nines.

Heather said she was delighted that Annie had asked, and that she'd definitely be home.

"She said she was 'honored' again," Annie called, running back up.

Gordon was stretched out on Robbie's bed, eyes closed and feet hanging over the end. He and Annie had slept here, in her cousin Emmett's double bed, the few times they'd visited Aunt Faye together. The bed took up so much of the room that to open the drawers of the clothes bureau at its foot, you had to kneel on the mattress.

"I left Heather's telephone number on the kitchen counter, Robbie, along with my cell number and Daddy's. We'll keep the phones turned on. You're sure you're okay with this? Your first babysitting job."

"Yup," he said, his eyes moving along the page. "The girls probably won't even wake up till you get back, they're so lazy."

Annie looked in on Meg and Lily, cuddled up asleep together in each other's arms. Funny—she'd heard them arguing about something up here during the Monopoly game. One of the Barbies was half-dressed and looked like she had been flung across the room. They must have been fighting about her outfit.

Sisters were so complicated. But maybe they inherently knew Aunt Faye's old house rule about never going to bed mad.

6

Lambert's Cove

Gordon was already dressed when he woke Annie up the next morning. It still seemed strange to wake up with her husband in Aunt Faye's room, rather than in her old lavender room upstairs.

"Let's go, gorgeous," he whispered, kissing her neck. "I made you some coffee. Today is the first official day of summer and it's a little foggy outside, but I bet it will clear."

Annie was cold and wouldn't have minded a little more sleep, but didn't want to let him down. Outside, the birds were singing *con brio* and she wondered how she could have slept through their racket. She pulled on jeans and Aunt Faye's Black Dog sweatshirt from last year and checked on the kids, all sleeping soundly.

Heather appeared crossing their field, which this morning smelled vaguely of hay and skunk. She was carrying a huge, colorful quilt in her arms, Apple trotting alongside her.

"I was thinking, if it's okay with you, we would hang out on your deck while you're gone. I'm making a quilt for when Nick comes home, and I like to work on it mornings."

Annie felt relieved and kept thanking her. "Let me show you around. If Robbie comes down, maybe you can say you're here for backup, because we told him he could babysit. But this is much better for my peace of mind."

They drove down the hill as two cardinals, a red male and a brown female, flew past the windshield. Gordon, thinking out loud, said he'd have to mow back the overgrown weeds and grass from the middle of the tire tracks so it would look like a driveway again.

Wild grapevines and honeysuckle tumbled over the old stone wall separating their property from the Aldens' next door. They turned onto Middle Road, where colorful blue chicory and yellow daisies brightened up the grass and clover along its banks. Endless stone walls, worn and dappled with mossy lichen, skimmed along the waves of the hills.

Annie had ridden her bike this way a thousand times, yet everything looked a little different now. Past the cows and bulls in the wide pastures, past the cozy gray barn nestled into the side of the field … but she didn't remember the barn being so close to the road. She remembered Middle Road as wider, she remembered it bordered by thicker stands of woods. And the old farmhouses along the way looked shabbier somehow, smaller.

The thick branches of the oak and maple trees met in a graceful arch overhead. They cast puddles of shade splashing across the pavement the way clouds sometimes create patterns on the ocean.

The road curved up and down. She still felt a little disoriented as they turned, on a sudden breeze of fresh-mown hay, onto the Pan Handle Road, past the white cedar shingles of the brand-new Agricultural Hall, and left again onto State Road. She looked over her shoulder toward the cemetery at the bend where Uncle Jared was buried, though she was not sure exactly where, then ahead over the little bridge and past the old oak tree with its sprawling branches pointing every which way around the Island.

They passed Humphrey's Bakeshop and decided to stop on the way back, so the doughnuts would still be warm. Past Vineyard Gardens, where Gordon had bought flowers to plant in Aunt Faye's rounders on the back deck. Past Cronig's Market and, finally, left onto Lambert's Cove Road. They didn't encounter a single car.

Gordon had remembered water bottles and a big beach towel. They set out down the nearly half-mile path lined with scrub oaks to the beach, hand in hand, listening to the happy chatter and singing of the birds. Almost there, they kicked off their flip-flops at the split rail fence just before trudging up the dune to the beach.

From the top of the dune they should have been able to see the water, but instead they could hear only the waves slapping against the pebbles along the shore.

"Pea soup," Gordon said, and they both laughed. That's what he used to say most mornings in San Francisco.

Their feet sank a little in the white sand, soft as confectioners' sugar, as they made it down to the water. They were walking through a cloud, but could consistently see about ten feet or so ahead.

"Which way?" Gordon asked.

Lambert's Cove is a perfectly shaped crescent; the path spills pretty much right into the middle of the arc. You can easily walk about two miles in each direction, maybe more at low tide, before the water collides with cliffs or impassable tracts of stone and brush.

"Let's go left," Annie said, without thinking. She was surprised to find herself here again. "It's all private, but no one will care this early. Can't go this direction during the day."

"Private? Great. Always exciting to get arrested first thing in the morning," Gordon said, putting his arm around her shoulders.

"We'll be able to hide in the fog."

He laughed. "Whatever you say … this is your island. I've never gone this direction. We used to go right, to that brownish brook you called the Coca-Cola Stream, toward that big rock."

Her island? What rock? Why couldn't she remember walking on Lambert's Cove with him? She remembered being on this stretch of beach only with Chase—and not by the town path, but by cutting through beach grass behind his parents' house a little farther up-Island, off Indian Hill.

The tide was far out and they strolled along the hard-packed sand, the water occasionally washing over their feet. Every once in a while, one or the other would pick up a pretty pebble or a shiny piece of what Vineyarders called "wampum," the Wampanoag word for the polished purple that lines the shell of a quahog, or New England clam, after the shell has been broken and tumbled smooth by the ocean. There didn't used to be as much wampum here on the north shore.

What had she done with that necklace Chase gave her, the one with the piece of wampum carved into the roughly triangular shape of Martha's Vineyard? Was it in the trunk in her parents' attic, along with his cryptic notes and postcards?

Annie explained to Gordon how the Wampanoag used wampum for money as well as for jewelry, and that the slang expression to "shell out" money derives from Wampum shells. But he didn't seem to be listening.

They waded through a stream where a salt pond emptied between dunes into the ocean, the chilly water coming up almost to Annie's knees. The fog was beginning to clear.

Carefully picking their way across several yards of small pebbles that had washed up over the last millennia of waves, they rounded a small bend along the shore. Above the dune to the left they could see the outline of a sail shack. The same slanting roof, but much closer to the beach than she remembered, less hidden.

Now she wished she hadn't brought them this way.

Gordon veered off the beach into the scrub brush to investigate. He spanned his long arms the length of the wide sill to peer in the front window. "A deserted shack. *Verrry* interesting."

"This is Katharine Graham's beach, I think. You can't see it now, but her big brick house is up there on the hill. It has a lot of chimneys. I think she used to lend this shack to what's-his-name, you know. The Vineyard painter." Annie scanned the land above the bank of the shore: the meadow, the scrub oak trees mixed with brush and brambles, still as they had been.

"No, I *don't* know. Vineyard painter? Looks like a love shack to me."

Gordon disappeared around the back and in a minute was inside, shoving forward the old single-paned window and somehow latching it open. He craned his neck to call out to her.

"Convenient nobody locks anything on this island. Kind of cozy in here, you know." Then, in a pretend English accent, "Won't you join me, please, m'lady?"

Annie's hands were cold, and she tucked them back inside the sleeves of Aunt Faye's sweatshirt. She didn't budge from her place on the sand.

"Thomas Hart Benton," she called back, biting her lower lip. "That's his name. He made that famous poster for the Agricultural Fair, you know, the one hanging upstairs. He built this as a place to paint. Or Katharine Graham let him use it ... I can't remember which. That's what I heard, anyway." She mumbled this last part more to herself than to him.

"Well, nobody's painting in it now. Just a bunch of old sailing and fishing stuff. Are you on your way up here or do I have to come get you?"

She hesitated. A halyard clanged on the mast of a sailboat moored just offshore. Chase had called it a love shack, too.

Confused, not knowing what she wanted to do, she slid her fingers over the glossy pieces of wampum in her hand and climbed past the beach grass that waved along the crest of the dune, up the same two flat, pink-granite rocks that served as steps. Someone had fashioned four slender tree trunks into pillars to support the roof. She ran her hand along the nearest one: fir, or maybe locust. She ducked her head through the door.

But ... this was it? Inside it seemed smaller, the knotty pine walls looked flimsier, less magical than she remembered. Her memory had turned everything into a technicolor movie, while the reality was—not black and white exactly, but not as vibrant, either.

"Welcome to my love castle," Gordon said, still in an English accent, bowing down to welcome her, extending his arm with a flourish. "You must be the Princess Anna."

The craggy gray planks of the floor, the narrow shelves holding large tin cans with faded labels of ripe plump tomatoes, all filled with nails and fishing lures; rafters the length of the peaked ceiling holding kayaks and paddles, fishing rods and reels; the speckled light coming through the sandy windowpanes. She felt as if she were trespassing on a sacred memory.

Gordon wrapped his big towel around her shoulders. "An ermine robe for you, m'lady. Your wish is my desire."

She tried to smile back, to go along. She was shivering a little, and kept glancing out the window. The halyard clanged in an erratic kind of rhythm; the beat was off.

"Nobody's out here this early, sweetheart," Gordon whispered. "Nobody but us."

Gently, he took her face in his hands and gave her a long kiss. She kissed him back, but looked sideways to scan the beach through the open window for any stray walkers. Could that possibly be Chase's sailboat?

A thin strip of morning dew lay on the weathered windowsill.

Gordon slipped one hand around her neck and down her spine, and pulled her toward him. She felt nervous, shy. Was it possible to betray your old boyfriend with your husband?

She let the towel drop behind her.

Gordon lifted her sweatshirt over her head, slowly letting his hands glide all over her. He undid her ponytail and combed his fingers through her hair, delicately teasing it out until it fell long down her back. The air felt crisp, sexy on her skin. He undid her bra and drew the tips of his fingers slowly back around to her breasts, tracing each one deliberately before cupping them with his palms. Her nipples stood hard and erect, and goose bumps rose along the insides of her upper arms and thighs, across her back, across her whole body.

He bent over to kiss her breasts, to kiss between them, underneath … to run his tongue slowly down the length of her stomach. He undid the top button of her jeans, unzipped them, eased them down around her hips. He took off his own sweatshirt and held her close, slowly rubbing his upper body side to side, his chest sliding back and forth against her breasts. He was drinking her in as his hands caressed every inch of her.

Still kissing her, Gordon, with one hand, reached up to pull a life jacket down from the rafters, then tugged out an old bunched-up sail that had been tossed aside, not properly furled. He slowly guided her onto the grainy floor and smoothed the sail beneath her, flattening out the life jacket for her pillow.

Could this be one of the same sails?

On clear nights, she and Chase used to sneak down here from his parents' house. They would sit in the pitch dark on the sand in front of the shack and talk, philosophizing about life and watching the shimmery waves and whatever else might be in store for them that particular night—the Milky Way especially deep, moonbeams across the water—and listen to the foghorns from the lighthouses. Sometimes they would make a bonfire.

Chase would wrap one of Piper's plaid blankets around their shoulders and they would kiss—hesitant at first, then quickening, then groping and throbbing into an out-of-control fervor. They would barely make it up to the shack. Rolling around on the sails, hands everywhere at once, whirling around like they did on the dance floor, their energy, exploding, would become sweaty passion and visceral, rushed lovemaking. Once they started, they couldn't stop: a torrent of charged young libidos colliding with unleashed desire.

Back then, it never occurred to her to watch whether anyone was coming.

The planks of the floor were hard and rough, probably washed ashore from some shipwreck, and her back ached on top of the crinkly sail. Gordon, from his knees, tugged another sail out from the pile, a faded rainbow-colored one—an old spinnaker—and pulled it up and over them for a top sheet. Then his body rolled slowly over hers like a long, gently breaking wave.

On the wooded path back to the parking lot, quite a few dogs trotted up to greet them, their owners trailing behind. The fog had dissolved into an azure-blue sky and the sun felt warmer than it had since they'd been on the Island. They encountered all sorts of people: couples, single women, groups of women. Everyone looked buoyant and fresh, excited to be resuming their summer morning rituals. The parking lot was nearly full.

"I guess we beat the rush," Gordon grinned, taking her hand. "I didn't know this was Doggie Central. Better remember for next time. The early bird, and all that."

"They all look so happy," Annie said. "But I feel sorry for anyone who isn't us."

They passed several large pickup trucks and SUVs heading the opposite direction, all of which looked cumbersome and out of place on these roads, so much narrower than she remembered. A speeding, shiny red Jeep Wrangler, like the one Chase used to drive, passed them illegally over the double yellow line. Annie craned her neck, but couldn't make out the driver.

At Humphrey's they bought some jelly doughnuts, known to the locals as "belly bombs," and powdery doughnut holes for Apple—the kind old Uncle Emmett used to buy for her and her cousins.

She remembered they needed milk.

"Think the kids are awake yet? We ought to stop at Alley's while we're out." She checked her phone, which she'd carefully left on. "Robbie didn't call, and I don't want to wake them up."

Alley's General Store, with its twin pointed roofs, gray shingles, and white trim, had been the heart of West Tisbury since even before the town was incorporated in 1892; the hanging sign next to the American flag declared they were "Purveyors in Almost Everything." People were already settled on the bench beneath the community bulletin board and in rocking chairs along the long narrow porch, chatting and sipping coffee. The red Jeep Wrangler was in the parking lot.

Aunt Faye used to send her here on an errand at least once a day. Annie, on her bike, would tackle the hills of Middle Road and race the flat of the Panhandle and Music Street with her cousins, and later by herself. There wasn't any traffic or fear of being run over, and she never had to worry about money because Aunt Faye had an account. Someone in the Alley family, someone familiar, always worked the counter, but her favorite was John Alley.

He would tell her the history of the store and of West Tisbury: how the store had been founded in 1858 by Mr. Nathan Mayhew and was originally across the street, next to where the new library was now; how it sold everything necessary for living on the Island—bridles, saddles, food, clothes, and at first oil, then kerosene, lamps; how Nathan's son, S. M. Mayhew, transplanted a barn from Chilmark to this spot for the new, enlarged store, which featured a separate ladies millinery section upstairs; how it was called S. M. Mayhew's until Albion Alley, John's father, took over at the end of World War II. Albion's first job had been making up-Island deliveries, initially driving a horse and wagon and then, in 1917, a Ford Model T truck.

It was different today.

A teenage girl with streaks of purple in her russet-colored hair and two tiny silver rings in her nose stood behind the oak counter. As she rang up customers on the old-fashioned cash register, a small tattoo of a mermaid performed a kind of belly dance up and down her left forearm. Frank Sinatra was singing "Fly Me to the Moon" in the background.

Annie and Gordon bought milk, a *New York Times*, and some

nectarines from a basket on a table. While Gordon perused the headlines, Annie peeked into the hardware section to see if perhaps Chase was there. He wasn't.

Gordon handed the salesgirl a fifty-dollar bill for the eight-dollar tab. She was cradling the store phone on her shoulder and moving deftly around the long cord that extended to the wall behind her. She had black circles under her eyes, as if she'd had a late night.

"I can meet you when I get off, at one," the salesgirl said into the phone. "Yeah, let's go to Lucy Vincent. I got, like, a walk-on pass yestaday. Can't believe how much it cost. We can go there all year for free when it's cold, but once the weatha's nice we have to pay for our own beach. So the show at the Hot Tin Roof, I mean *Outerland*, excuse me, whateva it's called now, was wicked good last night."

Three people were behind them in line.

The large till opened with a *ka-ching*, and she handed Gordon the change.

"You nevva heard-a him? Just another, you know, Vin-yed singa-songwrita, but he was awesome. Played until two. What? You got a *cah* pass for Lucy? Yeah, pick me up. Betta than hitch-hikin'."

Gordon counted his change. "Excuse me," he said.

The girl was still engrossed in her conversation. He waited, cleared his throat. "Excuse me, but you gave me an extra twenty."

She looked at him.

"What? Oh, shit," she said to her friend. "I gotta hang up."

"I think you gave me sixty-two dollars' change for a fifty," Gordon said. "Here you go."

The girl glanced around to see if the manager were within earshot, then smiled gratefully and thanked them both. She had pretty hazel eyes.

As they crossed the dirt parking lot, Annie took Gordon's hand. "Good grief, how things have changed around here. I love how honest you are, Gordon—you never cheat at anything. Not to mention you're good at arithmetic. Remember our anniversary in Bali last year, when they forgot to charge us for the champagne and you told the waitress? You have excellent karma."

He considered for a moment. "Yes, I do," he said. "I get to be married to you."

7

Long Point

Turning right onto the Edgartown Road, the kids were squabbling and Annie threatened to turn around.

"Would you rather spend the day at the beach or in time-out?" she demanded, stopping in a line of cars by the Old Mill Pond. There never used to be traffic jams on Martha's Vineyard.

"Look at the swans, they get along," she said, pointing her arm out the window—right into the open back of a red Jeep Wrangler. The driver, a blond man, did a double-take toward her at the same time he moved forward with his line of cars, and Annie was positive it was Chase. Same broad shoulders, same muscular back.

"Go, Mommy," Lily said, and the car behind them honked.

Annie inhaled sharply. So he was here, after all.

The weather had turned glorious on Monday morning—figures, after Gordon left—and Annie had brought the kids to Long Point, to this little sheltered pond set back from the ocean, both days since. This afternoon Robbie had been especially busy, building a castle with a moat that ran about ten yards along the edge of the pond with three boys from Connecticut, brothers whose family was renting a house for the week on Charles Neck Way.

As usual, he was the general and ordered everyone where to dig and exactly where to shore up the sides of the moat. It was quite an operation, but really—he could sound like such a bossy old man sometimes.

Annie had been involved too, digging and lugging water and

following directions, until she'd grown a little bored and sat down on her towel. She took a few pictures with her camera, careful to zip it back into its plastic bag. The sun, not too hot, was delicious on her face, and she felt very sleepy all of a sudden.

They had played in the pond earlier, the water as warm as the bath the girls shared every evening, but it was too shallow to swim in; so shallow that even Meg, wearing her floatie arm bands, could wade out quite a distance.

The kids had had regular swim lessons at the American Club in Singapore, but Annie wondered how they were going to become good swimmers, since they couldn't possibly practice their strokes in the rough ocean. Ironic that they could live on an island and not learn to swim—and, embarrassing—talk about the cobbler's children having no shoes! Adair used to brag to the other Wellesley mothers at their country club that Annie could swim before she could walk.

Brushing sand off her towel, Annie made a mental note to call the Sylvan Fell YMCA tomorrow, find out when the sign-ups were for fall swim lessons and maybe for those masters classes she'd seen posted, too.

She watched the castle-building, but could hardly keep her eyes open.

It was so serene here, worth the long walk along the beach from the parking area, although she wished someone would clear a shortcut through the scrub brush one of these days. Among the many magical things about Martha's Vineyard, South Beach's saltwater barrier ponds, separated by wide swaths of sand from the ocean, were near the top of Annie's list. She didn't know any place more placid than this pond—yet, less than a hundred yards behind them, on the other side of the dune, was the steady, tumultuous crashing of the South Beach waves.

They were probably staying too long, but the light was so exquisite in the late afternoon that it was hard to leave and, as the westward sun slid lower in the sky and the colors of the beach grass changed to gold, Annie ached with pleasure. Once the beach began to empty out around four-thirty, they had it all to themselves: a ring of sand devoid of other people, canvas chairs, striped umbrellas. Now, apart from the family from Connecticut, they were the only ones left.

A few white clouds scudded across the sky. If she didn't hurry up and dive into those waves on the other side and wake up, she wouldn't be able to manage the long trek back, the drive home, the process of getting everyone cleaned, fed, put to bed.

The kids were getting ready to fill up the moat. Independent as usual, Lily carved a detour, making part of it branch off and veer directly to the pond earlier than Robbie had instructed.

"No, Lily! You have to follow the plan. Don't make an opening there. Block that up with sand."

"This moat is stupid," Lily said. "The water is never going to make it the whole way up anyhow."

Annie agreed, but she didn't say anything. Moats work when you can build them perpendicular to the ocean and watch the incoming tide rush up and slosh apart in opposite directions, connecting in the back to make a complete arc. If you've done it right and the tide is strong enough, your castle will be surrounded by water and fully protected—for a few seconds, at least.

They would have to make do with sand castles along the pond until Saturday, when Gordon would be here and they could build along the ocean.

"Don't help, then!" Robbie snapped, and Annie suspected he knew his little sister was right. He stomped past the three boys to Meg, digging obliviously, and patted her shoulder. "Good work," he said.

Lily shrugged and came over to Annie. Curling up next to her, she reached into their canvas bag for *The Trumpet of the Swan.*

"Read to me?" she asked, running her little fingers over the smooth purple-and-white square tiles of Annie's new wampum bracelet.

They'd driven up to the Gay Head Cliffs on Sunday for lunch. While Robbie and Annie, with Meg on her hip, were still searching for whales through the viewfinders at the observation area, Lily and Gordon had sneaked down to the line of artisans' shopping stalls and bought it for her.

What if they had run into Chase and his family up there?

Gordon had given her the bracelet as they ate lobster rolls and fried clams on one of the picnic tables across from the Aquinnah Restaurant.

"This should keep you safe when I'm not here," he said, fastening the beaded clasp around her wrist, sealing it with a kiss. "Supposed to be a kind of talisman."

"They say wearing it means you'll always return to Martha's Vineyard," Lily reported.

The old Wampanoag man who'd made it happened to be sitting in a folding chair outside his shop and, smiling across at their picnic and noticing the bracelet was a little too big, offered to size it for her. He unstrung one of the purple tiles and matter-of-factly advised her to save it, in case she got fat one day and needed him to string it back in.

Annie glanced at the sky—it must be nearly five o'clock. This beach did not have a lifeguard, although a cute patrol guy cruised around periodically on his three-wheeled dune buggy and was responsible for locking the parking lot gate by six-thirty. They had been so slow packing up yesterday that, after shooing everyone else off, he had given them a lift back to their car.

"I'll have to read you the next chapter tonight, Lily, because I guess we should get going. I think I'll just dive into the waves first, to wake up."

"Good idea to go home," Lily said, taking off her blue baseball cap and pushing her matted blond hair behind her ears. "It's too sunny here, Mommy. Too sandy."

Annie told Robbie and Meg she was going to take Lily with her while she dove in, and they could stay at the pond until she got back. As she had the day before, she emphasized to Robbie that he was in charge of Meg and must not let her out of his sight. She asked the Connecticut boys' mother, who had been idly reading *People* magazine and eating Cape Cod Potato Chips all afternoon while Annie played with her sons, if she wouldn't mind watching them for a few minutes.

Of course, she replied, no sweat.

Annie took her towel and Lily's hand, and they plodded over the sand hill to the ocean.

Even this beach seemed different. The dune between the pond and the ocean used to be much higher, the beach wider. The past few years of winter storms must have eroded the dune, flattened it out a bit. So much of the Vineyard seemed different from how she remembered it, which was maybe why she constantly felt so disoriented. So out of focus.

What was Chase doing here so early in the season, in the middle of the week? Didn't he have a job? Maybe it wasn't him. After all, wasn't that a kind of stereotype—a middle-aged blond man driving a red Wrangler? It could have been anyone.

The sun's last rays angled from behind Squibnocket Point and glinted on the waves.

Ever since Annie had first swum at Long Point as a teenager, she would imagine herself here when she was trying to fall asleep, rising and falling with the swell of each wave. She had been relieved the last two days to find that, at forty, she could manage the surf now as well as when she used to come here with Chase after work at the Edgartown Inn. He, of course, had been a natural on the water: an intrepid sailor and windsurfer, a fearless swimmer.

Everything was easier then. Beaches were free, and they didn't have to worry about locked parking lots or patrols kicking them off the sand.

Long Point was notorious for its undertow, although Annie couldn't remember ever seeing anyone caught in it. Gordon, always so cautious, had asked her not to swim on her own, and last night, when she'd told him how spectacular the day had been, he'd sounded annoyed. He asked her please to find a pond not so close to such a steep beach—despite the fact that she hadn't even mentioned she'd jumped in! Maybe he suspected that, sooner or later, she might not be able to resist the temptation.

Anyway … another quick dip wouldn't hurt. The waves were moderate today—she had certainly managed bigger ones. She would dive in to feel that exhilarating sensation of cold salt water on her face, the strength in her arms as she swam underwater a few strokes, then swim out. Thirty seconds.

"Okay, Lily. You sit here on Mommy's towel and watch, like you did yesterday. I'll swim a little bit, wave to you, and swim right back. Don't move from this towel unless a wave comes. The tide is going out, so none should wash up this far. But always pay attention and remember," she admonished, repeating what she said all the time, "you must never …"

"Turn your back on the ocean. Got it," Lily said, starting to draw on the sand with a piece of driftwood.

Annie took a deep breath and waded into the water. Much as she craved it, the cold was still shocking. It was slightly rougher than yesterday but not too bad, and she let a few waves break in front of her before she dove into one headfirst. Her body tensed from the bracing chill—she felt wide-awake now. She swam in a strong crawl past where the waves were cresting. Treading water with one hand, she turned to wave at Lily. But the little girl was drawing on the sand, not watching her at all.

Putting her head back for a minute, Annie allowed the happiness to wash over her whole being. She couldn't think of any sensation that made her feel more *free*, more *glad*, than this. She closed her eyes, wished she could stay in longer, dove down one last time. Surfacing, she quickly turned to pinpoint Lily on the beach.

The waves seemed steeper here but the clear ocean was irresistible, and as she was treading water, her arms carving large figure eights, she turned seaward again and let the rhythm of the swells swing her body up and down.

She thought about her conversation on Sunday with the old Wampanoag man up at the Cliffs. He said there was something spooky about the power of wampum, something she needed to watch out for when she went swimming: a kind of double, conflicting force. Sometimes it could actually make you feel as if the ocean were trying to pull you out—tempting, *seducing* you farther than you meant to go, he said—but you needed to trust that, at the same time, the wampum would protect you, bring you safely back to shore.

Sounded a little crazy, but who was she to say? The Wampanoags arrived here 10,000 years before Bartholomew Gosnold from England did, around the year 1600. They had a relationship with the Island, with Nature and the sea, that she couldn't begin to fathom.

Facing the ocean again, she grinned broadly at the open water. Not even a sailboat interrupted her view, and she felt as if she were alone in the middle depths of the ocean, rather than just offshore. Remembering swimming here with Chase, things started to feel more familiar and she forgot she wasn't still twenty.

It was time to go back. She scanned the beach, spotted Lily drawing, and bent in toward her, once more falling into a swift crawl.

But despite a dozen strokes, she didn't make any progress. She swam harder, yet seemed to be staying in place. She looked west up the beach and saw Lily still sitting on her towel, much smaller.

With a flash of annoyance, Annie realized she must have gotten caught in a riptide. That was okay, she could handle it. She would just wait a minute, catch her breath, judge the drift. Angle her way out parallel to shore, the way she'd been taught. Pace herself.

She had to get back to the kids, though. She couldn't wait all day for the right angle.

Yet ... there was something strange going on here. Something didn't feel right. The current of the ocean seemed to be pushing the riptide eastward, toward Chappaquiddick. It was as if she were caught in two fast-flowing rivers: one pulling her out to sea and one pulling her along the shoreline.

Again she ducked into a forward crawl, more or less parallel to the beach. But again she made no progress.

Swimming in place but drifting sideways, Annie felt the water get darker, abruptly colder. She must be floating past a narrow, submerged sandbar, past some kind of underwater cliff, because all at once the water felt immensely deep, as if she'd been shoved off the continental shelf, the bottom a mile down.

She heard the *slap, slap, slap* of waves crashing and, drifting and looking over her right shoulder, sensed the tug of a swell gathering powerfully beneath her, of water surging backward. Before she knew it, she was sucked down, churned around, flipped over. Her neck snapped back, and she could see nothing except bubbles and foaming white froth.

Holding her breath, Annie kicked her way up, but the surface wavered farther and farther above her. Pulling through with her arms she began to panic, her chest strapped tight with weight, her head about to explode from pressure. She finally got her face out and, gasping, gulped a lungful of air just as another huge storm of water thundered over her. Somersaulting, she swallowed a stream of seawater—up her nose, in her mouth. Her eyes, arms, legs were tearing out of their sockets.

She kicked her way up again, sputtering, only to have the same thing happen again. The waves must be breaking against this weird underwater sandbar. She had to get away from it. Get her bearings. But the waves were coming too fast. She couldn't catch her breath. Water was filling her throat and she couldn't stop coughing.

These waves had come out of nowhere.

Another one suddenly slammed her down so deep, with such force, she swam for a minute toward the bottom thinking she was kicking up to the sky. Terrified, wrestling her way endlessly up, she reached the surface just as she was sure she would suffocate.

She was still too close to the sandbar. Gasping, her heart beating wildly, she saw another wave advancing toward her, but this time she mustered enough strength to dive straight into it, her limbs somehow pulling her all the way through so she didn't get tossed around.

She was farther out, but at least now she could try to stop coughing, keep herself buoyed on the swells. She tried to steady herself, sculling her arms and pedaling her legs. She had been pitched around before, but never like this. Never when she was by herself.

The ocean was roaring like an oncoming freight train and coming toward her was another steep, snarling, impassive wall of white water.

This was the worst yet. Again sucked down, distorted, thrown around—her body twisting, arching. The top of her bathing suit tore below her breasts.

Choking, she managed to reach her head above the surface. She tried to catch a breath but inhaled only more water. She couldn't get enough air through her nose, but if she opened her mouth to breathe, no matter which direction she faced, water sloshed down her throat. Another wave smashed over her, then another. Waves kept pulling her down; she kept fighting back up.

She had been pulled backward again, toward the sea, away from the surf. Her legs felt like lead, but somehow she managed to bob up and keep her head afloat. If only she could rest a while like this.

The ocean current was still pulling her east, but the waves had subsided. She had passed the sandbar, and began to sense she might also be out of the rip. She began a kind of weak breaststroke straight toward shore and this time, slowly, made progress. She started to regain her breath.

Up on the beach, she saw four people walking. She tried to swim harder, desperately trying to keep her face above water. Maybe she could get their attention. It was a woman with three children trailing behind. The woman stopped and, turning back to her children—boys, Annie could see now—paused to look out to sea.

Annie thought the woman saw her, but there was such a glare from the low sun and water she couldn't be sure. Couldn't she see that she was in trouble? Was she, in fact, looking at her? Or just looking out?

"I am drowning!" Annie tried to scream, just as she felt that petrifying tugging beneath her again, that backward surge. A lone wave slammed into her. She thrashed around frantically, like a wild dolphin ensnared in a fishing net.

Back up, panting, she could see the woman still staring in her direction. The boys had stopped behind her and were looking out too. Squinting, Annie realized it was the Cape Cod Potato Chip lady. They must be looking for her.

She tried to motion to the woman again. But she was so tired she could no longer hold her arm up and tread water. Couldn't they see her?

"*Help!*" she yelled, her voice swallowed by the howl of the ocean.

The family was staring toward her. Annie couldn't breathe. All she could do was inhale little blasts of air, water splashing into her mouth. She tried to catch the woman's attention but, impossibly, the woman turned away. She turned and continued walking slowly up the beach, toward the parking lot. The boys followed, tramping along the sand. They disappeared.

With the next wave, Annie realized that she was completely on her own. And as she continued gasping for breath, it hit her that she was drowning. No one was going to help her. That lady wasn't. The patrol wasn't. No one was.

Each time she opened her eyes, a torrent of salt water flooded them shut again. She had to get to Lily, to Robbie, to Meg. Where were they?

She didn't have any strength left. Everything was too heavy. Her arms couldn't figure-eight through the water anymore. Her legs weren't cycling her up. She had no lungs. She was dizzy. All she could feel was the cold, burning salt water in her eyes and nose and down her throat, inside all of her.

Suddenly, Annie's body, already so tense, became paralyzed, and a rage welled up within her. How *dare* that woman leave! How *dare* she not help! That woman had deserted Robbie and Meg—stranded them by the pond, not knowing whether their mother was ever coming back! She and her sons must have walked right by Lily, waiting on the sand—unless, what if something had happened to Lily, and she wasn't still sitting there? What if Lily had wandered off and gotten lost? What if—she had been carried out by a wave?

With a furious blast of adrenaline, Annie began kicking, pulling toward shore. She extended her arms as far forward as they would go, cupping her hands, moving the water, finally swimming, and then—for a weird, eerie split second, she felt Chase beside her. She heard his self-assured voice coaxing her to not give up, to trust herself in the sea, to try harder, to keep going. Telling her she could do this.

Once more she felt that petrifying tug, that now-familiar surge below her. Gasping for breath, she braced herself. But this time, instead of getting sucked under like a piece of flotsam, she managed to catch it just right. She stopped swimming and let herself be borne along the crest of the wave toward shore.

This was a tremendous wave. She aimed her arms together overhead, forced her legs in a flutter kick, willed the wave to carry her.

She and Chase used to swim out of the ocean and afterwards he would wrap her in one of his mother's huge velour towels. He'd hold her, quiet on the sand, until the warm sun dropped behind Squibnocket and left them, standing alone in the day's last bit of rosy light.

Unexpectedly, violently, Annie crashed sideways onto the pebbles.

She crawled forward through a wash of white foam up the sharp incline, grasping for the beach like the early amphibians in those evolution films. She pressed her weight forward and dug her fingers into the sand to prevent the same wave that had delivered her from sucking her back out.

Finally on dry sand, kneeling on all fours, her body went into convulsion, wrenching. Cold ocean water spewed out of her mouth. Vomit and tears streamed down her face.

She had no time for this! Had to get going, had to stand up. She couldn't feel her legs because her brain was not controlling her body, but somehow they managed to right themselves. She started walking. She had to find Lily.

What if a wave had washed over her? *How could she have left her there?* What had she done?

How *dare* that potato chip lady ditch her kids! How dare *Annie* ditch them? *How could this have happened?* Annie berated herself for panicking in the waves, for wasting so much time, for diving in the water in the first place. What if she had drowned?

Not a soul was on the beach. The shore stretched as far as she could see.

The bottom of her bathing suit was loaded with sand. Trudging forward, she yanked up her top from where it had slipped down around her waist and felt a fierce stinging across her breasts. Her whole upper body was ripped into a red rash, rubbed raw from the rocks.

Her hand was slippery with blood, but she couldn't tell where it was coming from. She kept on, eventually figuring out that she must have clamped her teeth down so hard on her lips and the sides of her tongue that she'd bitten right through them.

The sun was even with the horizon; it was way past six o'clock. So ridiculous, so trivial to have to worry about locked beach gates when she had almost just drowned.

She was too far down the beach, still couldn't see Lily. The sand from the low tide was wet, and her feet kept sinking. She bent forward and tried to propel her arms as if she were running, trying to set her legs in motion, but they refused to go. She supposed she was walking but she was barely moving, like in a nightmare.

Her teeth were chattering uncontrollably and kept slicing into her swollen lips and tongue. Now she was swallowing blood. The wind had picked up and was whipping her face. She was freezing cold and couldn't see her daughter; her heart was beating so fast she still couldn't catch her breath.

After what seemed a very, very long time, she was at last able to decipher what she thought must be the little figure that was Lily on the sand. She tried to run, but she couldn't because her legs still weren't moving normally.

"*Lily!*" she tried to shout. "I'm coming!" But no sound came out, and anyway there was no use because the wind just whipped the words right back in her face.

The little girl had not budged from her towel. She was standing up, minding her, still holding the driftwood and scanning the ocean. One small hand shaded her eyes in a kind of salute. She was crying, but somehow Annie sensed that she had faith, that she absolutely trusted that her mother would return.

Annie reached into the wash of a wave to rinse the blood from her face.

Lily looked down the beach and began running toward her. Annie tried to jog to meet her, but she still couldn't lift her feet.

"Mommy! It took you so long! I knowed you wouldn't drown! I was drawing then I couldn't see you. I wanted Robbie, but you telled me not to leave my towel. I was so scared, Mommy!" She wasn't speaking like her daughter who had just turned six, but like a two-year-old.

Annie collapsed onto her knees and held Lily tightly on the sand, hugging her, rocking back and forth, letting her sob. Her head was still reeling, but she felt too delirious, too cold, too exhausted, to cry anymore herself. She did not want ever to let go of Lily, but all she could think was that she had to get to Robbie and Meg on the other side of the dune and get them all off the beach before the patrol locked the parking lot, and she wasn't sure she had enough strength.

Later, she could never remember how she made it over the dune to the pond back to her children, who looked small and deserted on their blanket. Meg had fallen asleep. Robbie was sitting next to her, reading *The Trumpet of the Swan*. He had packed everything up.

He saw them approaching and stood up.

"Where did you go, Mommy! What took so long? I didn't know what to do. I was just about to come find you. Meg fell asleep. Those people left. The moat didn't work."

Annie didn't respond but, holding Lily with one hand, again sank down on the sand. She hugged Robbie hard. They were all right.

The castle had been squashed; she could see a zigzag of angry footprints where the turrets had been.

"Your lip is bleeding," Robbie said.

She could have drowned and never made it back. Did that even cross the Cape Cod Potato Chip lady's mind?

"Robbie, Robbie, Mommy almost drown-ded! I was watching and then she wasn't there." Lily was still crying.

Her breath was starting to come back. Annie tried to push some wet hair off of her face, but her fingers weren't working. Directing all her strength into her voice, she attempted to sound nonchalant.

"No, no," her voice said, sounding strangely hoarse and watery. "I did *not* almost drown. Just got carried in the undertow a little, that's all."

Robbie scowled at her. "You should be more careful. There's probably a rip current, like Daddy said. Didn't you read the sign in the parking lot? You're supposed to just go limp, like this, and you'll float out of it." He shrugged his head and neck forward and dangled his arms to demonstrate, then bent over a little farther to shake Meg. "Wake up, lazy. Time to go."

Annie *had* gone limp, but if she'd allowed herself to float out she'd be dead and halfway to Nantucket by now. She picked up Meg and hugged her against her hip.

At that moment, by some grace of God, the patrol appeared on the top of the dune. It wasn't the cute young guy but a different, older one.

"You need to leave the beach now, ma'am," he said.

The kids looked beseechingly at Annie, hoping she would somehow arrange things so they could hitch a ride the way they had yesterday.

The patrol gazed at her for a minute. She must look wild, like someone who had tumbled face-first out of the spin cycle of a washing machine. Like herself in her dream.

At that moment, her whole body started shaking uncontrollably again. She willed it to stop, to calm down, but it wouldn't.

Her teeth started chattering. Her body, freezing cold, was completely detached from her head.

"You all right, ma'am?"

"Yeah," she said, forcing control of her voice. "Maybe a little chilled. Dove in for a second and, you know, got caught a bit in the rip. I'm fine, though. Everything's fine." She'd slipped into a broader Boston accent than normal.

"Well, you're lucky," the patrol said. Squinting, studying her, his eyes rested on her bleeding mouth. "It looks like you might be shaking from shock. A little hypothermic, I'd say."

From the back of his dune buggy he pulled out one of those aluminum-looking space blankets, the kind Gordon wore at the end of his marathons.

Gordon was going to be so furious.

"What were you doin' swimmin' alone and leavin' these kids here, anyway?" The patrol switched off the motor and leaned back a little on the wide seat. "Didn't you hear what happened? A kid just drowned off Katama. A teenager."

Katama was about three miles farther east along the shore, in the direction she was being carried.

"The riptide got fierce this afta-noon, all of a sudden," he continued. "If it stays like this we'll prob'ly have to close the beach tomorrow."

Annie's eyes, dry and scratchy, welled up. Someone had actually drowned today?

The patrol climbed down onto the sand. Maybe because there were so many out-of-state tourists here now and recognizing from her accent that she was from Massachusetts, he treated her as if he'd always known her, as if she were one of them. In the club. A Vineyarder.

He reached into a cooler tied to the back of his buggy and pulled out a bottle of water, kindly averting his eyes as he handed it to her.

"Come on, kids, hop on the back. Mum, you sit here and hold the little girl. You'll be all right."

In the beach parking lot, the children were quieter and more cooperative than usual, rinsing off their feet with the hose and helping pack everything into the car. Annie could not stop shivering. Robbie silently pulled off his sweatshirt and handed it to her. She stretched it on under an old one of Jared's she'd tossed earlier into the car.

No one spoke as they inched down the long, rutted dirt road to the paved West Tisbury-Edgartown Road, where they turned left. She was careful to remember to turn into the right lane—to keep herself, as driver, in the center of the road, her left shoulder hugging the yellow dividing line.

Robbie sat in the front passenger seat, refusing to look at her, staring out the window. Lily rested her head on Meg's car seat, crying quietly, while Meg sucked her left thumb and stroked her sister's back absently with her right.

The airport runway was directly beside them, behind some woods and a fence, and Annie sensed the children were missing Gordon and wondering why they'd let him get on his airplane Sunday.

A small Cape Air Cessna flew low and loud overhead, causing them all to jump.

"Everything is okay, it's all right, it's over," she said. "We'll be home in ten minutes."

She put the girls in the bathtub and let Robbie have the first outdoor shower. The cardinal was at the bird feeder.

Robbie complained that the backyard smelled of what they referred to as "Island perfume," and was worried the skunk might still be hiding out there. "We have to leave the beach earlier from now on, Mommy," he stated.

Annie microwaved some sesame noodles she'd made the other

day, and warmed up frozen chicken nuggets and peas. Luckily, she'd bought a quart of cherry tomatoes and some fruit from the farm stand on Middle Road in the morning; there wasn't much else left in the refrigerator. She'd have to take them all to Cronig's tomorrow. Sounded ambitious.

From the top shelf in the kitchen, Annie reached for the bone china teapot, the one with the pink-and-red rose pattern, that she'd so carefully carried back for Aunt Faye from her college semester in England. She'd bought it, along with two matching cups and saucers, so they could have tea together in the afternoons. The spout, over the years, had acquired a little chip.

She remembered how Aunt Faye used to ask people, whenever they joined her for tea, whether they would like a cup or a mug. She was never one to inflict her preferences on others.

Each time Annie breathed in, her nose, throat, and lungs felt as if they were being stabbed with a thousand icicles. If she'd been alone for supper, which she couldn't remember ever being, she would have just eaten crackers or cereal straight out of the box and gone to bed.

Yesterday, her cousin Juliet had called from her office and commented, "No matter how well-behaved and nice your children are, three is an awful lot to manage on your own in a new place in the summer with no school. Unless, of course, you just let them stay home and watch television. I don't know many people who could do it."

"Well, maybe you don't know many people," Annie had replied.

"Are you sure you shouldn't get an *au pair?*"

"I'm managing just fine, thanks," Annie had said.

But maybe Juliet was right. Maybe, in fact, she couldn't manage.

She lit the wood stove in the living room and let the children watch an Arthur the Aardvark video while they ate supper, and she took a shower with what little was left of the hot water. It had really cooled off outside. Afterwards, she microwaved a bowl of

Campbell's tomato soup for herself, and not until then did she begin to warm up.

Aunt Faye used to make brownies from scratch for them on cold nights like this, so Annie pulled down her old tattered *Joy of Cooking* from above the stove. She felt that familiar pang of grief when it fell open to her aunt's brownie recipe, pleasantly seasoned with smudges of flour and chocolate. She stared at the words swimming around the page for a while before she put the book back on the shelf.

Instead she found some Pepperidge Farm cookies she'd bought the week before, and arranged them in a sort of heart shape. She poured glasses of milk and herself another cup of tea. She kept taking deep breaths to check whether the icicles, the frozen shards of glass in her throat, might have begun to melt. But they hadn't.

The kids looked as forlorn as she felt. She had to think of something.

"Did I ever tell you," she began, lifting Meg onto her lap as they all moved over to the old wooden pews that lined the long table, the ones Uncle Emmett had rescued from a nineteenth-century meetinghouse on Tea Lane, "about your, let's see, *great*-great-grandmother, Miss Liza Robinson?"

The kids rolled their eyes at being subjected to another one of her stories, but leaned forward a little to listen.

"Well, around when Abraham Lincoln was president, when she was twenty, Liza decided to take a trip out West to visit a cousin who had gone prospecting for gold in Colorado. That was considered the last frontier then, not even a state yet. Are you sure I haven't told you this story before?"

Annie sipped her tea and speculated about how many pots it would take to raise the temperature of the ocean water still gurgling in her lungs. "Liza used to tell Grandpa, Aunt Faye, and Uncle Dwight this story herself, because she lived to be a hundred and two. Well, back then people had to travel by covered wagon, and crossing the Great Plains they had to be especially careful. The Native Americans were pretty mad about being driven off their land, and occasionally they'd capture people in the night and scalp them, or set fire to their wagons."

Meg snuggled into Annie's chest with her pink blankie. Robbie shuddered. Lily had found her coloring book and paused for a second, her crayon suspended in the air.

"One night they parked their wagons in a circle in front of the fire, as usual, and ate dinner—I'm pretty sure they had baked beans and hot dogs—and fell right asleep. They forgot to leave a lookout. But Liza stayed awake and, suddenly, what did she see through the darkness but men running toward them, carrying torches. They were going to set fire to their wagons and steal their horses!"

Annie reached her arm around Meg to pour more milk for the older two and took another sip from her china teacup. She liked to prolong the suspense in her stories.

"How do you know they had hot dogs? Can we have hot dogs?" Lily asked.

"Liza shook the men awake, shouting at them to get the wagons ready. But her driver had drunk so much whiskey that he kept falling over. He couldn't sit straight enough to drive and the torches were getting closer, so Liza climbed to the front herself, swishing up in her long proper dress, and shoved him aside. She took the reins and held a rifle in her lap, ready to shoot if need be."

"Wait," Robbie said, at last impressed. "How is she related to us again?"

"It's not easy to drive a team of six big horses," Annie continued. "And it's not as if Liza had grown up on a farm. She didn't exactly know what she was doing, but she knew she had to do *something*, to help save everyone, and she trusted herself enough to know she was strong. She managed to steer the horses across the Great Plains all through the night. She and the other wagons didn't stop until they got to the Mississippi River. She was a hero-ine! People talked about her for years out there. Probably still do."

Robbie and Lily grinned at each other.

"All of our ancestors came to America a long time ago, on ships. We cannot even imagine how difficult *that* must have been. Liza used to tell Grandpa she wasn't scared while she was driving the wagon in the dark because she figured if her ancestors could make it across the great Atlantic Ocean, well, she could make it across the great American Plains."

The teacup rattled as she replaced it on the saucer. It had a little chip, too, just like the teapot. She rotated the cup so she wouldn't have to look at it.

"There was no way I was going to let anything bad happen to us today at Long Point. Was I smart to go in the waves by myself? To leave you alone on the sand? No, I wasn't, and I'm sorrier than I can say. I made a terrible, terrible mistake, and from now on, I will be much more careful." She bit her lower lip the way she tended to, and could taste it bleeding again. "I want you always to remember about Liza, though, because we take after her. We are a lot braver than we think."

Annie did not feel particularly brave. She didn't, in fact, know how she felt, other than very certain she would never again set foot in the ocean.

Lily tucked in the cover of her crayon box and climbed off the bench to where Annie sat with Meg. Robbie came over, too, and put his arms around her neck. The four of them hugged like that for a while.

"And now," Annie said, squeezing back the tears in her eyes and not wanting to let go of her children, "it's time for bed."

8

The Brass Ring

The next day it rained, so they were able to avoid any discussion of going to the beach. Instead, like everyone else, it seemed, they went to Oak Bluffs to ride the Flying Horses, America's oldest carousel, transplanted from Coney Island in the 1880s. Other families with small children wearing raincoats and hoods spilled off the sidewalks onto Circuit and Kennebec Avenues, bobbing along in front of the ferry terminal and the two movie theaters, flooding the front of the pinball arcade.

Annie searched for a parking place along the green oval of Ocean Park, pointing out the elaborate scrollwork that trimmed the roof edges of the Victorian houses and their unusual combinations of pretty colors. As opposed to San Francisco's "painted ladies," here they were known more innocently as gingerbread cottages and had given Oak Bluffs its original name of Cottage City.

A red Jeep Wrangler cut in ahead of her, coming up short at handicapped parking places and fire hydrants and then pulling dejectedly forward. At the top of Ocean Park, rather than circling again, the Jeep turned abruptly right to follow the beach road along Nantucket Sound. It was hard to tell through the windshield wipers and pelting rain, but Annie could have sworn she saw a blond man at the wheel. She recognized the back of his head. She wondered if he knew a secret place to park that she didn't know, or if he'd given up and decided to go to Edgartown instead.

Eventually she found a parking place, and she and the kids

headed down the hill to the Flying Horses.

Inside the musty, wooden carousel building, the wide planks of the floor were wet from all the dripping umbrellas and raincoats, and the air smelled like stale clams. Salty vapor seemed to rise visibly from everyone's bodies. The Tuckers filed behind the other summer people, in line between plastic sections of white-picket fence put there to keep order. Annie's hair, usually cooperative, was so frizzy it fluffed out about a foot off her scalp, like the Chia pets they used to have in Singapore.

This was not the time to run into Chase St. Clair and his purportedly beautiful wife.

When it was their turn, Robbie lifted Meg onto a purple horse on the outside of the platform and strapped her in, then helped Lily onto the horse opposite, on the inside, and showed her how to fasten the strap herself—even though these horses didn't go up and down like on new merry-go-rounds, and no one was likely to fall off. Then he climbed up behind Meg.

With each revolution of the carousel, riders would grab at shiny silver rings that spurted out of two chutes of incongruous, robotic-looking metal arms installed on either side of the platform. Annie watched, the humidity and hurly-burly music making her drowsy and dizzy, occasionally glancing around to see if any handsome blond men had joined the line.

As soon as the college-age girl in charge announced that the brass ring was *now in place*, older children, and all the teenagers and dads, became frenetic, whipping out as many rings as possible each time they went around—two, three, sometimes even four. She and Chase used to be greedy like that here, too.

Robbie and Lily, each holding one hand tightly onto their horse's pole, Robbie's arm stretched around Meg, both leaned sideways as they approached the chute, anticipating the grasping. But they could never manage to extract more than one ring at a time. And then the organ music slowed down, just as Robbie and

Meg's purple horse approached, and the lucky brass ring was there, waiting for them. Robbie pulled it out with a flourish and handed it to Meg, and everyone in line cheered.

Robbie said Meg should take the free ride, since she would have reached for the brass ring if she'd only been a little taller, and this made Annie's eyes well again with tears. She let them stay for two more turns and forgot to look around for Mr. and Mrs. Chase St. Clair.

When they got home, Annie laid out newspapers on the tiled floor of the screened-in porch so that Meg and Lily could finger paint, and she and Robbie embarked on a fresh game of Monopoly. Four rolls of the dice landed Robbie's race car on Boardwalk; a few moves later, she landed on Park Place. She hemmed and hawed and pretended not to be able to afford it, so he could have a match and start putting up houses.

While she didn't want Robbie to think she was letting him win, the truth was she couldn't have cared less. Instead, she took comfort in counting out the spaces with her old shoe token, smooth from thousands of laps around the board, and as "banker" she enjoyed meting out the tiny houses: wooden in this old set, not plastic like in the new one they'd bought in Singapore.

Playing Monopoly made her miss her cousin Emmett, Aunt Faye's son. She thought it interesting that Robbie wanted to be the race car, just as Emmett always had. When Robbie had first chosen it, a small part of her wondered if she should say no, hide it in her underwear drawer, retire it in Emmett's memory like a baseball jersey. But her cousin would have scoffed at her. ("What do you want a little boy to be?" he'd have asked. "The thimble?")

Although ... Emmett hadn't been the scoffing type. He would point things out considerately, never sarcastically. He was gentle. Not particularly tall or adventurous, not athletic or funny, but quiet, small boned. It took a while to get to know him. It was

Emmett who taught Annie how to play board games, Emmett who always waited for her on his bike, whereas Juliet always sped ahead.

Emmett's only complaint about the house on Middle Road had been that there was no piano, and he would often wile away sunny mornings inside the big pine hall at the Chilmark Center playing the out-of-tune upright there. He could play anything: all the standards, pop, Mozart, Beethoven. He'd met Chase only a few times before he was killed, and while they didn't have much in common besides the Vineyard, they got along: they were both the type who could see the best in everyone, always find something to talk about.

Annie threw the dice and landed on St. Charles Place. She couldn't remember a single thing about Emmett's funeral, except to say that it was the saddest event of her life. Much sadder than Aunt Faye's.

Her younger brother, Percy, really lost out, playing golf on the mainland instead of those intense Monopoly games with their cousins Emmett and Juliet. He'd missed getting to know them. That's probably why he hadn't bothered to come back from New Zealand for Aunt Faye's funeral.

When Robbie said he wanted to take a break from the game, Annie went into the kitchen to call Aunt Faye. She picked up the receiver and started dialing the Wellesley number on the rotary phone.

She wanted to tell Aunt Faye about her funeral, to fill her in on the details. She wanted to describe the yellow roses, the choir marching down the aisle in crimson robes and crisp white surplices, the choice of hymns ("All Things Bright and Beautiful"; "Joyful, Joyful We Adore Thee"). She wanted to recount some of the comments she'd overheard, because Aunt Faye would find them hilarious, and it would be fun to laugh right now.

First of all, it was funny how mortified Annie's mother, Adair, had been that the reception was to be held in the St. Andrew's church hall instead of at the Wellesley Country Club. Adair wasn't interested in the fact that Faye's will specifically dictated that the reception absolutely should be held there, not at the club. (Faye had never been a fan of clubs.) Then, mingling, Adair kept alluding to her sister-in-law's abrupt death as if it were some kind of enviable coup: "I can't be*lieve* she did that!" (As if anyone had control over a brain aneurism.) Adair repeated this so many times, she'd begun to sound competitive.

Annie wanted to tell Aunt Faye how Juliet had remarked, "Well, my *good*ness. Wasn't *that* the most capricious act of our dear aunt's most capricious life?" And how Uncle Dwight, Juliet's father, had downed a few too many glasses of sherry yet somehow managed to slur his way through a very touching eulogy, while Aunt Connie, Juliet's mother, gazed serenely up at her husband in a loaded-on-Valium kind of way.

Annie wanted to tell Aunt Faye how her own father, Faye's younger *brother*, consistently incapable of providing any emotional support whatsoever, kept muttering, "People die, Annie. For crissakes, don't make a scene."

Annie was halfway through dialing the Wellesley number before she remembered Faye wouldn't answer, and she slowly latched the receiver back on the wall. Aunt Faye would have gotten a real kick out of her own funeral. It was such a shame she had to miss it.

The night before she died, Aunt Faye had telephoned Annie; she'd always been wonderful about "checking in." She was a firm believer in two cocktails before dinner—Seagram's Seven being her drink of choice—and had sounded a little loopy. Aunt Faye loved the ceremony of sitting down in the living room and having a drink with cheese and crackers on the coffee table while supper waited on the stove, of using her parents' pre-World War I silver tongs to place ice cubes in the old crystal low-ball glasses. And, just as reliable as her Triscuits and Cabot's Vermont cheddar, was the way she'd pour her second drink with a wink and say,

"Can't fly on one wing, you know."

Standing there, her head resting on her clasped hands against the wall of the cottage, Annie could almost hear her aunt's crackling New England accent.

"How are you?" Aunt Faye had asked. "Making any friends down there in Maryland? Oh, who cares—get to know your children and your husband, that's what counts. *Get to know your family.* Me? Fine, fine … alone with this good dog, Tashmoo. I just miss people, that's all. I miss my husband, Jared; my son, Emmett; my first husband, Emmett; my parents … Everyone has died! I've got my two brothers, I suppose, and Juliet across town, and *you,* my dear, but you're busy with those babies, as you should be. I miss my young Vineyard friends, too. Never mind, let's talk about something else. Tell me, how is Robbie, the young professor?"

Robbie called her to play again. It was her turn. Annie sat down on the floor at the Monopoly board, and tossed the dice.

Gordon called several times a day: when he got to work, at lunch, when he got home, while eating his supper, while carrying the cordless phone puttering around fixing things in the house, and, of course, while flossing his teeth. A lot of times, Annie couldn't think of a single interesting thing to say—"*Breaking news! I just bought Ventnor Avenue!*"—and sometimes there would be long pauses. Gordon was preoccupied with financial problems in Thailand and Indonesia and apparently just needed her company on the other end of the telephone line. It seemed that the content of their actual conversations was, to him, irrelevant.

Wednesday night, despite one of their long pauses, she still hadn't mentioned what had happened at Long Point because she was afraid he would scold her. She hadn't intended to tell him Thursday, either, thinking she would tell him in person on the weekend, but that night there was something about that comforting lilt of his voice that prompted the story to spill out of her.

She toned it down quite a lot, which is maybe why he seemed unfazed. Distracted. Maybe he wasn't really listening, didn't realize she'd almost drowned, because he said hardly anything. Maybe it was all too far away for him to comprehend … maybe he had too much on his mind with the pending collapse of the Thai baht and how that would affect currencies and economic development throughout Asia and the world.

Whatever the reason, it hurt her feelings.

Ever since Long Point, Annie had slept in fits and starts. She'd wake up in the pitch dark just as she was alone drowning—not off some Atlantic beach but in the midst of a vast sea, way off the coast of some tropical Asian country. She could feel herself clammy and cold and would sit up shivering, reaching for Aunt Faye's old wedding quilt, while at the same time she could see herself floating in her dream, as if she were watching through an underwater camera. Another time she dreamt she was spinning, riding a real horse too fast off a merry-go-round.

She would go upstairs to check on the kids and lie down with Meg—cradling her, hoping to still breathe in even the slightest baby wisp of vanilla in the soft folds of her arms and neck—until Meg would stretch and kick and send Annie fumbling her way back downstairs.

When Annie woke up on Thursday night, she truly could not breathe. The bedroom had become unbearably hot and stuffy. Her heart was racing a mile a minute, and her whole body was covered with a skim of sweat. She wanted to explode out of her skin. Bolting upright against the pillows, she ran outside and lurched through the sliding kitchen door. Her lungs could not open; her head could not contain her brain. Her arms were shaking as she paced back and forth outside along the deck.

She must be having a heart attack, must be about to die. Her body had stopped, frozen shut—nothing inside her was moving except for her heart, which was pounding so vehemently she was afraid it was about to burst through her chest.

She couldn't swallow but she was gasping, the way you do in the last stage of labor. Or the way Louise, her college roommate the doctor, had told her once that people do right before they die. Your breathing turns into something called, what was it? Agonal respiration, that was it. Agonal for agony.

She was dying, that's why she was panting like this. She was going to die and abandon her children.

What if she had drowned? That had been really, really close. What would have happened to the children, deserted in the dark on the beach, if the patrol hadn't come? Robbie didn't even know how to get back to their house yet. He didn't even know their address. They had no friends here. Where would the kids have gone?

How could she have been so irresponsible? How could she have let herself get so clobbered?

She leaned over the railing and threw up.

Eventually she went inside and lay down with the telephone and, even though it was three in the morning, dialed the house in Sylvan Fell. But it just rang and rang. She thought maybe she had misdialed and called back, but again Gordon didn't answer. For a minute, Annie began panting again. Her insides stabbed.

What if he's not home? What if he has a secret life with, say, his new secretary from Zimbabwe, Kalisa, whom she hadn't gotten around to meeting yet? Annie had no real way of knowing what he was doing or where he was. He could be doing anything! Sleeping anywhere, with anyone!

What the hell was the matter with her? She had to calm herself down. With every bit of concentration she could muster, she began slowly counting her breaths the way she'd learned in Lamaze classes. Labor had been much easier to control than this.

After a while, counting, she remembered that all spring she kept forgetting to put a phone extension in their bedroom, and Gordon probably just hadn't heard the ring from the kitchen.

9

Tashmoo

The humidity woke Annie up, and at first she thought it must be noon. Starting Monday morning at nine o'clock, the kids would have to be at the Chilmark Community Center—where, in the 1970s, she, Emmett, and Juliet had also gone, to what was up-Island Martha's Vineyard's version of summer camp. There would be no more sleeping late.

The first thing she did was write an emergency contact list—Gordon; Kalisa; Juliet and her husband, Lonny, in Wellesley and in Maine; Aunt Connie and Uncle Dwight, also in Wellesley; her parents and brother in New Zealand—and tape it to the refrigerator. She had no one on the Island except Heather next door and Caleb the caretaker, so she added them too, quickly making copies to give to them both.

It was hot, like Hong Kong in summer, but at least it wasn't raining, and they were all excited about Gordon's arrival that evening. Annie made chocolate chip pancakes (bad choice, too heavy for the weather) and they discussed what to do to get ready. She wanted to organize things, finish the laundry. Lily and Meg wanted to make a welcome sign for when they met Gordon at the airport, and began taping construction paper together. Robbie wanted to set up the croquet game, even though he had never played before and didn't know the correct formation of the wickets. "Let me show you how to set them up," Annie offered, but Robbie, hauling the croquet set out from the shed, said he would do it his way.

In her bedroom, matching socks, adding to the piles of clean clothes that covered the bed, Annie mulled over exactly how she was going to keep the kids occupied all day. She didn't ever want to go back to Long Point, couldn't get a car sticker to Lambert's Cove because they technically didn't live in West Tisbury, and the kids, Robbie especially, would be bored at Seth's Pond. She wondered whether they should try Lucy Vincent Beach in Chilmark. The problem was—that was an ocean beach, too.

Suddenly Robbie ran inside, shouting. "Our cousin is here, Mommy! And he has a *dog* with him!"

Perched on the edge of a wooden chair at the round table on the deck, a large yellow dog at his feet, was Juliet's son, Emmett. At nineteen, wearing brand-new boat shoes, he looked as preppy as Lonny, Juliet's husband. The dog stood up when he saw Annie and wagged his tail.

"What a nice surprise!" Annie exclaimed, giving the dog's head a cursory pat. She and her cousin hugged, somewhat formally; she'd been away so long that she'd pretty much missed his growing up. Lily knelt down next to the dog.

"I haven't seen you since the funeral," Annie went on. She felt happy to have a visitor, though worried he might notice the blister on her swollen lower lip. Maybe he would be too polite to mention it if he did.

"Would you like some lemonade, Emmett? Jeez, you look like your dad."

"Yeah, I get that a lot." He smiled as he picked a strand of yellow dog hair off his faded red shorts.

"It's a compliment. How are you? How did you like your freshman year? Your mom said you're working at your dad's bank for the summer. Awesome that your sister won all those awards for her high school graduation. Heard from her yet? I wonder how she likes her art program. So lucky to be in Venice! Imagine, a whole summer in Italy."

She had to stop talking so fast or she'd scare him away.

Emmett nodded. "All good," he said. "Caroline called only once, when she got there. I wish she'd write a letter soon, or maybe find a computer and try emailing." He chuckled; that sounded complicated. "I just wish Mum would relax. She's been driving me and Dad crazy."

"Your mom can be a worrywart," Annie said, smiling. "I would've picked you up at the ferry, you know." She gestured toward the gravel driveway and noticed an olive-green Subaru Outback. "Oh! You brought your *car* over?" Seemed a bit extravagant. Did he always travel with Faye's dog? "I guess it must be weird for you to be here without Aunt Faye, your *great*-aunt. Weird for me, too."

"It's nice to be here, Aunt Anna. Nice to see you. The kids got, like, big. It's nice and peaceful here. But, well, I can't stay too long." Annie couldn't understand why he was so nervous. "Ah, I almost forgot. My mother sent these books down. *When We Were Very Young* for Lily, and this new one for Robbie. Cool you guys have the same birthday."

Emmett handed Lily A. A. Milne's classic book of poems featuring Christopher Robin and introducing Winnie-the-Pooh, and placed a hardcover book called *Harry Potter and the Philosopher's Stone* on the table. "This has only just been published in London, can't get it here yet. I'm looking forward to reading it, myself."

"That's very nice of you," Annie said.

How many times between them were they going to say "nice"?

"Well, um, this is, like, a little awkward," Emmett said, standing up. "You see Tashmoo here? Remember him, Aunt Faye's nice dog?"

"Of course. His bed is still in the downstairs bedroom. You can take it back with you in your car."

Lily was carefully balancing a bowl of water. She knelt back down and placed it before the dog.

"I knew he was thirsty," she said, stroking him as he lapped up the water. Then he stretched out on his side and put his head right in her lap.

"Dogs pant when they're hot. That's how they sweat," Robbie informed her from the yard.

He had finished placing the croquet wickets haphazardly all over the field and was building something with a lot of sticks and string just arm's length from the hammock, where Meg was now lying on her stomach, sucking her thumb and keeping a weather eye on Tashmoo. Robbie occasionally gave the hammock a gentle, reassuring push.

"That's nice," Emmett said, nodding at Tashmoo and Lily and looking truly relieved. "Good. My mother thought the kids would love him."

"Sure, we're okay with dogs," Annie said. "I mean, well … Meg sometimes gets a little nervous around them. But Tashmoo seems friendly. The last time I saw him was in Wellesley. Talk about loyal—he wouldn't leave Aunt Faye's side."

Her hair was making her neck itch, and she wrapped it into a ponytail.

"So, Emmett," she went on. "Can you stay the weekend? You can sleep in your namesake Emmett's old bed, and Robbie can sleep on the window seat in the sun porch. Gordon arrives tonight and would love to see you, too. Are you sure you want to work in town all summer? Why don't you live with us and be our au pair? I'm sorry I don't have any dog food for it, but …"

"Tashmoo. His name is *Tashmoo*. Aunt Faye named him after, you know, Lake Tashmoo, where Uncle Jared used to keep his boat. Do you ever go down there, in Vineyard Haven? Can be, like, a lot of mosquitoes. Anyway, we have that boat up in Kennebunk now at my dad's mooring, with his other boats. Dad and I sailed it up two summers ago, after Uncle Jared, you know, died. It's just a day sailer, but it's a nice boat." He took a long sip of lemonade.

A red cardinal appeared at Gordon's hanging feeder and began pecking at the birdseed, flapping its wings. Tashmoo surprised them all by jumping up and wagging his tail, excited for no apparent reason. He let out an urgent-sounding bark.

Annie wasn't sure where Emmett was going with all of this, but she liked having him there because he looked so … familiar. She studied him more closely and realized it wasn't his father he looked like but rather his namesake, his older cousin Emmett, around the time that he died.

Why was she missing him so much lately? Why had he had to die when he was only this Emmett's age? He, who rarely went out at night, but decided to go to a party on New Year's Eve, only to be hit by a drunk middle-aged couple on Route 128.

"Yeah, Tashmoo's a good boy," young Emmett continued. "Not your typical dog. Well-mannered and smart, like our old Amos. He died that same summer as Uncle Jared."

Emmett gazed across the field and combed his hair behind his ear with his fingers, and Annie noticed that his hair was almost exactly the same color as hers.

"You remember Amos, right? He was a release puppy from the guide dog place, same as Tashmoo here. I guess Aunt Faye was pretty impressed with our Amos, to want to get herself the same kind."

"No kidding," said Annie. The backs of her thighs were sticking to the wooden slats of the chair.

"Anyway," Emmett resumed, "my parents have been taking care of Tashmoo since, you know, well, February. My sister, Caroline, was a big help, before she took off for Italy. I'm not sure why, but last night I was out at the house for dinner and … well, my parents were getting ready to go up to Kennebunk and Mum just, like, *flipped out.* I guess she thought I was going to, like, move home and take care of him or something. But I got a sublet in town on Tremont Street with a guy from school, also an economics major. Dad's going to be in Maine so much this summer, it's not like I could commute with him. Not that I'd want to."

The cardinal hopped onto the deck railing and stood listening, and Tashmoo wagged his tail. Emmett reached across to the middle of the table and snapped off a dead bud from the petunia plant.

"My job is to assist one of the loan officers. It's kind of, well … so far, anyway, *boring*, to tell you the truth."

Annie's mind wandered to her clothes sorting and her quandary about how to get a Lucy Vincent Beach parking pass.

"Do you still play the saxophone, Emmett? I remember going to one of your concerts when you were in high school. Seemed like you were always standing up to play a solo."

He smiled. "Thanks. Yeah, I play in a jazz band at school. We have gigs … people actually pay us to play at their parties."

"Cool."

"How about croquet?" Robbie called from the field. "Do you know how to play that?"

"Yeah, sure I do." Emmett turned back to Annie. "Well, getting back to my mother. Yesterday she just got, like, *fed up*. She said she doesn't want a dog anymore, not with working at Houghton Mifflin, plus they just did a lot of decorating and whatnot in our house in Kennebunk. I don't know, maybe that's why she didn't want to bring Tashmoo up there. It's not as if he *did* anything."

"What color was Amos?" Lily asked, still stroking the now-asleep dog.

"Black, like your famous black dog here on Martha's Vineyard. I'll have to buy one of those tee shirts on my way back to the ferry. Did you get one from this summer yet, Lily? I don't remember ever bringing Amos to the Vineyard, but we should have—this is a nice spot for dogs. Amos used to love to swim. Tashmoo doesn't swim, though. Not sure why, since he's an Island dog."

"Wait," said Annie. "You're not *leaving* Tashmoo here? *Delivering* him?"

Lily, kneeling between the dog and the cardinal, turned her

face upward. She beamed a smile of what Annie later described to Gordon as pure wonder and beatific disbelief, as if a miracle had just occurred. Miniscule sun rays had always radiated from within the pupils of her blue eyes but somehow, at this moment, they reflected the light as if they were prisms. Looking into them was like looking into two tiny kaleidoscopes.

"He's a really good dog, like I said," Emmett continued. "You've had a dog before, haven't you?" He took another long sip. "I'm sorry to be like this, Aunt Anna. I told Mum we should call first, but she didn't want to give you a chance …"

Lily wrapped her arms around Tashmoo and burrowed her head into his yellow fur, and the bird shuddered its wings.

"I see," Annie said, inadvertently biting her blistered lower lip as she stood up. "It's not your fault, Emmett. I know what she can be like."

"Thanks. Um, well, there's one more thing. Sorry, now this is getting, like, awkward. Do you mind if I use the telephone? I really am sorry."

He disappeared into the house and slid the screen door shut behind him, but they could hear him whispering into the phone.

"Mum? I *cannot* believe you're making me do this. Can you explain to her, please?"

Silence for a while, then: "Okay, I'll get her."

"Aunt Anna?" Emmett called from the kitchen. "Excuse me, but my mother would like to speak to you, please, if you don't mind."

Annie took the receiver and stretched the cord out to the deck. The kids watched her curiously. The cardinal was strutting happily back and forth along the railing.

"Hi."

"How's it going down there?" Juliet's Boston accent sounded particularly English today.

"Well, we're a little …"

"Thanks for taking Tashmoo, Anna. I really cannot handle him anymore. Now. I told you I didn't forget the kids' birthdays, I've just been under water here. Emmie brought along that new book for you, didn't he, *Harry Potter*? You'll love it, supposed to be amazing. It's going to take England by storm. And then the world."

"Thanks, Juliet, but …"

"I thought Lily would enjoy the rhymes and illustrations in *When We Were Very Young*. I seem to remember sending Robbie *Now We Are Six* when you were out gallivanting in Timbuktu. We just announced our new list of children's titles … I'll send them down to you as well. Speaking of which, you remember Aunt Faye had a post office box at Alley's General Store. You may as well take that, I doubt John Alley has given it away yet. You'll have to pay an annual fee, but it should make your life easier down there. I'll have my assistant send the books to that p. o. box this afternoon."

"Okay. Thanks, Juliet. That's very kind of you. But …" Annie tried to take a sip of lemonade, but her hand was shaking, and the rim of the glass missed her mouth.

"Sorry about not calling first. I should have. But it's all been a tad too much."

"I'm kind of overwhelmed here, too—"

Juliet cut her off. "I told you to get some help, Anna. This is ridiculous, you being down there alone. Be flip if you want, but no one goes to Martha's Vineyard without some kind of au pair. You're supposed to be having fun. I have my hands full, what with work and getting Caroline off—"

"I think I can manage my own children, Juliet," Annie interjected, although Juliet kept talking over her, "and anyway, do you know how many women around the world would kill to be in my position?"

"Not to mention the estate lawyers and selling Faye's house— what a *behemoth*—and, frankly, Lonny's just about had it up to here." Juliet exhaled.

Annie got a wet paper towel from inside and dabbed the lemonade off her cheek.

"Faye's your aunt, too, Anna," Juliet said. "It wouldn't kill you to step up a bit."

The cardinal fluttered across the deck to the round table and peered up at Annie, as if eavesdropping.

"Okay," Annie said simply, surrendering. "I should probably ask Gordon first ... but he grew up with dogs, so I suppose, well—okay. We'll take Tashmoo. Don't worry about it." Lily let out a little cry and hugged the dog even tighter; Robbie held Meg and the hammock mid-swing. "I ought to do more to help. You're right, Juliet."

Juliet paused, clearly not expecting such quick acquiescence. "Okay, then. Well. Thank you." Now Annie could hear her taking a sip of something. "Well. Thank goodness that's done." Another sip. "That dog needs a real family, and there are just too many comings and goings around here. Caroline was helpful, for a teenager, but now she's gone, and Lonny and I head up to Maine soon. It's been a lot to wrap things up at the office, and the church vestry ... oh, my goodness, don't get me started. Talk about *Peyton Place*."

Annie felt her ears getting tired. Why did Juliet gush so much? And when had this become her personality, anyway? She hadn't been like this when she was younger, back when they used to sleep in the lavender room upstairs.

"Now, Anna, there's one more thing. I honestly hope you don't mind ..." Annie heard a spoon stirring in a glass. "I know you won't." Coffee? Iced tea? Bloody Mary?

"This might seem somewhat ... peculiar," Juliet continued. "You remember we had Faye cremated? And everything was so frozen around here we couldn't bury her after the funeral? Well, I *assumed* she'd want to be next to her husband and son, the two older Emmetts, here in Wellesley at Woodlawn Cemetery. Of course, we'd never gotten around to, you know, actually discussing it. Had you? But the other day I found a letter addressed to me, as executor, in her desk drawer. Who knows why she didn't include this little caveat in her formal will." Juliet took another sip. "Maybe she didn't want that old lawyer friend of Uncle Emmett's to know. Or, more likely, she didn't want to pay for another amendment." Another sip.

Annie sat down and tried another sip herself, but the lemonade stung her blister.

"Well, are you ready for this? She wants, *wanted*, I mean, to be buried next to *Jared*. In West Tisbury. Apparently his family has a nice shady plot or something. I don't know when I can get down there, and it seems ridiculous to have her sitting in the hot living room all summer, so …" Her speech seemed to be accelerating. "Emmie has her with him in the car."

Juliet laughed nervously, the way children do when they're trying to get away with something.

"Excuse me, Juliet? What did you say?"

"If Emmie could just leave Aunt Faye with you. You can call the warden over there at the cemetery and, you know, bury her yourself. With Gordon, of course. Lucky for you he's so handy at this sort of thing. Won't take a minute. We had enough pomp and circumstance at her funeral, don't you think?" Juliet sniffed; she had been the one to organize it all. "In fact, I'm not sure I would have bothered to put you to all this trouble if not, well—this is probably the worst part: her letter said she'd already had her name etched alongside Jared's on the headstone. She said it was more *economical*. Two for the price of one, some sort of thing." Annie heard a glass thud against a table. "I think it's *so odd* she didn't tell us."

Juliet had never deemed Uncle Jared, who was from Brooklyn and eschewed the whole Wellesley country-club scene, quite up to par. He hadn't been particularly close to either one of Faye's conservative brothers—not to Annie's father nor to Uncle Dwight, Juliet's father—both of whom no doubt had already bought their own respectable plots at Woodlawn Cemetery. Having Faye choose to be buried next to Jared, rather than next to old Emmett, her husband of thirty-five years, would be an awful lot for this propriety-conscious family to digest.

But it was so like Aunt Faye, and Annie grinned to herself. It was funny: her parting shot at the snobby mainland establishment.

When Annie was in high school, her mother's worries that she was too much of a "tomboy" and would never find a "suitable husband" reached a feverish pitch. Adair insisted Annie be presented at a debutante ball the way Juliet had been and made a big to-do about the cost, as if Annie should feel guilty about and grateful for something she didn't even want. The night of the first practice, Adair dropped Annie off at the country club on her way to her bridge game but, instead of going inside, Annie ran away to Aunt Faye's house and stayed there a whole week. Aunt Faye eventually marched her back home, whereupon she and her sister-in-law had a showdown. It wasn't a shouting match, because Aunt Faye wouldn't have shouted. All Faye had to say was *"Listen to your daughter,"* and Adair backed down.

"You'll have to get the date Faye died engraved on there," Juliet was saying. "Once you figure out who does that, send the bill along and I'll have the estate pay it." She sighed. "Women in general, you know, tend to be buried next to their first husbands and any offspring who happen tragically to predecease them. But *our* aunt ... well, she never was much of a rule follower, was she? A free spirit if ever there was one. Oh God, it just occurred to me. Where was Jared's *first* wife buried, what's-her-name, you know, Priscilla? You don't think right there along with him?"

Annie was still smiling to herself at Aunt Faye's irreverence, but her throat was so dry she could hardly speak. In five minutes she had managed to inherit a dog and her favorite aunt's ashes.

Juliet took another long sip before starting to accelerate again. "No matter! Caroline and Emmie are always telling me, 'You have to let go, Mum! Let go!' Easy for them to say." She snatched some air before racing to the finish. "Any-hoo, Annie, maybe you could take a photo of the plot once it's all done. Although I have no idea where you get film developed—"

"We have stores here," Annie said.

"I did think about journeying down there for a small grave-side service, you know. But most of her friends are gone, and with your parents in New Zealand … How long are they planning to stay with Percy and Fiona, incidentally? Well, it just seemed like overkill." She was starting to sound like the old Juliet. "Emmie is a bit embarrassed. I'm sorry I didn't mention any of this on the phone the other day, but I really did only just find the letter. Oh! There's my other line. Call waiting: what an invention! Toodle-oo!"

Holding the receiver for a minute before latching it onto the phone, Annie visualized Juliet's red pen crossing *Bury Faye* off her to-do list.

She went back out to the deck and scanned everything around her: the field, her children, a relative she hardly knew, the gray shingles of this little house, this dog who was suddenly hers, the rhododendron and azalea bushes, the stalking cardinal on the railing.

In a flash, it seemed, Emmett had unpacked his Subaru. In one hand he carried Aunt Faye's ashes and in the other a huge bag of dog kibble. Robbie and Lily brought in yet another round dog bed, this one covered in beige tartan and inscribed with Tashmoo's name in blue. There was also a large metal water bowl, an inscribed ceramic dish, two leashes and matching collars, a folder listing all of his vaccines, and a note in Juliet's prim handwriting that said, "Feed 1 cup 2x a day." Like a plant.

Once that was done, Emmett said he had to leave to catch the noon ferry out of Vineyard Haven. He waved at Robbie, who was back swinging two croquet mallets in the field hoping he would play with him, hugged Lily and patted Tashmoo, both of whom studied him wordlessly. Just like that, he was gone.

The kids and Tashmoo stared at each other for a while. Meg refused to leave the hammock, and wet her pants. Robbie flung the mallets into the woods as far as he could throw. Lily arranged her crayons and started to draw Tashmoo's picture.

It occurred to Annie that Gordon hadn't phoned yet this morning, and she went inside to call his office.

She recounted everything to him before even asking how he was. She assumed he wouldn't mind too much about Tashmoo, since he'd always wanted a dog, and he didn't. She talked nonstop.

"I can't believe Juliet still calls him *Emmie*," she said at last. "My cousin Emmett, and my uncle Emmett, must be rolling over in their graves. A college sophomore called Emmie? For heaven's sake."

"Well, it can be confusing, how everyone in your family has the same couple of names," he said, alluding to the fact that, the three Emmetts notwithstanding, both her father and brother were named Percy. "It helps to keep them straight if you vary them a little."

Annie bristled. "Oh, well, you get used—"

"Annie," Gordon interrupted.

"Hmm?"

"Annie," he began again, hesitating. "Sweetheart, something horrible has happened. I was on the phone most of the night." He sounded distraught, not like himself, and spoke very slowly. "Remember Samir, the Indian guy I hired to replace me in Guangzhou? You met him in Hong Kong that time?" She could hear him closing his eyes to speak. "He was killed yesterday. He and three field officers were flying across Guangdong and their plane crashed. The four of them killed, plus the pilot." Forgetting to exhale, she realized he was crying. "This is really bad, Annie. My office has been nearly wiped out."

Shortly before they'd moved to Maryland, Annie and Gordon had dinner with Samir and his young Hindu wife, whose name was Pretti, at a Chinese restaurant in Repulse Bay. Gordon wanted to welcome them formally to Hong Kong, since he'd made them relocate from Mumbai, only recently renamed from Bombay.

Formal Chinese dinners always have lots of courses, and a few dishes in, they had each been served an entire slippery-looking fish with its head intact. When the waiter politely asked if they would care to eat the eyeballs first, Annie had been the only one to giggle. Gordon had frowned at her for being culturally insensitive, unsophisticated. Pretti hadn't seemed to mind and, smiling demurely, had also declined the eyeballs.

Pretti is a common enough name in India and Annie had heard it before, but nonetheless thought it adorable during the introductions when she'd said in careful English: "I ... am ... Pretti." She was, too. Very. She had large breasts and huge brown eyes, which she'd accentuated with an exotic application of make-up, drawing the eyeliner past the corners of her eyelids and curving it up into those so-called cat eyes. In her turquoise silk sari that night, she looked like a Bollywood film star.

If Gordon had still been working in the Guangzhou office, would he have been on that plane instead of Samir?

Annie took the phone out to the deck and knelt down next to Tashmoo and Lily, who was patiently working on her sign, coloring in the middle "D's" of "DADDY" in strips of parallel colors. She had already colored in all of "WELCOME HOME."

"I can't believe it," Annie said to Gordon, stroking Tashmoo's silky fur. He really was a beautiful dog. She still couldn't think of anything helpful to say; she felt she was floating above somehow, and looking down at herself on the deck. "How awful. I'm so sorry, Gordon."

Tashmoo wagged his tail slowly and gazed up at her with golden eyes sparkling with tiny sunbursts, like Lily's.

She couldn't remember when she'd last taken the time to look into a dog's eyes. But she could swear Tashmoo actually looked, she wasn't sure how to put it, *concerned* for her. Empathetic.

"So," she said. "When do you have to go out there?"

"Now, Annie. *Today.* That's what I'm trying to tell you. I'm leaving at five."

"Five? Five, tonight? So you're not coming?" Her eyes filled spontaneously with tears.

"Yes, tonight. I found out yesterday at work. I didn't tell you on the phone last night because—I don't know why … I didn't want to worry you. I wasn't sure what I was going to do."

Annie traced her fingers along Tashmoo's wiry whiskers. "Can't someone else go, Gordon? Why does it always have to be you who has to fix everything?"

"Because that's my job."

"What about …" she began. She wanted to tell him how she hadn't been able to sleep since she'd almost drowned and about how she couldn't breathe in the middle of the night. How she'd thrown up over the deck railing. She was about to say, "What about *fixing me?*"

"I want to say I'm sorry a thousand times, Annie, I really do." He took a deep breath. "I'm flying to Hong Kong tonight; a car will drive me up to Guangzhou. Having a helluva time getting flights because of the Handover on the first—the Return, I should say, since that's what the Chinese call it. Can't find a hotel room anywhere."

He paused, and Annie muffled the phone while she blew her nose. "Everybody's been so panicked about the Thai and Indonesian currencies collapsing and how our projects are going to be affected … and now this has happened. Once I get things fixed I'll come straight to the Vineyard. Zhen said I could take an extra couple of weeks when I get back. She's trying to be a good boss. Listen," he said, regaining his composure and once more sounding stoic, rock-like, fixing what he could from afar. "You need to hire someone to help you. This is too hard, on your own up there, not knowing anyone. I'm so sorry, Annie, but I have no choice. I have to go."

"Okay," Annie said in a faraway voice, looking across the field. She still felt detached from her body. She would have to get someone to mow the grass. "I see. Yes, of course you need to go." Tashmoo sat up and licked the length of her cheek. "Amazing you'll be there for the Handover now, after so much talk about it when we were there."

She rested her cheek on Tashmoo's warm neck and ran a finger down the length of his face to his wet nose.

10

Split Rock

The next morning, Annie woke to see Tashmoo peering at her by the side of the bed, his head cocked to one side. It wasn't six yet. Her husband was still on airplanes traversing his way to the other side of the world and here she was, on her own. He had called from Dulles Airport to say goodbye and they'd chatted until the flight attendant told him to turn his phone off. He wouldn't be able to call her from Tokyo, he reminded her, because Japan was on a different cellular network, but he would call the minute he got to his hotel in Hong Kong. They had both sounded bereft.

She felt awful about the plane crash. She also felt guilty, selfish for being disappointed Gordon wouldn't be coming to the Vineyard in light of what those families were going through.

He would have changed planes in Tokyo and be somewhere over the East China Sea by now. Maybe he was asleep on the plane, maybe working, maybe watching a movie—while she was on a vacation island that was supposed to be paradise with three children, a big dog, and no friends, and had nearly drowned in the ocean.

When they had lived in Asia, being a single mother, so to speak, had been normal. It had taken a couple of months to find Susheela, and Annie had managed lots of long stretches alone with the kids. This was nothing new. At least she was in her own country now! She could handle it.

Why, then, did she feel so overwhelmed? Why did this seem so different? She'd had an infrastructure in Asia, what with school and the American club. And all the other expat women's husbands were also traveling, so she'd had a lot of company and instant friends. Aunt Faye had been alive, checking in on her periodically and boosting her spirits, and her mother used to call more often, come to think of it.

Annie wanted to sleep but somehow willed her body to get up. Tashmoo padded lightly behind her into the kitchen and sat regarding her even after she placed his full bowl of kibble in front of him. He cocked his head again.

"Go ahead," she said. "Jeez, you're polite."

He wagged his tail—such glee!—and devoured his food before she'd even filled the coffee pot. He sidled over to the door and sat down until she slid it open, looking grateful that she seemed to be catching on to their conversation.

She watched as he trotted alongside the azalea bushes down to the driveway and behind the little shingled garage that had served mostly as a workshop for Aunt Faye's husbands. The fact that he knew not to go on the grass was very convenient, since the kids liked to run barefoot. But instead of coming back, he sat down next to her parked station wagon and cocked his head again, his gaze floating up toward her on the deck. Obviously, he had some morning routine of which she was unaware. Nice of Juliet to give her so much direction.

Annie remembered overhearing a couple of women at Cronig's arranging to meet with their dogs on Lambert's Cove "to walk out to Split Rock," whatever that was. One of them had long, loose gray hair and seemed like an interesting, down-to-earth type, and (this was ironic to recall) as Annie had eavesdropped in the cereal food aisle that day, she'd almost wished she had a dog so she might get to know her.

It occurred to her that she could probably take Tashmoo to Lambert's Cove and be back before the kids woke up. She spotted Heather across the field, gardening by the side of her house as usual. As Annie started to jog over, Tashmoo caught up—but when he realized where they were headed, he accelerated ahead. Annie watched as he greeted Heather and she dropped to her knees to hug him, nuzzling her face in the fur of his neck. Of course. Heather was his neighbor! They had been friends since he was a puppy.

Annie, handing Heather the list of emergency telephone contacts, explained about the plane crash and how Gordon wouldn't be coming back for a while, and asked whether she would mind watching the kids while she took Tashmoo to Lambert's Cove. Heather, still patting Tashmoo, nodded as she repeated the word "honored," and wiped a few tears from her cheeks.

Back in her kitchen, Annie checked that she had her cell phone and wrote a note to Robbie, instructing him to call her as soon as the girls woke up.

Tashmoo was again down in the driveway, waiting next to the car. Annie flipped the rear seat over so he could stand in the back of the station wagon and he jumped right in, as if he'd been doing this his whole life, as if he were absolutely sure of where they were going.

With a start, Annie realized all she had to do was listen to this dog, and she would know what she had to do to take care of him. This was his house, for heaven's sake, his life on Martha's Vineyard. The reason Juliet hadn't spelled out specific care instructions was because she didn't know what they were.

Annie steered carefully down the dirt driveway, better at avoiding the potholes now, and remembered how Juliet had left work early that terrible afternoon last February and driven over to Faye's house when she hadn't answered the phone for the third day, only to find her dead in her four-poster. Her shoes were off but otherwise she was fully dressed on top of the made-up bed, as if she were just lying down for an afternoon nap. Tashmoo had been rooted beside her: his haunches on the floor, his neck bowed across the quilt, his head resting under Faye's hand. The coroner said she'd been gone for two days.

An older man, one of Jared's professor friends, told Annie and her parents all this at the funeral, but she hadn't thought of it until now. The dog couldn't have left Faye's side since before she'd fallen asleep.

Juliet had let herself in and wandered through the house, starting to panic when Tashmoo didn't bark or run to greet her as usual, the professor told them. He didn't budge until the mortuary men came. The unsettling thing was that when they lifted her body up, he dutifully crept aside and allowed them to take her away; he never barked or made a sound. Juliet said he just watched, as if he understood exactly what was going on and had been waiting for them, and that it was one of the most heartbreaking things she had ever seen.

Turning onto Middle Road, Annie dialed the radio to WMVY. An old James Taylor song was playing. It had rained again in the night, and she could almost smell the fresh colors: the cool blue of the sky, the wet green of the fields and trees. Tall telephone poles lined the road, evenly spaced and measuring the way. Opening all the windows, she drove faster than usual through West Tisbury, barely slowing down for the wide turn onto Lambert's Cove Road.

Tashmoo, his tail wagging high, stood tall in the way back. He looked straight ahead as if he were captain of a ship: his head and neck strong across the prow of the seat, his gleaming black nose breathing in the glorious summer morning.

He had simply been waiting for someone to bring him home.

When they reached the beach lot, a few cars were already parked in a cluster. Tashmoo leapt out the back and trotted right over to the start of the path, turning his head to wait. His tail, still raised and proud, beckoned like a flag.

Annie hiked the long path to the beach trying to get the hang of how to use the retractable leash, and again had that eerie feeling that she was watching herself from above. Tashmoo, beside her, tried to hurry her along yet kept tilting his head up, looking at her curiously as if he, too, were surprised at this mutual inheritance. She couldn't articulate it but sensed he knew that she was familiar, a safe relative: that he wasn't betraying Faye by being with her, that Faye, in fact, wanted him to be hers now.

The woods were full of the happy calls and songs of birds she glimpsed flitting from tree to tree and foraging among the bushes: warblers, chickadees, bluebirds, eastern phoebes, bobolinks. The cardinal's whistling soprano soared above them all.

Annie remembered her romantic morning with Gordon in the sail shack, and how awkward she had felt. She wondered if it really had been Chase driving that Wrangler she'd seen on the way to Long Point and looking for parking in Oak Bluffs.

"Why did you flunk out of the guide dog program?" she asked Tashmoo, her voice breaking the stillness. "What did you do, anyway? Your brothers and sisters are busy escorting people across city streets, opening doors, helping navigate escalators."

Last night, Robbie had told her he'd read that guide dogs had vocabularies of several hundred words. They could be trained to turn on televisions, even to detect a particular aura epileptics give off prior to having a seizure.

Tashmoo perked up his ears and wagged his tail in response. Annie undid the leash from his collar and let him run ahead.

Jogging to catch up, she tripped on a rock hidden beneath some dried-up leaves and fell down flat, barely putting her hands out in time to break her fall.

She must have let out a little cry because Tashmoo galloped back to her, his ears flapping behind. She quickly picked herself up lest anybody come along and see how clumsy she was. Tashmoo licked her hands and searched her face with his concerned eyes and then, with his gentle mouth, began to pick the leaves carefully off her jeans, one by one.

He was brushing her off.

Her left knee ached where she had landed on a rock and her palms stung, but mostly she felt embarrassed. Between them they smoothed away the leaves, and then Annie knelt down to stroke her dog for a while. She looked up and there was another red cardinal, studying them intently from a tree branch along the path.

They resumed their walk but now Tashmoo, still off the leash, stayed glued to her side. Juliet's son Emmett was right: this was no ordinary dog.

At last they climbed up the path as it wound between the high sand dunes to see, spread out below, the immense blinding shimmer of Vineyard Sound. There wasn't a trace of fog today: instead, the pale early-morning light and blazing sunshine glinted off the water to create a dazzling glare. Out above the Elizabeth Islands, the sky was a patchwork quilt of clouds stretching toward Cape Cod.

Annie sank down and wrapped her arms around her knees. The same lone sailboat she'd noticed with Gordon bobbed lazily, and the only sound was its halyard against the mast, clanging rhythmically in a breeze. Were there other moorings in this cove or just the one she knew of, the one that belonged to the St. Clairs?

It was as if they were inside an Impressionist painting. Tashmoo sat down on his haunches beside her, his head high, smelling the sea. They drank in the view together until Annie, to her further embarrassment, began to cry.

As she stared, unfocusing, across the Cove, she sensed some movement on the water. Someone was on the boat, crouching, moving nimbly around the cockpit, preparing to raise the sail. Annie pushed herself to her feet and impulsively raised her arm above her head to wave.

Just then the woman from Cronig's appeared beside them, the interesting-looking one with the long gray hair, today tied back in a loose single braid that reached nearly to her waist. Three wampum bracelets lay flat against each wrist, and a wampum necklace wound around her collarbone. Something about the way she stood on the sand, her hands on her hips, announced a kind of fearlessness: she was clearly a year-rounder, a real Islander, and this beach was her place. She had soft, flat features, and Annie wondered if she might be part Wampanoag. Thin but very muscular, she was taller than Annie, and was wearing faded jeans rolled up at the cuffs and a Save the Whales tee shirt with a picture of a breaching Orca. A black fanny pack was belted around her long waist.

"Incredible morning, huh?" the woman said. "Heaven."

Tashmoo suddenly sprang up to greet her, wagging his tail in a rapid blur, the kind a hummingbird makes with its wings. At precisely that moment the woman's dog, a coppery collie mix, flew down at them from the top of the sand dune and, barking wildly, nearly bowled them over.

"Zoey!" The woman shouted. "Calm down!" She stepped toward her acrobatic dog with a leash. "I apologize," she said to Annie. "She's three already, but still acts like a puppy."

Tashmoo, barking ecstatically in reply, leapt high into the air in a kind of Snoopy loop of exhilaration, his body a soaring, tail-to-nose arc.

Annie stared in disbelief. Was this her quiet dog?

Tashmoo landed essentially on top of the collie and reared back on his hind legs, waving his front paws at the woman like a frantic horse, careful not to touch her but seeming to be dying to embrace her. Barely able to contain his joy, he began pacing back and forth brushing crazy U-turns against her legs and rolling on the sand with the collie, who was just as exuberant.

"Whoa," the woman said, laughing and putting down the leash. "How do you do, too! Aren't you gorgeous! Do you give all the girls this kind of greeting, handsome?" She scratched him behind both ears and talked to him as if he were a person.

The dogs continued to jump on top of each other, kicking up a lot of sand.

"So much for the stillness," Annie said, swallowing. When it came down to it, Tashmoo was just a dog. She watched as the sail—white, with a blue sunfish in the middle of it—fluttered up.

"Wait!" the woman burst out. "This is *Tashmoo!*"

Annie nodded, adjusting her sunglasses. The sailboat glided away from its mooring.

The woman turned to stare at her. "*Faye's* Tashmoo! So you're Annie!"

To Annie's amazement, the woman began to cry.

"I was a close friend of your aunt's," the woman said. "She told me all about you! Tashmoo is Zoey's best buddy!" She hugged Annie hard before sitting down on the sand to hug Tashmoo. "How've you been, pup? Good to be home?" She patted him vigorously and he wagged his tail some more, appreciating that she finally recognized him, before zooming off with Zoey to gambol at the shore.

"Faye and I walked out here almost every day, clear through Thanksgiving," the woman said. "I couldn't believe the news when I heard. How could that happen? She was so strong! Kept up with all of us." She lifted her sunglasses off her nose and wiped her eyes with the bottom of her tee shirt. "Sorry. I just really, really loved her. And I was so glad when I heard you'd taken Tashmoo."

"Pardon? How'd you hear that? We only just got him yesterday."

"I don't remember who told me," the woman said. "But I knew you were supposed to end up with him, anyway. Not Julia."

"Juli*et*."

"I don't know why I should be surprised to meet you here, Annie. It only makes sense we'd find each other eventually," the woman said. "I'm Lindsay, by the way. Lindsay Trout. A group of us usually walks out in the morning to Split Rock." She scanned the beach. "But I'm in a hurry today and can't really wait. I've been helping take care of a baby seal that washed up on South Beach two days ago, and I'm anxious to get over to her. Care to walk with me? The others will probably catch up, or maybe not. Never really know with summer people."

"Split Rock?"

"Have you been out to it before? It's amazing, a true geologic wonder. Plus, it calms me down every morning. Centers me, you know." Lindsay grinned, tears still in her eyes.

"I'm not sure I've even heard of it."

"Well, you're in for something special, Annie, because it's magnificent. About a mile walk."

They headed down the beach, away from the old sail shack, and chatted idly until the dogs ran up into the dunes. Annie watched the sailboat tack and head toward the middle of the Sound.

"The dunes are not okay," Lindsay told her. "Lots of ticks, and bad for erosion." She cupped her hands around her mouth. "Zoey!" she shouted, whipping her long braid behind her shoulders, "Come!"

"Tashmoo!" Annie yelled, trying to sound like she knew what she was doing but feeling silly, like a dog owner imposter. She had never shouted his name before, and it sounded strange. "Come!"

To her surprise, both dogs zoomed over. They sat down in front of Lindsay and raised their shiny black noses, looking at her expectantly. She handed them each a treat from a plastic bag in her fanny pack, then handed the bag to Annie.

"Cheese," Lindsay said. "Tashmoo loves these. Take them."

Annie was beginning to appreciate that other people were missing Faye, too; that she had friends and a whole life here Annie didn't even know about. And for some reason, almost as soon as they fell into a steady pace down the beach, Annie started talking, and everything spilled out of her: the plane crash in China and

Gordon not coming, how she had almost drowned at Long Point and left her kids orphaned on the beach, her amazement at inheriting the house and now Tashmoo, how much she missed Hong Kong and Singapore and San Francisco, how displaced she felt in Sylvan Fell, how she didn't know if she could manage everything here by herself.

Lindsay didn't say a word except to call the dogs occasionally and reach into Annie's bag to dole out more treats.

"And then, the other night," Annie continued, "I freaked out in my sleep. Woke up, couldn't breathe, ran outside like a lunatic. Thought I was dying."

Lindsay looked at her sympathetically. "Sounds like you had a panic attack."

"Is that what it was? Nothing like that has ever happened to me before."

"Sorry to be the one to say it, but welcome to the real world, Annie. Is that when you cut your lip? Or did you do it at Long Point?"

"Long Point."

Lindsay nodded and stroked Annie's arm. "That riptide sounds terrifying. A wake-up call, my husband, Noah, would say. He surfs off Stonewall Beach and used to love to go out just before a hurricane, when the waves are gigantic. But he had a bad accident last year and has more respect for the sea now. For his own limitations."

"What happened to him?"

"He broke his back. He's only just been able to return to work. He runs a landscaping business here out of West Tisbury, though he's starting to do more landscape design. Noah said that accident put his life in perspective. In sharp relief, I think, is how your aunt would have put it."

"Your poor husband!" Annie said, wondering if she had ever heard Aunt Faye use the expression "sharp relief." She decided she hadn't.

They continued walking and, after a while, Annie said, "But I've always been able to handle everything before. I played competitive tennis, ran a magazine in China, had three children with no anesthesia."

"Maybe things are a bit much even for your amazing superwoman powers," Lindsay said, laughing. "Maybe the ocean is trying to teach you that there's a limit even to what *you* can do."

Lindsay threw a piece of driftwood for the dogs to retrieve; she didn't have the greatest arm. "You'll figure it out," she said. "Maybe that's why you're meant to be here this summer. The Vineyard, not to mention the ocean, has an uncanny way of simplifying things. Reminding you of who you are, what it is you're supposed to be doing, what it is you *can* do."

The sailboat, on a broad reach through the water, ran parallel to them now. The man at the helm threw a glance over his shoulder at the two of them, then leaned back into the heel of the boat. It could be Chase. She couldn't tell for sure.

Annie heard Lindsay say, "Hmm, Annie? Have you tried it, yet?"

"Tried … ?"

"Yoga. We were talking about yoga."

Embarrassed, Annie shook her head.

"Never while you were in the Far East?"

"Maybe a few times—but it seemed, I don't know, too slow or something."

"Yeah, I can see how you might think that," Lindsay said, laughing again. "Well, Faye and I love it. Love*d* it, I mean." She took a deep breath. "We used to go to a place in West Chop. Maybe you'd like to come with me, try it again sometime."

Lindsay picked up the wet piece of driftwood that Tashmoo had dropped at her feet and, wiping dog slobber onto her jeans, threw it inadvertently into a bed of kelp along the shore.

"I didn't know Tashmoo was such a good retriever," Annie

commented, trying to ignore the slobber.

"He's good at everything except swimming," Lindsay said, and stopped to turn toward her. "You know, I think this is playing out exactly as your aunt would have wanted. I mean, how great that you and your kids can be here instead of in humid Delaware—I mean, Maryland—for the summer, while your husband has to deal with that mess in China. You have a built-in community on the Vineyard, Faye's community, ready and waiting for you."

She did?

"But how terrible for Gordon," Lindsay went on, resuming their walk. "He's under so much pressure."

Lindsay bent down to pick up a small rock in the shape of a heart, her thick gray braid sweeping the sand. She handed it to Annie. "Lovely," she said. "Something to welcome you and Tashmoo back."

Annie was barely over her surprise at the heart when Lindsay handed her a second one.

"You'll see them all over the place, if you look," she said.

Annie thanked her. Sweet, if a little corny. "The accident is really terrible, horrible, but Gordon's okay," she said. "He's always traveled a lot, he's used to it. We all are."

The sailboat tacked and headed back out across the Sound.

Tashmoo and Zoey galloped up to them, globs of seaweed dripping out of both their mouths. Zoey seemed to be gagging.

Kneeling on the sand, Lindsay wrenched Zoey's jaw open, stuck her whole fist into her dog's mouth, and extracted a long wad of stringy, saliva-coated kelp. "Oh, Zoey. Is this how you welcome back your buddy?"

She kissed Zoey's nose and looked over at Tashmoo, at the seaweed dribbling out of his mouth, and turned her head expectantly up toward Annie.

"Mind if I … ?" Lindsay asked, yanking open Tashmoo's mouth. The seaweed was tangled so far down his throat she had to pull it out overhand, like a rope.

"For someone so gorgeous, you sure have some disgusting eating habits," she cooed, kissing his nose, too, and patting him some more.

They rounded a tiny cove and could at last see the famous Split Rock.

A reddish glacial boulder that loomed huge out of the water, it spread about twenty-five feet across and was cloven entirely in two, from its flat top all the way down to where it disappeared beneath the water. The waves, at high tide now, parted behind it and met again a couple of feet before the shore. A few smaller boulders were scattered around in front; another large boulder was to its left. Up close, the surface of the mammoth rock looked very splotchy, almost as if the granite face were peeling.

"Here we are," Lindsay said. "So majestic. At sunset in the fall and spring, if you stand in exactly the right spot, you can actually see the sun shining through the crack. Magical."

Annie nodded, but it wasn't as if this were the most beautiful rock she'd ever seen. It was fun to have a destination, but in her opinion this rock, in and of itself, was not particularly worth the trek. It bothered her that it wasn't symmetric: the fracture was about a third of the way over from the left.

"Sometimes I wonder what distant mountain this boulder was carried from, back when the Island was being formed during the Ice Age," Lindsay continued. "It's what's known as a *glacial erratic.* It probably developed a slight crack in its journey, and the crack got bigger bit by bit as water seeped into it and kept alternately freezing and melting over, I don't know, tens of thousands of years."

The tide receded with a *swooosh* and Lindsay quickly reached down to pick up another stone. She waded across the pebbles and extended her left hand to press it against the big rock. Leaning on her arm as the waves swirled around her knees, she bent her head for a minute and closed her eyes, silently adding her pebble to a row of like-size ones nestled along a small crack on the opposite side of the big split.

"Every morning I say a prayer as I do that," she said, smiling a little and gesturing to the line of stones. "A lot of these are for your aunt. And Faye placed her fair share of them herself, come to think of it. I'll bet a lot of them are for you and your family."

"It is magnificent," Annie said, not thinking. "But I don't think I'd say *beautiful*, on account of the huge split, so off-center. Not to mention these uneven patches all over the place." She peered more closely across the lapping waves, not bothering to wade out. "Jeez, it's *full* of cracks."

Lindsay contemplated her quietly.

Annie, not wanting to offend, quickly added, "Maybe if it were smooth and in one piece, it would be … It's definitely a geologic wonder, though. I'll give you that."

The sailboat disappeared behind Makonikey Head.

"Hmm," Lindsay said, wading back. "I never thought of it that way."

11

Water, Water, Everywhere

It started sprinkling as she drove home along State Road. Robbie hadn't called, so Annie took the long way and stopped for coffee (she couldn't seem to drink enough of it lately), hoping to find John Alley. He was in the old-fashioned, one-room post office sorting yesterday's mail, hidden behind stacks of the *Boston Globe* and the *New York Times* tied with string.

"Hi, John," she said from the doorway. "I don't know if you remember me …"

"*Mis-sus An-nie Tuc-ker!*" he exclaimed, like a sportscaster announcing a star batter. He took two steps over to embrace her. A portly, kind-faced man, he looked exactly as he had years ago when he had run the general store that he had inherited from his father. "Come out of the wet. Heard you were here, getting a jump on the season. I was wondering when you were going to stop in and say hello."

"Someone told you I was here? I guess you know about my Aunt Faye, then."

"Know? Damn straight. Not the same around here. Terribly sad. She was one of the *kindest* ladies I have had the privilege to … didn't you see that nice write-up in the *Gazette*? Good picture, too. I have a copy around here someplace, saved it in case you missed it. Don't know if you subscribe to the *Gazette* down there in Virginia, or wherever it is you live at the moment …" He began sifting through the stacks of mail and paper. "Everybody sure loved Faye. She used to pick up her mail and tell me about you and your smart kids and her other niece, what's her name, the stuffy one there, Julia."

"Juli*et*."

"Yeah. You'd think she'd be more the romantic type."

"Juliet's taken care of nearly everything regarding our aunt's estate. She's been heroic."

He grouped together some catalogs. "Righto. Didn't mean to offend."

"We were all stunned," Annie said.

"Don't I know it." He stared ahead for a minute, lifted his voice. "Well. Are you going to take her p. o. box? It's here waiting for you, paid up through the end of the year."

Another gift, here waiting for her.

"Juliet mentioned she was going to send down a box of books," Annie said. "They should arrive any day now."

"I'll keep an eye out. Hmm—maybe you'll help me sort the mail some time. It's a big job and I'm always on the prowl for an assistant. All this is from a late delivery yesterday afternoon ... some traffic snarl up on the Cape." He gestured to three huge Santa Claus bags of letters on the floor. "Your son and daughter just had their birthdays, didn't they? Robbie and Lily? Born on the same May day? Let's see ..." he looked up at the ceiling. "Nine and six now, am I right?"

Marveling at his memory and also at how fast news traveled around here, Annie asked whether he was still in charge of the cemetery.

"Yup," he said, squinting at an envelope and reaching across Annie to slide it into one of the little cubbies.

"Well, this is kind of odd, but—Juliet just sent down our Aunt Faye's ashes. Her son, Emmett, brought them, and I'm supposed to bury them. Her, I mean. Bury her."

John Alley stopped what he was doing and considered her again over his bifocals. His eyes were watery.

"You don't say. Well, I was wondering about that. I buried

Jared at his family plot, two years ago. She had both their names added to the stone. Holy mackerel, she was cut up about him dying. Never really recovered, I don't think. They sure were a special couple. Love affair of the twentieth century, in my humble opinion. Then Jared had that heart attack, remember? Coming out of Seth's Pond? Terrible. She should have died like he did, on-Island, here with us. Not on the mainland in hoity-toity Wellesley." He took a handkerchief out of his pocket and wiped his eyes under his glasses. Annie pretended to be interested in the headlines of the *MV Times*.

What was he talking about? What about Aunt Faye's thirty-five-year marriage to Uncle Emmett?

"You know, Annie," John Alley continued, lowering his voice to a whisper, "there's been so much rain lately, the earth is soft. You can bury her yourself if you don't want to wait till your husband gets back from dealing with that horrendous plane crash. I mean, unless you want to make a big production out of it."

How did he know about the plane crash?

"Oh," Annie said. "You knew my husband was away?"

"Word travels. Some people, they set up chairs," he continued. "The Bryants rented a tent on Memorial Day, had a ceremony, the whole nine yards. But you can do it yourself so you don't have to pay my fee. Not my doing, the town requires it, you know. Then, well, I don't have to dig the hole. I wrenched my back again yesterday … My sweet wife, love of my life, gardener extraordinaire, is always making me move some damn bush or another."

"Dig the hole?"

He chuckled. "The shovel's in the shed, in the back toward Scotchman's Bridge Lane. Just dig right in front of the stone, wide enough for the box. A foot down's enough. Soil's sandy. Easy, for a Vineyarder like you."

Vineyarder?

"Just make sure you have your cousin Julie*t* send me the cremation certificate so I can pass it along to the town clerk, have it properly recorded."

Annie nodded.

"You'll notice your aunt was smart, had a real green thumb. Maybe not quite like your old friend Mrs. Piper St. Clair on Indian Hill, winning prizes for her roses left and right, but good enough." He raised his eyebrows, and Annie wondered if he was angling for a reaction. "Faye planted some pretty perennials there for Jared: black-eyed susans, geraniums, day lilies, if I remember correctly. Daisies, too. Last I checked, they'd all come up pretty. Tidy, too. You can water them with the bucket by the old spout. Just be sure to return it back where you found it."

"How is Piper?" Annie asked, taking the bait.

"Lovely as ever," he said, grinning at her sideways as he slotted more letters. "After her little whatchamacallit, her *mishap*. Dropped by with some of her blueberry jam the other day. She sure does love a full house."

Annie caught her breath. "Mishap? Full house?"

"Some things never seem to end, do they," John said, and Annie wondered if he were being deliberately evasive. "That fellow just bought himself a new car. You'd think a person would want to vary the style and color once in a while."

He took a few steps past the newspapers to peer out the windowpanes of the old mailroom door. "Looks like it's clearing, but I don't think for long. You know what they say: if you don't like New England weather, wait five minutes and it'll change. You may not have to water anything until September if this keeps up. Good you got out so early with the pup."

"How … ?" she began, but he waved her off and resumed his sorting.

Heather was playing a game with Apple and Meg on the table outside while Lily was talking on the telephone to Adair in Auckland, on "speaker." Lily was telling her grandmother about a new picture she was drawing, and Adair was telling her how she couldn't wait to take her to the National Gallery of Art in Washington. Lily handed Annie the phone.

Skipping over the hello and how-are-you, Adair stated that she'd seen a woman who reminded her of Annie that morning, alone with three small children, looking a frumpy wreck.

"You're not letting yourself *go* or anything, are you, darling? I just can't see how you wouldn't. Now that you're forty you'll need a little more, how shall I put it, *upkeep*. Lily said Gordon had to go on a trip. Why doesn't he send your Susheela back from Indonesia? Couldn't he track her down?"

"She's already working for another family in Hong Kong," Annie said, trying not to sound annoyed. "Besides, Susheela would hate it here: the food, the climate. Even if I could steal her away, it would be too expensive."

"That's ridiculous. If you can afford to spend the summer on Martha's Vineyard, you can afford a babysitter. Put an ad up at that quaint general store."

"A lot of women would kill to have my problems. It's beautiful here."

"Sounds to me like the weather's been just awful."

"Are you ever going to tell me what's going on, Mom?"

Adair pretended not to hear and went on instead about New Zealand's distress at the latest rumors about the misbehavior of Princess Diana with some billionaire Egyptian named Dodi Fayed, whose father owned Harrods' department store in London, and Annie went about making breakfast.

What were her parents doing down there? Her brother Percy had stunned them all by this move to Auckland—ditching his wife, Annie's friend Kathleen, for Fiona, a professional golfer with whom he'd apparently been carrying on a torrid affair for years.

Percy used to run a spectator tour company to golf tournaments around the world and had met Fiona in Pebble Beach. He'd settled in with her and her two young children and, from the sound of it, taken the place of her first husband, who had recently died in a mountaineering accident.

The very day his divorce from Kathleen was official, Percy had gone so far as to *marry* Fiona, without informing anyone, and recently declared he was considering becoming a New Zealand citizen!

Annie kept assuming this must be why their parents had dropped everything and scurried down there, to talk him out of it, though Adair wouldn't say. Annie had always considered herself a dutiful daughter, even if her parents did get on her nerves—her mother with her incessant judgments and outdated sense of decorum, her father with his questionable ethics. Admittedly, Annie and her brother hadn't had a real conversation in years. But it was still a slap in the face to be excluded like this.

They hung up, and the skies grew suddenly dark and blustery. It was raining hard before Annie had finished putting away the dishes. She and Robbie ran around closing the windows, but the windowsills were already soaked and everything began smelling like salt.

They played games and built forts and read stories, but it was boring. Everyone felt lazy, yet no one was tired enough to nap, and she couldn't think of anywhere to go. The Capawock Theater in Vineyard Haven would be mobbed, there would be no place to park, and anyway the one matinee that was playing sounded too grown-up for the girls. She couldn't handle Oak Bluffs again. It seemed all-around easier to remain stranded and wait for the kids' camp at the Chilmark Community Center to start on Monday.

Tashmoo had fallen in love with Lily and followed her everywhere. Occasionally the rain would let up and they would start to walk him down the driveway for something to do, thinking the downpour was almost over, but then they would hear water shushing through the treetops. "The raindrops are whispering to each other again, Mommy," Lily said. "Better turn back."

Having a dog was proving to be a lot of extra work. No matter how vigorously Annie dried him off and wiped his wet paws after he went out, he smelled terrible, like clammy, dank mildew, and he dragged sand and mud into the house. Dog hair was everywhere. Balls of it coagulated in the corners, yellow strands wafted endlessly through the rooms and landed on the counters, their clothes, in her coffee cup. Her housekeeping, so perfect in Sylvan Fell, had gone by the boards in precisely two days with a dog.

At one point in the afternoon the downpour turned into a drizzle, and Annie took Meg and Tashmoo to Cronig's to get supper and then to Lambert's Cove, but it wasn't fun to walk in the rain and they didn't run into Lindsay and her collie.

After supper, Annie decided to plug in the hairdryer she'd brought (and hadn't yet bothered to use on herself) to see if that would help dry Tashmoo's smelly fur. Just as she did so, all the downstairs lights switched off. She had blown a fuse. Gordon hadn't gotten around to showing her where the fuse box was, but she and Robbie managed to find it, groping their way through the dark cellar with a flashlight. They located the culprit fuse, blackened through the miniscule window, and screwed in a new one from a little cardboard package Gordon had left on top of the box. Five minutes later, even without turning the hairdryer back on, the lights went out again. This happened two more times until there were no new fuses left.

Rain was pounding against the roof, beating against the windowpanes.

"I think it must be raining the ocean," Lily said, and Meg nodded in agreement.

"When that happens in the Wampanoag culture, it means that it's time for bed," Annie said.

Each taking a flashlight, they trundled upstairs.

Under one of Aunt Faye's quilts, lying cozy and all connected on Robbie's big bed, Annie read them whimsical rhymes from Lily's new book, *When We Were Very Young,*

> *Where am I going? I don't quite know.*
> *Down to the stream where the king-cups grow—*
> *Up on the hill where the pine-trees blow—*
> *Anywhere, anywhere. I don't know.*

They all fell asleep and a few hours later in the pitch dark, forgetting her flashlight, Annie stumbled downstairs to answer Gordon's telephone call—he had finally arrived in Hong Kong—only to slip on a sheet of sticky wet plastic that Tashmoo had apparently knocked out of the trash, rifling after some leftover hamburger meat. Something disgusting stuck to the bottom of her bare foot.

A clap of thunder woke her up later, the telephone receiver on her chest: she must have fallen asleep mid-conversation with Gordon. She rolled over to hang up the phone and in the dark knocked over a glass of water, which made Tashmoo bark sharply until she took him out.

The low clouds brightened the night sky a bit, but the dog refused to go down the path in the storm unless she walked a little way with him—and there she stood, shivering outside in the cold pelting rain that smelled like the sea, wondering if she were about to get struck by lightning.

Caleb, the caretaker, came over on Sunday morning and fiddled with the fuses until he got the power back on. Not long after he left, the rusty old washing machine broke. Water gushed out the bottom and it took an hour, plus every towel in the house, to mop up the cellar. Annie was afraid to put the soaking-wet towels in the dryer lest that break, too, so they hung them up on Aunt Faye's drying rack, which promptly collapsed in pieces; they ended up draping them over the furnace and some folding chairs stored there for parties. Annie turned up the dehumidifier Gordon had installed (the electric bill would be sky high), but the musty smell from the dripping towels, combined with the monsoon-like rain and the oppressive stench of wet dog, was nauseating. It reminded her of the outdoor fish markets in Southeast Asia.

She had no idea what kind of washing machine to replace it with or even how much money she had to spend, which made her more irritable yet. Her hands were raw from wringing out the towels and washing so many dishes. She wanted to jump out of her skin.

No sooner did they have the towels hung up then the upstairs toilet got clogged, and that was so revolting she almost threw up again. She managed to find an old rubber plunger in the basement and cleared it out. Dirty water sloshed over the sides of the toilet onto the floor.

The kids were on top of each other squabbling, making a big mess. Robbie slammed the door to the girls' bedroom so hard that the handle fell off in his hand, and the girls were locked in there until she could find an Allen wrench to fix it and get them out.

Everything was breaking, and Gordon wasn't here to fix it.

The kids would not stop antagonizing each other. She couldn't keep up with them. This was what her mother meant when she used to complain that she couldn't hear herself think.

She put on Frank Sinatra to calm them down, whereupon the two girls burst into tears because they missed Gordon so much. Robbie turned it off, glaring at her for upsetting them.

"What are we *doing* here?" he demanded. "We should have stayed home. Why can't we go back to our apartment in Singapore? Hong Kong, even? It's too crowded here. When is Daddy getting back? I hate this place."

Annie's Zen-like Vineyard house had become claustrophobic, and the rain was still coming down in sheets.

Lily and Meg fought over everything and eventually got in a

big slapping fight and pulled each other's hair; Lily ripped the head off Meg's favorite Barbie; Meg ran to Robbie for retribution and he, furious at Lily in the first place for not playing Battleship with him, poured a whole bucket of water on top of her head.

So much goddamned water.

The bucket-dumping cost Annie her temper. Aware that her temples were throbbing and she might collapse from a stroke any minute, she yelled at them. They were out of control! How were they going to mop up this water when they were out of towels?

She grabbed one of Aunt Faye's plates from the counter and smashed it on the floor, and screamed at everyone to go to their rooms.

Petrified, the three children stared at her, and even Robbie started to cry. They had never, ever seen her lose her temper. Huddling together, Robbie and Lily helping Meg, they clambered up the steep stairs.

Annie had never smashed anything in her life. She was not one to holler. What *were* they doing here? Why *had* they come?

She stared at the shards scattered on the floor and under the table, tasting blood again from her lower lip. She kneeled down to pick up the pieces one by one, then leaned against the refrigerator and cried.

That night on the phone, Annie neglected to tell Gordon about the plate-breaking or temper-losing or how much self-loathing she felt after yelling at the children. (It wasn't their fault it was raining, or that they had come here, and she had spent a long time apologizing to them.) In the cellar, she cradled the portable phone against her neck, twisting the bottoms of the towels one more time so hard that her wrists hurt. How could these towels still be so soaking wet?

She wanted to tell Gordon that the small matter of her nearly drowning the other day had knocked her more than she liked to admit, but she didn't want to upset him when he was preparing to meet the other families of the victims, so she didn't mention it. Her mouth clenched shut when he described how, straight from the airport, he had taken Samir and Pretti's son for a rainy walk through one of their favorite parks along Kowloon Bay. She suppressed an urge to tell him off: *he had his own son who needed him.*

Gordon offered to try researching washing machines for her on this new AOL that everyone kept talking about, on the so-called World Wide Web.

"A lot of good that will do," she snapped, as if it were his fault the machine had broken. "Fat chance they'll even sell that particular brand here. I'll take the kids down-Island tomorrow after camp. What do you say I buy a dishwasher while I'm at it?"

"Where would we put a dishwasher in that tiny kitchen? Let me figure this out for you. The Internet is amazing! I'll look on it this morning from the computer in the office."

She ungripped the phone to hang up, but could barely straighten her neck.

12

The Percherons

Somehow on Monday, a blue-sky morning and also the first day of camp at the Chilmark Community Center, Annie and Tashmoo managed a fast, early hike out to Split Rock with Lindsay and Zoey. It was impossibly lucky to have Heather on call to mind the kids, and Annie decided to place a pebble in one of the cracks and silently thank Aunt Faye for whatever she had done to earn her this favor.

Driving back along Lambert's Cove Road, Annie had to slow down behind a long line of cars slowly passing a team of two draft horses. One black and one gray, the horses were well over six feet tall and wore wide leather blinders on either side of their eyes so nothing could distract them. A strong man was driving, sitting in a little pull cart, holding the reins.

Tashmoo jumped from the way back into the middle seat of the station wagon to see.

"Aren't they magnificent? They're called *Percherons*," Annie said, talking to her dog the same way she talked to her children.

Tashmoo thrust his head out the open window and barked as they passed, even though Annie, steering carefully, immediately barked back that he should leave them alone.

But the horses ignored Tashmoo and the cars and everything else, and kept walking undeterred. They weren't bothered by what they couldn't see. It must be lovely to live like that, with no interruptions, to get to focus merely on putting one foot in front of the other.

She drove on, fiddling with the radio in the car to get the

Boston NPR station, but whether or not it came in seemed to depend on that minute's breeze. They couldn't get any radio stations on Middle Road, either, just like they couldn't get many television stations or much cell phone coverage, and suddenly she felt stranded, desperate for news. She had to remember to buy a paper every day or she would definitely go crazy.

From what she could decipher from intermittent, crackling newscaster voices, Hong Kong was getting most of the air time because tomorrow, July 1, Britain would hand it and the New Territories back to the People's Republic of China, and the world was anxious to see what changes Communist China would make. Prince Charles was there on the royal yacht *Britannia* and the Chinese army was rolling in tanks and, for some bizarre reason, dozens of black Audis for the official ceremony.

Annie was also able to make out that Pete Sampras was poised to win Wimbledon again; that a young golfer whom her brother Percy had raved about named Tiger Woods had just made number one in world rankings; and that Princess Diana had cleaned out her closets and auctioned her beautiful fairy-tale dresses at Christie's on Park Avenue for several million dollars, all proceeds donated to AIDS and cancer charities.

Annie resented the way people who were interviewed said it was a fitting end, pun probably intended, to the "fairy tale gone sour" and "the last great Cinderella story," but maybe she hadn't heard correctly because of all the crackling.

She really wished she hadn't smashed that plate and terrified the kids like that, and couldn't quell the voice in her mind that kept berating her. The children would probably never forget it, and bring it up at Christmas dinners in ten, twenty, thirty years, squeezing around their polished, long table. It would become a family legend! The way she would be remembered!

Her great-great-grandchildren would beg their parents for stories not about the adventurous Annie, but about the stark-raving-mad one.

She passed a peaceful flock of sheep grazing in a meadow, and made a mental note to bring the kids back here for a picnic.

Camp at the Chilmark Community Center started at nine, but they were so excited to have somewhere to go that they were early, among the first to pull into the dirt lot at the top of South Road. It was hard to find a place to park that wasn't a puddle.

Annie had loved the occasional weeks she had spent here over the years with her cousins Juliet and Emmett—although, funny, she hadn't made any friendships that had lasted. People looked familiar, but she didn't recognize any faces.

Everyone else seemed to be meeting up with lifelong friends, squealing and hugging and asking about each other's winters. There were a lot of fathers.

Chase and the St. Clairs had never gotten involved with the Center because they had more than enough to keep them occupied in West Tisbury—what with their own beach, sailboat, and tennis court, plus a lot of extended family scattered about. It was odd to think that she and Chase had spent so much of their childhoods on the same island without knowing that the other even existed.

Annie and the kids stood apart until some teenage camp counselors, who managed to temper their enthusiasm with a confident mellowness earned from spending every one of their summers here, led Robbie and Lily to their age groups under designated oak trees. Everyone wore old Chilmark Center tee shirts and cut-off shorts, and some of the counselors went barefoot. That was an old up-Island thing: people used to take off their shoes the moment they landed on the Vineyard and leave them by the ferry docks until the end of summer.

Alone and self-conscious, and relieved to have Meg on her hip for company, Annie set out across the wet, wide field past the art shack. Kids were still playing racket-smacket on the worn baseball diamond as she used to in the '70s, batting a tennis ball with an old wooden racket. Meg arched her back to watch the kids playing. She was almost too heavy to carry anymore.

They passed the back of the library and cut behind the tiny post office, sidestepping more puddles. Annie appreciated the way the buildings were all of a perfect piece: squat, and shingled with weathered, gray cedar in the traditional Cape Cod style. Their sloping roofs reminded her of the tiny Monopoly houses she'd been doling out to Robbie all weekend.

Seeing an older woman walking into the post office, Annie was sure it was Aunt Faye and lunged forward, nearly calling out her name.

They crossed State Road to the old one-room Chilmark School but were crestfallen to see a handwritten sign that said the little kids' camp didn't start until tomorrow. Something about flooding.

"Isn't there some other place I could go play?"

"Not that I know of," Annie said, laughing, but she was disappointed too. "You're stuck with me. I have something to do, but we can just do it together. First, though, I need coffee."

The high-backed, white wicker rocking chairs that lined the big front porch of the Chilmark Store were already filled with summer people picking up conversations they'd left off last Labor Day. As Annie and Meg stood in the pressing throng of people trying to catch the attention of the overwhelmed counter staff, Annie's eyes met those of the owner—a trim, bald man who was tossing pizza dough by the back ovens. They smiled at each other.

She had to angle her head between lots of shoulders and raise her voice to carry over the chatter. "Hi, Primo. Do you remember me? You knew my ..."

"Faye's niece, right? Annie? She talked about you all the time! Is this Lily or Meg?" Primo put down his dough and in a few strides was at the counter, leaning across to hug them.

The coffee crowd, parting, stared at Annie with open curiosity: knowing Primo seemed to have granted her sudden status. "Welcome to the summer of '97. So pleased you're using the house." He lowered his voice. "Mary and I were devastated, love. She is *missed*. What a great spirit. Living kindness, she was."

Next to Annie, a burly guy wearing large glasses interjected in a loud voice, "Hey Primo, any slices up yet? And how'd you get so skinny?"

Who on earth eats pizza at nine o'clock in the morning?

"Doing yoga now. Check it out." Primo flexed his arm muscles at the guy and bent closer to Annie. "Your aunt was awesome at yoga, did you know that? Now, if you need *anything*, anything at all, you just ask, okay? When is your husband supposed to get back from Asia?"

"How did you ..." Annie began, swinging Meg to her other hip so she wouldn't have to shout. But before she could respond, she was shoved along by a swarm of other parents who had just dropped their kids off and were jockeying to be heard. Everyone seemed to know each other, even in here, and she felt as if she were crashing a party. She got her coffee and gave Primo a little wave goodbye.

13

Chase

————

"Home again, home again, jiggety-jig," Annie sang to Meg, as they headed back up Middle Road away from Beetlebung Corner. They waved to Heather and Apple on the road, on their way somewhere—maybe to yoga in West Chop. Earlier, Heather had mentioned that they had babysitting at the yoga studio; maybe Annie would like to try it sometime.

Tashmoo lay on the deck dozing in the warm morning sun. He thumped his tail at her a few times and opened one eye as if to say, "Have a nice time wherever you're going next. Let me know if you need me."

Annie brought up the boxes of Aunt Faye's old clothes and left them on the deck for Lindsay, who had tactfully asked her about them on their walk and offered to bring them to the Boys & Girls Club Thrift Shop in Edgartown. She then picked up the backpack she'd organized earlier, wheeled her bicycle out of the shed and carefully strapped Meg into the child seat, tucking her spiky bangs under the new safety helmet Gordon had bought. The pack was heavier than she'd anticipated.

"This won't annoy you too much, will it, Meg?"

The large pumpkin-colored fiberglass helmet fit so snugly around Meg's little head that her features looked like the carved face of a jack-o'-lantern. She shook her helmet side to side.

"Mommy, are we going to get the ... *you know* ..." she whispered, even though nobody was around, "the *Life* Savers?"

"Of course," Annie said. "We have to stop by Alley's on our way, anyhow."

They rode down Middle Road under an endless umbrella of leaves, still whispering with leftover raindrops. The air was full of the sweet smell of hay, and the houses and picket fences that lined Music Street gleamed after the rain.

As they cycled along, Annie told Meg the story of how it had come to be named Music Street in the nineteenth century, when one whaling-ship captain bought a piano for his daughter and all of his ship-captain neighbors decided to buy pianos for their daughters, too. Even then, parents were competitive.

The lawns and fields glowed a kind of electric green, and Annie pointed out that they were the color of *chartreuse* in the Crayola crayon box, though it was Lily who would have been more interested. They passed the tiny old library with the mansard roof on the right, and the old weathered town hall with the see-saw in the playground. Maybe it was the comfort of being on her bicycle, but she didn't feel as disoriented today.

"Later maybe we can go on the swings," she called back. "But first we have a job to do."

Turning left onto State Road, Annie steered them along the sandy shoulder to Alley's, carefully navigating the stones and wet sand. She leaned her bike against the shingles behind an old clunker and unstrapped Meg, stuffing the backpack on the ground behind her front tire. She took off her helmet and strapped it to the handlebars, not bothering to take off Meg's.

On the porch notice board, Annie thumbtacked the little sign she'd made that said, Needed: Mother's Helper. Then they went inside and she had a long talk with John Alley about how to change fuses. He told her she had most likely replaced them out of order, and helped her find two more four-packs on the crammed shelves.

Meg picked out some Life Savers and Annie grabbed several bottles of water, and they joined the back of the line for the cash register. Annie tapped her foot; she didn't have all day. But at least here in West Tisbury, people were polite and didn't shove and cram around the counter.

With all the confusion getting the kids ready for the first day of camp, Annie had forgotten to eat breakfast, and she impulsively grabbed a Milky Way bar from the rack. She squeezed the wrapper: fresh and soft, as opposed to the ones she used to sneak in Asia, which were invariably hard and stale. "God bless America," she said to Meg.

She took a slow mouthful of the chocolate, and her impatient foot-tapping ceased.

"Want a bite?"

Meg shook her helmet, busy trying to find the string to open the pack of Life Savers.

Craning her neck, Annie noticed that the salesgirl with the mermaid tattoo and purple streaks in her hair was working the register today, and debated whether she should just leave a few dollars on the counter and take off. The guy in front sure was taking his time.

Deciding not to be pushy, she shifted Meg onto her other hip and savored another bite of Milky Way, letting the malt nougat and sweet, gooey caramel stretch along her tongue. She didn't ordinarily eat this kind of stuff; in fact, her mother had mentioned that Fiona referred to her as "Miss California Organic." Two more bites and it was gone.

Still hungry, Annie reached for a bag of potato chips and tried to tear it open without making an obvious ripping sound, which naturally it did, but everyone seemed to be minding their own business. Meg lunged from her hip to pull a box of Lucky Charms off the top of a shelf, and Annie let her keep it.

She studied the line ahead, and then she stopped breathing.

"Mommy, let *go*," Meg complained. Apparently, she had tightened her grip.

Instinctively, she almost called his name, but caught herself. A bit shorter than she remembered—not as tall as Gordon. Sunglasses on top of his head secured by one of those thick, preppy straps that wraps around the neck. Hair still wavy and blond. Same muscular shoulders from college. Same broad back, same strong arms.

She was pretty sure he was the one she'd seen driving around.

He was chatting to the salesgirl with the mermaid tattoo about the heavy metal music now playing in the store. Annie edged to the side and could see his face was kind of scruffy, as if he hadn't shaved in a couple of days. He still had those arms.

Why, oh why had she eaten that candy bar just now?

"Hey, Meg," she whispered, baring her smile, "do I have chocolate smushed all over my teeth?"

Meg peered into her mother's mouth, inspecting. It wasn't easy for her to angle her eyes because of the huge helmet. "Not *on* your teeth, Mommy," she said at last. "Just *in between* them."

Annie began intently trying to pick out the chocolate with her tongue.

He turned to leave but glanced over his shoulder. She watched as his eyes darted sideways for a second, even after she was pretty sure he had seen her. Then their eyes locked and, hesitantly, they both grinned.

"Annie."

"Hi, Chase."

She grabbed a newspaper from the stand, as if to hide the chocolate between her teeth.

"Jesus, it *is* you. I can't believe it," he said, taking a few steps toward her but stopping short. "You look great … haven't changed a bit. You kept your hair long." He started to reach out a hand to touch her ponytail, but caught himself.

"You do … did, too," Annie said, referring to his hair but suddenly feeling confused about grammar and verb tenses and the English language in general.

He was swallowing rapidly.

They were quiet for a second, having forgotten whose turn it was to speak, but eventually his eyes floated toward Meg and he smiled again. "Hello," he said, touching her shoulder lightly. "What's your name?"

Meg answered and smiled sweetly back.

"I'll bet you keep your mom busy."

"No," Meg replied, resuming her quest for the Life Saver thread. "I keep her *company* sometimes, though."

Chase laughed; he had regained his footing. "I like your orange helmet."

Annie wondered if he could see her heart beating through her shirt, or if maybe he could hear it pounding. She was grateful for the thudding heavy metal.

Brushing his hair back with the fingers of his hand the way he used to, his palm sliding over his forehead, he hugged the side of her that wasn't holding Meg. It was awkward.

"Awesome to see you, Annie," he said, swallowing again. "I was wondering if you came here anymore."

There was a little hole in the right shoulder seam of his tee shirt.

"Oh, well … I haven't, actually, been here in years." She felt her face getting very hot. "My aunt died. Aunt Faye. She left me her house." All of a sudden there was a lot of phlegm in her throat and her voice sounded strange and raspy. The Milky Way, probably.

"Yeah, my parents told me," he said. "We were all really sad to hear it. I'm sorry, Annie. She was such a cool lady." He was silent for a respectable amount of time. "I would have sent you a card, but I didn't know your address." He cleared his throat. "Her house on Middle Road?"

Annie nodded, keeping her lips closed while she ran her tongue over her teeth one more time. He seemed strangely distant, as if he were dying to leave, and she was trying to think of some small talk to keep him there. But all she could think was to ask how he was.

He seemed to be searching her face in a strange way, uneasy to see her again. It was his impeccable manners that kept the conversation going.

"We're renting a place on Abel's Hill," Chase said. "My wife, Élise, didn't want to be so close to my parents. We still see them every day—at least, the twins and I do." He flashed one of his grins: he'd always liked hanging out with his parents. It was strange to hear him use the word "wife."

Élise. Annie could practically see the *accent aigu* in the air.

"Twins?"

"Can you believe it? A little younger than you, Meg. Two girls. Antoinette and Hope. Élise let me name one ... guess which?" He laughed. "Figured we'd need some—with twins," he added hastily.

Hope was Annie's middle name. Did he remember that? And *Anne*-toinette ... ?

He pronounced it Anne-*twahn*-nette.

"*Très Français.*" Annie didn't mean to mumble, but she couldn't seem to get any air behind her words. She opened one of the water bottles and took a sip.

"Oh yes, Élise is the real deal. Sorbonne, Cordon Bleu, summers on the Côte d'Azur. We met teaching skiing in Chamonix." He brushed his hair back again. "I thought I wrote you that."

"About Ay-leese? No, I don't remember any letter about her."

He paused. "What?"

She shook her head. Her mouth felt like chalk.

"My letter. It was long. You never got it?"

What letter? Annie had received only postcards.

He'd broken up with her at the end of their graduation trip around Europe, the night before she was to fly home, in a light September rain in the arched middle of the Pont Neuf, the most romantic bridge in the world, the one in her awful dream. Staring down at the Seine together, he'd explained that he wanted to live in Europe for a while, meet other girls, not hold her back. She had a career to get to; he didn't. He didn't even know what he wanted to be when he grew up! All he did know was that he didn't want to feel guilty about anything now, or remorseful later.

She asked him why he hadn't mentioned this before. They'd had plenty of time to discuss it—riding trains, hiking goat paths winding between terraced white houses in Santorini, driving up to Delphi in a rented car, sipping a steady stream of cappuccinos in cafés across the Continent—but all he said was that he'd been having too much fun to worry about the future.

She cried, she yelled, she nearly pushed him into the river; she didn't believe him. It seemed to her that breaking up after three years ought to take some undoing.

She didn't believe he meant it because of a moment the week before, when he'd fallen asleep with his head in her lap on the train, traveling through Tuscany at twilight. An amber glow from the setting sun on the wheat fields flooding their compartment, she'd drawn her fingers through his pale hair, along his lovely face, and begun to cry. She'd never expected she could feel so much. And while she wanted to hold that precise feeling forever, along with and in equal measure to her gladness she felt a dread because she knew that, soon enough, they would have to get off the train and it would all be lost. Her tears fell onto his cheeks and he opened his cornflower-blue eyes, sleepy and smiling. He stroked her face, and she knew he understood.

"You're as happy as I am, aren't you, Annie," he said. It wasn't a question.

Why had he let her go if he was so happy? That's what never made sense.

She returned to Boston to work at Juliet's publishing house, still not comprehending. He called sporadically, but the connections and time zones were bad and he was always in some different ski lodge in the French Alps, so when she telephoned back he was never there. When they did manage to talk they would often argue, about what she couldn't recall.

He had written those few cryptic postcards and she'd written several newsy, blue aerograms to the American Express office in Chamonix, but their correspondence petered out and at Christmas, when her family asked how he was, she had no more news than she'd had at Thanksgiving. Not until she'd run into Piper St. Clair on the Vineyard in July and she'd said how sorry she was things hadn't worked out (something about bad timing), did Annie begin to believe it was really over. But she had never heard Élise's name until now.

It was her turn at the counter.

"How are your parents?" Annie tried to slide the empty Milky Way wrapper under the newspaper, but her free hand was trembling and got bungled up with the waters and crumpled potato-chip bag, and a few chips spilled onto the counter. Meg handed down the Lucky Charms. The salesgirl smiled.

For a second, Annie felt Chase searching her face and everything quickening. He opened his mouth to say something, then changed his mind. He shuddered his head and shoulders like a discombobulated dog when he bounds out of the ocean.

"Good, thanks." He was smooth again. "Dad's getting the sailboat ready. Mom broke her back in March moving a hydrangea, but she's nearly recovered now."

Annie's face was on fire. She had definitely received only postcards. They were still in a trunk in her parents' attic.

As they inched toward the back porch, he switched his grocery bag from one arm to the other to pull the screen door open for her.

Annie felt acutely aware of her cheap flip-flops and old shorts and tee shirt, and how frumpy she must look—especially compared to Élise. Really, it wouldn't kill her to make more of an effort. Thank goodness she'd at least taken off her bike helmet. Noticing his faded navy shorts, she missed him all over again, even though he was standing right beside her.

For some reason they both looked at her toes, and she wished she'd painted them as she used to in Asia. But when was she supposed to have gotten around to doing that? They switched their gaze to his feet. He had on those expensive leather sandals sailors wear.

"I don't paint my nails, either," he said, and they both laughed. He could still read her mind.

Meg finally extracted a butterscotch Life Saver, popped it in her mouth, and decided to join the conversation.

"What's your friend's name, Mommy?"

"Chase, Meg. This is my old friend, Chase."

Two teenagers brushed by them on the porch, making it hard for Meg to hear, not to mention the helmet crammed over her ears and the fact that Annie had kind of swallowed the name.

"What?" Meg extended her arms, her whole face lighting up. "You *are*? James? James *Taylor*? I *love* you!"

"No, no, not James," Chase said, catching her little hands with one of his. "Glad your mom's bringing you up right, though. My name is *Chase*—you know, like when you run after somebody and try to catch them." He looked straight at Annie and softened his voice. "But you can't, because they run faster than you do."

A man and woman in Lycra racing-bike clothes approached, forcing them to turn sideways, shoulder to shoulder. When they faced each other again they stood closer and she sensed the familiar smell of his breath.

"I'd love to see you sometime, and meet all your kids. And your husband. What's his name, again? Gary?"

"*Gordon*. Actually, he's in Southern China. Detained there for another month, probably."

Chase raised his eyebrows. "China? You're kidding me. Wow. Well, then," he lowered his voice again. "How do I find you?"

She pretended not to hear. He certainly wasn't nervous anymore. She'd forgotten how flirtatious he could be.

They reached her bike; his, naturally, was the clunker parked in front.

He handed her the backpack. "What's in here, anyway? Rocks?"

"Aunt Faye."

He stared at her.

"Faye? Cripes, Annie. Exactly what are you two planning to do? Just take her for a ride?"

"Well, if you really want to know, I was going to go bury her." She strapped Meg in carefully and stood with her legs on either side of the bike. She couldn't bear to put on her goofy helmet in front of him, so she left it on the handlebars, although it was starting to get so humid that her hair must look terrible. "As a matter of fact, I have to hurry up because I have to pick up my older two at the Center at noon."

"Ah, the Center. Still hippie-dippie up there? Tie-dye and macramé and water balloon fights? Our girls do educational activities with the nanny all morning while Élise and the many friends she ships up from New York gad about tanning. Bury her? By yourself?"

"Yup, and I better get going." She put her right foot on the pedal. "Well … it's … amazing to run into you. I guess I'll see you around, Chase." Despite not being at all aware of her legs, she somehow shoved off, her helmet whacking against the front wheel.

"Wait! Can I call you? I still remember your aunt's number!" He recited it the colloquial Island way, using the last five digits only. "Can you ever sneak away? Do you have a nanny up here?"

He broke into a jog to keep up. Annie's body seemed to be

riding her bicycle without her. She turned, Meg between them, and waved.

Her legs were cycling furiously out of the sandy parking lot, but she was in too low a gear as she turned onto the pavement and her foot slipped off the pedal. Please let him not have noticed.

"Hey!" yelped Meg, as the corner of her child seat nearly side-swiped a telephone pole.

Annie picked up speed around the bend to the left on State Road. A car approached and honked, and to her horror she realized she was riding on the wrong side of the street, against traffic.

Somehow, her bike cruised into the cemetery.

14

A Modern Family

John Alley had told her where the plot was, by the old white-picket fence. The smell of hay was thick in the air. Annie rode slowly across the sandy crabgrass between the scattered headstones, again in the lowest gear, looking across to the red barn where the sorrel horses were grazing in the far pasture.

Jared's family plot was in the new part of the cemetery, with other people who had died in the twentieth century. The old section held people buried from long before the American Revolution and was supposed to be haunted, as if any graveyard weren't.

Meg was singing in her seat.

The stone—with its bright, distinct lettering—didn't take long to find. Annie dismounted and unbuckled Meg, but her legs still felt so wobbly from having seen Chase that she could hardly hold the bike steady.

Faith Robinson Wright Holloway.

Faith. Precisely what Annie needed a little of herself, these days.

And it was inscribed with three names: Jared's, Faye's—and Priscilla's.

Juliet would have a heart attack.

Priscilla and Jared had one son who worked in computers and had moved to Seattle a long time ago; Annie wasn't sure if she'd ever met him. Did he know Faye was to be buried here on Martha's Vineyard, alongside his parents? Would he mind? Well, too late now.

A pretty row of perennials was in bloom, just as John Alley had said. Black-eyed susans, day lilies, geraniums, daisies. Aunt Faye had thought of everything.

A red cardinal stood on the stone, gazing at her.

"Figures you'd be here," Annie said to the cardinal.

"Hi, Aunt Faye," Meg sang, mimicking a bird's song. "Nice to see you! Nice to see you!"

"What did you mean, Meg, when you said the red bird in Sylvan Fell told you she, it, he, was Aunt Faye?"

But Meg ignored her and wriggled down to wander, humming to herself.

Annie traced the chiseled letters on the stone with her fingertips. She had to remember to call Alan Gowell in Edgartown to finish the engraving.

When Aunt Faye had been economizing and decided to have her and Jared's names engraved at the same time, at least she had refrained from having that expectant dash put next to her birthday, hanging suspended, waiting to be rounded off by the inscribed date of death.

Yet ... maybe that's how we should all live our lives. Maybe we should live every minute knowing a dash is there, holding the space that will one day be filled in after finding its way to an engraver's to-do list.

Annie wasn't in the mood to do this anymore and it was getting cloudy, but she had made it this far so she might as well get the shovel. She and Meg crossed the cemetery's dirt road and meandered through the old section, looking for the garden shed. Sunlight filtering through the leaves of the trees created a misty yellow haze. Reading a thin, faded stone, she saw that a Mr. Mayhew had been buried in 1820 with his first and also second wives. At least, that's what it looked like it said. The lettering was so faint she couldn't be sure.

Annie decided she'd dig up the geraniums on the right side, reasoning (she couldn't explain why) that Priscilla was probably buried on the left, under the small stand of daisies.

Oh, who cares whether this was unconventional? It's what Faye and Jared had wanted. And he would definitely be in the middle, under the day lilies and black-eyed susans.

Meg wandered over to a flat tombstone and began playing dolls with some sticks. Annie started digging.

The flimsy box of ashes, out of the backpack now, looked forlorn resting alone on the ground. She started talking out loud to her aunt, which she hadn't thought to do when Faye was in her bedroom closet all weekend. But rather than actually talking to her box of ashes, Annie kept glancing up at her chiseled name on the stone.

"I just ran into Chase at Alley's," she told the stone, jamming the shovel into the dirt. "Remember that glamorous French girl my roommate Louise said he started dating after me, in Chamonix? He married her. I thought he was going to marry me."

She dug with a fury that would have impressed Gloria Bradshaw and the entire Sylvan Fell Garden Club.

"Gordon's in Hong Kong and my parents are in New Zealand and we're back in the States and now Chase ..."

It was getting stickier by the minute.

"I'm so tired, Aunt Faye." Part of her wanted to keel over right there on top of Priscilla and Jared. "But who am I to complain to you? You're dead!"

Aunt Faye would have thought that was funny.

John Alley had been right about the soil: it was soft and easy to turn. After about six inches, though, it hardened. Her back ached and her knees were getting sore from the scratchy crabgrass. Gordon would have thought to bring a mat and some nifty tool that cut through rocks.

Heavy clouds had replaced the blue sky. Annie contemplated the stone.

"What do you think was in that letter?"

She lifted up her tee shirt to wipe her nose and face, something that would have mortified her mother. Oh, so what? Adair would never in a million years pick up a shovel.

After a few minutes, Annie had managed to dig down about a foot; all she had to do now was make the hole a bit wider. She really should have waited for Gordon. Doing this alone was ludicrous. Terrified she would jam the shovel accidentally into Jared or Priscilla, she put it down.

And then Annie, sitting cross-legged on the grass, all of a sudden could not stem the tears anymore and they began coming very fast. Thank God the cemetery was deserted: she must look pathetic, like some histrionic Gothic heroine, wailing on the proverbial gravestone.

Splintering pain began in her belly, seared through her ribs, cut through her throat. Her neck was about to burst. The sobs had a primitive force of their own, and she felt helpless to control them. This is what it means to be wracked with grief, she thought, but she didn't think any words after that. Her mind, usually so busy, went suddenly blank. She didn't see the gold pasture or hear the buzz of the insects around her. She sobbed and sobbed, and the only thing she thought was that she might break in half.

After a while she felt Meg's small hand softly patting her back. Annie pulled her daughter into her lap and, closing her eyes, pressed her little head against her chest.

She was getting Meg's hair all wet. She hugged her close and kept crying, and slowly they rocked back and forth.

Annie's fierce sobs gradually subsided, as even ocean waves will after a tumultuous winter's storm.

"Hi, Mr. Chase," Meg said.

Annie opened her eyes to see him standing before them, out of breath and pushing his hair out of his eyes.

He gave her a minute.

"I started riding back up toward Abel's Hill, made it all the way to Meeting House, and thought, what the hell am I *doing?*" His shirt was dripping wet. "On the way back down I got a flat tire, had to ditch the bike at the Mobil station, run from there. Sorry I'm so sweaty."

She thought he looked wonderful.

"And sorry I wasn't here to help you dig the hole."

She gazed up at him from the crabgrass, unable to register that he was standing here in front of her.

"Looks like you did a good job, though, Annie. Jeez, it's humid."

She felt as if a steamroller had just driven over her body, too spent to react. Her voice, however, sounded surprisingly normal. Maybe that was what happened after you were run over—you surrendered.

"I'm not sure I went wide enough." She spoke to him as if they had just spent yesterday sailing in his Sunfish. "The thing is, I'm afraid of running into ..."

Chase read the tombstone and seemed to put it together at once. "That's okay, that's cool," he said. "A modern family."

He took up the shovel and dug wider to the right, and deeper.

"Hey," he said. "When did your Uncle Emmett die, anyway? I remember it was right after your cousin. Wasn't that the same year as poor Priscilla here?"

Annie thought for a moment. It had been their sophomore spring. She nodded.

"Kind of interesting that your old Uncle Emmett and this lady Priscilla happened to die the same year, wouldn't you say? A little suspicious. Convenient, anyway."

Uncle Emmett had died of a heart attack; what about Priscilla? Annie would have to ask her mother.

Chase's forearms were so strong that it took him only a few minutes to finish the hole.

"Ready?"

She nodded. Her legs were all pins and needles, but Meg was almost asleep in her lap and she didn't dare move.

"Would you like to do the honors, or shall I?"

"You can, thanks, Chase."

Carefully, he lowered the box. He had to busy it in a little, since the sides weren't perfectly square as they would have been if, say, Gordon had dug the hole. Then he began shoveling the pile of dirt back over the box, and Annie placed the sleeping Meg gently on the ground. Together, they packed down the dirt and smoothed it over with their hands. Then they replaced the geraniums.

He wasn't wearing a wedding ring and, with a start, she realized she wasn't wearing hers, either. She had taken it off during the weekend towel washing and wringing, and forgotten to put it on again. She didn't want him to think she wasn't happily married.

Wiping her hands on her shorts, she felt something in her pocket: the two heart-shaped pebbles Lindsay had given her on the beach Friday when they'd first gone out to Split Rock. That seemed like a long time ago.

She placed the pebbles in front of the row of flowers, and another red cardinal flew over and landed beside them. Or maybe it was the same one. It hopped over to the base of the gravestone.

"Aunt Faye planted these flowers herself and here they are in bloom, ready and waiting for her. How ironic," she said quietly. "She's left me so many gifts."

They stood up, both stretching their backs the same way. Meg was still asleep on the grass. Chase put a sweaty arm around Annie and she leaned against his shoulder, feeling as if she had never stopped standing this way next to him. There was something about the way her body fit into the crook of his arm.

He reached around to wipe a tear, or something, off her cheek with two fingers. "What'd you do to your lip?"

"Oh, that," she said, touching her blister and hesitating. "Got caught in the riptide the other day. Long Point."

"Ah," he said, nodding. "That's not like you. The waves must've been brutal."

She smiled weakly and nodded.

They both looked at the cardinal. It still hadn't budged from the grave.

"Bold bird," Chase said.

"I know this might sound kind of weird," she began. "But sometimes I wonder if this cardinal is—Aunt Faye. Checking in on me, or something. There was a cardinal outside our kitchen in Maryland and—one seems to follow me around everywhere, here."

Chase nodded again; no idea ever sounded weird to him. "The Island has a lot of red cardinals." He laughed in a kind way, not mocking her at all. "I'm pretty sure it's the state bird of Martha's Vineyard."

"I don't know if this is the *exact* ... Probably impossible for it to fly all the way ..."

"Remember when I traveled in Ecuador around the Amazon with Haven Ladd, my roommate at Deerfield? The people down there believe a person's soul can become an eagle, or a jaguar or a serpent, I think it is, after they die. The spirit lives on in that form for a while. Lots of cultures believe that sort of thing."

She smiled weakly again.

"I think, when you're grieving, you see things like that. You're more open to it, or something. When Haven died in that skiing accident—remember, senior year?—I saw a bald eagle after we buried him in New Hampshire and was positive it was him. At first it kind of freaked me out. Then it made me feel better."

The cardinal hopped onto the top of the engraved stone and, once again, looked Annie right in the eye. "It does, actually," she said, "make me feel better."

Chase reached into her backpack for one of the bottles of

water he'd watched her buy at Alley's, unscrewed the top, and handed it to her.

"Seems like you might be fraying at the edges a bit, Annie." He put his arm back around her, pulled her closer. "Grieving is a lot for one person to handle. You'll be all right, though. You're tough." He paused, looking across the field at the pretty sorrels, and wet his lips.

Amazing how it seemed no time had passed between them. He had been her best friend for a long time.

"Do you want to know what it said?" He released her shoulders to bend over and straighten one of the day lilies that had flopped over onto Jared. "The letter?"

He knelt down to pat back the dirt, not looking at her, and now it was his voice that went hoarse. "It was long. I remember, because it's the longest letter I ever wrote." He let out a little laugh and she froze, listening. "I wrote asking you to come back to Europe, to Chamonix." He turned to look up at her. "But you never wrote back, and then I heard you'd married Gary."

"Gordon."

"Yeah." Chase stood up and took a few steps away from her. "Kind of on the rebound, wasn't it?" He took a deep breath. "So who *is* he, anyway?" He crossed his arms. "Where the hell did he even *come* from?"

"What?"

"None of our friends from Brown even knew the guy, never heard of him!" He raised his voice, and it sounded even louder in the graveyard. "He came out of fucking left field! Why didn't you *tell* me you'd met someone? That you were going to *marry* him, for crissakes?"

"What? You broke up with me! I was supposed to ask your permission?"

"You didn't even give me a chance!" Chase kicked some fresh dirt onto Aunt Faye, tamped it down with his foot, then paced a few yards farther away, over to someone else's grave. "*Fuck!*" Annie heard him say, and watched as he kicked at whomever that dead person was. He pounded the sides of both his thighs with his fists.

Standing there drenched with sweat, Meg asleep on the ground at her feet, Annie's hands started shaking.

Chase stamped over and faced her again.

"Well, why didn't you *call* me from France when I didn't write back?" she demanded, surprised at her own raised voice. "*Wouldn't* I have written back? I always wrote back!"

"You were married before I had fucking time!"

"I didn't think you'd care!"

"Like I said, textbook rebound move."

Annie glanced at Meg, still sound asleep. How insane that she and Chase were arguing, shouting at each other in the West Tisbury Cemetery, after all this time.

They hesitated, each waiting for the other, glaring indignantly in the heavy air. The cardinal fluttered away.

"Anyway," Annie said finally, exhaling, "I heard you were living with Ah-*leese* in Paris."

"What the hell are you talking about? I never lived with *Ay*-leese in Paris."

"You didn't?" Annie inadvertently bit her blister. "Oh. My roommate Louise said you did. Charlie Pembroke told her."

"What?" Chase scowled—then, pausing, cocked his head to one side, trying to remember. "No, no, no," he said, his voice returning to normal. "That was Chan*tal.*"

"Oh. Chan*tal*? Sorry. I guess Charlie got your girlfriends confused."

"Élise and I actually broke up pretty quick," Chase continued, ignoring her. "I didn't see her again until we happened to run into each other in Manhattan a few years ago. You already had a couple of kids. Then we decided to get married. Or, allow me to rephrase that. *She* decided."

"What happened to Chan*tal*?"

"Who?" He scuffed the dirt again. "Cut it out, Annie. You know you were the one I cared about. Not any of them."

She studied the ground and then gazed back and they continued standing like that, staring stupidly at each other as if in some dumb contest.

"Oh, well," they said at precisely the same time, the way they used to. "Destiny."

They rolled their eyes and smirked.

"Kismet," she whispered, also the way they used to, and he drew her back into his arms.

She pressed her cheek against his damp chest and gazed across the meadow. He smelled salty, like the ocean. The sorrels were ambling over to the far side, back to the barn.

"Cripes," he said. "I thought you blew me off."

"I thought you blew *me* off."

They stood there, breathing, until Chase, resting his chin on the top of her head, chuckled. "I hate to say it, Annie, but you look like hell."

She chuckled too, and touched her cheeks. They were puffy from so much crying.

"So," he said. "Want to meet Élise while we're here?"

"Let's not get carried away."

They hugged again and lingered a while longer. Chase had always had such a nice quiet. And his body felt so comfortable, so familiar. She started to tell him how he had saved her from drowning at Long Point, but instead turned her face up just as he gazed down, and for a split second she thought they might kiss.

He was the one who held back.

"Looks like it's going to rain again," he said.

"I need to wake Meg and head back to the Center," Annie rushed, stepping backwards. "Oh, my gosh. I nearly forgot something."

She reached into the backpack and pulled out a fifth of Aunt Faye's Seagram's Seven she'd found in one of the kitchen cupboards.

"Ha!" Chase laughed. "I remember her liking that stuff."

Annie twisted off the cap and handed him the bottle. "I know it's early, but let's have a toast."

"Here's to you, Faith Robinson Wright Holloway, for a life well lived," Chase declared, reading the tombstone. He took a long swig. "And I'd still like to know how you and Jared managed to knock off your spouses the same year."

"Thank you for saving my life, Aunt Faye," Annie said, taking a sip. It tasted sweet, and felt good and warm on her throat. "Who knows where I would be without you."

She held the bottle high and watered the overturned bit of earth with the rest of the whiskey. "I hope this doesn't kill her perennials."

15

Yielding

——

After seeing Chase on Monday, Annie suddenly—stopped. She stopped trying to keep things going. She stopped tidying the house, yielding to the disheveled mess and letting the dirty dishes and laundry pile up. The voice in her head that ordinarily told her what to do stopped talking, which pretty much meant she stopped thinking.

She truly *had* intended to take the kids to Vineyard Haven to order a washing machine the afternoon after seeing Chase, but it was too hard to mobilize in the rain and she just—didn't. Miraculously, Gordon, in Hong Kong, went ahead and ordered a new one for her, somehow using the new-fangled World Wide Web.

Annie never got around to taking the kids to see that sweet flock of sheep, either. And it kept raining and raining.

Did she truly believe she could wrap up losing Chase so easily? Just let the crazy fact that it happened—go? Nonchalantly accept, after wondering about him all these years (off and on, of course), that one lost letter had determined their whole lives, the way they pretended at the cemetery? They were Americans, for heaven's sake! Can-do, river-diverting Puritan stock! Since when did they believe so passively in "destiny"?

Maybe it was their combined good manners that had momentarily rescued them from the agony of asking more questions, or at least delayed the rescuing—but she did not feel wrapped up. Not one bit.

She and the kids were starting to run out of clean clothes. But instead of fretting about when Gordon's new washing machine would be delivered, Annie told the kids not to worry, it was okay to wear the same thing every day in the summer. And to simplify dishwashing, they started using paper plates and plastic cups she found in the basement.

She did manage to walk Tashmoo with Lindsay and her dog, Zoey, and to get the kids to camp on time, but spent the greater part of the morning wandering aimlessly around the house or resting in bed, staring at the ceiling. Tashmoo began following her around constantly, refusing to let her out of his sight.

She made herself get up and brush her teeth and hair for pick-up, but stayed in the car and let Robbie bring the girls over in the rain. She didn't feel like meeting anybody and, even though Chase mentioned when they left the cemetery that he was on his way back to New York, she was afraid she might run into him or, worse, Élise. She was sure she'd recognize her.

During the rainy afternoons and periodic thunder and lightning, Annie allowed Robbie to employ every one of Aunt Faye's sheets and blankets to build a fort that stretched the length of the downstairs, in which the four of them played Monopoly with flashlights. Later they would curl up together on her bed and she would read them chapters from *Harry Potter* or, when that got too scary, more of A. A. Milne's whimsical poems,

> *They're changing guard at Buckingham Palace—*
> *Christopher Robin went down with Alice.*
> *Alice is marrying one of the guard.*
> *"A soldier's life is terrible hard,"*
> *Says Alice …*

until, one by one, they fell asleep.

When the kids weren't having fun and being adorable, of course, they were practically killing each other.

Annie spent a lot of time on the telephone. Her mother, a day ahead of her in New Zealand, suddenly seemed to call every day; she must have signed up for some special telephone plan. After a quick catch-up on Princess Diana, Adair would tell her how roomy and comfortable it was at Fiona's house even if it was cold, being the middle of winter; how Fiona's children were polite and quiet and still had their live-in Maori nanny, even though Fiona had quit the golf circuit; how Percy was trying to start another golf-tour company but wasn't sure it was feasible considering the vast distances. At this, Annie had scowled. Was this news? Had Percy bothered to consult a map before he moved down there?

Unfortunately, during this particular conversation, Meg and Lily happened to get into a big fight over some silly thing and chased each other, stomping and screaming, until Adair said she wouldn't call long distance again if that's how they were going to behave and advised her daughter to hang up before the roof caved in.

Juliet called from Maine to apologize once more for Tashmoo at the very moment he launched into a strange barking spree, mainly because Robbie had locked the girls in the bathroom. There was a lot of shouting and door-pounding, and Juliet once again claimed something about call-waiting and hung up in a hurry.

At least twice a day, Annie spoke with Gordon, twelve time zones ahead. The kids fought and threw things at each other while she talked to him, too, but she went into her room and closed the door and lay down on the bed under Aunt Faye's wedding quilt.

Things were not going very well in Hong Kong. The Handover had been surreal, and everyone was freaking out wondering how different Hong Kong, the most capitalist city in the world, would be under the communists. Gordon said there was a "palpable feeling of anxiety," which didn't sound like something he would say.

It was raining there, too, and had ruined the Handover ceremonies, but the skies cleared at dusk and rainbows had popped up all over the place, and the Chinese had taken this as an auspicious omen. Gordon described how he had taken Pretti and her children in the downpour to Nathan Road near Victoria Harbor to watch the parade of People's Liberation Army tanks rumbling down Nathan Road, which used to teem with long black limousines and little red taxis. He used the word "teem," which didn't sound like something he would say, either.

Nathan Road was known in Hong Kong as the "Golden Mile" and a lot of it looked like Times Square, and Annie could not for the life of her envision it full of tanks. It would be like the Russian army bulldozing down Broadway. She should have watched the news on Aunt Faye's old television, but she hadn't gotten around to turning it on yet.

"Does Pretti wear her elegant saris out in the rain? That turquoise one?" Annie asked.

"Pretti? *Saris?*" Gordon laughed. "She's not that traditional, Annie. She has her PhD in psychology from the University of New Delhi, for Pete's sake. She was about to start working again. Nope. She wears Western clothes."

He went on to tell her how the bodies from the plane crash, or what was left of them, had finally been found and returned, how he was trying to hire new people but having no luck because of all the confusion with the Handover, how he was trying to spend as much time as possible with each victim's family.

He pronounced her name *Pree tea'*, emphasizing the accent on the second syllable as if his tongue were going straight through his front two teeth.

A few times he asked Annie if everything was okay, but she simply directed the subject back to him. She didn't mention her awful dreams about drowning or her new terror of the ocean, since he would have been angry with her for getting in that situation in the first place; it wouldn't have been helpful with all he had going on. She didn't mention burying Aunt Faye, didn't mention Chase. Gordon didn't understand their history, and she didn't feel like explaining it.

16

Lucy Vincent Beach

"My new friend Ben's dad invited us to meet them at Lucy Vincent Beach after lunch," Robbie said on Thursday, snapping Meg into her car seat after camp. "Can we go?"

The dirt parking lot of the Center was more pitted than ever with mud puddles, thanks to the last few days of wind and steady rain, but at noon the sun was blazing and the sky clear and dry. The stormy weather seemed finally to have blown offshore; maybe, Annie hoped, the earth would at last have a chance to dry.

As they headed up Middle Road, Lily said, "Robbie wants to go to that beach because he has a crush on Margaret." She began taunting him in the familiar singsong, "Robbie and Margaret, sitting in a tree, K-I-S-S-I-N-G ..."

"*Shut ... up!*" Robbie turned around from the front seat and punched her in the arm. Lily pretended it didn't hurt and continued to mouth the singsong.

Annie pulled over to the side of the road above the panorama of Keith Farm, generally considered the best view on Martha's Vineyard. With all this rain, it reminded her of her family's trip to "the British Isles." (Of Vermont, too.) Green-and-brown mallard ducks and white swans paddled around the little pond at the bottom of the field, while chestnut-colored cows amiably grazed about. They looked perfectly placed, as if Thomas Hart Benton or some other famous Vineyard painter had specifically positioned them there. Hovering along the horizon, above a long stand of trees at the end of the pasture, the ocean rose dramatically to meet the sky.

She had an impulse to jump out of the car and roll sideways like an Egyptian mummy down the verdant hill, the way she and her brother, Percy, used to do in their backyard in Wellesley.

"Please, *please* will you get along," she said, too fed up to raise her voice. Tears trickled out of her eyes. "This fighting has *got* to stop. You're wrecking everything." She gestured toward the view. "You're so lucky to have each other, to have built-in company, to be here. You need to figure out how to get along."

Robbie turned to glower at Lily. "*Idiot*," he muttered. "Look what you started."

Annie closed her eyes. She pressed her forehead against the face of the steering wheel and dropped her hands into her lap. She sighed in a despairing way.

"Okay, okay," Robbie said, stricken at her crying. "Sorry, Mommy, sorry. From now on we'll be better, I promise." He stroked her arm. "Please don't cry."

The girls whimpered in the back seat.

"It's time for us to go back to the beach, Mommy. We're on an *island*. I told Ben's dad we would meet them after lunch if you said we could. Please?"

Annie wiped her cheeks with the backs of her hands. Slowly, she opened one eye. "If you can be nice to each other and help me pick up the house, maybe."

Somehow, she had mustered enough ambition to get the necessary sticker for the car after drop-off that morning; Primo's wife, Mary, had explained how to go about it on the telephone. It probably was time to return to the land of the living, as Aunt Faye herself would have said.

Annie had never been there, but Lucy Vincent Beach worried her because she'd heard it was vast. While part of it backed onto Chilmark Pond, the pond beach was a sliver compared to the one at Long Point. It wouldn't be enough for Robbie: he would want to swim in the ocean. The town made it clear that they had monitoring "beach patrols," whatever that meant, but no official lifeguards to save anyone. There was no way she could take Robbie in those waves and no way he could go alone.

Lucy Vincent Beach had been donated to the town in the 1980s and was named after Lucinda Poole Vincent, a lobsterman's widow who happened to be the longest-serving librarian in Chilmark history. Her family had owned it since the Island was first settled by the English. It used to be known as Jungle Beach because it was overgrown the way a New England jungle would be, with blueberry briars and rosehip bushes spilling across the sand, but also because it was notorious for being a nude beach where people could relax in their "primitive" state. In the 1960s and '70s, artists like James Taylor, Carly Simon, and John Belushi used to slap red clay from the cliffs onto each other, giving themselves so-called mud baths. At least, that was the general lore.

Annie had a feeling Aunt Faye and Jared used to hike to Jungle Beach to skinny-dip. Jared once told her that being naked was simply part of the unfettered up-Island spirit begun in the 1930s and '40s, when people started buying summer houses up here; that it was part of a larger anti-establishment rebellion in the United States about being free and authentic. For Bohemian artists and intellectuals who lived in New York City like Jared, the scruffy, wild woods and shores of up-Island were paradise.

The fact that Annie appreciated and "got" this about the Vineyard was, she knew, one of the things Faye loved most about her. Unlike Percy or Juliet, Annie had never been content to go along in lockstep with the establishment; she liked to make up her own mind, to question authority, and coming here when she was younger had been her way of rebelling against her parents' obsession with keeping up with the so-called Joneses. They didn't know who they really were apart from their country-club life, and clearly they didn't know Annie. Imagine, her a debutante!

Up-Islanders, Jared had once explained, maintained that living on land in its natural primitive condition would allow their minds to expand, unbound from oppression and convention. It was actually important to shed clothes and shoes. They were constricting, and if you truly wanted to be a liberal thinker and have your mind roam and comprehend things without any preconceived judgment, you needed to free your body.

Sounded like a line Chase might have used back when they worked at the Edgartown Inn.

In their driveway, an olive-green Subaru station wagon was parked beside a Crane Appliance truck, and young Emmett was there, helping a deliveryman wheel the broken washing machine out the cellar door. Looked like they had just finished installing the new one Gordon had ordered. Tashmoo lay relaxed on the ground, supervising, beside a large duffel bag and a long, rectangular instrument case.

"Hi Aunt Anna, hi everyone!" Emmett called. "Surprise! My mother said maybe you could use another pair of hands."

Annie stared at him as if he were some kind of mirage.

"Are you all right there, Aunt Anna? Does your offer for me to be your au pair still, like, stand?"

She reminded herself to close her gaping mouth and hugged him.

"I quit that job at my dad's bank on Tremont Street. I wasn't, like, cut out for it. My roommate's girlfriend moved in and took over my rent. By the way, would you mind calling me Emmie from now on? Everybody else does. Emmett's a little formal for me."

The kids jumped up and down and tore around the driveway, acting as excited as Tashmoo when he first saw Lindsay and Zoey at the beach.

"We're so happy to see you, Emm*ie*. You have no idea." Annie kept her arm around his shoulders; she wasn't going to let him escape. "So, so happy."

They walked up the path to the house and she noticed Robbie and Lily share a sideways, knowing glance.

Robbie immediately leapt into action and led the operation to move Emmie into his little room upstairs, cheerfully swapping it for the sun porch next to Annie's room.

"I can keep an eye on things better from down here," Annie overheard him say to Lily. "And we need to stop fighting. So just do what I say, will you, and stop making me so mad."

After lunch he immediately began issuing commands, like a general, to dismantle their elaborate fort and put away the puzzles and toys. Determined to get to the beach, he began packing up snacks and lathering sunscreen onto his sisters.

Emmie quietly surveyed the mess left over from the weekend—dishes stacked in the sink and on the counter, small mountains of laundry piled across the cellar floor. If it was all the same to her, he said, he'd rather skip the beach and unpack and get settled, maybe walk Tashmoo and practice his saxophone a bit. Was there anything he could do to start supper? Any errands he could run?

Soon they were trailing to Lucy Vincent Beach along the narrow, planked boardwalk the town had installed to preserve the sandy path, so much shorter than the one to Lambert's Cove. It was dotted with little pyramids of pebbles, miniature cairns people had created for a bit of whimsy. *Deceptively* welcoming and child-friendly, Annie commented, since the waves were probably treacherous.

They emerged onto the beach and, as if in a cartoon, together dropped what they were carrying, so stunned were they to see this sudden spectacular swath of sand stretching to the sea. The famous iron-red cliffs shot up majestically on either side of the path, but the most striking thing of all was the slew of reddish boulders strewn haphazardly across the shore, dozens of small Split Rocks gleaming in the sunlight.

"Is this Heaven?" asked Lily.

The water was calm and the beach bejeweled with a strange, colorful spread of towels—strange because the towels had no people on them. Rather, clusters of men and women Annie recognized from the Chilmark Store and the Center were gathered chatting, in circles of chairs or circles of standing groups. It looked to her like one exclusive clique-y cocktail party.

"How will we ever find your friend?" Annie asked, passing the tanned, blond, twenty-something beach patrol sitting in a tall lifeguard's chair.

"I just will. Come on," said Robbie, leading the way.

In single file, they threaded between the towels and groups, and Annie couldn't stop herself from scanning the shore to see if maybe Chase and Élise were here. But it wouldn't be like him to come to a crowded town beach. He would be on Abel's Hill, surely, or Quansoo.

He must have been detained in New York. That's why he hadn't called.

"Aha!" Robbie pronounced, as they came upon the burly, tall man Annie had seen ordering pizza that first morning at the Chilmark Store, lying on a huge towel reading *Stuart Little* to three children, their eight arms and legs entwined.

Ben leapt up to greet Robbie, and the man disentangled himself.

"Excellent!" the man declared, in a deep voice. "You made it! We've been waiting for you. Your sizes match up. Three boys, three girls. *Mechayeh.*"

He introduced himself, Freddy Rosenthal, and one by one his children: Ben, Tommy, and Beatrice. He made them all shake hands. The boys had very short buzz cuts, making them look as if they had just stepped out of the barbershop.

"I've been meaning to ask you, Freddy," Robbie said, clearly comfortable with him from waiting for Annie at pickup time. "What's that language you always speak?"

"Yiddish. You must have heard Yiddish before."

Robbie shook his head. "My dad and I speak Chinese."

"Chinese? My *goodness!*" exclaimed the younger brother, Tommy, revealing a little mouth crowded with big buckteeth.

"That's Tommy's favorite expression," Freddy said, grinning. "Sometimes he even wrings his hands. Gets it from my mother."

Tommy nodded, beaming.

"Let me tell you something, Robbie," Freddy continued. "Yiddish comes in handy when you're looking for exactly the right word. It's a great language. But I don't suppose too many people speak it here on Martha's Vineyard."

"Hmm. Maybe you could teach it to me," Robbie replied. Then, barely able to suppress his excitement at being back on a beach with a boy his own age to play with, he yelped something to Ben about building a fort out of driftwood, and off they ran toward the rocks that separated the top of the beach from the dunes. Apart from their haircuts, their lean, lanky builds made them look like brothers.

"Watch the poison ivy!" Annie reminded, watching them go with a lump in her throat.

"You have such pretty hair," Lily said, kneeling down next to Beatrice and glancing guiltily at her little sister.

"She cut mine," Meg piped, pointing at Lily before sticking her thumb back in her mouth.

Beatrice looked like an unkempt, brunette Shirley Temple, with long ringlets that fell every which way around her face.

Annie, with Meg on her hip, stood facing Freddy awkwardly; this was an unusual play date. He had wide shoulders and a big barrel chest, and was very tall. With his coral-colored Hawaiian bathing suit scrunched below a good-size belly, he reminded her of Hoss from *Bonanza*, if the Cartwrights ever happened to go to the island of Maui.

Freddy took off his thick Ray-Ban Wayfarers and studied her with sharp brown eyes. Those big sunglasses covered a lot of an unexpectedly handsome face.

"Hey, I know you," he said. "You're Primo's friend."

"Well, a new one, I guess," Annie said, hoping he wouldn't notice her still-blistered lip. "My aunt was his friend, though."

"Who is your aunt?"

He was certainly direct.

They chatted until Beatrice and Tommy begged him to lie back down and read some more.

"Do you mind?" Freddy asked. "We can shmooze later."

"I like that book," Lily said. "Did you get to where Stuart drives around in his little car yet?"

"What, are you psychic? We just read that part. You girls sit down and listen, too."

Lily sat beside Freddy on the towel as if she'd known him her whole life, and Meg snuggled next to her and sucked her thumb. Annie felt self-conscious. She had brought only a book to read to the kids, not one for herself, and she didn't particularly want to listen to *Stuart Little*—although she was beginning to think this guy Freddy had a career doing books on tape. He adopted special voices for each character, the way Annie herself tried to do, and was good at keeping them straight. She'd never heard a dad read like this before.

When at last Robbie and Ben returned, they were covered with sand.

"There you are, guys," said Freddy. "I'm *shvitzing*. Let's fold down the page and go in the water. The waves are like nothing today."

Robbie looked at Annie, imploring.

"Why not?" Freddy bellowed. "What, do you have an ear infection or something?"

"My kids aren't very strong ocean swimmers yet," began Annie. "If he goes in, would you mind staying with him?"

"*Oy vey.* Okay, okay. You have to watch Beatrice, then. Tommy, you come with me. I'll take care of everybody so Gavin can keep working on his tan up there on his lifeguard chair. You girls can read the book if you want, but don't dare lose my place. I want to know what happens." He folded his glasses into a leather case and slid it into the pocket of a brand-new Black Dog canvas bag and galumphed into the water.

"He looks like the friendly giant in *The BFG*," Lily mused.

So, with the three little girls, Annie got to stay safely on the sand. She watched Robbie bravely dive into the cold sea, swim out past the break, turn to tread water and wave at her, then bob in the waves and even ride a few in, all while having Freddy remain safely beside him.

Next to their towels was a circle of beach chairs, full of women about Annie's age. They all wore the same kind of fancy, one-piece printed swimsuits with translucent chiffon wraps tied around their waists, as opposed to Annie's sporty two-piece and simple cotton cover-up. The women also had the same kind of dark Chanel sunglasses, and were all very tanned despite the recent rain. Some wore wide-brimmed straw hats and others baseball caps with New York Yankees or Mets logos. Didn't they know they were in Massachusetts, home of the Red Sox?

They looked out of place and silly here, up-Island; they certainly didn't look "unfettered" or hell-bent on freeing their souls and minds from the modern, material world.

Her eyes skimming the sand again on the off chance she might see Chase, Annie noticed that their circle, and all of the circles around here, were closed. Even if you wanted to, you couldn't have wedged in another beach chair.

The women were keeping an eye on their children while discussing the latest troubles of Princess Diana. It seemed to be all anyone gossiped about these days, and Annie was sick of it. She felt sad that Prince Charles had thrown her over for some horsey-looking woman named Camilla with whom he had purportedly been carrying on their whole marriage, and found it unnerving: hadn't people compared her and Gordon's wedding to Charles and Diana's? Annie adored Diana, and her divorce made her sad; she had enjoyed envisioning her fairy-tale princess life. These women seemed to be recounting her litany of troubles with glee, eagerly anticipating her coming to a bad end.

They were so tactless. Didn't they know the princess had visited the Vineyard three summers ago? Aunt Faye and Jared had caught a glimpse of her playing tennis at the Edgartown Yacht Club.

A short, dark-haired woman with a New York accent said, "Puh-*lease*. Do we need any further proof that fairy tales do not exist?" They all laughed. Then someone brought up Jackie Onassis, and what a "phony baloney" she was.

How *dare* they judge Mrs. Kennedy, which is how her mother, and Aunt Faye and Aunt Connie and everyone Annie knew, would forever refer to her? Jackie Kennedy was American royalty, as far as New Englanders were concerned, and it was particularly crass, in light of all she had endured, to criticize her when her estate on Moshup Trail was no more than five miles from where they were presently sitting.

Annie felt her shoulders tense up as she built a sand castle with the little girls. Jackie Kennedy was inspiring, a role model in all manner of things, and not merely fashion. She demonstrated how to live with grace and create an elegant home, how to be a supportive wife, how to play the long game. Adair used to joke that her Wellesley friends never said, "What would Jesus do?" but rather, "What would Jackie do?" They deeply lamented, when Mrs. Kennedy died in 1994, that there would be no one to show them how to grow old.

Annie wasn't ashamed to admit she'd often taken solace in Jackie's famous comment, "If you botch raising your children, nothing else much matters." It had kept her going when she felt stranded sometimes in Asia. Maybe, in light of last week, she ought to take Jackie's words a little more to heart.

At dinner once in Wellesley, when Jared was visiting Faye from New York before they were married, he mentioned Mary Jo Kopechne and Ted Kennedy's 1969 Chappaquiddick tragedy. Adair had practically bitten his head off. "Hasn't that family been through *quite* enough?" she snapped. "We don't discuss it."

Chase and Annie had known John F. Kennedy Jr. slightly at Brown; he had been a freshman when they were seniors. Well, actually he said hello to Annie only once or twice on campus, but he had gone out drinking a few times with Chase in Providence and, one summer Saturday, invited him and a couple other guys from Brown up to Gay Head (as it was called then). Chase drove his Jeep Wrangler around Jackie's property, called Red Gate Farm, with JFK Jr. in the front seat, and Annie had felt jealous when he described it: miles of dunes and rolling hills sweeping above the Atlantic Ocean and Squibnocket Pond.

Chase liked John Junior well enough, but what he really admired was his magnificent land. He couldn't stop talking about it, and kept saying he felt very privileged, as a Vineyarder, to get to see it. Annie smiled to herself, remembering how Chase's mother, Piper, pestered him for details about the house only to have Chase shrug and say he hadn't noticed much about it.

This sand castle could use some water, but Annie didn't dare leave the girls alone. She smacked a palm-full of sand firmly against its side, causing it to crumble once and for all. Like a school of fish, the women turned to gape.

All at once Ben and Tommy raced up, swilled some lemonade right out of a thermos, and searched in the beach bag for baseball gloves. Tommy slowed down only to remove Freddy's glasses from their case. The boys ran back to the hard-packed shoreline and Ben tossed a glove to his father precisely as he blundered out of the surf with Robbie, both tugging up their swim shorts.

Tommy waited for them to collect themselves before carefully handing Robbie a glove and Freddy his glasses. What a sweet little boy he was!

Annie watched the brothers fire the baseball easily at Freddy. Tommy was quite a bit smaller than Ben, even though he was only a year younger, but his arm was just as strong. Robbie's throws, unfortunately, went hither and thither.

"Don't let the ball go in the water!" shouted Freddy, exasperated. "Wait, wait, guys. Time out." He plodded over to Robbie. "Stop," he said. "What is this? Let me teach you how to throw." Methodically, he took Robbie's arm and, over and over, showed him how to point with his left hand, extend his right arm down his back, and step into his throw.

"Okay, guys, let's try again."

Robbie improved slightly.

The brothers, for their part, kept shouting words of encouragement and cheerfully chasing after Robbie's bad throws. They seemed to be enjoying this new game of running into the water to make a diving catch before the ball splashed and got hopelessly waterlogged.

After playing for quite a while, Freddy left the boys and, weary, came over to Annie and the girls. He plopped down on his oversize towel, oblivious to the way he sent sand flying all over everyone. He reached right across Annie into his cooler for a bottle of water, which he unscrewed and poured entirely on top of his head. Then he reached across her again to get his thermos, gulping down lemonade before she could extract a plastic cup for him from her bag. He took a huge, deep breath.

"Where the heck is your husband?" he asked, and Annie wasn't sure whether he was being funny or not. "How come your son doesn't know how to throw?"

Freddy was so blunt she couldn't think how to answer, but luckily he blustered on ahead.

"Were you watching? Your son shows up throwing like a girl. But I just taught him, and he's got it now. Thank God he's reasonably coordinated … I've seen a lot worse, believe me. I'll work on it every day with him, and he'll make Fall Little League, I guarantee. Tomorrow morning I'll go to Brickman's and buy a whole bag of balls."

"We just moved back from Asia," she started to explain. "My husband is more of a cross-country runner type, not one for ball sports …"

It hadn't occurred to her that Robbie didn't know how to throw; it had been too hot to even think about joining any kind of baseball league in Singapore or Hong Kong. How would she find Fall Little League? She must write to Gloria Bradshaw tonight. And she needed to ask her to please forward the mail, since Gordon was no longer there to collect it.

"Who doesn't like baseball?" Freddy swigged more lemonade. "Oh, well. Lots of time to practice before school starts. Right, Beatrice?" The little girl beamed and nodded. "Come here, princess. Let me get this *shmutz*." He wiped her nose with the corner of his towel. "This is why God gave us summer—to figure out what we want to do with the rest of our lives. Learn new skills, discover who we are."

He kissed Beatrice on both cheeks and squeezed her so hard she virtually dissolved into his chest. "Beatrice is learning how to swim at our friend's pool in West Tisbury, aren't you? And she and the boys are all practicing their violins. Beatrice, did you tell our new friends you have your very own violin? I'm supposed to be losing weight. So *aggravating*. Gave up bread."

He retrieved a pack of Humphrey's butter brickle cookies from his bag and ate two at a time, sandwich-style. "Can't give up everything at once."

Freddy went on to tell her how he'd bought their place in Chilmark two years ago; how he had recently become separated from his wife, Lauren, who was currently in Scarsdale commuting on the train to Manhattan to her job as an investment manager while he was here with the kids and Rosa, their housekeeper, because she never would have agreed to this plan otherwise; how he had a realtor looking for an apartment for him in a nearby town in Westchester County; how he was originally from Staten Island; how he was taking July off from the musical-instrument leasing business his father had started over fifty years ago.

"We lease to three states, and the five thousand kids at our schools renewed their instruments in June. They're supposed to be practicing them this month. That way I can have time to play with my own kids."

Annie listened, enjoying the sun on her face and his idiosyncratic New York accent and how well the six kids were playing together. Somehow she felt less distraught, sitting here with Freddy, than she had lately. Less shaky.

Lily took the hairbrush out of their beach bag—Aunt Faye's old one, from L.L. Bean—and began brushing Beatrice's hair. She and Meg clucked in awe at how full it was of sand and snarls.

"The separation is terrible," Freddy went on, his voice descending from *fortissimo* to *pianissimo*. "I never wanted to do this to my kids. But Lauren is a crazy person, and I suppose it was going to happen sooner or later. Aagh, so much *meshugas*. I can handle the boys, but I'm not so good with Beatrice. She's a beauty, don't you think? I'm nuts about her—although unfortunately, she inherited my ridiculous hair." He gestured to the gray messes of curls that covered his head and huge chest. "If it was up to me and this wasn't a temporary situation, I would chop it off for the summer, short like you did for your girls. But I have them only until July thirty-first, and Lauren would slap it onto the divorce settle-

ment if I returned Beatrice with her hair cut. She might sue me
outright."

"You would miss her long hair, believe me," Annie said, attempting a laugh. "Maybe you could try braiding it."

But Freddy, whose hands had been gesturing in sync with his
words in a kind of sign language, flicked her suggestion toward the
waves.

"If you really want to know, the real reason I wanted time off
is because my father dropped dead of a heart attack in March, and
I'm having a helluva time dealing with it. What a *mensch* he was.
Aagh, I don't know. His death is worse than my own divorce."

"I think I might know what you mean," Annie said slowly.
"My aunt, Primo's friend … she died this winter, too. She was my
favorite relative by a long shot. Grief is—well, I had no idea. No
one talks about it. I wasn't prepared."

"Yup. Uncharted waters." He dug his heels into the sand.
"Lauren's parents play tennis every day in Florida … she doesn't
get it. It's almost like a club—those who have lost a parent, or
in your case sounds like your parent substitute, and those who
haven't." For someone who talked so much, he was pretty per-
ceptive. "What killed my father was, last year I put my mother
in a nursing home on Long Island because she almost burned
their house down." He twirled his finger at the side of his head.
"*Tsedoodelt.*"

"I find I can't manage as well as I used to," Annie said, not sure
why she was confiding in this person she'd just met. "I don't know
why things seem so hard all of a sudden."

"Me, neither. Maybe we underestimate the power of grief."

"Then I feel like a spoiled brat because here I am on this
beautiful island, and I'm not having fun." She lengthened her legs
out straight on her towel and pointed her toes, smoothing away
some sand with the back of her hand.

Freddy laughed. "Maybe you are a little spoiled. But that's

okay, so long as you're grateful. You're still adjusting."

They sat without talking, watching the kids, until, eventually, he asked about her. This time he waited for a response. When she told him Gordon would be in China a few more weeks, all he said was, "What kind of *putz* leaves a woman like you alone on Martha's Vineyard?"

17

My One and Only Love

———

Annie and the kids arrived home to find that Emmie had set up the croquet game in the field, placing the wickets in the traditional formation. He had walked and brushed Tashmoo and cleaned his teeth with a dog toothbrush he'd bought at Cronig's; he'd vacuumed and swept all the floors. He'd unpacked his clothes into the cramped dresser at the foot of his bed, tackled the laundry, and even made a salad and shucked five ears of corn. He had hamburgers waiting to grill.

Annie's eyes welled up. "Who taught you to be so good at housework?"

"My dad," Emmie said, laughing. "Comes from spending so much time on a sailboat. He insists on things being, like, ship-shape, and to be honest I prefer to spend time below deck." He looked around to make sure the kids weren't listening. "I used to sneak downstairs after Mum went to bed to, you know, organize things. Try to cheer her up. Caroline and I used to vacuum and run the laundry with our babysitter after school."

The washing machine buzzed. "Another load finished," he said. "By the way, your new machine is awesome. Has, like, a nice rhythm to it." He was wearing the long strap for his saxophone around his neck. "We improvised a pretty sweet little duet."

Annie grinned. She didn't know that anybody else noticed, the way she did, the sounds of rhythms in everyday things.

"Oh, I almost forgot—someone just called for you. He didn't leave a name or number, but said he'd call back after the weekend."

Chase?

"It's really nice here, Aunt Anna," Emmie continued. "Thanks for letting me stay. I didn't feel too appreciated on Tremont Street. By the way, Mum said not to worry about paying me. She's going to take what I was making at the bank out of Aunt Faye's estate. Transition expenses for Tashmoo, she called it." He pointed to the dog, sunbathing on the deck. "Cool how he doesn't bother this red bird hanging out on the railing. I guess he's not much of a retriever. Our old dog Amos would have, like, barked at it, or chased it. Scared it away, at least. These two spent the afternoon together—coexisting. Bizarre."

"There is something special about that cardinal."

"Yeah," Emmie agreed. "Tomorrow I'll buy it more birdseed."

The cardinal fluttered over to the windowsill and tilted its head, looking in on them. Annie could have sworn she saw it smile.

Robbie and Emmie began their game of croquet after supper, and Annie wheeled her bike out of the shed. She wanted to see how Aunt Faye had weathered the storm.

She rode down Middle Road, splashing through puddles of both shade and water this time. Gliding across State Road onto Scotchman's Bridge Lane, the sun casting its glow on the green fields, she turned right up a sandy driveway and held the bike steady as she wobbled between pine trees. She steered through a hole in the fence to the back of the groundskeeper's shed and emerged into the wide, honey light of the cemetery. Everything was still but for the busy chatter of birds settling in for the night.

Annie could see a woman kneeling down, a dog at her side, in the vicinity of Aunt Faye's grave. As she rode closer along the dirt perimeter road—it didn't seem considerate to ride her bike over the grass—she saw that the woman was Lindsay Trout, her long gray braid trailing down the middle of her back. Annie rested her bike on the ground next to her navy blue pickup truck and inched up the little incline to the graves. She didn't want to startle her.

Hands full of weeds and passed blossoms, Lindsay turned around, a trowel and pail on the ground next to her.

"Ah," she said. "I was wondering if you ever came over to this neck of the woods. I keep forgetting to ask you on our beach walks."

"I didn't think you even knew Faye was buried here."

"I didn't. I mean … I knew the grave was here, and that Jared and Priscilla were, but I didn't know if Faye had made it. Yet. Last I heard, she was still with your cousin Julia."

"Juli*et*." Annie explained how Emmie had brought the ashes down with Tashmoo, and about the burying. She neglected to mention Chase.

"You buried her by yourself?"

"I needed to get it off my to-do list," Annie said, unbuckling her bike helmet.

Lindsay raised her eyebrows. "I would have helped you, you know. For some reason, I thought you didn't garden." She sat back on her heels. "Anyway, thank you. I feel better. I like chatting with the stone, but it's good to know she's actually here."

"John Alley told me Faye planted all these flowers after Jared died."

"She did! Well, together we did. Got the flowers from Noah's big garden. I spruced things up a bit in the spring, after I'd heard the news, before you got here. She would have done the same for me."

Lindsay didn't mention that the flowers looked any different after the recent digging and scuffing, so apparently Chase hadn't messed anything up with his extra foot-tamping. And the rain would have helped, of course.

"I've just been transplanting some more of these day lilies. What do you think? Thought the stone could use a little more height. Lilies are hearty, which will be good if it's going to continue pouring all summer."

"Looks perfect," Annie said. "Elegant and colorful, not too orderly, with a bit of added whimsy. Like Aunt Faye."

"I hope I'm not imposing," Lindsay said.

Annie laughed. "Your green thumb is just another of my Vineyard gifts."

She sat on the grass and patted Zoey's coppery fur while Lindsay finished pinching and plucking, and they talked about Faye—whether or not it was scandalous to have her buried with her second husband and his first wife (who cares, they decided); whether there was anything suspicious about Emmett and Priscilla dying the same year (an unsolved mystery); how lucky it was that Faye had convinced Uncle Emmett to buy their summer house in Chilmark only a few dozen yards over the West Tisbury line since, in general, conservative academics like him preferred the more traditional down-Island towns, which Jared would never have cared for; and how wasn't that just like Faye, always the diplomat, to find the perfect place, smack dab in the middle of the Island.

Annie asked Lindsay whether she thought Faye and Jared might have gone skinny-dipping at Jungle Beach.

"I certainly hope so," she replied, giggling. "I know she was happy beyond words when they eloped. Noah and I had a small fifteenth anniversary dinner for them at our house, with some of our yoga friends. God, they were crazy about each other."

Until this summer, Annie had never really thought much about Aunt Faye as a woman her own age. A younger woman in love, or not, with her first and second husbands.

"Faye was full of marital advice at that party," Lindsay continued. "She said, I forget how it came up, that secrets were bad for marriages. Thank God she didn't look at me directly, but she might as well have. I'd told her earlier that I'd gone skinny-dipping myself with Patrick Harrington after our high school reunion and hadn't told Noah, and she was of the mind that I should." Lindsay put down her trowel. "She didn't usually tell me what to do."

"So, did you tell Noah?"

"Not yet."

Annie laughed. "Amazing, isn't it, that Faye happened to find Jared after such a staid life with Emmett."

"Faye used to say the highlight of her week as a Wellesley professor's wife was hostessing tea for the young ladies at the College, dressed in their white gloves and pearls." Lindsay stood and picked up her watering bucket, gesturing to Annie to walk with her over to the pump. "Faye didn't just happen to *find* Jared, though, Annie, you know. They met in high school." And she told Annie a story she hadn't heard before.

Riding her bike up their driveway through the twilight, Annie could hear the children laughing and shouting in the field. A round moon had risen from the east, and she watched as Robbie and Emmie played croquet and the little girls chased tiny fireflies that, one by one, lit up their warm field. Tashmoo was trotting around proudly, making sure no one tripped or cried and that everyone was safe and sound.

Gordon called once the kids were in their beds with their teeth brushed, and they passed the phone around upstairs on "speaker." Annie enjoyed listening to their different perspectives on Freddy and the Rosenthal children and that morning's all-camp game of Red Rover, and noticed that Gordon didn't sound particularly surprised to hear that Emmie had shown up out of the blue. Come to think of it, he hadn't been too surprised to hear of Tashmoo's arrival, either.

When it was her turn to talk, however, he had to hang up to go to work.

The girls asked Emmie to read them a story, and as Annie folded laundry, she overheard them recount how Gordon used to read and sing them to sleep. Meg seemed especially melancholic all of a sudden, and asked him to play a song on his saxophone. Emmie's tenor sax was much too big for the upstairs, but he agreed to play from the back deck if they promised to go to sleep. Annie heard the rapid sixteenth notes of his feet pattering down the staircase.

Deep, sultry notes began wafting through the air, each blending into the next, as he began improvising on Brahms' lullaby under their window. Who knew Emmie, Juliet's son, had so much emotion? No one else in Annie's family had ever displayed a fraction of what Emmie was releasing on his saxophone tonight. No one she knew of, at least. No one she'd ever noticed.

Maybe Aunt Faye was right: she should get to know her family. That's what counts.

Robbie had fallen asleep on his new window-seat bed, and Annie slid open the sun-porch door to watch her cousin. Low white clouds were drifting across the dark sky. His back to her, absorbed, Emmie was literally playing to the moon. He sounded like John Coltrane, for God's sake. What a loss if he'd spent the summer stuck in the bowels of some bank.

She took Aunt Faye's tartan throw from the living room and went outside and lay in the hammock, not too damp thanks to the full branches overhead. Everything smelled like cool, fresh pine needles. Through the leaves of the oak trees and the branches of the wispy evergreens, she could make out twinkling stars and the bright yellow moon, almost full tonight.

"Hey Emmie," she called across the field. "Can you play 'My One and Only Love'?"

Without a word, he segued smoothly into the old ballad that had been the first dance at their wedding, the song Gordon loved to sing to her,

> *The shadows fall and spread their mystic charms*
> *In the hush of night while you're in my arms*
> *I feel your lips, so warm and tender …*
> *My one and only love.*

The touch of your hand is like Heaven
A Heaven that I've never known.
The blush on your cheek, whenever I speak,
Tells me that you are my own ...

You fill my eager heart with such desire
Every kiss you give sets my soul on fire
I give myself in sweet surrender,
My one and only love.

Annie closed her eyes, floating in the swaying hammock, imagining herself slow dancing with Gordon. Chase used to be her default daydream, especially when it came to dancing. But now it was her husband's body she longed to feel pressing against hers, it was his chest she wanted to nestle her cheek against, his hand she ached for in the small of her back. She could almost feel his body rocking gently, holding her close. A tear etched its way into her mouth.

She went inside and called his cell phone, but there was no answer.

On Sunday, they took a picnic lunch to the beach and shared their second afternoon with the Rosenthals. The kids still missed Gordon but, Annie could tell, they were becoming used to him not being there. And it looked like Freddy might prove to be a pretty good daddy substitute, especially when he played catch with Robbie long after his own boys had lost interest.

They went home about four-thirty, and could hear the telephone ringing as they lugged their beach bags up the path. The cardinal was flying briskly alongside them, telling Annie to hurry up and answer.

It was Chase. As soon as she heard his voice, her mouth went dry and her heart started beating like a marching snare drum.

"I almost hung up when I heard the man's voice the other day, but I decided he sounded too young to be Gary. He sounded like your family, not some flaky Californian."

"Ha, ha," she said, setting the picnic cooler down on the counter. "Are you going to persist in calling my husband that?"

"Calling him what?" Chase laughed. "Prob'ly."

She shook her head, but couldn't help grinning.

"Thanks again for helping me the other day, Chase. I don't know what I was thinking, trying to bury my aunt myself."

"It was an unusual way to spend a morning, I'll admit. But incredible to see you, Annie."

"Sorry I cried so much."

"Forget it. Any time you need to deep-six someone, I'm your man. Did you have a good Fourth?"

They hadn't, actually, done anything to celebrate the Fourth of July, although Annie had driven down-Island in the morning and bought a present for herself. She couldn't seem to get her act together enough to take the kids to the parade in Edgartown, and going to the fireworks later on the Harbor seemed way too ambitious.

"Great," she fibbed, and began wiping out the cooler.

"Good. I had to go back to New York after I saw you, but all this coming week I'll be here." He took a breath. "So. Can I see you?"

"I never even asked what you do for a living."

"Real estate. Now, quit stalling," he said, being funny. "What's your routine? And who was that who answered the phone?"

"Emmie. Remember my cousin, Juliet? Her son. He looks, he *sounds*, just like our cousin Emmett, Aunt Faye's son—the one who died in that car crash when he was about this Emmett's age. Remember?"

Chase had no trouble following which Emmett was which, maybe because he was the fourth or fifth Chase in his own family.

His father was called Skip only because he loved to sail.

"Emmett and I were buddies," Chase said. "I was with you when you got the telephone call. Remember?"

That's right. Of course.

Chase had been tremendous—going to the funeral, sitting quietly with Aunt Faye and old Uncle Emmett in their Wellesley living room when there was nothing anyone could say; even helping sort through his clothes and stuff with Adair and Aunt Connie.

"Remember later, when Juliet had her baby and named him Emmett? We drove up from Providence to visit the hospital."

"We ran out of gas on Route 95," Annie said, giggling. "Across from the Howard Johnson's."

Chase laughed. "I forgot that part. Your Aunt Faye was at the hospital, too. Juliet was mad at what's-his-name, her husband, for missing the birth because he was at an important sailing regatta, and she signed the birth certificate while we all were milling around the room. She named him Emmett, instead of after her husband, what's-his-name. I thought that was so funny."

Annie slid the cooler to its place under the counter.

"Juliet's baby was the first newborn I ever held." Chase was sounding downright nostalgic. "You know something else? When I was riding my bike home after seeing you, I couldn't figure out who your Meg reminded me of. Her little face looked so familiar. Finally it came to me ... she looks like your Aunt Faye. Have you ever noticed? Something about her."

Annie's throat closed up. How lovely. Of course she had noticed. No wonder she had never gotten over Chase: they had too much history together.

"Well, young Emmie is going to help me out the rest of the summer," Annie said brightly, after a minute. "Divine intervention. I was getting a bit stressed out."

"Maybe old Juliet rallied the troops and sent him down."

"It's a wonder she didn't send in the Marines."

Chase laughed again. "Nice for you to have company. You should see Élise: she can't make it five minutes without a nanny by her side. In fact, I don't think she's ever been alone with both twins. She wants a nanny for herself." His voice dropped into a whisper. "Okay, so this is tricky because we have a house full of her friends and I don't think we're up for a shared family day at Quansoo quite yet. How about this: Why don't you have young Emmie there take your kids to the movies tomorrow night to see *Air Bud*? It's playing at the Capawock at six-thirty. They'll love it. I'll come over for a drink." He stopped whispering and his voice became abruptly formal—someone must have come into the room. "Yes, that's fine. I'll be over to pick it up. Thank you very much, then." He hung up.

The phone rang again in her hand before she had latched it back on the receiver. "*Ye-e-esss?*" she answered, expecting Chase again, and an explanation.

But it was Gordon calling from Hong Kong in his tomorrow morning, sounding increasingly forlorn as he told her that the first of the funerals was to be held in three hours; how Pretti had told him last night that both her family and Samir's had disowned them when they'd married in India because they were of such drastically different castes; how what was left of Samir's body had been cremated at a place off Nathan Road, in Tsim Sha Tsui, but Pretti planned to take his ashes to the Ganges to spread by herself sometime later; how confusing it was to get anything done in Hong Kong since the Handover; how unbearably humid it was; how so many expats were packing up to leave, including people they knew from their two times living there, now that Hong Kong was part of Communist China.

Annie murmured supportive things as she carried the phone around and put in another load of laundry. She arranged the wet bathing suits on the drying rack.

She carried the phone to the kitchen and began chopping

vegetables for dinner, listening to her husband explain how frightening the currency collapse in Indonesia was, how it could spell doom and gloom for Asia, and wondered whether her old boyfriend had called back and gotten a busy signal.

18

James James Morrison's Mother

The morning of the Fourth of July, after walking with Lindsay out to Split Rock and dropping the kids at the Center, Annie had driven down-Island to the windsurfing store on the lagoon to buy herself a kayak. Now that Emmie had fallen out of the sky to help them, maybe it was time to sneak away by herself some mornings, get her confidence back.

She remembered her cellular phone for once and actually kept it on, and to her surprise Gordon called as she was stuck in ferry traffic at Five Corners in Vineyard Haven. He persuaded her to buy a double kayak instead.

"You can still take a double out by yourself, but it will be fun for us to explore together, and we certainly don't need two kayaks. Why would you want to go out alone, anyhow?"

Annie bristled. She wanted the adventure of paddling her own little boat whenever she wanted, and couldn't really think of anything lovelier than quiet solitude on still water.

But rather than say this, she agreed and bought a big blue plastic double and two paddles, although she kept running her hand over a small yellow fiberglass kayak on display.

The surfer guy who tied the long blue boat on the car roof said, "Why don't you take this one home and come back for that sweet goldie? I think you want it."

"I couldn't possibly," Annie replied. "Who needs two kayaks? Can't afford it, anyway."

"That's what credit cards are for. Lots of people have two kayaks. Besides, that yellow one is designed for a woman just your size.

It will be easier for you to haul around so you can check out different ponds."

Annie drove up-Island feeling deflated and, after wrenching her lower back sliding the double kayak off the roof—it looked even more ungainly in the driveway than it had in the store—she retraced the fifteen miles back to the shop. Gordon would just have to deal with it.

"I hoped you'd be back," the surfer guy said. "I'm glad to see you celebrating your own independence this Fourth of July."

Now, Annie carried her little gold kayak easily under one arm and a new, orange life jacket under the other, euphoric to be getting back on the water. Since Chilmark Pond was so close to the Community Center, at noon she planned to stash the kayak in the reeds, zip over there in five minutes, and come back for the boat later. Emmie had offered to pick up the kids today, but she told him not to bother: she'd have plenty of time. She couldn't get over that he actually thought it was fun to go to the grocery store, and gave him a long list for the Edgartown A&P. That's where she would be stuck now, if he hadn't shown up.

Annie savored the subtle splash of her paddle as it sliced through the pond, smooth as silk. Not a soul was here. With two strokes she could have floated straight across to a deserted stretch of beach, part of the long south shore, but instead she wanted to meander, to explore, to go nowhere in particular.

She headed up-Island to a narrow channel of tall marsh grass called Doctor's Creek that snaked its way to the upper pond. The town had recently cut an opening in the barrier beach east behind her, making the pond brackish and tidal. Her little gold kayak sashayed by itself in the gentle current. It was low tide now, low enough that, if she felt like wading, the water would come only to her knees. At high tide, and also once what people referred to simply as "the cut" closed up by late summer, the pond would fill, she remembered, and the water would be deep again. She and Chase had kayaked here lots of times.

She hoped her little boat wouldn't scrape bottom in the very shallow water and get stuck, like it used to, because she really didn't want to have to be the one to get out and push it in the squishy mud.

She passed the small jetty at Abel's Hill and smiled at two teenagers laughing, putting a big cooler in their boat, ready to row across to the beach. Had Chase and Élise rented their place at North or South Abel's Hill? If South, then they were right here, up that dirt road.

She wondered what Gordon was doing now in Hong Kong. It was around evening there, still hot and humid. She should have brought her cell phone in case he wanted to say goodnight, but there was no coverage up here and anyway, she was sick of talking. They spoke so often they didn't say anything, and when she did have something to say, she was too sick of talking to say it.

The waterway had become so narrow that Annie had to separate her paddle and row with one half, alternating sides like in a canoe. She laughed out loud at how much fun she was having. This is what it would have been like to be a Wampanoag a thousand years ago.

She finally emerged from the reeds at the edge of the upper pond. She clicked the two sides of her paddle back together and glided across, eventually drifting into a cove ringed with small camps. Rowboats and canoes were tied to tiny worn docks, bobbing peacefully and waiting for the afternoon people to load up and row them across to the beach. She saw some younger kids dangling their feet in the water.

What was Chase expecting, coming over tonight?

These cozy cottages, called camps, were what the Vineyard used to be about. There didn't used to be any huge houses, like the ones now under construction on the hill above the pond. She turned her eyes back to the quaint camps. Insects buzzed atop the pond's surface on all sides of her boat.

She'd giggled a lot, talking on the phone last night to Chase. She'd probably sounded silly, girlish.

What would Élise say about her husband dropping by? What would Gordon say? Oh, God. What the hell was she doing?

She paddled easily across the water and decided she could get right down to the end of the pond and be back in time for pickup. She felt as carefree as she had when she was twenty. Maybe it was carrying Meg so incessantly, but she was strong, lithe. Those morning aches and pains she'd had in Sylvan Fell had all disappeared.

From the far end of the pond she hadn't noticed the tide coming in, increasing through the cut, so heading back was harder and quite a bit slower. It was also more humid. Her hands slipped on the paddle, and more than once she accidentally splashed herself with the sticky, brackish water. Two dragonflies buzzed right onto her lap.

This was too risky. She didn't *do* this sort of thing. She needed to tell him not to come. But how could she reach him? She wasn't about to call his mother and ask for the number of his rented house.

Over the years, on more than one occasion, Gordon had complained that she didn't think things all the way through systematically, that she wasn't logical. This seemed to be one of those times.

She reached Doctor's Creek just as a family of four emerged from the grass in two kayaks. The father was belting out instructions and making a big expedition out of it. Annie recognized one of the boys from Robbie's group at camp. Was she late?

Needing to separate her paddle again, she rowed with one half as fast as she could through the channel, back to the put-in. The surfer guy had been right about her little gold boat: it tracked perfectly. It really was great not to have to deal with the hassle of a rudder—which was more than she could say about herself. *She* needed a rudder!

Her boat bumped against the pond bottom next to the dock, and she swung her legs into the mucky water. Yanking the boat, she stepped right out of both her flip-flops, stuck in the mud and tall sea grass. She reached into the thick water to grab them, but could find only one. Cursing, she ran barefoot to the car, lugging the boat under her arm and shoving it and the lifejacket in the reeds.

The station-wagon clock said twelve-thirty. She had never been this late for any pickup. Meg would be beside herself, and the camp counselors would be annoyed. It was one thing to make Robbie and Lily wait, but how could she be so late for a three-year-old?

The Community Center lot was empty except for a lone black Suburban. She pulled at the doors of the building, but they were locked. She ran the length of the huge field and across State Road to the Chilmark Store. The pavement was hot and burned her feet.

The porch rocking chairs were full of people eating sandwiches and pizza. She didn't care if they noticed her or not. Right away, Primo called out from where he was tossing pizza dough. "Your kids are over at the library, Annie. Relax. It happens." He winked at her. "You're getting into it though, baby, I can see that."

Back across State Road, biting her blistered lower lip and feeling the bottoms of her feet starting to blister, too, she opened the library door to a blast of air conditioning, so incongruous in this old building with its low-beamed ceilings. Aunt Faye used to take them to the original one-room West Tisbury Library on Music Street. This place was a confusing rabbit's warren of small rooms.

Her hair was a disheveled mess and the bottom of her bathing suit was wet and itchy under her cover-up dress.

She followed the low rumble of a voice into one of the side rooms and there, sitting on the floor, was Freddy, reading out loud in his prodigious baritone. Their six kids tumbled over him like puppies. Meg sat on one side of his lap with her blanket, sucking her thumb, and Beatrice sat on the other; his big arms encircled them both. Tommy and Lily were on either side, leaning in, while Ben and Robbie faced him on the floor. With perfect expression and cadence, Freddy recited,

> *Whenever I walk in a London street,*
> *I'm ever so careful to watch my feet;*
> *And I keep in the squares,*
> *And the masses of bears,*
> *Who wait at the corners all ready to eat*
> *The sillies who tread on the lines of the street …*

Annie stood behind the boys, holding her breath. Freddy looked up and paused, whereupon Robbie leapt to his feet and hugged his arms around her waist. The others, absorbed in listening, smiled mildly, unsurprised to see her.

"Where *were* you? I thought you had drowned again." Robbie's brown eyes brimmed with tears.

"I was in my new kayak and I'm so, so sorry … I totally lost track of time." She stroked his hair and worried she might start crying, too.

Robbie buried his face in her dress.

Freddy put the book down. "Come on, kid, let up. Nobody's perfect. I told you she just got tied up. Moms get to be on vacation, too." He grinned. "They just need to wear a watch, that's all."

"*Wandering vaguely,*" Robbie burst, quoting A. A. Milne's poem *Disobedience*. "Page thirty-two. That's what you do, Mommy!"

"Goodness!" exclaimed Tommy.

"Calm down, quit it," Freddy interjected. "Sheesh. Everybody deserves to escape once in a while."

"No," Robbie said adamantly. "No more escaping. It's too dangerous!"

"I'm sorry, sweetheart," Annie said. "I'll be more careful from now on." She hugged him while everyone stared. She forced herself to recover her breath, to distract. "So. You're reading from *When We Were Very Young?*"

Robbie refused to let go of her.

"I didn't know you were a fan of Christopher Robin," she continued, forcing a smile at Freddy. Their eyes met and she mouthed, *Thank you.*

"Never read these before," Freddy chuckled. "Didn't know he and Winnie-the-Pooh were even *in* poems. This book just happened to be here."

"Yes, Mommy. My birthday book from Aunt Juliet was right here, on this purple bench," Lily said. "Isn't that funny?"

"It's just a coincidence, Lily. Your book is at home," Annie said.

"Yup, and it's a darn coincidence that we were on our way to the library and so were you," Freddy said, covering for her. "A hundred percent lucky coincidence. Your kids know all these rhymes, Annie." He looked impressed. "I really love your kids. They are tre*men*dous. We love them, don't we, guys?"

His three nodded politely but looked impatient to get back to the reading.

I love you for picking them up, Annie almost said out loud.

Robbie was trying very hard to hold back his tears. "You're just like James James Morrison Morrison's mother, Mommy," he said, struggling to control his voice. "He was only three, that's why he couldn't keep track of her. *He lost his mother and she's never been heard from since!* I'm nine now and I do try to take care of you, but you just … *go off.* My camp counselor said someone drowned in Chilmark Pond and nobody knew until they found her car in the parking lot."

"Did you know Mommy almost drowned?" Lily asked, turning toward Freddy. "I watched her."

"What?"

"Goodness!" Tommy exclaimed again.

"I waited a long time. It was boring." Lily fiddled with her pink sneaker, adjusting the little ruffle on her sock. "Mommy came back out of the *sand*, not the water." She giggled. "I *told* Robbie. Don't worry. Mommy always comes back. Plus, she was wearing her wampum bracelet."

Meg took her thumb out of her mouth and waved at them to stop talking. "*You* guys are what's boring." She patted the page of the book. "Keep reading about the bears and the cracks in the London street." She smiled sweetly, almost flirtatiously. "Please. *Freddy*." She snuggled into his chest and gazed across at Annie. "I like him, Mommy. He's nice."

"He is a very good reader," Lily added.

The pages had blown over in the breeze from the air conditioner.

"What? I lost the page. Bears? Which one was that?" Freddy adjusted his glasses, not taking his eyes off Annie.

"Page fourteen," Annie and Robbie said, together.

On the way home, they retrieved her kayak. Annie wanted to show Robbie how shallow the pond was, how virtually impossible it would be to drown there, but she'd forgotten that the tide was coming in and the water was, unfortunately, now quite deep. A few more teenagers, ignoring the weather, were piled in a rowboat headed across to the barrier beach. No one was wading.

Robbie recounted further tragedies and near-death aquatic accidents his camp counselor had itemized while they had all been waiting for her. Annie made a mental note to thank him.

They groped around in the mud by the shore for her flip-flop, but it was gone.

Tashmoo cantered down the path to meet them and the cardinal greeted them from the railing. Emmie, sensing something was amiss but too polite to ask what, offered to take the girls to Nip 'n'

Tuck Farm on State Road to see if old Mr. Fisher was giving pony rides today, or maybe to Takemmy Farm to pat the llamas and the miniature horses, or else to feed the swans at the Old Mill Pond at the corner of the Edgartown Road. Annie handed him some money to do all of the above plus get a treat at Alley's, because she needed time to get ready. The last thing she wanted was to be caught off guard again.

Emmie asked if he should buy any Island tomatoes at the farm stand since they hadn't looked too good at the A&P, and … he'd met someone on the porch at Alley's who liked to play jazz standards on the guitar. Would it be all right if he invited her over sometime?

Of course, Annie said, whispering the movie plan by him as they loaded the girls into his Subaru.

Back in the kitchen, Annie peered into the refrigerator. "I thought I'd make pancakes and bacon for supper, Robbie. Okay with you?"

"What?" he grumbled. "*No.* Pancakes are for breakfast. Meals are supposed to *stay put.*"

He headed with his book to the hammock, and Annie watched Tashmoo, for the first time, stretch along the middle step of the deck stairs, blocking his way, and the cardinal begin busily flitting from side to side above them.

Annie quickly went outside, whereupon the cardinal fluttered down to its usual place on the railing and Tashmoo ambled off.

Annie and Robbie sat down together on the top step.

"Do you really think this bird is Aunt Faye, Mommy?"

"I have no idea. But it seems entirely possible."

"It's a male, though. That's why it's red."

"Well, if you're going to think a person's soul is in an animal, you can't overthink too many details. It requires what's called a leap of faith. The spirit is what's important."

"Sorry I was rude about the pancakes. I think she, it … was

scolding me." He glanced at the cardinal, who was still eyeing him, but kindlier now. "I just get sick of everything moving around all the time."

"Me too."

Annie put her arm around her little boy's hunched shoulders, and they sat that way for a while.

While Robbie read his book, Annie showered inside. She wasn't really thinking, and had entered that dazed, semi-conscious state of going through motions without being quite aware of what she was doing. She had a vague recollection of her mother referring to this as being on "autopilot." She felt as if she were hovering above her body again—like a hawk, not a cardinal—watching someone else shave her legs, wash and blow-dry her hair, apply eyeliner and mascara and foundation.

Underneath a casual pink sweater and jeans, Annie had put on the matching lacy silk lingerie Gordon had given her for Valentine's Day, just after Aunt Faye had died. She had no idea why she did this, because her brain had switched off.

This cotton sweater reminded her of one she used to wear in college. That one was also pink, but it had a loose cowl neck, the fashion in the late '70s. Someone, Aunt Faye or Piper, had taken her picture in it, tanned and relaxed in the gold of the setting sun.

Emmie came back with the girls and took a double take when he saw her. "Wow. You look nice, Aunt Anna," he said, and asked what he could do to help with the Chinese chicken dinner she was making, even though it was only four forty-five.

"I thought I'd call my friend Lindsay and see if she wanted to do something while you were at the movies," Annie lied.

During their early supper, she announced what the surprise was: *Air Bud* with Emmie. The girls jumped up and down ("What Bud?" Meg asked), but Robbie stared at his mother, astonished. Or maybe he was suspicious. "Don't we have enough real-life stories about dogs in our own house now? You never allowed me to go to silly movies like that when I was the girls' ages. This sounds like a big fat waste of my time."

The other day at Lucy Vincent Beach, Freddy had said to her, aside, that Robbie reminded him of a little old man trapped inside a kid's body. "Kind of the opposite of me." Annie had laughed and agreed, and said he was becoming more and more like Gordon. "He'll make a great professor one day," Freddy had remarked. "So will Gordon," she'd replied.

"Come on," said Emmie now, straightening Meg in her chair, "your mom deserves a night off. Besides, we can get ice cream cones afterward at Mad Martha's. Have you ever tried their black raspberry? It's a New England specialty."

Robbie was eventually persuaded, but he kept glancing over his shoulder the whole way down the path, as if to reassure himself that his mother hadn't disappeared, disapparated like one of the witches in *Harry Potter*. Annie had a feeling A. A. Milne's *Disobedience* was still ringing in his ears,

LOST or STOLEN or STRAYED!
JAMES JAMES
MORRISON'S MOTHER
SEEMS TO HAVE BEEN MISLAID.

19

Vodka Gimlets

Annie ran inside to put on lipstick, and through the window saw Chase skid up in a brand-new red Jeep Wrangler, just like the one she thought she'd seen him driving, just like the one he'd crashed into a tree, spring of senior year. She watched as he hoisted himself through the roll bars and hopped over the side—not quite as gracefully as he had back then, but almost. The red cardinal, perched on the railing, swooped off to the woods for the night.

Tashmoo ran across the lawn to greet him, and Chase patted and scratched him for a while behind his ears. Annie met him on the path.

"So Prince Charming gets to have this awesome dog, too?"

They kissed on the cheek.

"He was Aunt Faye's." Her heart was beginning to do that snare-drum thing again. "You got here quick. Were you stalking the driveway or something?"

Chase grinned. "Do the Aldens still live next door? I camped out on their road."

"What would you have said if they happened to pull in?"

"That I couldn't remember exactly which was your driveway and could they help me. Classic up-Island line. Works every time."

"Every time you want to whisk in to see a woman the moment her family drives out, you mean?"

"Time is of the essence." He laughed. "Surprised to see me?"

She smiled back. "My kids were pretty shocked I let them go to that movie."

"I heard it's pretty good." He was wearing creased khakis and a blue brushed-cotton windbreaker over his pressed white polo shirt.

"Nice jacket." She started to run her hand along the polished sleeve, but caught herself.

God, he was handsome.

"You know the French," he was still grinning. "Élise would have me fully dressed before I open the door of our apartment just to get the paper."

"Well, at least you didn't give in on your flip-flops."

"She's got us going to some dinner party at eight up at Quitsa. Another one of her New York friends." They had fallen into step as they made their way up to the deck. "Élise used to work in television in Manhattan, did you know that? She made quite a name for herself, actually, pretty talented. She doesn't like to miss a chance to network with her contacts, no siree." He was talking oddly fast. "Chilmark's a different crowd from our day, you know—a lot of her fashionista movie and TV types come here now. They wear loafers in the summer. Would fit in better at the Hamptons, if you ask me." He slid open the kitchen door and followed her in. "Got anything to drink?"

She shook her head; she hadn't gotten around to driving down to Oak Bluffs to the liquor store. "A couple of beers—I might be able to find another bottle of Seagram's stashed in the back of a cupboard."

"Figured as much," he said, producing three nips of vodka from his jacket pocket. "Any tonic?" He started to open the refrigerator, but paused to examine the photos stuck all over it with shell magnets. A lot of them were from the week Gordon was here.

It was remarkable how at home the two of them felt in Aunt Faye's old house.

"So this is Gary, huh?"

Annie nodded, not bothering to correct him.

"Great-looking kids, Annie. And Gary looks like a swell fellow. Life has worked out for you, hasn't it? Looks kind of perfect."

He rummaged around the fridge while she washed up the supper things, appreciating the warmth of the water on her hands. Her heart would not stop pounding.

He held up a glass six-pack of Schweppes tonic bottles.

"Might be flat," Annie said.

"Nah, it'll be great. Any limes?"

She shook her head.

"Look at this," he said, inspecting the condiments on the inside rack. "Rose's lime juice. Remember this? Your Aunt Faye was a class act. We can make vodka gimlets, straight out of the '40s."

He poured a couple of glasses and put hers on the counter then, starting in on his, resumed studying the photos on the fridge. Out of the corner of her eye, Annie saw him trace a finger over one of them.

"Jesus, Annie, you still look so young and innocent. Like you did in college. *Wholesome.* Maybe it's your long hair."

She felt her face get hot. "You say that as if it's a bad thing."

"Not at all. I guess … I just thought all your traveling might have, I don't know, changed you somehow. Jaded you. But you look as pink as ever."

"Well, thanks, I guess," she said, drying her hands before sipping her drink. "Or are you saying I'm unsophisticated?"

Chase laughed. "You never could accept a compliment. I'm saying you look wide-eyed and innocent, that's all. Safe from the worries of the world. Gary must take good care of you." He squinted at a picture of her in her Shanghai office, wearing a traditional Chinese silk brocade jacket with a mandarin collar and covered buttons; Aunt Faye had kept it on the fridge all these years. "Even with your big job, there's something, I don't know— childlike about you. Yeah, *wholesome.*"

"That's an old photo. That picture was at the start of the great magazine career I forgot to have."

"Haven't had *yet*, maybe."

He didn't look wholesome, not at all.

"You look beautiful tonight, by the way," he said. "A helluva lot better than when I left you at the cemetery." They both laughed. "Is this picture from Long Point?"

She nodded.

"When you got caught in the rip? Looks like you're healing up." He tapped his lower lip.

"That picture's from before. I went in by myself after Gordon left for Hong Kong, got pretty thrown around."

He raised his eyebrows, listening.

"It was kind of ..."

"Scary? I bet." He turned away from the refrigerator and started to take a step toward her, caught himself. "Good thing you're on your game."

She smiled, noticing how soft his eyes were, and still that extraordinary cornflower blue. "I'm not too sure about that," she said.

He took another sip and looked around. "I love how you kept it all the same in here. Or Faye did, anyway. Didn't remodel, make it all fancy-shmancy. My parents haven't changed their house, either. It's exactly like it was in the '70s. Élise likes everything spanking new. Drives me nuts."

"How does she like the Vineyard?"

"Well, as a matter of fact, I would have to say she doesn't. She's so paranoid about getting Lyme disease that she's practically afraid to go outside. Checks for ticks every ten seconds."

"Where does she think you are right now, anyway? Visiting your parents?"

"Yup."

"What if they happened to call your house?"

"They never do, but on the off chance they did, I would say I ran into someone on the road. Tad Alden, for instance."

Had he always been this glib?

"Not sure why, but my wife usually buys my cockamamie excuses."

Just as when they had run into each other at Alley's, Annie winced slightly when he said "my wife."

She laid out some Vermont cheddar cheese and Carr's crackers, and they took their drinks out to the deck and sat down at the round table.

Chase told her about his sister, Brooke, who had been Annie's friend and lived in Connecticut now and spent the summer with her kids at their parents' house here on Indian Hill, which he wished Élise would do, but no, she wanted her "space." How their twins were adorable but, being in real estate, he had lots of work dinners and so forth, so wasn't home much; he expected they would be more fun when they could talk more, "like your little girl." He sort of wished they'd had a boy, but Élise had a hard time getting and being pregnant and had made it clear she didn't want any more children. "We went through the whole infertility thing, in vitro, jerking off into test tubes, the whole kit and caboodle. That's how we ended up with twins."

Annie sliced another thin piece of cheese and handed it to him on a cracker.

"I haven't drunk vodka since ... last time with you, prob'ly," she said. "Gordon never lets us drink it."

Chase raised his eyebrows again. "Never lets you?"

She cleared her throat. "I mean, he grew up in California, you know, and we pretty much drink only chardonnays and cabernets ... We did try those new Australian wines when we lived in Singapore—" She was rambling. "But Gordon is sort of an expert on California wines, and ..."

"Of course he is." Chase took a long sip before flattening his lips in a kind of grimace she didn't recognize. "I thought maybe you meant—" he glanced at Tashmoo and, as he had so many years ago at that party at Brown, tightened an imaginary dog collar around his neck. "Well, Élise won't touch anything *but* French wine. Not that I'm complaining. I'm just more of a purist." He stretched back in his chair and reached a hand into his pocket for another Absolut nip, which he quickly poured into his glass.

"Your pocket is like Mary Poppins' carpetbag," Annie said, giggling.

He looked at her with a blank expression, clearly not knowing what she was talking about.

"Bottomless," she prompted.

"Hmm," he said. "So. Does Gary abandon you like this often?"

Annie's smile faded, and she stiffened. "Gordon didn't abandon me. It's his job." She took a long sip herself, noticing that the grass in the field was getting awfully high—she'd forgotten to find someone to mow it. "Once, when we'd just moved to Singapore and the kids were little and I didn't know anyone or have help yet, he went off to Thailand to deal with some crisis and we all got really, really sick with the flu. I had to write up a chart to keep the medicines straight, I was so out of it. *That* was hard."

"Hard? That sounds *brutal*. Élise would have given me an ultimatum: fly back pronto or pack my bags forever."

Impulsively, he reached across the table to cover her hands with his. He held them for a moment, turned them over in his palms. He smelled like Old Spice, and his blond hair was still thick.

"Sweet." He traced his finger over her gold wedding rings. "I like the single diamond."

"What kind of rings did you get for Élise?"

Why had she just asked that? It's not as if she'd ever wondered. At least, she couldn't remember ever wondering.

He must still lift weights, or something. She had an impulse to feel his upper arm muscles through his jacket, to run her fingers along his forearms. To rest her cheek on his chest.

"Engagement rings are not very French," he said. "They're considered, you know, a bit of a *gaucherie*. But her New York friends rubbed off on her and she wanted three of these." He tapped her diamond with his left forefinger, his right hand still wrapped around hers. "Supposed to be for past, present, and future." He grimaced again. "I try not to think about it."

"About what?"

"The future. Freaks me out sometimes."

It was getting a little buggy and cold, so they went inside. She turned the radio on to WMVY and an old Ashford and Simpson hit was playing.

"We used to love this song, remember? Solid, solid as a rock ..." She sang a few notes.

He looked at her, uncomprehending again. "We did? I don't remember listening to this song with you. I remember, besides the Beatles and Carly and JT, you used to like Fleetwood Mac. Earth, Wind & Fire. Diana Ross. Maybe you're getting your *boy*friends confused." He was alluding to her sarcastic comment at the cemetery.

The radio announcer said it was a blast from the past to 1984 and, with a start, Annie realized Chase was right. She used to dance to that song with Gordon, not with Chase, before they were married and Gordon began making up excuses about why he couldn't dance.

"Do you still like to dance, Chase?"

He chortled. "Nah. My knees are shot." He pulled two more vodka nips from his pocket. "Work out in the gym, that's about it. May I make you another?"

She shook her head; she was only halfway through the first. He helped himself to more ice.

"Let me freshen it up for you, at least."

He handed her back a full drink and downed all of his. Then he took a few steps into the living room and sat on the faded plaid armchair by the wood stove, nodding toward the kids' drawings taped up all over the place. "You named your son Robbie after your family? I like that."

Annie sat down on the rattan sofa. She was dying to touch him. How could he still be so ridiculously … sexy?

"So exactly what is Gary doing in China this time, that he has to be gone half the summer?"

She tried to explain, but had trouble focusing on her words and was pretty sure she sounded incoherent. She mentioned how amazing it was that Gordon was there for the Handover, and Chase looked at her blankly again. "Handover? What Handover?"

"It doesn't matter," she said, shrugging.

She hadn't expected him to be so tanned and muscular, to smell so good. He still had those shoulders, and his forearms hadn't changed much either. She felt a very distracting swelling, and crossed her legs.

Chase gazed at her and listened, his lips twitching before flattening out together again. He jumped up to light a fire in the stove.

"You really don't mind that he takes off and leaves you here alone to steer the ship?"

Annie shook her head. "He's really important to his Foundation. He earns a good living."

Chase raised an eyebrow in an exaggerated way as he perused the cozy room, implying that she wasn't exactly living in Buckingham Palace. "Whatever you say, Annie. Other women wouldn't be so cool about it. My sister Brooke's husband used to take business trips, until she put the kibosh on it."

"She did?"

"Yeah, and Élise would have a cow if I had a job with a lot of travel. Not that I would mind a few adventures." He swirled the ice cubes in his glass. "I guess you sort of abandoned him to come up here in the first place."

She hadn't thought of it that way.

"Well," he said, "you always were patient. Except for the fact that you didn't wait for me, of course."

He made two more drinks for them. She was vibrating a little inside.

"Remember how we used to make out right here?" he asked, sitting down in the chair across from her.

"I wonder if Aunt Faye and Jared knew."

"They totally knew. They would come home and we would be all disheveled-like, and I'd have a hard-on up to the ceiling."

She shifted, embarrassed; she didn't remember him being so crude.

"They were always going to dinner parties, like I have to go to now. Generous of them to let us commandeer the living room, though."

He pulled a paperback-size photo album off the bookshelf next to the sofa. "Look at this—my, my. Weren't *they* the swingers?"

Faded color photos showed Aunt Faye and Jared windblown on the ocean, leaning close around the table on the deck where Chase and Annie had just been, at a bonfire on some beach. Chase turned the page, and a few pictures slipped out from behind the plastic. There they were on what had to be Jungle Beach, naked with clay patches all over themselves.

"Ha!" Chase laughed, handing Annie the photos. "And you thought she was so prim and proper. They had the time of their lives down here."

Annie peered at their faces under the Tiffany table lamp. They looked so in love. Young, not like people in their midsixties. Maybe John Alley was right: theirs had been the love affair of the twentieth century.

"I have a new friend here named Lindsay Trout," Annie said. "We walk the dogs together. The other day I ran into her at the cemetery—she's the one who planted all those flowers—and she told me the most amazing story: that Jared and Faye had actually been sweethearts since high school, and secretly engaged before the war. They wrote each other every day while he was in France, but then his letters stopped and everyone assumed he was dead. He'd been taken prisoner and no one knew. Faye was devastated. My grandparents, I guess, didn't want her to be an old maid, so they made her marry Uncle Emmett."

Chase stared at her. "Cripes," he said. "That's the story of *my* life! Except no war, thank God. That's just like us, huh? Shows what happens when a guy ships off to France." He forced a laugh. "But, well, they ended up together after the interlopers—Emmett and what's-her-name there, Priscilla—died off, right? And they got to be buried together after all. So that's poetic justice, or something like that."

"Everyone always assumed Aunt Faye loved Uncle Emmett. Lindsay said yes, she did, *and* she was also still in love with Jared the whole time. And he was, with her, even though he was happily married to Priscilla."

"Like I said, pretty convenient Faye and Jared both became single the same year."

"Odd coincidence." Annie really couldn't imagine Aunt Faye murdering anyone.

"You think we'll get married when Gary and Élise die and we're in our sixties, then? Cripes, we can all four of us be buried together in West Tisbury, stacked side by side. Élise would love that. But first we get to be twenty-first-century swingers."

Tashmoo pawed the door, and Chase jumped up to let him out.

"There are lots of stories like this, I guess," Annie said, inspecting all the pages of the album and attempting to reattach the pictures that had fallen out.

"There's an awesome full moon rising, Annie," Chase said,

sitting back down and pulling his chair a little closer. "You know, I still can't get over that you didn't get my letter from France. I'm glad to know that's the reason you didn't write back, though. I've always wondered. What d'you think: Would you have come over?"

Annie slid the photo album back onto the shelf. "I suppose I would have loved skiing in the Alps, trying my hand at teaching," she said. "But my French is hopeless. You know that."

Chase smiled. "You would have learned. But if that's all that was holding you back," he said, "I would have been on the next plane."

Tashmoo barked sharply from outside.

"Jeez, it's as bad as being at church in here—up, down, up, down." Chase let Tashmoo back inside.

"Your dog gives me the hairy eyeball," he said. "Thought we'd be pals at first, but now I'm not so sure."

He'd always been able to make her laugh.

"Sorry," she said. "He doesn't usually bark."

This time, Chase sat down beside her on the rattan sofa and stretched his arm around her shoulders. Her heart was now beating in an extended drum roll of about a thousand beats a minute. Her mouth was dry, even though she had somehow finished most of her drink. She'd forgotten how good a vodka gimlet could taste.

"I went to our Brown reunions, you know, to see if you'd show up. But you were too busy being a jetsetter. Your old roommate Louise said you had quite the career with that decorating magazine in China."

"Home furnishings," Annie said. "Nice while it lasted, which wasn't too long. Seems like someone else's life, now."

"Yeah, I know what you mean. Awesome that you came back to the Vineyard, though. I wasn't sure you ever would. You could have sold this house for a bundle; great location." He turned sideways to face her. "Why *did* you come back, exactly?"

Why had she?

"I guess I felt I needed one constant place," she replied, a little too quickly. "Something consistent for me and the kids."

"Tough on your own, with no family here."

Tashmoo sank down in front of the fire and contemplated them for a moment, then folded himself up on his haunches, his chest and head erect like a sphinx. He wouldn't stop staring at them. Annie was probably imagining it, but he looked downright reproachful.

"I can't get over how you've lived in all those countries. I didn't take you for someone so adventurous, although I do remember how much you loved traveling. As for me, well, Manhattan is far enough afield."

She tilted her head and looked at him quizzically, the way Tashmoo and even the cardinal looked at her sometimes.

"I loved everyplace, once we got unpacked."

Maybe he was right: she should insist Gordon come home, get someone else to deal with the stupid plane crash.

"You really took the wind out of my sails for a while there, you know," Chase said.

She realized he was running his hand lightly up and down her arm.

"Anna-banana," he said, under his breath, tensing his fingers around her upper arm. "Banana" had been his college nickname for her. Almost always, when she heard his voice in her head, he was calling her "Banana."

She was afraid he might feel the goose bumps through her cotton sweater.

"You're the one who broke up with me," she said, biting her lower lip and closing her eyes for a second to feel the warmth of the fire.

"Yeah, well, that was a rash mistake."

He was silent for a while until, as usual relying on his good manners to navigate out of uncomfortable territory, he changed the subject.

"That was something else, you trying to bury Faye by your-self."

Relying on her own good manners to let him, she said, "Seemed the least I could do, when Juliet's been doing everything else, managing the estate and all."

"Why didn't you wait until Gary got back?"

Good question.

"I always think I can do everything myself," she said slowly, aligning her hair over her breasts. She should have worn a different bra, one not so see-through. "I guess I thought I owed it to Aunt Faye—to put her where she wanted, in place next to Jared."

Chase nodded. "Makes sense."

They sat without speaking on the chintz slipcover sipping their drinks, watching the flame through the cloudy glass door on the wood stove. Annie forgot that she wasn't still twenty and forgot to tell him it was probably time to leave. His body next to hers felt just like it used to.

There was so much she wanted to say: how she had been heartbroken after the Pont Neuf, how she'd missed him—probably more than she was willing to admit—in all the places she'd lived, how not having Gordon here to tell her what to do wasn't actually all that bad, now that she had Emmie to help ... how sexy he felt sitting next to her, how gratified she was to find out about the lost letter, how she wondered if she was still in love with him, but how could that be since she hadn't spoken to him in eighteen years and was, as everyone knew, madly, perfectly in love with her husband?

She wanted to tell him everything at once and that made her feel overwhelmed, so, consequently, she didn't say a word. Instead she let herself relax into his arm as he tightened it around her. They listened to the crackle of the fire and finished their drinks.

"When I heard you got married, I bummed around France and the UK for another few winters, you know," he said, breaking the quiet. "Teaching sailing in the summer, skiing in the winter. My parents finally sent out the Charge of the Light Brigade to bring me back."

"So you *do* like adventure."

"Not really. Can't say I loved it. Hanging out with a lot of spoiled kids, same as me. Just didn't know what else I was supposed to do."

He gazed into her face and she felt herself dissolving into his tantalizing virility, his breathtaking *maleness*. The long summer twilight outdoors cast a gentle glow through the house that made his skin the color of honey. With her head on his shoulder, she felt she was back with him in the train car in Tuscany.

"So how have you been, Banana, really?" His blue eyes had a way of boring into her soul, and she was caught off guard.

Her eyelids were fluttering. "A little tired, I guess."

"Well, sure, of course you are." He stroked her arm. "All by your lonesome, taking care of the kids and two houses now and all this constant packing up and settling in you've had to do, not to mention losing Faye. My mother stayed in bed for a month, practically, after Ooma died."

He poured another nip into both their glasses. "By the way, what happened, exactly, at Long Point? Ready to tell me?"

She turned her head to look at him and took a deep breath, and embarked on the whole story. This marked the first time she'd told anyone the way it really happened—how terrified she was, how close she'd come to going under. With Gordon and even with Lindsay, she'd played it down. Or maybe she was exaggerating it now.

He didn't interrupt her once, although he tensed his arm around her shoulders and shook his head and gasped and otherwise punctuated her story, so she believed he was fully empathizing with her.

"And then suddenly I thought of you, Chase. It was so bizarre. Like I could feel you right next to me in the water, telling me to go with it. And next thing I knew, I was on the sand."

His forefinger had been tracing her cheekbone back and forth while she talked. Now, he opened the rest of his fingers so that he was holding one side of her face in the palm of his hand.

"What a tale. Sounds like you were caught in a fucking *maelstrom*. That's how you cut your lip?"

He ran his thumbnail over her blister, and she nodded.

"I remember you bit your lip like that in our race on Sengekontacket, that time."

She felt energy, tension, seeping out of her entire body, and she crumpled a little.

"I was really afraid."

"Yeah," he said softly. "Sounds way too close. But I'm glad to know it was me there with you, at least." She let the full weight of her head fall on his shoulder.

There was some kind of current passing between their two bodies, side by side on the sofa. She couldn't tell where she stopped and he began, and she was having so much trouble concentrating that she couldn't talk anymore. How could she be so attracted to him when she was so happily married to someone else?

He really needed to leave.

She closed her eyes again, and his arm slid off her shoulder down to the curve of her waist.

"Poor you," he said, stroking her face.

She knew she should will herself to resist. He turned toward her again and now the back of his cupped hand began stroking her face while he ran the fingers of his other hand through her hair and along the front of her breast.

Her left hand somehow lifted itself and its fingers ran along his firm jaw. He kissed her palm, kissed her bracelet. Her breasts veered into his chest and with an irresistible desire she knew they both wanted to kiss, but there was some unspoken code going on. He was waiting for her signal, acting like a gentleman.

What gentleman cheats on his wife with a married woman?

But they weren't just anybody. They were Chase and Annie, the couple that people used to crowd around to watch dance in college. The "golden couple," her roommate Louise used to call them.

"Sounds like you were really brave," Chase said, rubbing her back.

Annie closed her eyes and raised her face and he bent down and floated his smooth lips back and forth against hers, tantalizing her, barely touching. His fingers began gliding lightly along the length of her throat, and she stopped breathing. She held her face next to his, not kissing but not arching away, either.

She was drifting a bit from the vodka.

"Nobody will know, Banana," he said quietly. "Just us. C'mon. For old time's sake."

He poured his shoulders into her body, engulfing her, and together they sank into the sofa. He skimmed his hand up and down her breasts to her waist and kissed her neck. Her right hand was pinned between them but it managed to extract itself and, on its own, slid up and over his thigh, approached the swell that was his rising erection.

"You know I never stopped loving you," he whispered. He undid the top few buttons of her sweater.

She couldn't hold back any longer. She lifted her face.

There was no angry thunderbolt, no earthquake either. He pressed his parted lips against hers and his tongue began circling inside her mouth until she was kissing him back.

He hugged her in tight toward him and they started falling over each other, kissing like they used to, their hands moving fast up and down each other's bodies. Everything sped up. He yanked her sweater over her head and the palms of his hands swirled over her breasts as they fell out of her bra. He kicked over the coffee table with his foot while holding onto her, knocking her tumbling onto the floor. He tore off his white polo shirt and wrestled his way on top of her.

For a second, their skin felt silky together, like when they used to swim together underwater, but they were so entwined, so frantically groping each other, that soon it was only his hard muscular body she felt. They were both trying to feel all of each other everywhere at the same time.

"You're so sexy, Annie," he said, still whispering. "You're still the same."

She kissed him back so deeply she couldn't breathe. She was on the floor beneath him and powerless to stop.

He pulled her legs apart and swiftly kneaded the tops of her thighs with his thumb and fingers, then cupped his hand over her middle. He rested it there for a split second, holding, and she could feel herself swelling fast beneath his hand.

He unzipped her. Everything was accelerating out of control, the way it used to in the sail shack. He wedged himself up on his knees between her legs and tugged off her jeans, but in his hurry he pulled only one pant leg off, leaving the other stuck around her ankle. He unbuckled his belt and pushed his own pants down as far as his knees. He leaned down to kiss her mouth with his tongue, desperate and hard, and reached around with a quick flick to undo her bra. Lying on top of her again, his chest squeezed her bare breasts so flat they hurt.

She was keeping up with him. He pressed fast and close, rocking on top of her with no space in between, and she could feel him pushing strong against her panties. She couldn't stand the empty throbbing inside her. She wanted him inside, wanted him to fill her up.

He pulled down his boxers and positioned himself along the

center of her belly, his mouth still hard on hers. He slipped his fingers beneath her silk, exploring, stroking the soft sides of her.

He stretched the bottom of her panties over, alongside her thigh, so he could angle himself in … And she froze. These silk panties were from Gordon. *Gordon.*

This was not Gordon.

What the hell was she doing?

She tried to veer her body away from underneath him.

He was still kissing her, but all at once he tasted cold. Like vodka, like a hospital, like her father's ice cubes rattling in his martini shaker. The Rose's lime juice felt grainy on her teeth and tasted sickeningly sweet, like green Jell-O, like the artificial air fresheners in those Singapore taxis that always smelled so nauseating when they used to land there at midnight on those interminable flights from California.

Tashmoo leapt up and let out a piercing bark, and just then the telephone rang.

Annie lay frozen on the floor, next to the knocked-over table, stark naked but for her sideways silk panties and one leg of her jeans around her ankle. Chase was on top of her with his khakis and boxers around his calves, still rocking.

What time was it in Hong Kong? Gordon would want to chat as he ate his breakfast and got ready for work.

"Let it ring," Chase urged, his voice a hissing whisper. He leaned up on one elbow to push himself in around her silk.

Tashmoo was barking furiously now, his neck thrust forward, and Annie felt as if she were hearing him bark the words, *Watch out! Danger!*

What if it was Emmie, and something had happened with the kids in Vineyard Haven?

What the hell was she doing?

She shoved Chase off and turned over on all fours next to Tashmoo, her breasts swaying, and crawled over to Aunt Faye's red tartan throw on the floor. She wrapped it around herself like a towel and somehow managed to stand up. Dragging her jeans behind her from one ankle, she hobbled into the kitchen to answer the telephone.

Tashmoo flattened himself against her like a bodyguard.

"Good morning, gorgeous," Gordon said, cheery as ever. "How is my love today? I couldn't sleep, I missed you so much. I'm so happy you're home to answer the phone."

For a second she thought she was going to be sick. She turned her back away from Chase and cradled the phone to her ear, checking her impulse to whisper lest she make Gordon suspicious. Tashmoo barked again and looked up at her with concern while he brushed his body back and forth against her legs, herding her against the wall.

His father had pneumonia, Gordon was saying. It occurred to him—maybe they should think about visiting Sacramento at Christmas. Incidentally, had she thought any more about ideas for the kitchen remodel in Sylvan Fell? The appliances were fine, but everything else looked so dated. They could put in a hardwood floor, pull up the linoleum. He heard a little girl singing today on the Kowloon ferry who sounded exactly like Meg.

Chase slid open the kitchen door and crept out, tucking in his shirt. A faint smell of skunk wafted into the house. The telephone clapped against her ear, she and Tashmoo watched as he strode down the path under the full moon.

20

So Many Floating Annies

She could hear her father's rebuke: And what exactly did you think was going to happen, Miss Muffet, sitting with him on the sofa drinking vodka in front of the fire?

She never should have invited him in from the deck. Everything had happened so fast. Why on earth had she drunk so much?

She had been seduced.

Correction: nix the passive voice. She had *allowed* herself to be seduced. She never should have agreed to let him come over in the first place. What was she thinking, shaving her legs and getting dolled up and putting on lingerie?

She hadn't thought, that was the problem, and never in her life had she been full of more self-hatred.

Pretty soon Gordon, oblivious Gordon, would be back in his service apartment after work and she could call and tell him how much she missed him and that this was not working out and please, please could he come home. She wasn't planning on explaining everything right now, she just wanted to hear his voice.

Theirs was the first car in the parking lot.

Annie and Tashmoo walked along the dim wooded path to Lambert's Cove, her thoughts drowned out by the birds chattering and rustling in the woods, but there was no avoiding the silence on the beach. The air was cold and pale and there was not a trace of wind. The Sound was smooth as glass.

"Thanks for not saying I told you so," Annie said to her dog, walking along the shore.

More than once she nearly tripped, he was fastened so closely to her leg.

"Chase was just like the riptide," she continued, looking down at Tashmoo and breaking into a slow pounding jog in an attempt to shake out some of the self-disgust she felt. "Sucking me down. Thank God I came to my senses before we ..."

Well, yes, that would have been worse, but what happened was bad enough. It wasn't like tennis, where the ball was either in or it was out. She was guilty: she had been unfaithful to Gordon. Even if it *was* only with Chase. If you're naked on the floor with a man not your husband, that's infidelity.

They passed what was left of a yesterday's sand castle, mostly washed away by the tide and trampled over by someone, like Robbie's stomped-over construction at Long Point.

The beach today was narrow and rocky. She didn't permit herself to sidestep the pebbles but made herself walk straight over them, relishing the pain on the soles of her feet.

Just before Split Rock, at the bend in the beach where smaller boulders had washed up long ago, rain had mixed with ocean water to form a little standing pool above the shoreline. Annie dropped a rock into the puddle and it sank, the water too shallow even to make a ripple.

She and Tashmoo kept on their way.

Last night's moon had been full, and in this morning's flood tide Split Rock was swimming, rather than walking, distance away. She waded in anyhow, Tashmoo's eyes carefully tracking her, but the earth gave way and she tripped into a divot and lost her balance, drenching her shorts. The water was freezing.

She turned around and staggered back across the rocks to Tashmoo and the boulders, whereupon she stripped off her sweatshirt, tee shirt, and shorts, started to leave on her underwear, decided to strip that off, too.

Tashmoo cocked his head to one side, confused. She had been

holding five pebbles but, considering, bent down for a sixth, one for him, and then ran straight into the chilly water. She plunged forward, kicking off with her feet into a kind of breaststroke. Tashmoo let out a nervous bark behind her.

Feeling for the bottom with her toes, she stood up when she got to the giant rock, the water swirling as high as her breasts. She looked back at her dog sitting resolutely on the sand, watching her. After a minute he waded into the water and stood, waiting in the wash of the waves, until his worried expression eased into one of resignation. Gingerly, bracing for the cold, he began to pick his way across the stones.

Annie leaned against the granite for support with one hand and placed her six stones in a row along the small crack with the other, mumbling wishes for Gordon, for each of her children, for Tashmoo … for herself. When she came to that last one, all she said was, "Please, please forgive me."

The sky was lighter now and the water blue and glossy, so still that she was able to see her reflection.

For a fraction of a second the water held her face as distinctly as a mirror, but then it would slowly shatter into a distorted pyramid of prisms: ten Annies shimmering one on top of the other, the tiny top one disintegrating into the waves. The light would refract and in another instant she would think she could glimpse herself, but somehow her face would become blurry, like one of Georges Seurat's luminous pointillist paintings when you get too close.

So many Annies, all floating away.

She had been truly in love with him. His playful blue eyes, his hair. The muscles in his shoulders. His wicked boyishness, his sense of humor. And his manners. His lovely New England courtliness.

But maybe it was more than just his sexy Chase-ness that had collapsed over her last night, like one of those waves at Long Point.

When he was her first love and everything was new, they used to have so much fun. When they'd been twenty, she'd felt as confident and as daring as any explorer. With him, everything was the future. Everything was possible.

Because Paris hadn't happened, yet. He hadn't broken her heart, yet. Their complicated married lives hadn't happened.

She couldn't make out her entire watery self in the pulse of the tide, but she could catch enough to know that the real Annie was not the one who had been on the floor last night. That was not who she was now. Without her even knowing it, she had become different. Chase's Annie was gone.

"I am not that person," she said to Tashmoo, across the rippled blur of images. "Chase said nobody would know. But *I* know. And I don't want him! I want Gordon. I want our children. What I *don't* want is to wreck anything. That's not who I am. I love my husband! I am happily married!"

Tashmoo looked sorrowful and took another cautious step into the water.

"*I am happily married,*" she repeated, whispering this time. "Maybe not perfectly, but happily."

Annie stretched out her arms, and Tashmoo took a few more steps until it got too deep and he floated, astonished, because he thought he was still walking but now actually he was paddling. He looked as dumbfounded as she did that he could swim.

It was not easy for him to keep his head up. He swam all the way to her and was so proud of himself, so overjoyed, that he lunged forward with his front paws to embrace her ... and gouged both her arms with his razor-sharp claws.

Three parallel scratches streaked from her shoulders down to her elbows. Her arms stung, but she didn't care about the blood or the smarting pain. He certainly hadn't meant to hurt her.

"You *are* a water dog!" she cried, hugging him back, startled at how much larger an animal he seemed in the water than on the land.

And she and Tashmoo, side by side, began swimming around Split Rock.

Last night, Chase had asked why she'd come to the Vineyard. Why had she?

To see if what happened on the floor would happen. To look for that old Annie, the one who used to belong to Chase. She had come to be seduced. And seduced she had been—not only by him, but by something else ... by, maybe, some kind of girlish yearning to be young again.

What if she *had* married him? Was he more than a good-looking guy who let himself be carried wherever the wind blew him? Really, what had he done with his life? Bummed around Europe until his parents hauled him back, drifted into a career he didn't particularly seem to care about, married a woman mainly because she asked him. Oh, and clearly screwed around on said wife—he had been so comfortable on the floor with her, his seduction so polished, that this could not have been his first stab at adultery. Not his first encounter. Where was the character or backbone in a person like that?

And yet ... he had been so great at the cemetery, helping her. He shared her culture. He read her mind. He was so funny, so entertaining. There was nothing dull about him. They had so much in common. They finished each other's sentences.

He used to be loyal. During the years they had been together, Annie never once suspected he had been anything less than faithful, never had reason to be jealous. Her roommate Louise and their other girlfriends used to mock-serenade her with that old Flamingos' song, "Chase only has eyes for you." That aggressive Chase on the floor wasn't her old Chase.

Maybe if he had married her, he wouldn't cheat.

No. She had absolutely married the right person, even if Chase and her roommate Louise were right and it *had* been on the rebound. Gordon was charismatic, conscientious. His morals and goals had never blown in the breeze! He always steered carefully, devoting his life to taking care of his family and others. He was committed to helping the developing world, for heaven's sake!

She missed his warm, crinkly eyes and his square jaw. She missed her place on his breastbone.

Annie and Tashmoo were back where they'd started, at the crack with the line of pebbles, and she stood up. Tashmoo continued swimming, still churning next to her, his snout barely above the surface. "I guess you don't know how to tread water yet," she said. "And I don't know how to teach you." She caught her reflection again. "First thing I do when we get back to Sylvan Fell is chop my hair off. Who the hell do I think I am, pretending I'm still a naïve college girl? Miss Muffet? Yeah, right."

It was all Tashmoo could do to keep swimming his circle.

Rays of sun were beginning to streak across the North Shore and Vineyard Sound. A flock of seagulls landed above her on the rock.

"I'll tell you one way *I'm* split," she continued to Tashmoo, who gave her a beseeching look. "My crack is that I felt really turned on by Chase. I think I thought I was above that, too high and mighty. Too married. But I really, really wanted to make love to him. There was some fissure in me and I didn't protect it. I allowed him to get in, just like the water that got in here and made this."

She ran her hand down the major crack that split the huge rock almost in two. But there were scores of additional cracks, all sorts and sizes going in all directions. And the way it was splattered with patches was almost as if it were peeling, shedding its skin to reveal richer, reddish-brown colors beneath its light topcoat. Was this how granite reinvented itself? Or showed its true, deeper colors? This monolith was immoveable, impervious, constant. Yet despite that, it was still changing, still growing.

It was not okay, what she had done, and she would never fully forgive herself. She'd wrecked it. She'd wrecked the absoluteness of their happy marriage.

"My marriage isn't perfect anymore," she said aloud.

But had it, really, been so perfect? Perfect simply because she and Gordon hadn't been unfaithful to each other? Could she even be sure that Gordon *had* been completely faithful? She didn't really know what he did on all his business trips, did she?

That old man in the bowtie at the bric-a-brac shop near Sylvan Fell was right about "perfectly, happily." Nothing was that simple, and it was unrealistic to wish it were so. She would throw away that pillow when they got home.

Five black cormorants stood still on one of the smaller boulders staring at her, ignoring a sudden, larger flock that flew by in a roughly shaped V, low across the water, their beating wings breaking the quiet.

Annie belly-flopped over to Tashmoo's circle and swam around with him overhand before leading him out toward where the larger flock of cormorants had been. Tashmoo had gotten the hang of swimming. He needed a little more practice keeping his nose up, that was all. He was downright grinning at her.

She would not let herself get carried away again, ever.

Annie swam way out past the rock in the placid water of Lambert's Cove, under and over the surface with Tashmoo paddling beside her, until all her salty tears had dissolved into the sea.

On the path back to the parking lot, they ran into Lindsay, Zoey heeling perfectly beside her on a leash. Tashmoo, dripping wet and peppered with sand, wagged a polite hello but didn't budge from Annie's side.

"Everything okay?" Lindsay asked, placing her gray braid behind her shoulders and tactfully looking at the dogs rather than at the soaked demarcation of Annie's bra and underpants through her clothes. "Looks like Tashmoo has his paws full, walking with you today. And like you forgot a towel."

"Everything's fine, fine," Annie said, starting to press forward. "Sorry I can't walk today ... got to get back to the kids."

Lindsay, deferentially nodding, suddenly exclaimed, "Wait *just* a minute! Those are some serious scratches you've got there, Annie!" She peered at her bleeding arms, then at Tashmoo's wet fur. "He went *swimming* with you?"

Annie grinned. Tashmoo stood up taller, practically puffing out his chest.

"But he *never* swims! He doesn't like to swim!"

Annie shrugged. "Maybe it's not true what they say about old dogs and new tricks."

The next morning, on the drive back up Middle Road after dropping the kids off at the Center for today's big racket-smacket tournament, Annie pulled over to admire the view across Keith Farm and the way the ocean shot up to the sky at the horizon.

She'd skipped her walk on Lambert's Cove and instead stayed in bed and had a long, lovely conversation with Gordon before the kids woke up. No more multitasking while she spoke with him. He was sorry, he said, he couldn't come home quite yet, but what if she flew out to see him in Hong Kong? He had already spoken to Zhen, and the Foundation would pay for her ticket.

Annie didn't see how that could be possible, yet she was grateful for the invitation, relieved that he wanted her. During their conversation, she tried listening harder to what he was saying, concentrating on his details about rebuilding his department and the aftermath of the crash. She tried not to feel jealous when he mentioned taking the tram up Victoria Peak with Pretti and her children.

A pair of white swans joined the ducks and geese on the pond, and she felt she was in another painting—an oil, this time. On that morning's drive to camp, Robbie happened to explain how he'd read in the Chilmark Library's *Encyclopedia Britannica* about the famous Austrian ornithologist Konrad Lorenz's experiment on "imprinting," when baby geese followed Lorenz around mistakenly thinking he was their mother. Maybe Robbie had become interested in waterfowl that day she'd bawled them out in this very spot, before Emmie came to their rescue.

Annie watched the mother goose glide around the pond with her tawny goslings in an orderly line behind her. It occurred to her that she was just like Lorenz's baby geese. She'd fallen in love with Chase, her first real boyfriend, at some critical time in her development, and he had become imprinted on her brain. In college and, more important, during summers here on Martha's Vineyard, when she was just spreading her own wings and gaining independence from her constrictive upbringing, figuring out who *she* was, she had gotten used to envisioning herself with Chase, or with the idea of Chase. He had become a habit.

It was almost as if, since the Pont Neuf in Paris, she didn't believe she could be herself *without* him, as if part of herself had truly been chucked into the Seine that day he had tossed her aside. Somehow, when she had been as impressionable as these goslings, she had managed mistakenly to tie Chase up with her concept of who she really was. She hadn't lost herself from all of the moving with Gordon. She'd lost herself with Chase.

It was time for her to untangle him.

Aunt Faye used to recite her favorite Shakespeare quote all the time, and had it inscribed on a little plaque in her kitchen in Wellesley. *To thine own self be true.* Annie would have to ask Juliet if she could have it.

One of the goslings veered from the line and, rebellious, scuttled alone up the other side of the embankment, just as a shiny red Jeep Wrangler passed behind her on the road.

21

Just Another Midlife Crisis

The next morning, Annie met Lindsay and Zoey on the beach where the path spills onto the sand.

"Were you all right the other day, Annie? You didn't look like yourself," Lindsay said, bending down to unclasp Zoey's leash.

"Oh. Yeah, well, I had an argument with Gordon on the phone," Annie lied.

"Understandable. You guys are under a lot of stress. Things resolved?"

"Think so," Annie said, inventing.

"Did you put some antibiotic ointment on those gashes?"

Annie nodded, even though she hadn't, and they headed out toward Split Rock. Lindsay seemed more subdued than usual.

"Everything okay with you?"

Lindsay didn't respond, and as they walked, she picked up a heart-shaped rock and put it in her pocket. "I need some of these today," she said. "Noah and I had an argument, too. I wasn't going to tell you all this, but I suppose you'll find out sooner or later so you may as well hear it from me. Remember when I told you about Noah's terrible surfing accident at Stonewall Beach, how he broke his back? And he looked at it as a wake-up call to begin examining his life—you know, asking whether he was living the life he wanted, making the most of his time here on earth, etcetera, etcetera? Typical midlife stuff." Zoey, tail wagging, brought her a stick and fell into step beside her. "Well, unfortunately, as part of that process ... he left me for one of his landscaping clients."

Annie felt a little sick to her stomach as Lindsay went on to say the woman was a "washashore," someone not from the Vineyard who decided to move here year-round. She was in her thirties, divorced from a guy in Los Angeles, owned a dress shop in Edgartown. Noah had lived with her for a year but had recently moved out and taken an apartment over someone's garage in Oak Bluffs. He was begging Lindsay to forgive him and "reconcile."

"Are you positive you *want* him back?" Annie asked, picking up another heart-shaped stone. It was the third she'd found already this morning.

"Well, that's a very good question. And the answer, I've decided, is yes. We've been married over thirty years." Lindsay flung another stick far into the water and grinned as Tashmoo swam after it alongside Zoey. "Believe it or not, until this happened, Noah was a really good husband and dad. I've decided I'm not going to let some spineless woman from down-Island destroy us, destroy our family."

"And you're sure you'll be able to forgive him," Annie asserted, rather than asked. "You'll be able to love him again." Would Gordon be able to forgive her, assuming she told him what she had done?

"Noah is my best friend. He was seduced." Lindsay scowled, yanking the stick out of Zoey's mouth. "Just another midlife crisis."

Rounding the bend, Annie turned the heart-shaped rocks over in her hand. "You won't always hate him for hurting you."

What if she told Gordon what she'd done and he said, "I cannot love you anymore"? What if he didn't believe that almost having sex with Chase didn't have anything to do with him, that she loved and wanted to stay married to him but had some twisted, immature need for closure? What if Gordon divorced her because she hadn't been able to prevent herself from being seduced?

"I guess this is what's called *working on your marriage*, Annie. It's not like he's some stranger. He's *Noah*. What would you do if Gordon did this?"

"Oh," Annie said. "He never would."

Which is what Gordon would no doubt say about Annie: that she would never do what she had done.

"That's what everybody says. Until it happens." Lindsay scuffed the sand with the sole of her bare foot as she walked. "He and our kids are the only family I've got. My parents and my sister are dead. I have friends who've gotten divorced, and it doesn't seem to solve anything. Right now, to be honest, I think it would probably be easier to break up than to have to live with this hurt and forgive him, to try to love him while I still feel so betrayed. It might be harder to stay together. But I truly do believe that it will be easier, and better, in the long run." She wiped her nose with the back of her hand. "God, Annie, I wish your aunt were still here."

"Me too."

Lindsay clearly didn't want her to notice her crying, so Annie pretended to be busy looking out at the shimmering Elizabeth Islands, perfectly defined this morning. It was the kind of day she and Chase used to wait for all summer so they could sail over to Cuttyhunk for lunch. Tashmoo was swimming alongside them in shallow water, wearing a smug "what's-the-big-deal" expression. He had gotten good at keeping his head up and his mouth closed.

"I hope you won't hold it against Noah too much when you meet him," Lindsay continued. "Hopefully, you'll be like Faye. She appreciated that we all fuck up occasionally, we're all works in progress."

They finally reached Split Rock.

"Maybe that's why Faye and I love—loved—this rock so much. If we thought something wasn't beautiful because it was cracked and splotchy, well, we wouldn't be left with much to admire in this world, would we?" Lindsay blew her nose on a blue bandana from her fanny pack. "We're *all* some version of Split Rock."

The rock looked magnificent today, to Annie. She thought of the famous line from *Hamlet*, "For there is nothing either good or bad, but thinking makes it so."

She stepped forward to embrace her friend, who seemed to have given up on her tears not being noticed. The dogs flicked their tails nervously at their feet.

"I need to get going if I'm going to make it to Woods Hole this morning," Lindsay said. "Mind if I jog back? I'll see you tomorrow, unless I have to stay overnight at the Institute." And, Zoey at her heels, Lindsay made a beeline across the sand.

Annie sank down exactly where she had stripped off her clothes the other day, and Tashmoo flopped his head into her lap. She felt as if she had just been walloped in the stomach. Poor Lindsay. Poor Gordon. Poor Élise!

She stroked Tashmoo's fur, coarse and grainy now from swimming but still the same sublime color as the sand. The scratches on her arms stung. "I am no better than Noah, getting seduced. And I have a million more cracks even than Split Rock."

Tashmoo coughed, and Annie pried open his mouth and reached down his throat to pull out a wad of seaweed. She wiped dog slobber on her shorts.

"Remember when I used to be a perfectionist?"

Tashmoo belched a rank smell of dead fish and salt water. She hugged him and looked out at the Elizabeth Islands, and he licked her face.

After drop-off (the annual basketball knockout tourney was today), Annie was ahead of Freddy in the checkout line at the Chilmark Store.

"Fancy meeting you here," Freddy said, trying to manage a large coffee and two huge blueberry muffins. "Have you tried these yet? They make them here, with Island blueberries."

"I'll save you a seat," Annie said, spying two empty chairs and making a sprint toward them. He was only a few minutes behind her, but she had to wave off four people and finally hold a protective hand on the back of the rocker. It was more competitive every day, up here.

Freddy sat down with a big thud and a creak, and lined up three warm muffins on the wide arm of the rocking chair. "Guess what—Primo gave us a cranberry one for free. He said it was a present for you. I don't know your definition of heaven, Annie, but ..." He broke a big edge off a sugary, crumbly top.

People lined the length of the wide porch reading newspapers in the rockers or else chatting in pairs, the way they were. There was a lovely feeling of calm midsummer.

"Tommy made me stay up and finish reading *Charlie and the Chocolate Factory* after you'd started it with him on the beach," Freddy said, berries staining the corners of his mouth. "I didn't want to put it down, either. You've got us all crazy about reading, especially Tommy. Going to get the next one out of the library now, what's-it-called."

"*Charlie and the Great Glass Elevator.*"

"Yeah. Don't you love summer, getting to stay up late and read?"

He caught her up on the latest about the irascible Lauren, at one point saying, "The thing is, besides not having anything particular in common, she and I never had any real *chem*istry. And you want to know something else? I was never *all in*. I don't think she was, either. So if we play it right with the kids, our splitting up won't be any Greek tragedy."

The muffin really was delicious. So was the coffee.

"You and Gordon, now, you two have much more at stake. Sounds to me like the only negative thing about the guy is that he flosses in bed. Oh, and that he's ambitious. You don't know how lucky you are, Annie. Take my cousin Muriel. Her husband is everything *but* ambitious. Talk about a lazy, no-good ... By the way, did I tell you my company just received a huge new order yesterday, while I was sunning myself at the beach?"

He then delved into the intricacies of the musical instrument leasing business, in case she was interested. He really could go on and on. But one thing she'd learned this summer from having Tashmoo, she said to herself, nibbling a piece of muffin, was how to listen.

Suddenly, a red Jeep Wrangler turned off State Road and skidded into a parking place on the other side of the stairs. Her heart, ignoring her better judgment, picked up the beat, pattering into a fast snare-drum roll again. Annie watched Chase hold onto the cross bar, swing himself up and over the side, dash into the store. She couldn't decide whether to go inside and pretend to bump into him, leave, or stay where she was. It would hurt Freddy's feelings if she left, so she decided to stay there, rocking.

In a minute, Chase dashed out again, carrying a plastic pack of Pampers in one hand and a stuffed paper bag in the other, out of which peeked the telltale pale blue of a box of Tampax. He tossed the diapers in the back and opened the door to climb in, and as he did so noticed Annie in the rocking chair. With one foot in his Jeep, standing there with tampons spilling out of his bag, he paused, his shoulders falling somehow as if he were deciding whether to linger.

She raised a sweating hand from her lap in a little half-wave and he half-smiled in that new, flat way he had, and for a few seconds they held each other's gaze across the sea of rocking chairs. He then carefully placed the shopping bag on the front seat and drove back the way he'd come, toward Abel's Hill, while Freddy went on about the merits of trumpets over trombones.

The next morning, as the kids were finishing up their breakfast, her mother called from New Zealand. The red cardinal was at the bird feeder.

"Isn't it kind of late there, Mom?"

"Midnight. We were at a Maori festival with your brother and

Fiona."

"Percy took you to a Maori festival?"

"Fiona's idea. It was out of this world. Fantastic."

From there, Adair plunged right in as usual. Princess Diana was now rumored to be carrying the Egyptian guy's child: it looked like the nail was in that fairy tale's coffin, once and for all. At least Fiona was better, and Percy had begun his certification to be a golf pro and had found someone to help set up their golf academy, so the coast was clear, she said: they could finally book their return tickets. They thought they'd stop first in Sydney to see the famous Opera House and then in Melbourne to visit some cousin Annie had never heard of; would be a shame not to, when they were practically in the neighborhood.

"Too bad about the timing, isn't it, darling? We could have visited you in Hong Kong."

"That's how it goes, Mom, I guess," Annie said, pressing down the toaster.

Her parents didn't expect to be back in Massachusetts until Labor Day, but would visit them on Martha's Vineyard next year. "Maybe you can keep your ear to the ground for a hotel *sans* mold," Adair said. She was anxious to get back to her volunteer job as a gallery guide at the Museum of Fine Arts in Boston. And they would like to come down to Sylvan Fell for Thanksgiving, assuming Annie didn't mind roasting the turkey; she and Lily already had a date at the National Gallery. So lovely they had this shared interest in art, wasn't it?

"Are you ever going to tell me what happened to Fiona?" Annie asked, finally, the phone on her shoulder, extending the cord to the sink.

"*Must* you run the water now? I don't know why I have to keep reminding you I am calling long distance."

"Mom?"

"I'm surprised you haven't figured it out yet, darling," Adair said, after a moment. "Fiona had a little … episode."

"A little what?"

"In April she just … disappeared. Left the two children. Your brother is going to legally adopt them, by the way, did I tell you that?" Adair took a moment to breathe. Annie realized she'd never noticed how much Juliet and her mother had in common, even though they weren't blood relatives. "Percy eventually retrieved her, vanished up some canyon, and installed her in, you know, a rehabilitation place. A sanitarium, we used to call them."

"Why didn't you tell me?" Annie scraped butter across the toast.

"We were pretty beside ourselves, dear. Well, everyone is entitled to one midlife crisis … hopefully, this will be hers."

"But why didn't anybody *tell* me?"

"Oh. Well, you already had your hands full." Adair sighed. "But if you really want to know, darling, Percy specifically asked us not to. He and Fiona seem to think you can be a bit, how shall I put it, judgmental."

"They do?" She stopped scraping.

"Makes it a bit hard to confide in you when there are problems."

"Oh," Annie said. "I'm sorry that's their perception."

"You can come across sometimes as a little too … perfect. That is, until you hear those hooligan children of yours on the other end of the telephone line." She was probably referring to the time Robbie barricaded the girls in the upstairs bathroom.

How little did she know, Annie thought, kneeling down to tie both girls' sneakers.

"Although, I dare say, they're much quieter today than last time I called."

"We've all settled down. And it stopped raining."

"Thank heavens."

Annie didn't respond.

"Incidentally," her mother resumed, "I meant to mention something. Percy told me you weren't particularly polite to Fiona when you met her in Boston at the Parker House, I think he said it was. Remember?"

"You mean, when he was technically still married to Kathleen?"

"There is never any excuse for rudeness, Anna. You know that."

"I don't believe in abetting adultery," Annie said, forcing her voice to stay level.

Her mother sighed again. "No one does, darling. That doesn't mean it doesn't happen."

Annie's father had never allowed her to quit anything growing up, which was why he had been so furious when she'd given up tennis in college. If you got away with breaking a commitment once, he used to say, you'd think you could get away with it again. (Obviously, he was speaking from experience, considering the hookers and his affair with Mrs. Pedrick.) The whole reason Annie *quit* tennis was because she hated cheaters (and *now* look what she had done)! But what about Percy, quitting his *marriage*? How could her parents be so nonchalant about that?

"I don't know why you insist on living in the past the way you do, Anna. This has been extremely difficult for us. Very painful, what Percy did to Kathleen. But he is our son and we must support him. Got to move on, get ready for the twenty-first century."

Annie wrapped hair ties around the ends of Lily's braids. "Anything else you want to mention, Mom?"

"Well, yes." Adair cleared her throat. "You might as well know … Fiona's expecting. She's stopped drinking entirely, that's the good news."

"Wow," Annie said, standing up. "It's going to kill Kathleen to hear this. I think she still hopes Percy will come back to her. Unless—is Fiona … ?"

"Of course she's going to keep the baby! What kind of question is that? Due beginning of December."

Her mother sounded almost compassionate. Wasn't she the one who used to view any kind of addiction as weakness? Since when had she become so forgiving?

"Aren't they—?" Annie began, but caught herself. She was going to ask whether they were worried about fetal alcohol poisoning, but that probably wouldn't be helpful.

"Your brother is married to Fiona now. I'm sorry, but Kathleen needs to move on. You do too, Annie. It's time for you to accept Fiona and forgive your brother."

Annie rubbed sunscreen on the backs of her children's necks as they watched the red cardinal strut up and down the deck railing. The three kids were wearing the tie-dyed shirts they'd made at camp, and the cardinal seemed to be admiring them.

"Now," Adair continued. "It's high time your children got to know their cousins down here. What would you think about us all meeting in Auckland after Christmas? Meet the new baby? Your father and I will handle the airplane tickets. It will be midsummer here. Maybe Percy can organize someone to take us sailing."

"What's going on down there, anyway, Mom? Some magical elixir in the Kiwi waters?"

Annie could sense Adair debating whether or not to respond to her sarcasm. "Fiona and Percy have us doing this, whatchamacallit, family counseling."

"Marriage counseling, too, Mom?"

"Please, Anna. Stop being so ridiculous. Why would anyone want to open that can of worms?"

Annie threw a ball across the field for Tashmoo. She had to stop making these snarky comments.

"Say hello to your father," Adair said. "He's just back from taking out Fiona's little terrier."

Annie heard her mother whisper to her father, under her breath, "I think she's making progress."

And, after another minute, "How are you holding up, dear? That cottage still standing?"

Annie couldn't remember the last time she'd spoken with her father on the telephone.

"Sounds a bit intense down there, Dad."

She handed Lily and Robbie their tennis rackets.

"It's been quite a journey for us, Annie. You'd be surprised. The counselor lady comes right to the house. And you thought California was touchy-feely." He chuckled. "Remember those self-improvement lists you used to keep when you were little? You're not the only one trying to get better. We're learning to be more open-minded. By the way, did you ever consider putting *Be more forgiving* on there?"

"Hold on, please, will you, Dad?"

The kids were lined up on the deck, ready to go to camp. Annie called upstairs to ask Emmie to drive them.

"It's been great to have Emmie here," she said into the phone, kissing the top of each head and deciding not to address her father's last comment.

"Yes, your mother thought he would be a big help," her father said.

"What? So Mom was behind it?"

"As I recall, she and Juliet were in cahoots."

"Oh." Annie leaned on the deck railing, just inches away from the cardinal. "I didn't realize."

"In cahoots with your children, I ought to say. With Robbie and Lily."

Annie inhaled sharply and Tashmoo, at her feet, wagged his tail anxiously. She hadn't realized she had been quite so obviously out of control. It was just laundry and dishes. Oh, and a smashed plate.

"How do the Beatles put it? *We get by with a little help from our friends.*" Her father chuckled again. "The other one I like is *Love is all you need, love is all you need.*" He hummed a few bars. "Fiona's crazy about the Beatles."

Annie coughed. She had never in her life heard her father hum. "Well, having Emmie here has made all the difference to the summer." You could say that again: his being on the Vineyard enabled her to wind up naked on the floor. "So, Dad, tell me. Fiona just ran off and left, huh? Up some canyon, Mom said? I can't imagine."

Really? What if Emmie hadn't happened to sail in when he had, and the rain hadn't stopped? Who knows what she might have done, or how many plates she might have smashed?

"You might find this hard to believe, Miss Muffet, but everyone does the best they can. And you know what they say … there but for the grace of God go I. Or maybe you haven't heard that expression."

"Actually I have, Dad. Believe me."

Who the hell was he to give her advice?

Tashmoo, and the cardinal, seemed to be looking sympathetically into her eyes.

"Fiona is like you. Tough."

"I'm not, actually—"

"Did you know she grew up on a sheep farm on the South Island? You might admire her if you got to know her. Think about Christmas. You ought to have visited your brother when you lived on this side of the world." She could hear Fiona's terrier purring like a cat. Was her father actually patting him? "It's never too late to change, Annie. You might try calling once in a while—it wouldn't kill you. Your brother's been through the wars down here."

Annie felt her bones soften with that now-familiar feeling of surrender. This was what Aunt Faye meant when she used to admonish her to *get to know your family, that's what counts.* Her family was just a bunch of regular, cracked human beings with messy problems, same as she was. But they certainly rallied around when she needed them, she had to admit; maybe she should start paying more attention. It would, actually, be nice to have her little brother back, to get to know him again. Maybe she could be friends with both Kathleen *and* Fiona.

Was she really taking relationship advice from her father?

"Thanks for the invitation, Dad. I'll talk to Gordon about Christmas," she said, and hung up.

22

A Very Intellectual Beach

A stretch of perfect July weather followed, and they settled into a routine.

In the mornings, after Annie hiked to Split Rock with Lindsay, she would hurry everyone out the door so they wouldn't miss a minute of camp. Emmie complimented her efficiency and how well the kids made their beds and tidied up and put their dishes in the sink. He said she ran a tight ship.

Summer was fading away and she spent her two hours alone biking, running, or else kayaking or swimming across one placid pond or another. It felt good to be fit again; maybe she wouldn't have had so much trouble at Long Point if she'd been in better shape.

She wasn't sure whether it was the cleansing water or the sea air, but she actually did feel twenty years old during her mornings, and carefree ... except that she bought, and wore, a waterproof watch in Edgartown and was careful to leave plenty of time for Center traffic at pickup. She was never once late.

She tried to ignore it, but every time she saw a red Jeep Wrangler her heart slid up to her throat and she craned her neck to try to make out the driver. It was, more often than not, a skinny, middle-aged bald guy she saw sometimes at the Chilmark Store. Chase must have gone back to New York.

After lunch, they'd head over to Lucy Vincent Beach and sit with the Rosenthals, always in the same spot, and Annie would play with the girls while Freddy took the boys into the ocean. Robbie became such a strong swimmer that, when it wasn't too rough, Annie let him go in alone.

Gavin seemed like a responsible-enough lifeguard, but having Freddy around made her feel safer. She trusted him. She also liked that no matter what the surf, he stayed with Tommy. He was not demanding like some of the fathers; he never forced him to keep up with the older boys. And he never once pressured Annie to join them in the waves, never asked her to explain why she refused to go in.

Some afternoons, when it was not too hot, the Tuckers would bring Tashmoo along and, once all the kids were safely out of the water and playing or reading on the sand, Annie would walk him east, down-Island, since the other way was private. It didn't take long for them to get to the section of Lucy Vincent that had remained "clothing optional" after the town had gentrified Jungle Beach; in other words, the naked beach.

The first time she encountered nudists, Annie tried to avert her eyes, pretend the beauty of the sea had happened to take her in at that second, but it wasn't so simple. Apparently, people who like to go naked also like dogs, and they were constantly stopping to ask if they could pet Tashmoo, how old he was, did he have trouble with ticks, etcetera.

When she remarked to Freddy that she really enjoyed these walks but wished she didn't have to wade through a dam of naked sunbathers, his retort was, "What, are you a direct descendant of the Pilgrims or something? So prudish. Lighten up on the WASP *shtick*, will ya?"

So she decided not to discriminate, and began chatting with people who happened to be buck naked as she would with anyone. They turned out to be very friendly, particularly compared to the Chilmark set in their closed beach circles, and she found their unselfconsciousness refreshing. Conversing normally despite paunchy breasts, stomachs, and penises sagging, they were as relaxed and comfortable as toddlers, and Annie later admitted to

Freddy that she envied their lack of inhibitions. She began to wonder if she was a little rude, not being nude.

She and Tashmoo would stroll through the naked section to the flat stretch of wide-open beach that unfolded between the ocean and lower Chilmark Pond. They would trail the tiny sandpipers that always managed to scurry to safety just ahead of them, alone in the midst of nothing but sand, sea, and sky. If they happened to be walking later, the ocean would turn dark and they would follow not only the seagulls and sandpipers, but their own tall, narrow shadows along the shore.

Annie's mood tended to mirror the sea. She felt calm and strong on tranquil days, ready to dive in. But when the swells were raging and tumultuous, she felt anxious and kept high on the sand. She never tired of studying the breaking ocean waves, but she didn't dare set foot in them. Not now, at least, and maybe not ever.

Sometimes, on windy days, the wail of the wind and surf together sounded so mournful that she could hardly stand how much she missed Aunt Faye and, still—more than she would have liked to admit—Chase. But she missed Gordon most of all.

Tashmoo always stayed by her side and waited patiently while she picked up a shell or piece of wampum or spoke to someone; it never occurred to him to chase the piping plovers or the oystercatchers, with their sharp orange bills, the way he did on Lambert's Cove Beach, and he certainly never ventured into the big waves on this side of the Island. Something about the afternoon sun on the south shore brought out the gold in his amber eyes, and she felt more understood and loved than she ever had before by any living being. Together, they shared an unmistakable simpatico—a love on the same spectrum she felt for her children but constant, uncomplicated—and helped very much by the fact that he didn't speak.

Dogs were generally not allowed on Lucy Vincent Beach, but Tashmoo had connections.

The first time they brought him, he'd been a stowaway. While they were inside the house getting ready, he'd slipped down to the station wagon when no one was looking and darted in behind Lily when he saw his chance, burrowing low beside her. The girls said nothing, and Annie and Robbie in the front seat hadn't noticed him until they'd reached the parking lot.

It was too hot to leave him in the car, so they decided to try their luck sneaking him past the guard. Robbie, wanting nothing to do with this ploy, raced ahead to find the Rosenthals, and Annie, fully aware that she was not modeling responsible behavior to the girls, pretended not to see the sign with the big red X slashed through the dog icon. Tashmoo seemed to know his way around; probably Aunt Faye had brought him here off-season.

Annie held him on the leash, doing her best imitation of an invisible person, but practically lost her arm when, without warning, Tashmoo spurted forward and dragged her toward Gavin's lifeguard's chair. He sat down squarely at the base and gazed up at Gavin, the one person they were trying to avoid.

Noticing the dog out of the corner of his eye, Gavin looked down, annoyed and about to scold them, but instead leapt off his chair.

"Tashmoo!" he cried. "It's you!"

And they enjoyed a reunion reminiscent of Tashmoo and Lindsay's on Lambert's Cove.

Turns out that when he wasn't lifeguarding, Gavin was training dogs, and he was the one Aunt Faye had hired to train Tashmoo when he was a puppy.

"This isn't just any dog," Gavin told Annie and the girls, taking some dog treats out of his backpack, "so I'll tell you what. You can bring him on cool days when it's not too crowded in July. But never in August, okay? Promise?" And then he demonstrated how Tashmoo could roll over three times on command and suspend a biscuit on his nose for a whole minute.

Thanks to Gavin, these afternoons along the south shore became one of the best parts of Annie's summer.

Once, watching the sky sweep out to sea, she went as far as the stretch designated for Abel's Hill residents, across from where she'd put in her kayak that morning. With a strange lump in her throat, Annie scanned the families, trying to find a woman who might look like Élise with a nanny and twin toddler girls. She didn't notice anyone and, instead of berating herself for bothering to look, told herself that it was just habit, and that habits took a while to break.

After these walks, Tashmoo would sleep under the umbrella Freddy always set up in case, he said, one of the kids had too much sun. Then Annie would keep watch so Freddy could take a nap or swim, and sometimes she actually got to read a few pages of her own book, checked out of the adult-fiction section. The kids started playing close to the dunes on what they dubbed the "reading rock," and Robbie or Ben would often read aloud from one of the chapter books Annie took out for them from the Chilmark Library.

It was a very intellectual beach.

When the kids were out of earshot, Freddy complained in his pianissimo voice about Lauren—"Figures she would hire the most expensive lawyer in New York"; "I never imagined she could be so vicious"—or recount stories of how his father as a little boy had been smuggled out of Poland before the war to relatives in Belgium, stuffed in a bass violin case—leaving his grandfather, a prominent surgeon in Warsaw and also a talented cellist, and his grandmother, a singer, at the hands of the Gestapo. Freddy's father made his way to Brooklyn and worked a series of demeaning jobs before scrounging up enough money to start his instrument company.

"And here my children are, spending the summer on Martha's Vineyard," he said. "I came to Chilmark once in college and made it my dream to buy my own vacation house here one day. Such a blessing, a *brocheh*." He winked. "And this month I get to be Mr. Mom!"

Freddy missed his father terribly and described him so well that Annie felt she knew him: how his real ambition had been to sing on Broadway; how he donated instruments every year to inner-city schools; how a thousand people came to his funeral. She, in turn, tried to describe Aunt Faye: how she knew every verse of every Christmas carol; how she and Annie had jumped off the *Jaws* bridge; how she never held a grudge.

During their reminiscing they had a tacit agreement not to interrupt, but to hold any memory that might be triggered by the other until the one talking was through. And in this way, they created a conversation that spanned their summer afternoons.

The next Wednesday morning, Meg didn't feel like going to the Center, so Annie took her instead on her bike down to the playground behind the West Tisbury Town Hall. They played on the seesaw and Annie pushed her on the swing until they decided to head next door to the farmers' market for some lemonade. They had come here the last two Saturdays, and once with Gordon before he'd left.

Other parents were fussing with small children in single and double strollers, struggling to push them along the bumpy dirt surface between the two lines of overflowing farm stands, but Annie carried Meg on her hip as usual, even though her feet dangled down past Annie's knees now. A lot of people walked dogs on leashes.

They admired the greens and cucumbers and tomatoes, and tried tastes of jellies and jams, before buying two big, cold cups of lemonade.

"I could make a whole pitcher for what each of these cost, so enjoy it," Annie said, giving Meg a little toast. "Let's try not to spill on our clean white shirts."

They strolled back toward the playground and Annie's bike, stopping to listen to a salty up-Island combo play banjo and harmonica. They decided to visit their friend the Vietnamese lady, who sold delicious spring rolls like the ones they used to eat in Singapore and Hong Kong.

Standing in the long line, Meg suddenly twisted on Annie's hip and, pointing behind her, shouted, "Hey, Mr. Chase!"

Annie jumped, her lemonade sloshing in its cup, and there he was, at the Morning Glory Farm stand across the way, cradling a gigantic bouquet of long-stemmed, pink-and-white stargazer lilies. He was fishing his free arm above the red and yellow peppers, above the rutabagas, waving cash at the salesperson.

"He's wearing a white shirt too," Meg said.

They left their place in line and went over.

"Annie," Chase said, off guard, trying to stuff the change into his wallet with one hand.

"Need some help?" She started to put Meg down but, noticing a man coming toward them with an enormous Saint Bernard, changed her mind.

"I got it," he said, sliding his wallet into his back pocket. "How are you, Meg?"

Meg grinned.

"Your lilies are amazing," Annie said.

"Thanks. I bought out every stand." He tried to edge away, but it was awkward because of the leafy stems poking out. Summer people thronged around them to get to the vegetables, and he and Annie and Meg got pushed closer together.

"Someone's birthday?" Annie asked.

Chase paused. "Been driving all over the Island. Have more in my Jeep."

Just then, a stocky woman Annie recognized from Lucy Vincent reached way behind Chase for a large head of romaine lettuce soaking in a pan, and began vehemently shaking out the water. The Saint Bernard began barking. The woman lost her balance and tipped into the back of Chase, who in turn toppled into Meg and Annie, knocking Meg's cup out of her hand and spilling lemonade all over everyone and bumping the flowers into all of their chests. The orangey-yellow stamens in the centers of the lilies smeared across their white polo shirts, and the Saint Bernard continued barking.

No one in line noticed, and no one spoke. A man in pink shorts wedged into Chase's place and the lady paid for her lettuce.

Annie and Chase stood, their mouths open. Meg looked down at her cup on the ground. The Saint Bernard ambled on.

"I owe you, Meg, sorry," Chase said. Then, aligning the stems of his lilies, he stated, in an unfamiliar, measured way, "*I need to go.*"

Annie stared at the orange dust brushed all over their shirts.

"Forget it," he said, moving away as fast as he could. "That stuff never comes out."

23

Heart-Shaped Rocks

——

What was *that* about? Annie described the scene to Freddy that afternoon, back in their usual place on the beach. He threw up his hands. "*Oy.* That poor guy sounds like he's under a lot of stress. White shirts are such the pain here, don't you think?" He then asked for some laundry advice.

Annie, shaking her head, laughed. She gave him a brief tutorial on the importance of sorting colors, then surprised herself by telling Freddy stories—not about Aunt Faye, but today about Chase, about how quiet the Vineyard used to be in the '70s and '80s, about out-of-the-way places they'd gone together—places Freddy hadn't discovered yet and that may have been lost to development, for all Annie knew.

She'd never really talked about Chase to anyone before. When she recounted how he'd helped her bury Faye, which she still hadn't told Gordon, Freddy was so quiet she began to think he'd dozed off behind his big sunglasses. But when she finally stopped talking, he said, "What a mensch this guy is. How terrible to lose such a friendship, Annie, and I hope, for your sake, you don't. A friend like that is one in a million. Forget about the lilies."

Annie never knew how their conversations began. Once, another afternoon, she mentioned to Freddy how purposeful Aunt Faye had seemed, at eighty still driving back and forth alone between Wellesley and the Vineyard, volunteering at the nature center, staying in touch with everyone. Annie admitted that she envied her that sense of purpose—that sometimes she felt life was happening *to* her, that she was merely meandering along, being buffeted rather than actually steering, that she didn't know what her purpose was.

"Believe me, your aunt felt that way too at different times," Freddy said, his mouth full of Humphrey's cookies, *Doctor Doolittle* in his lap. "Everybody does. Maybe you should try going a little easier on yourself, Annie. You're still grieving. It's an awful process, and it puts us at our most vulnerable."

She liked how he put himself in the same boat with her and implied that he, too, felt adrift. So this is what happens when someone you love dies, she conjectured: your carefully constructed wall of emotional defenses collapses, the pain you have perfected yourself from feeling cannot be stayed any longer. You're hit over the head with the realization that, despite your best efforts, you have no real influence over much of anything.

"You have to be brave enough to let yourself feel the hurt," Freddy said. "It will pass through you sooner or later. There are no shortcuts. And as for control …" he flicked his hand, reaching for another cookie, "nobody has any. That, plus thinking about how you're also going to die someday and do this same thing to your kids, is what gets you when someone you love dies. Sure gets me, anyway. All we can do is try to make life better for our children and feel grateful for every moment because, believe me, are these moments ever numbered."

"I guess you're right," Annie said, her throat swelling. She stood up. "Nice that the weather's cleared."

Freddy smiled at her. "It's you, Annie. You make the clouds blow out to sea." And, jumping up to play catch with the boys, he returned to his fortissimo, boisterous self.

Emmie never came with them to Lucy Vincent. Having made a few excuses, he eventually admitted that he was allergic to the sun. So, as the summer days went on, Annie assigned him errands and odd jobs, hugely helpful to her, and she was happy to think of him on the shad back deck with the cardinal and his saxophone, composing and rehearsing songs with which to serenade them later. From across the field, Heather said that she and Apple loved listening to his music, too.

Freddy and Annie never spoke on the phone or even acknowledged their friendship; never said "See you tomorrow." But when she would pull into the beach parking lot at two o'clock, his Suburban would be right behind her station wagon. When she'd pull into the Center at drop-off and pickup, he would be parked next to the only available space. And invariably, when she decided to get coffee at the Chilmark Store, he'd be sitting on the porch with two muffins, an empty rocking chair beside him.

Every day, as promised, Freddy would practice throwing with Robbie, even after his own boys had run off to play something else. When Annie said she ought to take Robbie down to Brickman's in Vineyard Haven to get him his own glove so he could stop borrowing theirs, Freddy said, "It might be nice if you waited and let Gordon take him to do that. It's a special moment between a father and son, buying your first glove."

While Freddy took the kids in the waves, Annie often braided Beatrice's hair and listened to Tommy read. He was not a fast learner and needed a lot of prodding to sound out words, but he was steadily getting more confident. It took about the same amount of time for Tommy to get through a Dr. Seuss book as it did to organize Beatrice's hair.

Annie had never seen hair like Beatrice's: no one had. In fact, people constantly marveled at it, and strangers commented upon her wild curls as often as they asked to pat Tashmoo. Beatrice had so much hair that, depending on the humidity, Annie couldn't always corral it into two braids and would enlist Lily to help her divide it into five or six. "New England–style Bali braids," they called them.

The closed circles of women on the sand didn't widen, but

they did multiply, and at one point Annie counted three tangential rings surrounding the Tucker/Rosenthal camp.

"Those ladies don't like me too much," she once said to Freddy, not particularly caring but wondering what she'd done to offend them and why they never spoke to her.

"They're full of *shtuss*, that's all. Nonsense and jealousy. But they're not all that bad. For some reason, I don't know why, you just don't want to get to know them. You don't *need* to feel so outside the circle, Annie, but you seem to want to stay there." He chuckled. "Or, I suppose—you could be onto something. Maybe they really *don't* like you. Maybe they think you make life look too easy."

"Me? If they only knew the truth."

He laughed loudly in agreement. "Ah, who knows what's going on in their lives? They might be miserable." He passed her a butter brickle cookie.

Freddy was right. Why let people like that rain on her parade?

On Friday, Lindsay and Zoey were waiting for them where the path spills onto the sand.

"Sorry I wasn't here the past few mornings," Lindsay began, as they set out toward Split Rock. "Another sick seal pup. Cool job I have, huh? When I was a little girl growing up in Philadelphia, my dream was to work at the Woods Hole Oceanographic Institution, and now I do! I still don't know how I got to be so lucky. My baby seal is better now, by the way. She's going to make it."

"You saved her life," Annie said. "But Tashmoo and I missed you."

There were some white caps today, despite being no wind. After discussing the unpredictable New England weather for a hundred yards or so, Lindsay said, "I wonder whether maybe I shouldn't have told you about Noah. I really want us all to be friends. He and Faye were buddies, and I want you to like him, too."

"I'm sure I will."

"You won't judge him, will you?"

"Wasn't planning on it," Annie said, remembering what both her parents had said and feeling that familiar pit in her stomach, the way she did whenever she was criticized.

"It's very hard, this stuff, and living on a small island where everybody knows each other's business doesn't make it any easier. Ever tried to forgive anyone, Annie?"

The thing about Lindsay, as opposed to Freddy and almost everyone else Annie knew, was that she waited for a reply, didn't let you off the hook. The question hung over the beach until finally Annie had to answer.

"I don't think I've particularly tried, but I'm working on it. I think, before, rather than going to the trouble of forgiving someone and going forward with them actually still in my life, I tended just to write them off. It's a little hard, though, when you want to …" She caught herself. She was about to say, *It's a little hard when you want to write off yourself. You can't exactly avoid yourself.*

Although plenty of people do, come to think of it. Take her father, for instance. Maybe he used to drink too much because he was so mortified after the Mrs. Pedrick incident that he couldn't bear to look himself in the mirror. (Or else because he missed her when Mr. Pedrick moved her away to Palm Beach!)

Maybe that's why Chase drank so much, too.

Why couldn't she get her mouth around the words to confess to Lindsay what she'd done? Maybe she was too proud, or didn't want to let her down, or wasn't yet ready to admit out loud to anyone besides Tashmoo how imperfect she was.

"Well, you're right about forgiveness taking trouble and hard work," Lindsay said. "But anger is toxic. If you stay mad and don't forgive someone, it's like drinking poison and hoping the other person will die. Faye told me that! No question, Noah broke my heart—he broke everything. But, you know what they say—a heart that's cracked open is more expansive."

"Did Aunt Faye say that, too?"

"Nope." Lindsay laughed as she bent down to pick up a pebble. "You know, Annie, I have a theory. Anyone whose heart has *not* been broken has most likely not been paying attention. They're probably oblivious. Or in denial, wearing blinders like those Percheron plow horses you see sometimes on Lambert's Cove Road. People hurt each other every day, whether they intend to or not."

Annie tossed a piece of driftwood, but Tashmoo ignored it and remained trotting along beside her. Face it: she used to wear blinders about a lot of things.

"*I still have much ado to know myself,*" she said, quietly quoting Shakespeare to her dog.

"I don't know why I thought my marriage would be different from anyone else's," Lindsay continued. "Where I got off thinking Noah and I were somehow special. We're just like every other couple, working out our problems. I got mad the other day because he had the nerve to say we're the love affair of the twentieth century, even though he's been shacking up with what's-her-name in Edgartown the past year. There's no such thing, I told him. Noah was literally on his knees, Annie, begging me to forgive and forget and take him back."

"John Alley told me Faye and Jared were the love affair of the twentieth century."

"Oh, for heaven's sake," Lindsay said, yanking a stick from Zoey's mouth and whipping it back into the Sound. "Jared used to complain about her cooking, remember? Said she put too much salt on everything. And Faye got tired of all his photography talk. She'd want to go swimming and he'd want to go to art galleries on a sunny day. Theirs was a work in progress, same as everyone else's."

"Labeling these love affairs seems to make things worse, harder to live up to," Annie said.

"Especially when reality sets in." Lindsay picked up another stone. "But you and I really are so blessed, Annie. We have pretty awesome husbands, warts and all. Life isn't some romantic comedy, unfor—" She stopped abruptly. "You know, I started to say 'unfortunately.' Don't get me wrong—I love romantic comedies, how everything wraps up in a neat, pat way, how happily-ever-after is just … implied, assumed. But that's not real life. Not mine, anyway. Not anybody's I know, either."

It was Annie's turn to throw the stick.

"Like I said, everything is a work in progress," Lindsay said, "and we need to be able to relax in that, that *chaos*, and have faith that things will work out more or less the way they're supposed to … which will definitely be a lot more complicated than in the neat, pat, romantic-comedy kind of way. There are always going to be loose ends. The trick is to be grateful for the messiness." She laughed. "Of course, whether we live long enough to see how things come out is another matter."

Lindsay had found five or six heart-shaped stones while she'd been talking, and Annie had found several, too.

"I think it would be boring to live a romantic comedy, don't you, Annie?"

They had reached the bend in the beach at Split Rock. Tashmoo paddled into the waves first, swimming as if he owned the place.

"I don't think I will ever find out," Annie replied.

Lindsay put her hands on the backs of her hips and arched her upper body toward the water. "Do you see the rock, now?"

Annie still hadn't told Lindsay about the morning she and Tashmoo had swum around it, but grinned as she followed Tashmoo into the waves. "It's an emblem for each of us, corny as it may sound," she said, her back to Lindsay. "We're all split, we all have our cracks." *Many, many cracks,* she added, in a whisper.

"Just like our marriages," Lindsay said. "The cracks are actually what make it perfect. Oh, forget I said that. Perfect is an irrelevant concept." She picked up a pebble. "*Another* one," she called, holding it up and wading in behind Annie. "It's my lucky day."

They stood in the water and surveyed the huge boulder.

"I'll tell you what *I* think about Split Rock," Lindsay said. "This fissure was formed by water freezing and melting a million times. It's what's left from a long process of what you could call *glacial forgiveness*. I believe it's here to inspire us in all sorts of ways."

They held hands and placed all their pebbles, and the water twirled at their feet.

24

The Little Ketchup Dish

─────

The next afternoon, Lucy Vincent Beach was so exquisite that no one wanted to leave. Past the time they ordinarily would have said goodbye, the Tuckers and Rosenthals instead angled their beach chairs west toward Squibnocket. The sand was flecked with a million crystals and the sun, glinting off the cliffs, gradually cast a dusky light on everything until the beach was bathed in an almost surreal reddish hue.

Freddy took the boys in for one last swim, and Annie wandered down to the shore to watch them.

The water quickly became so blinding in the fiery reflection of the setting sun that, squinting and shading her eyes, Annie could barely see. She was relieved when they rode in their last wave.

Robbie and Ben looked tanned and strong as they raced past her, taller than typical fourth graders; they were both starting to look remarkably like their fathers. Tommy, still short and skinny, always came out after them. Knowing he would be especially cold, Annie had brought his towel.

"Goodness!" Tommy exclaimed, thanking her.

Freddy lumbered past—"What? No towel for me?"—and Annie enfolded Tommy in the velour. For an eight-year-old he was a very good swimmer, and had once explained how his mom had driven him to lessons every Saturday all winter, and how he had managed to tread water for fifteen minutes to pass his swim level. But there was something fragile about him, and of Freddy's kids, Annie unabashedly favored him. She hugged his shivering little frame and he clasped his arms around her waist, pressing his head against her stomach.

"You're like my mom when she's not at work," he said.

The kids didn't talk about Lauren much, although Annie knew they spoke to her on the phone every night, after they called their grandmother at her Long Island nursing home. Freddy had mentioned that the kids didn't technically know, at the suggestion of their marriage counselor, that this was more than a separation or that he was moving out of their home in Scarsdale. Lauren had always worked full-time, so maybe they didn't rely on her being around every day the way they did, say, on Rosa, or the way Annie's kids relied on her—but still, they must be missing their mother like crazy. They must be wondering what was going on.

The thing was, it was impossible to believe she was as *meshugah* as Freddy said: it didn't make any sense. The kids were too nice.

Annie gazed down at Tommy's delicate face and combed out some of the sand in his hair with her fingers. He must take after Lauren, and she must be lovely. She hugged him and felt a surge of affection—for this little boy and also for his mother, whose face she had never seen even in a picture.

As they were packing up, Freddy said, in his stentorian voice, "I have some burgers in the fridge. Why don't you bring the kids over for supper?"

"Supper?" Annie echoed.

"Hamburgers, Mommy?" Lily said. "Please can we go?"

"Of course you can. I want you to see where we live. You know, guys," Freddy said, switching from his sunglasses to his big black-framed clear ones, "I love you all so much."

Whenever he went on like this, which he did regularly even though they had met only a couple of weeks ago, Annie wished she could be similarly effusive. But it wasn't her personality, and it would have sounded forced. What was nice, though, was that rather than finding fault with her, he seemed to understand and accept this about her.

"Do you know that when we're in the waves, I hold you guys as I hold my own," Freddy continued, sounding almost as surprised at this as anybody else might be. He grinned toward the ocean. "Okay, let's go. It's getting freezing, and I'm super hungry."

Annie, with Meg on her hip and Tommy's hand in hers, looked behind to make sure they hadn't forgotten anything and saw Beatrice's little sandals and a bottle of their suntan lotion.

"These wouldn't be here tomorrow after the tide came in," she said to Beatrice, who smiled and silently reached up to hold Meg's trailing hand.

In parallel they stuffed their gear into the backs of their cars, as usual parked next to each other, and Annie began having second thoughts. She was cold after swimming across the pond, and her whole body felt dry, her hair like straw.

"Maybe we should go home first," she said.

"No, no, please don't do that," Freddy said. "I live just across the way. We'll be quick. Anyhow, I have some work to do afterwards and the kids need to practice their violins."

She followed him down South Road a mile or so back toward West Tisbury, then left up a hilly, dirt road. His driveway was overgrown and full of potholes, and led to a brown clapboard house that was, unlike Freddy, somewhat dour looking. It was a regular American house, more suburban than Vineyard.

"If you don't mind, the kids can change here," Annie said, opening the back to get the spare bag she always carried and to let Tashmoo jump out. "Less likely we'll leave anything behind."

"You know, your mother is odd," Freddy commented to Robbie. "For someone who comes across as a bit spacey, she's actually pretty organized, remembering a change of clothes and everything for you guys."

"Yes, she is organized," Robbie agreed. "She always brings our sweatshirts."

"She is a very good mother," Lily said.

Meg pointed at Annie's hair and giggled. "Your hair looks like Beatrice's, Mommy."

Annie realized she hadn't brushed it since her swim across the pond, and knotted a loose bun at the base of her neck.

"I love that," Freddy said. "Lauren won't take two steps without a comb and mirror."

"Our mom puts on make-up to pick us up from school," Ben interjected. "Such a waste of lipstick."

"Goodness," Tommy said, grinning with his two buckteeth.

"It's a lot of responsibility for me, you know, having these little sisters, and her remembering our sweatshirts is a big help," Robbie continued.

"Is that so," said Freddy, winking at Annie. "Well, I'll let you guys finish getting organized. Come around the back when you're ready."

This was the first time they were acknowledging they were actually friends, not just people who happened to run into each other at the Chilmark Store or beach and take care of each other's children, who happened also to settle into long discussions about life and death—and Annie was surprised at how nervous she felt. She didn't feel *attracted* to Freddy: she wasn't about to let *that* happen again. What she wanted was to keep his friendship, that's all. She didn't want to blow it.

The Rosenthals, unbeknownst to the Tuckers, had a small white dog, a Maltese named Cookie, who yipped a nonstop, nervous greeting on the other side of the split-rail fence that defined their backyard. Annie was amazed that Freddy had never mentioned her before.

"It's Lauren's dog, not mine," he said, opening the gate for them. His kids were rinsing each other off in their bathing suits in the outdoor shower. "Lauren said it would comfort the kids to have it here. But all it does is shit in the house and be a living magnet for deer ticks, and all I do is clean up and pull them off."

He brought Annie a bottle of beer and she sat at the brand-new glass patio table on the deck above the flat lawn, attempting to comb out Beatrice's hair ("Tomorrow I'll bring you some conditioner and detangler," she said), while the other kids, shouting happily, chased after the dogs and the fireflies. With Cookie, as with Zoey in the mornings at Lambert's Cove, Tashmoo stopped acting like a person and instead behaved like what everyone sometimes forgot he was: a dog.

"I'd better get these burgers started," Freddy said. "You might be surprised to hear that I am an excellent barbecuer."

Rosa had left a salad for them in the fridge, along with thick hamburger patties and shucked corn in aluminum foil. Cooked rice was in a pot on the stove. Freddy began bustling between the kitchen and the gas grill on the deck.

"Let's eat inside," he said. "Too buggy out here. Can you set the table?"

Annie quickly wove Beatrice's hair into two braids and went inside. Freddy had already placed eight new, laminated map placemats of Martha's Vineyard around the table, which stood on a sisal carpet two steps away from the linoleum floor of the kitchen. Despite it being very well organized and logical, Annie found it awkward to find her way around another woman's kitchen. Lauren must have spent a lot of time setting everything up, before she'd decided so abruptly to divorce, and Annie felt like she was sneaking around. Maybe she wasn't supposed to be here.

She ducked into the bathroom to borrow a hairbrush and retie her bun, and wished she'd brought the Red Sox cap she'd taken to wearing lately. Later, she spied Freddy doing the same, checking himself in the mirror.

Freddy grilled while she poured milk and tossed the salad, and they chatted easily through the screen door—both aware, it seemed, that they were crossing some invisible line. It was almost as if they were pretending to be married, pretending to be the

Brady Bunch or something.

The six kids piled onto the chairs that encircled the table.

"Isn't this *magnificent*, to all be together," Freddy bellowed, wedging his chair in next to Annie's. He reached for two hamburgers. "Thank you, guys, for coming. You're our first dinner guests. It's as if we are one big family now, almost *mispocha*." He turned to gaze at Annie, and she heard him add softly, "Maybe."

No one knew what he was talking about, but everyone laughed.

A breeze carried the faint sound of the ocean through the double-hung windows that lined the wall from the table to the living room, or maybe it was the traffic on South Road. Annie was a little cold, but she loved the sound so much, and felt so happy, that she didn't want anything to change. All at once the familiar smell of skunk spray wafted across the table, and Ben jumped up.

"What is it with skunks around here, Dad? I hate it." He began closing the window sashes.

"Be po*lite*, Ben," Tommy whispered into his brother's ear. "We have *com*pany." He beamed at Annie.

"Who cares about skunks when we are in such a place?" Freddy took a big bite of one of his hamburgers. "You want to know the Yiddish, Robbie, for how I feel right now? I am *kvelling*. That means I am overflowing with pride and joy at seeing your beautiful shining faces—"

He stopped and stared at Annie.

"You put the ketchup bottle right on the table."

Everyone froze.

"So?" Annie said, smiling and shrugging, looking sideways at the kids.

"Lauren would never do that," Freddy said, changing to a faraway voice. "She always puts ketchup in little bowls. No containers allowed on the table."

"For hamburgers? With six kids?"

"Mommy does too use little bowls. For Thanksgiving," Lily said. "For Christmas."

"You know what I just realized?" Freddy went on, his voice returning to its normal *forte*, talking to no one in particular and still staring straight ahead. "I don't *want* to spend my life with somebody who puts ketchup in little bowls."

Ben slammed the last window shut; Tommy looked bewildered; Robbie and Lily looked alarmed. They all stared at Annie.

Freddy turned to Robbie beside him and blurted out in that extroverted way he had, as if this idea had suddenly dawned on him and he needed to share it with the group, "I think I have a crush on your mother!"

"Well," replied Robbie, not missing a beat, "she doesn't have a crush on *you*. She talks to my father on the phone about ten times a day. And he's coming back on August first."

"Is that so," said Freddy. He grinned, still looking dazed, and the moment—as moments will when there are six children around a table—passed quickly, and the conversation turned to baseball and funny things about camp and what they were going to do for the talent show next week.

After they'd cleaned up, Annie and Freddy stood on the side of the lawn while the kids resumed their game of tag, their conversation no longer flowing the way it usually did.

In an instant, Tashmoo, chasing after Cookie, tore in front of them and knocked over a potted plant. Dirt spilled everywhere. Annie righted the plant and heard Freddy mutter under his breath, "I don't know if I could do this dog, though."

On the dark drive home, Robbie said, "Mommy, I don't think we should go there for supper again."

"No," Lily said. "Freddy likes you. He wants to marry you. But you can't, because you're married to Daddy."

Meg started to cry. "But I like going there," she said. "I love my

Beatrice."

"You're an idiot," Robbie said to Meg. "From now on, Mommy, let's just see them at the beach."

"I think you're right," Annie agreed, turning onto Music Street back toward Middle Road. "The last thing I want is to wreck our friendship."

They walked in the door to see Emmie sitting on the couch beside the girl from Alley's, the one with purple hair and the myriad nose piercings. An acoustic guitar lay across the coffee table.

She and Annie recognized each other, and they both laughed.

"I didn't realize *you* were Emmie's aunt," the girl said, in her broad Boston accent, smiling with her pretty hazel eyes. "My name's Jazzy."

"A perfect name for a friend of Emmie's," Annie said, shaking her hand.

"Short for Jasmine," she said, unconsciously pushing up a black sleeve to reveal her mermaid tattoo.

"We were just jamming," Emmie said, looking happy and proud to have company. "By the way, Uncle Gordon called."

"I think it's excitin' he's in Hong Kong, watchin' history be made," said Jazzy. "D'you want to call him back and we'll put the kids to bed? Emmie and I want to play them the lullaby we've been workin' on."

"You certainly never know about people," Annie told Gordon later, holding the phone so he could hear the guitar and saxophone duet before she caught him up on dinner with the Rosenthals and the latest on the New Zealand situation. "I can't wait until you get here next week and can hear their music for yourself. You think you have an idea of who a person is from their accent and how they mess up making change at Alley's, but you can be totally, unequivocally wrong."

25

Naked on the Sand

—

The next morning, Annie waited for Lindsay at the usual time. Tashmoo stood expectantly, his tail wagging high, but after a few moments even he looked dejected and the tip of his tail dipped and brushed the sand, like Lindsay's braid. Rather than walk to Split Rock, for no particular reason Annie decided they should set off in the opposite direction.

Alone without Lindsay's chatter, there was nothing but the gentle *slap, slap* of the waves and the occasional clanging of that halyard.

Tashmoo zoomed ahead of her, jumped in for a quick paddle, raced back to check in, waded out chest-high for an unobstructed view across the water—always looking back for Zoey and Lindsay, hoping perhaps they were on their way.

Annie forded the little stream and kept on, appreciating that her feet had toughened up and didn't hurt anymore when she crossed washed-up strips of pebbles. Ahead was the old sail shack. It didn't seem very far above the beach now, at high tide.

Tashmoo ran up to it, wagging his tail feverishly, as if he had been here before or else smelled something familiar inside. He hadn't been with her and Gordon that morning in June because he had still been stuck with Juliet in Wellesley. Had he come to the shack with Aunt Faye and Jared? But Faye didn't get Tashmoo until after Jared died. Could she have brought someone else here? Heavens.

Tashmoo refused to budge from under the window of the shack, despite Annie calling him twice. He wasn't as well behaved when Lindsay wasn't around, that's for sure. Finally, exasperated, Annie climbed up to get him. As she bent down to clasp his leash onto his collar, she glanced through the open window and saw two people heaving rhythmically together, a blond man thrusting on top, a red-haired woman lying beneath him on the unfurled sail.

Annie jumped back, embarrassed at how stark the man's white ass was against his tanned body. She stepped on the leash and stumbled against a rock and looked in again inadvertently just as the man turned his head.

It was Chase. Their eyes locked; they both froze.

And then she and Tashmoo tore off, running side by side back toward the main path. Evidently, she wasn't the only one with whom Chase had a magnetic attraction.

Tashmoo had to canter to keep pace with her.

"Annie!" she heard Chase yell, but she kept running. "Annie! Please! Stop!"

She didn't turn around but sensed his presence, naked on the sand and shouting like a fool.

She was still out of breath when she got home, but somehow managed to make breakfast for the kids and act relatively normal as she spoke to Gordon on the phone about the person he was considering hiring to replace Samir. Her arms and legs, however, would not stop shaking, and she wasn't sure whether Emmie noticed this or not when he offered to drive the kids to the Center and, rather than wait for her response, went ahead and shepherded them into his Subaru.

Cradling the phone on her shoulder, Annie made herself a cup of tea instead of her usual coffee, hoping to calm her nerves.

Gordon was falling asleep on the other end of the line and, after saying "I love you" several times, reluctantly hung up. Annie glanced down to press the button on the telephone receiver and looked up to see Chase, striding up the path in cool tennis whites, a bunch of wildflowers in his hand.

Tashmoo remained rooted to the deck and didn't get up to greet him. He didn't even wag his tail. The cardinal fluttered over to the bird feeder.

"I don't suppose that was your wife," Annie said.

Chase studied his feet. When he at last lifted his head, he surveyed the field. His eyes rested on the cardinal.

"Emmie will be back in a second," Annie said.

"All right, well, that's cool, because I'm going to stay only a second. I'm playing a tournament at Abel's Hill with my father. Just wanted to explain, that's all. Say I'm sorry."

"You don't need to explain anything to me. Maybe to Élise, but not to me. Why should I care?"

"Look, Annie. My marriage has problems. I'm the first to admit it. But I don't want you to think I just run around screwing everybody right and left, because I don't. That redhead is some single friend of Élise's from New York who's been staying with us. She's been after me for months. Means nothing."

"Whatever."

"Sorry about the lemonade, by the way. And the orangey stuff."

"Were those stargazers for her, or for your wife?"

"For my wife, if you really need to know."

"I don't understand why you waste your time with women like that, Chase, when you're so crazy about your wife that you drive all over the Island looking for her favorite lilies."

He hesitated. "She's available, I guess."

"I see. Well, I'm not."

"I know, Annie."

She started to go inside.

"Listen," he called after her. "I know you're mad at me. But seems a shame for us to lose each other again. I'd like to give you this: my cell-phone number and new email address. Email is awesome. It's going to change everything. No more letters lost in the deep blue sea." He held up his cell phone and waved it at her. "This is going to be a game changer, too. Dad and I just invested in the technology."

He extended a business card from where he stood on the grass, and she took it. Tashmoo stiffened.

"Is this the cardinal you were telling me about at the cemetery?"

Annie shrugged; she didn't feel like discussing her cardinal with him.

"It probably is the same one, you know, and I bet it is your Aunt Faye. Stranger things have happened. Like us figuring out how to be friends, for instance."

Annie bent over to pick up Meg's sweatshirt, left behind that morning on the deck, and folded it to her chest.

"*Just* friends. Cripes, Annie. Can't you help me out a little? I'm trying to apologize here." He pushed his hair out of his eyes. "Losing you will always be the biggest regret of my life, don't you get that? And who the hell knows ... maybe you and I will reconnect in our sixties, like Faye and Jared. But for now—well, you're married to Gordon. And I'm married to Élise." He flattened his lips, shifted his weight. "As to last week, well ... I'm not sorry it happened. I don't regret it one whit. We had to have it."

The wildflowers were drooping toward the ground in his other hand. He stepped forward and handed them to her, and Tashmoo made a weird throaty noise, like the beginning of a growl. The flowers smelled sweet and earthy, as if he had just picked them from that big field on Music Street.

"Had to *have* it?" Annie asked. "Like what, we had to reconnect, in order to regain Paris? Is this your Humphrey Bogart last-scene-on-the-tarmac routine?"

"Yeah, I suppose, maybe it is."

"Pretty cliché."

Chase stuck his empty hands in his pockets and pulled out a tennis ball he apparently didn't know was there. He half-heartedly tossed it across the field, looking unsurprised when Tashmoo ignored it.

"We had a helluva lot more than Paris. Face it." And as if reading her mind again, he added, "The other night with you meant a lot more to me than that floozy redhead."

He turned down the path and got into his Jeep, opening the door this time. He started down the driveway, immediately pulling to one side so that Emmie's Subaru could pass.

Annie crumpled up the business card and buried it in the trash.

She pulled her bike out of the shed and asked Emmie if he could please pick up the kids at noon. She rode down to the West Tisbury-Edgartown Road and turned right on New Lane, past the pretty red barn, past where the pavement ended. Without stopping, she pedaled hard onto the dirt trails of Sepiessa, bumping over branches and roots and rocks and through sandy patches and puddles. She rode all the way to Tisbury Great Pond, and when she got there she stripped down to her underwear and dove in. She swam across, sobbing the entire way.

When she got home later, she noticed that Emmie had stuck the wildflowers in an old orange-juice carton—but he never asked where they'd come from.

26

Aquinnah

Annie knew Robbie was right about no more suppers with the Rosenthals, but she couldn't resist the coparenting gig she had with Freddy. She should probably have taken the kids to another beach, or made Emmie come along, but he had his sun allergy and Jazzy had requested early morning shifts at Alley's so they could rehearse together in the afternoons. So instead she pretended to forget Freddy's comment about his having a crush and not to have heard the remark about Tashmoo, and things went on as before— not only because she couldn't resist the enticing beach weather, but because, after seeing Chase and the redhead, she truly needed Freddy's friendship.

Neither did she resist, the following Sunday afternoon, when Freddy asked if they wanted to drive up to the Cliffs for dinner at the Aquinnah Restaurant to watch the sunset. The perfect temperature and glorious skies were too tempting.

"You'll have to keep your dog in your car up there, though," Freddy said. "He has a personality change off the beach, away from Gavin's eagle eye. Let's take two cars."

They drove over the little bridge between Stonewall and Nashaquitsa ponds, past the sailboats bobbing in the gilded light, and wound up State Road. In the Wampanoag language, Martha's Vineyard is known as "Noepe," which means "land among the currents and streams, land among the waters." Annie loved driving up-Island Sunday evenings, passing all of the weekenders driving down to the ferries in Oak Bluffs and Vineyard Haven. The crowds had to leave the Island to go back to work, but they got to stay.

She wondered if it was this breathtaking view of Menemsha Pond and Vineyard Sound that had inspired James Taylor,

> *Now if all my golden moments could be rolled into one,*
> *They would shine just like the sun for a summer day …*

"Want to know why there aren't many trees up here?" she asked the kids. "It's because of a Wampanoag named Moshup. He had an enormous appetite—he was a giant, after all—and he liked to eat whales. To gather enough wood to make fires big enough to cook them, he had to tear up all the trees. That's why there aren't many left."

Freddy zoomed ahead, but Annie slowed down and pulled into the overlook so that a tailgating Mustang could pass, sweeping her arm toward the view as she turned around in her seat.

"Instead of using a harpoon, Moshup would throw stones into the water and step on them so he could scoop up the whales with his bare hands. That's how those big rocks that sailors have to be careful to watch out for, on the other side of Cuttyhunk, got there." She pointed across the Sound in the general direction. "The Wampanoag people loved Moshup because he always shared his whale meat, so for his birthday they gave him an entire ton of tobacco for his great giant pipe. He dumped his ashes into the sea, and that's how Nantucket came to be."

Annie pulled back onto the road and chuckled at her rhyme and at this little affront to Nantucket, electing not to share that the Wampanoags believed the Cliffs were red not because of the iron-rich soil, but because Moshup would whack his catch against them and it was the whale blood that had stained them that color.

"That's just legend," Robbie told the girls. "It's not true. Do you want to know the real reason why there are no trees up here? My camp counselor told me. It's because the early Wampanoags cut them all down to make canoes."

Everyone was silent.

"That's it?" asked Lily.

Meg pulled her thumb out of her mouth. "Bor-ring," she said, and popped it back in.

They followed the shady road straight up to Aquinnah, and Annie backed into a parking spot beneath the Gay Head Lighthouse.

"Listen, guys," she said, realizing she was beginning to sound like Freddy. "This place is touristy, and I have a feeling it's out of our price range. I think we should just order big bowls of chowder, and I'll give you more to eat when we get home."

"*What?*" demanded Robbie. "Why are we going there, then?"

"Well, for the view. For the sunset."

"Then we should have brought a picnic," he grumbled. "Besides, I thought we weren't going to have supper with them anymore."

"Just come along," Annie said, swinging Meg onto her hip.

The Aquinnah Restaurant, at the top of a row of clam shacks and souvenir shops, was across from where Gordon and Lily had bought Annie's wampum bracelet. Freddy, obviously a regular here, greeted the Wampanoag woman at the hostess stand by name. She brought them to the porch outside, to a picnic table perched a hundred feet above the Atlantic Ocean, between sea and sky. The water below was turquoise here today. They felt as if they were at once at the very top and the very end of the world.

They ordered on separate checks, but it was too awkward for Annie to confine her kids to chowder when Freddy's kids ordered hamburgers, so she let them get what they wanted and she ordered a lobster roll for herself. Everyone laughed and joked and seemed more relaxed around the table than they had the other night at the Rosenthals' house, and when they'd finished eating, Freddy gave the kids money to buy ice cream at one of the stalls.

"This is for ice cream, not for *tchotchkes*," he said, telling Ben and Robbie they were in charge and to beware of the skunks that scavenged around after French fries the tourists left behind.

"Ahh, so they can make their beautiful Island perfume," Lily giggled, holding Beatrice and Meg by the hand.

"*Kenahorah*," Freddy said. "These kids make me so happy I could *plotz*."

"I never know what you're talking about," Annie said. "But I sure love the way the words sound."

They sat alone on the deck sipping coffee while Freddy ate a big piece of blueberry pie à la mode; the other diners had left as soon as the sun had disappeared into the sea. The sky was now ablaze in stripes of orange and fuchsia, and a milky white moon was rising.

"Red sky at morn, sailors be warned; red sky at night, sailor's delight," Annie recited, admiring the colors before turning back to Freddy and noticing his blank expression. "It means it will be a nice day tomorrow. Chase used to say it."

"Oh," Freddy said. "The thing about you is, you appreciate all of your friends' expressions."

He then embarked on Lauren's latest wrongdoings and how hurt and offended he felt. He couldn't understand why she was so unreasonable on every single point of the separation. In the fall, he would be allowed to see the kids only on Saturdays, allowed to take them only every other weekend to his new apartment. Lauren said it would be too distracting for the kids to see him during the school week, and he couldn't bear it.

Annie listened, but finally she couldn't stand it any longer. She asked the question that had been burning inside her.

"I've been wondering, Freddy. I just don't get this. You're such a great guy, such an amazing dad. What did you ever do to Lauren to make her punish you like this? I cannot fathom why she is so out to get you. She must be a nice person, or your kids wouldn't be the way they are. What did you *do*?"

Freddy paused, obviously not his custom, and put down his fork. The waitress had gone inside, and he glanced around to make sure no one else was on the deck. The fuchsia sky had faded, and fog was gathering below them on the water's surface.

"Do you really want to know?"

She nodded.

"You sure?"

Again she nodded, and immediately regretted it.

He took a deep breath. "Okay. Well, here goes." He looked at the horizon, rather than at her. "We hadn't had sex since Lauren got pregnant with Beatrice. I already told you we never had any chemistry, and why we got married in the first place is a mystery to me. So, last year, I hired an agency, and started going to call girls. Nice ones, not tacky." He reported this matter-of-factly, as if he had hired someone to help him buy a car. "Lauren got suspicious and had a detective tail me."

Annie felt she had just swallowed sand. *Call* girls? Wasn't that a euphemism for *prostitutes*?

"You?"

He must have noticed her expression, or maybe how wide her eyes had become, since they felt like stones about to fall out of her face.

"Oy, what have I done?" he said. "I shouldn't have told you."

Annie's mouth had been sandblasted shut.

"I didn't want to have an affair with someone I knew, break up their family, make things complicated, messy. A mom on Ben's baseball team was interested in me but … this just seemed easier. Five years with no sex is a long time, Annie."

She stared at the table and began arranging packets of oyster crackers around her empty coffee mug, trying to hide her expression.

"My father used to talk about people being perfect in their imperfection. Have I told you that already? I wonder if I'll ever find anybody who will see me that way, who will love me despite my screwing up. Or even love me at all." He searched Annie's face. "It's not as if I liked going to those places. Well, I guess I thought I *would* like it, but—hell, I hated everything about it, believe me. I beat myself up every day, Annie. Such a *schmuck*! When I think I have to live the rest of my life knowing I did this to my wife, to my family—"

His voice had been in a steady crescendo and suddenly he slammed the table with both hands. "I was so fucking stupid! I've wrecked everything. *Oy vey iz mir.* But now it's done, you see? What can I do besides ask forgiveness and move on? Is she going to punish me forever? What does she want me to do, kill myself?"

This was exactly how Annie felt sometimes. Nonetheless, she wished he would stop talking. But instead he kept steamrolling over her like the fog, which was now creeping over the restaurant deck.

"The girls were shadows, really. Most didn't even speak English! It didn't *mean* anything. Not as if I *kissed* them or anything. With Lauren there was, I don't know, so much *rejection.* I felt ... so miniscule, like a speck of ... cosmic dust. They helped me feel like I was human. It was ... just three-dimensional masturbating, Annie, a natural extension of porn magazines. Yeah, that's what it was."

She could taste her lobster roll again, and was pretty sure she was going to throw up.

"Say something, Annie, for God's sake!"

Her oyster crackers fit end to end in a little circle.

"I don't know what to say." She still couldn't look at him. "I think it's ... smarmy. Gross." And then, not intending to articulate this and having no idea why she did, she asked, "You know, Freddy, I've always wondered ... What do they look like, anyway? All caricatures? I've never really seen one, except maybe twice."

"*What*? What are you talking about, never seen one? With all your years in Asia? Give me a break, Annie. For God's sake. Talk about not seeing what you don't want to see."

Annie stood up. "It's getting foggy."

"I swear, sometimes I think you go out of your way to keep blinders on, like—"

"Like the Percherons on Lambert's Cove Road," she said hastily. "I know. I know."

She had been trying very hard lately to change, to be more open-minded, more forgiving. But *prostitutes*? This was too much.

"You housewives don't get what it's like to be out in the real world every day," he went on. "You stay home with your kids in your tiny orbit and think that's the center of the universe. You have no idea how tough it is out there, how much pressure."

"We should go," she said.

Still seated, Freddy placed his huge hands flat, fingers splayed, aiming at her across the table.

"I don't get your shtick, Annie, I really don't. I thought you'd understand. You've been a great friend to me this summer, but maybe I misjudged you. Now you'll probably never talk to me again. There you are … married to Mr. Husband of the Year, always with your kids … you don't know what it's like to be lonely. Sometimes you remind me of, I don't know, that silly Princess Diana you love so much, some ditz like that. Living in a fairy-tale world. I really wish you'd get over yourself."

Annie's eyes filled with tears. She had given up on fairy tales, and she probably could have handled anything else he'd confessed; she could have understood an affair with a soccer mom. Why did it have to be *prostitutes*?

She felt betrayed, worse even than when she'd come upon Chase and the redhead. Freddy had no character, no morals. No wonder Lauren couldn't get divorced fast enough!

Thankfully, the kids came filing back onto the porch just then. Meg's and Beatrice's faces were covered with chocolate, and Annie took her time cleaning them up in the bathroom.

They left, and as soon as Freddy pulled his Suburban into the road, the fog swallowed his blinking taillights. Except for a pale glow from the moon, barely visible through the mist, and for the intermittent long red and white flashes from the lighthouse, Aquinnah was dark and deserted. Everything looked extremely gloomy all of a sudden.

"Why don't you guys wait inside the car for a moment and I'll let Tashmoo out," Annie said. "He's been such a good dog, waiting here."

She held the leash along the sandy shoulder of the road, trying to catch her breath in the salty cloud of sea air, and walked up the road toward the lighthouse. The fog was pouring up and over the cliffs as if from a backstage machine in a Shakespearean tragedy.

Freddy was as pathetic as her own father! Why hadn't he worked it out with poor Lauren, tried to figure out why she didn't want to sleep with him? She was probably disgusted because he was so fat! There was no excuse for any of it.

"Hurry up," she said to Tashmoo. It was downright spooky up here. They had become so enveloped in a cloud that she couldn't see her car, couldn't see anything. If it weren't for the rhythmic red and white flashes, she wouldn't even know the lighthouse was there—despite being directly beneath it. She shortened the leash to keep Tashmoo close against her leg.

The Wampanoags crave fog; to them, it is a comforting blanket of love. They believe it to be smoke wafting up from Moshup's giant pipe, smoke he sends over the Island to reassure everyone that although his body may have traveled offshore, he is actually still there with them in spirit. Like God. Like Aunt Faye. Like everyone you've loved who has died or moved on.

Out of the fog, a skunk waddled in front of them and, in an instant, exploded his wet spray all over Tashmoo and all over her, too.

27

Skunked

Tomato juice didn't work. Annie doused it on both herself and Tashmoo on the grass outside next to the outdoor shower, but they still reeked. She wasn't prepared for how thick and oily the skunk spray was, and kept screaming "*No! Don't shake!*" to Tashmoo, but he, confounded, apparently hadn't learned that command from Aunt Faye or Gavin and kept shaking the slime all over.

Annie ripped off her clothes, including her underwear, zipped them into a plastic bag along with Tashmoo's collar, and dumped the whole lot into the trash can by the shed. She stomped back into the kitchen and slammed the sliding door shut so hard the whole house rattled. Tashmoo, seeming to accept his banishment, gazed at her through the glass with his big droopy eyes, the tip of his tail brushing the deck, and waited.

In tears, Annie called Lindsay, who drove straight over from her house on Makonikey with a concoction of hydrogen peroxide, baking soda, and Joy dish soap. Lindsay tried to make light of it all and, after introducing herself to the kids, hauled Tashmoo over to the hose. She pronounced Annie a real Vineyarder, now that the Island's state animal had officially christened her.

In the noisy solitude of the indoor shower, Annie cried. She leaned her head back and let the hot water run down her throat. She washed her hair three times with shampoo and baking soda and tried to scrub the skunk oil off her body, but there was no use. Her hair and skin would smell forever. She punched her fist against the tile. How could this have happened? Why had she allowed herself to get a dog? She and her little house, not to mention her new car, would never stop smelling of skunk. Nothing would be the same. How could she have been so sucked in by Freddy? By Chase? Where was Gordon? *Why were they even here?*

Freddy had seemed different.

She wrapped herself in Aunt Faye's flannel robe and her hair in a towel, turban-style, and slumped at the table while Lindsay finished drying Tashmoo with a hairdryer, chatting with the girls as they flitted between their Barbies and yesterday's jigsaw puzzle. Robbie had already barricaded himself in the sun porch.

Meg, standing next to Annie, stroked her back and giggled, trying to make a joke of it. "What's done is done, Mommy," she said.

Lindsay gave a start. She was holding up one of Tashmoo's floppy ears and aiming the hairdryer underneath. "That sounds just like something Faye would have said," she remarked quietly to Annie.

"It's not his fault, Mommy," Lily said, indignant, drying Tashmoo's paws with a hand towel. "You had the leash."

Emmie brought the girls upstairs with a new stack of library books, and Lindsay, who knew her way around her old friend Faye's kitchen, gently placed the rose teapot in front of Annie.

"I have so enjoyed watching you fall in love with your dog this summer," she said, pouring steaming tea into the two porcelain cups. "And part of being in love, as you know from your children and your husband, is having to deal with the occasional skunking."

Lindsay seemed to be searching Annie's face, and Annie wondered if she suspected something else was wrong—say, that her new best friend had just proven himself to be an adulterous, immoral, unscrupulous asshole, or that Annie herself was not as virtuous as she seemed.

"It goes with the territory, Annie. Forgive me, but into every life a little skunk juice must spray. Listen to Meg: it's not the end of the world. I wouldn't carry on so."

Lindsay's concoction helped, but as soon as she left it started raining and that made it terrible all over again because, despite Tashmoo's fur being blown dry, the smell was reactivated when Annie let him out in the night and his fur got wet. She couldn't *stand* Tashmoo anymore; she resented him and resolved to give him away, give him to Gavin.

For his part, Tashmoo looked sad and apologetic and confused at this sudden putrid mix of wet dog, garlic, and sulfur that he was emitting. Annie ignored his beseeching looks because she wasn't going to get sucked in by him, too.

The skunk smell had permeated the seats and floor of the station wagon on last night's insufferable drive home from Aquinnah, and Annie's throat was full of bile as she drove the kids to the Center the next day. Whether it was skunk or Freddy, she wasn't sure. The girls held their noses while keeping up their usual chatter, but Robbie was so furious he hung his head out the window in the pouring rain and refused to speak except to mutter, "I *told* you we shouldn't have gone up there in the first place." And, later: "Exactly how old do I have to be to get my own driver's license?"

Annie spied Freddy, with no raincoat, sitting in a rocking chair alone on the covered porch of the Chilmark Store, and ignored how forlorn he looked. Instead, she drove straight back up Middle Road in the windy rain; she could make her own coffee there. She would erase him from her mind, officially write him off. It was almost the end of July, Gordon had hired new people, had airplane reservations for the first of August. She would not need Freddy's coparenting help ever again.

At home, she heard the cardinal calling to her from the protection of its pine tree. What a silly idea, that this was Aunt Faye. It was just some random bird. Annie asked Emmie, noisily eating his cereal, if he would mind driving the kids for the next few days in his Subaru, in which case they should transfer the child seats.

"I don't mind, but you can't stay marooned at home because of the skunk smell in your car, Aunt Anna. Let's try deodorizing it."

He zoomed off to Shirley's Hardware to buy special cleaning ammunition.

As she was running the laundry, squirting spot remover onto the kids' shorts, she heard Emmie move her car closer to the cellar door. He hauled the vacuum cleaner out of the coat closet, lugged it down the rickety stairs, and embarked on sucking up all the sand in her station wagon. Faye's lousy old vacuum cleaner would probably cause all the fuses to blow again.

She decided to join him outside and they began cleaning, keeping the car doors and windows shut because it was raining so hard. The smell was overpowering, but Emmie assured her they'd get used to it soon. Starting on opposite ends, they blasted every inch with more Joy dish soap, glass and leather cleaners, and plenty of all-purpose, deodorizing, antibacterial spray.

"I bet nothing like this has ever happened to your mother," Annie said, working up a sweat as she scrubbed the dashboard. It didn't matter that Tashmoo had remained in self-imposed exile during the drive, huddled in the way back of the car; skunk spray could travel.

"She's not really an outdoorsy type," Emmie said, as if Annie didn't know her own cousin. He was scrunched underneath the rear window swirling both hands in double helixes of Windex. "I think she walked Tashmoo on the sidewalk in broad daylight, and only then a couple of times. My dad and Caroline mostly took care of him. Never in a million years would Mum allow a dog in the car."

"Smart."

"We do have skunks in Wellesley, just not a *plethora* like we do here."

Annie was finished with the dashboard. She twisted her body like a pretzel to attack the front seat, glimpsing the cardinal through the window, watching them.

"How's it going with Jazzy, by the way? Any romance there?" Annie was beginning to get out of breath.

"Me? No, no," Emmie said, ripping off more paper towels and pausing to look at her. "We're just friends. She's really good at the guitar."

"She seems like a very considerate person," Annie mused, scrubbing with even more zeal. How she hated Freddy—and, come to think of it, her father! Did he actually hire that woman she'd seen at South Station, so many years ago? Did her mother know? She, and everyone else in Wellesley, certainly knew about Mrs. Pedrick. What hypocrites! Who were they to criticize her, anyway?

"Wow, Aunt Anna," Emmie said. "You're really going at that armrest."

Call girls? How *could* they?

"It's just skunk, Aunt Anna. It won't last forever." Emmie hung himself upside down over the back seat to rub saddle soap into the leather. "Nice to wash the car, though. It was pretty dirty. Dusty, like."

The front seat looked brand new. The skunk odor had been replaced by an unbearable smell of cleaning chemicals.

"Mum's all right, don't get me wrong," Emmie said. "She's happy when she can read on the porch in Kennebunk. Keep to the clock."

"How so?"

These fumes were probably toxic; maybe they shouldn't be talking.

"Well, she doesn't like disruptions. Golf after breakfast, same foursome. Lunch at the club. Two hours at the beach, tops. Cocktails at five-thirty, always with friends. Dinner at seven."

"So social."

Annie opened the door to take a deep breath of the rain, and the cardinal flew right over to her.

"Sometimes Mum gets, like, worked up. And then she blames Dad."

Annie was suddenly exhausted, dripping wet. She realized she was gasping.

"Dad sails every day, no matter the weather. He's late sometimes to meet their friends, or else all he talks about is sailing. She thinks that's why they don't, like, get invited to every single thing. A boat's a lot of work. Talk about cleaning! I think he stays out there to escape, but don't tell her I said that."

Annie had always assumed Juliet and Lonny had the perfect marriage. They had dated all through college and married right after graduation. Maybe if Annie had married Chase, he would have turned out to be like Lonny—always a little checked out.

"Seems like Mum always has some beef. That's what I like about the Vineyard: people are more understanding. Sympathetic. They're not mad at each other all the time."

Aunt Faye wouldn't be freaking out like this about her friend's confession that he was miserably married and went to call girls. She would try to understand. So would Lindsay.

Annie wedged paper towels down the sides of the seats. No telling how far the skunk oil had spread.

"Nobody's perfect," Emmie continued. "No *thing's* perfect. But all in all, Mum and Dad take pretty good care of each other, I guess." He unlatched the rear door. "Mind if I get out now? I think this is probably as good as we're going to get it, and I told Jazzy I'd meet her before I pick up the kids."

He came around to the front and looked in. "Jeez! It's gleaming in here, Aunt Anna. You oughta come up to Kennebunk next summer and help with the boat. Dad could use someone like you. You'd be great at the brightwork."

Annie climbed out of the car. She arched her back and let her head fall back, closing her eyes and opening her mouth, drinking the raindrops. She extended her arms to her sides and turned up her palms, allowing the rain to wash everything away. The cardinal fluttered to the shelter of its pine tree.

Annie was so soaking wet, she had to wring out the bottom of her tee shirt.

"What d'you say we do the outside, Emmie, since we're already at it? Can you stay a few more minutes?"

She squirted soap around the outside of the car and, with renewed vigor, began scrubbing away the dirt. Her right arm, like all of her, was seething.

"What I like about the Vineyard," Emmie continued, obligingly wiping the back license plate, "is that people don't *judge* like at home and in Kennebunk. I don't have to worry that people are going to get mad at me for some dumb thing I didn't even mean to do. I feel free here, like I can be myself, who I'm supposed to be. Or maybe it's you who makes me feel that way, Aunt Anna. Anyhow, I think being on the Vineyard is helping me, and helping my music. I think I'm getting better."

She didn't judge?

Tashmoo must have sneaked through the kitchen slider and was watching now from across the gravel driveway, afraid to come closer. He still had no idea what he'd done, but he knew he was in some kind of doghouse.

Annie went over the hood once more. The rain was invigorating.

Her father had sounded like a different person on the phone the other day—wise, mellow. Had he really hummed the Beatles? Was he experiencing a fleeting personality change, due to a few stiff drinks at the Maori festival? Or was this something more permanent, a happy consequence of whatever was going on with Fiona's rehabilitation and their bombs-away family therapy in

New Zealand? Or—could he possibly have changed sometime earlier, maybe while Annie had been away in California and Asia, and she hadn't taken the time to notice?

She had no idea what her parents' situation had been. Maybe her mother, God forbid, had cheated on him first! Who knew what it was like to be Freddy, or Noah Trout, or her father, or her brother, Percy? To be anyone? And really, what was worse—missing and thinking about your old boyfriend during your whole marriage, unbeknownst to your husband, or hiring anonymous prostitutes? Moving across an island to live with someone else for a year, or deserting your wife to follow a woman to the other end of the world? There was no answer!

It all depended on what you could tolerate, what you could understand or forgive, how contrite the person was, what their other long-standing virtues happened to be.

Maybe she should stop worrying about other people's marriages and focus on her own.

Emmie stretched. "Seriously, Aunt Anna. I think we did, like, enough."

Annie glimpsed Tashmoo fix his gaze and creep stealthily toward her in the rain. Each time she bent over the car he inched his way forward, like in that children's game red light, green light when you run as fast as you can to try to tag the person whose back is turned.

Back and forth, she flexed more muscle. She almost had the mud off. A combination of sweat and rainwater was beading down her face and neck.

"It's *enough*, Aunt Anna."

Her parents had been married for forty-five years. Her mother had apparently forgiven her father, forgotten about it, or else she would have gone crazy by now. Would Gordon forgive her, assuming she told him? Would he bring up her transgression on their fiftieth anniversary, with their grandchildren all crowded around that polished Indonesian table?

The red cardinal fluttered down from the pine tree and dawdled above the driveway. Aunt Faye would never have held a grudge.

"*Please, Aunt Anna!*" Emmie repeated, opening the cellar door and going inside. "*I think you can stop now!*"

Annie's arm was about to fall off. She let go of her rag, and dropped it in the bucket. The rainwater could clean off the rest.

Tashmoo had crept closer. It wasn't his fault this had happened. It wasn't anyone's fault.

Annie sank down hard on the gravel. She opened her arms and legs wide, and her dog smothered into her, hugging her as best he could with his front paws. He licked her face and slobbered his wet head on her shoulder, and she squeezed her arms around him as she buried her face in his soft, skunky fur.

28

Still a Bit Unsettled

The next morning, Emmie went down-Island with Jazzy in search of new sheet music, and Annie, on her way to Cronig's, stopped by the little post office at Alley's. Gloria Bradshaw had been religious about forwarding the mail from Sylvan Fell; Annie had never had such a helpful neighbor.

Among the bills and letters from friends in Singapore and Shanghai was a familiar-looking light blue envelope, *Annie* written across the middle in a recognizable scrawl. In front of the thin rows of wooden mailboxes among the stacks of newspapers, hoping John Alley wouldn't be in early today, Annie opened it.

It was written on Piper's signature stationery. A pressed flower fell onto the floor when Annie unfolded the paper, and she picked up what was a single, dried violet. Standing there in her shorts, her bare feet and ankles breaded with sand, she read Chase's sloppy cursive.

Dear Annie,

To express my recent humiliation, I looked in the Riverside Shakespeare from that seminar you made me take senior year. It was still in my old bedroom on Indian Hill, where I'd left it. Thinking I'd write, "Oh, what fools these mortals be," I wanted to check whether it was "Oh" or "Ah," knowing how important it is to you that things be perfect. The book happened to fall open to this dried violet on a page with an even better quote, highlighted in yellow. (Must have been your highlighter, since I don't remember owning one.)

"The fool doth think he is wise, but the wise man knows himself to be a fool."

Since I am the only person in my family who has ever read Shakespeare, and this is my book, and I have only ever read Shakespeare with you, I have to assume that you were the one who gave me this violet.

Have I apologized to you with the help of the Bard before? Or, heaven forbid, could you possibly have been apologizing to <u>me</u> for something? Because it was pretty lucky to find the quote I needed on the same page as this flower.

However this happened, I hope you will accept it back, along with my very humble apology.

I also hope you will allow me to explain myself sometime— because, now that you are finally back here on Martha's Vineyard where you belong, we are going to see each other every summer for the rest of our lives. It would be a lot easier if we could get along … or, dare I hope (does that sound Shakespearean?), be friends.

Your embarrassed, foolish knave,
CSC

P.S. Since I know you are wondering, it is actually "<u>Lord</u>, what fools these mortals be."

Annie had given Chase a bouquet of wildflowers one spring day at Brown and read him this quote, from his own volume of Shakespeare, in an attempt to apologize for forgetting a date. But she never imagined he would press and save one of the violets.

Pushing her cart through Cronig's not fifteen minutes later, Annie ran into Chase's mother, Piper St. Clair. She looked tanned and fit in her tennis whites in front of the olives and cocktail dips.

They kissed on both cheeks, and Annie was glad she'd grabbed her baseball cap on the way out to hide her hair, which had been looking really awful lately, probably from the salt water.

She slid Chase's light blue envelope farther into her back pocket.

Piper didn't seem especially surprised to see her, almost as if she were expecting to bump into her one of these days, which meant that Chase had mentioned that Annie was on-Island. He probably hadn't mentioned borrowing her notepaper, and Piper was too polite to let on whether she'd heard about Annie's histrionics at the graveyard. Chase certainly wouldn't have mentioned any other encounter.

They chatted about the weather—"still a bit unsettled"—and the increased traffic, the untimely loss of Faye, how Annie and Gordon had decided to take the kids on a big Christmas trip, first to Sacramento to see their Tucker grandparents and cousins, then to New Zealand to meet their new Robinson cousins. Annie told her that she and Gordon thought they might take up golf, something she'd never anticipated doing, starting with lessons at Percy's new golf academy. Like everyone, they touched briefly on Princess Diana.

"How is your back?" Annie asked, trying to steer the subject away from the demise of fairy tales and British royalty. "I was so sorry to hear you'd broken it."

"Oh, that was a silly thing, dear. Such a stubborn hydrangea! Do you know, in the end Skip had to hire a man with a truck to move it?"

Annie tried to look sympathetic. "Why did you have to move it in the first place?"

"Well, I just thought, you know, it would be happier on the other side of the garden. There's a little less sun there."

Annie picked out a fancy cheese—might be good to have on hand. "Of course," she said. "Was there something wrong with where it was?"

"Well, no, nothing particularly, I just thought ..."

Why did everyone think they could go around moving things

all the time? Why did they have to create so much havoc disturbing everything, presuming things would be better off somewhere else? Why couldn't they just leave things alone?

"So, *is* the hydrangea happier now?"

Piper frowned. "Well, as a matter of fact, no. Not yet. I'll get some more food for it on the way home, now that I think of it. Should do the trick." She reached for another crab dip.

Annie caught herself. Why was she picking on poor Piper about her anemic plant?

"How are your roses?" she asked, changing the subject.

Piper still looked slightly crestfallen about the hydrangea, but perked herself up. "Lovely, dear," she said. "Just beautiful. That was fun when you used to help me in the garden, wasn't it? Remember tying all those tiny rambling roses to the wooden stakes Skip made for us? They're thriving bushes now. I always say, roses need a little boost to get started, same as people. Anyway, I've added some new varieties since then. Must stay with the times, mustn't one?"

Annie smiled. "One must."

Piper squinted to check the expiration date, and smiled brightly. "Oh, Annie, you must come to our garden party this Sunday. You'll forgive such late notice, won't you, but I wasn't sure you were still here. You remember our little soirée, end of July? Summer has that way of slipping by and if you don't have a party, well, you might lose touch with people and next thing you know, they've forgotten you. Chase is flying up Friday night—they still have that place at Abel's Hill. Brooke and her three children have been staying with us all month—I just love every minute. You know, I was hoping you and Brooke might run into each other again."

Piper reached in for some olives, rifling around until she found the kind she wanted. "It would be so nice if you could all be friends. I know you just told me Gordon—that *is* his name, isn't it? I don't know why I always want to call him Gary—is still away, but at least you could meet Élise. The twins are darling, starting to speak a few words of French." She coughed. "Skip's family was originally from France, you know."

Annie smiled and nodded as she restacked some dog bones in her cart.

"Yes, of course you would remember that." Piper started to push her cart toward the aisle with the tonics and sodas. "By the way, dear, no one else will be bringing children." She smiled at Annie's baseball cap, her hand smoothing her own short-cropped white hair. "And how are the Red Sox? Having a good season, I hope?"

Piper was right, just as Freddy was. They had so much shared history, it would be nice if they could all be friends. Was a shame not to be. Chase wasn't Annie's husband—who gave her the right to judge him? She would just have to be very, very careful not to get skunked again.

"I would love to come to your party," Annie said, kissing her again on the cheek. "Thank you for inviting me."

Piper St. Clair, polite woman that she was, called that afternoon while Annie was at the library with the kids and spoke with Emmie. She wanted to make sure Annie remembered how to get to their place from Indian Hill, and dictated detailed directions: "Down the dirt road, left at the new split-rail fence, right at the third tall pine, left at the stone wall." Annie laughed when she saw Emmie's meticulous note. As if she might have forgotten! But it could be a bit awkward, receiving party invitations at the grocery store, and she was grateful to have it formalized. She stuck the note on the refrigerator with a wampum magnet.

After dinner, the telephone rang and Annie answered, hoping it was Gordon. He was so busy now that he didn't call as frequently as he had before, usually just once a day, and he told her about rebuilding his office more than anything else. Freddy's confession, plus all of Lindsay's talk about reuniting with Noah and his moving back into their house at Makonikey—not to mention Chase's behavior, both with her and in the sail shack—had hammered home to Annie how trivial the things were that used to annoy her about him, how silly and irrelevant. They had to make a few changes, but he was a great husband; he was her family and he was her best friend, and she couldn't wait to be back in his arms.

Instead, it was Tommy on the phone, asking in his little voice what they were doing tomorrow after the Center.

"We would really like to see you guys," he said. "There aren't many days left until we have to leave. Please could you meet us at the beach? Dad says it's not supposed to rain."

Annie stood in her messy, still skunky-smelling kitchen and looked across her field, newly mown by the caretaker Caleb's grandson. An eight-year-old voice was impossible to resist. It was time to move on.

After lunch the next day, she procrastinated leaving—throwing in another load of laundry, deciding to clean out the refrigerator—and they got to Lucy Vincent later than usual, only to be met on the dirt road by a stopped line of cars. The lot was full, and they'd have to wait until someone left and freed up a space.

The parking attendant, who was their friend now, poked her head in the window. "You might as well turn your engine off, Annie," she said. "This is how it's going to be until Labor Day. The August people seem to have arrived a few days early, oh joy."

It was hot sitting there with the windows down, and the heat seemed to activate the skunk smell, even though they'd left Tashmoo at home today.

"*Everything* activates this *pestilence*," Robbie growled.

"I think you mean *pungency*," Annie said. "Good word, though."

"I mean *pestilence*. My camp counselor said."

The girls, who had been bickering in the back seat, began swatting each other. Hoping to preempt a fight, Annie unsnapped Meg from her car seat and brought her to her lap, putting a towel down between them, they were so sweaty. As she reflexively kissed her little girl's neck, she noticed that it, too, smelled slightly of skunk, and that any trace of baby vanilla was officially gone.

"Robbie, why don't you pour everyone a glass of that nice cold water?" Annie suggested, sliding her seat back. She didn't mind waiting here on the road, since she wasn't exactly dying to face Freddy. "Hmm, water. That reminds me. Did I ever tell you the famous Wampanoag legend of Tashmoo?"

"Here we go again," muttered Robbie.

"In olden times on Martha's Vineyard," Annie began, "finding fresh water was a real problem. One day, a Wampanoag princess dreamt that her son Tashmoo, the swiftest runner of all her children, had discovered a beautiful, clear lake that no one knew about yet. The next day she told Tashmoo where she'd dreamt that this lake was, and he ran down from the Aquinnah Cliffs to look for it. He raced all over the Island looking, and was just about to give up, when at last, sparkling through some woods, he saw a crystal-clear lake exactly as his mother had described. See? He had confidence in his mother, he trusted her. He didn't give up, because he had faith that she knew what she was talking about. That's why they named Lake Tashmoo after him."

"So if we mind you, we might find a lake," Lily giggled.

"They named it Lake Tashmoo because he was the one who discovered the lake, not because he minded his mother," Robbie pointed out.

"Because of both," said Annie.

29

The Rescue

———

Eventually one of the cars left, and they were able to park.

"I don't know why we're *schlepping* all this stuff," Robbie grumbled again, as they trudged practically the whole length of the big parking lot up to the beach path. "We're probably going to stay only an hour anyway, we're so late. The sun is barely out."

He was right: dark clouds were suddenly scudding across the sky.

Lucy Vincent was more crowded than they had ever seen it, with a lot of new people who seemed to be sticking to themselves and lying on their own blankets, as people do on regular beaches. It no longer looked like a giant cocktail party. The Tuckers waved to Gavin up on his chair and he held his hands up as if to say, "Where've you been?"

The Rosenthals, in their usual place, looked ecstatic that they'd finally shown up. Freddy opened a beach chair for Annie with more politeness than usual. Tommy gave her a long hug and showed her his new book.

"So many people are here today, we almost couldn't find you," Annie said. "I feel as if our beach has been invaded."

"Time to return to America and the real world, I guess, sad to say," Freddy said, lowering his voice to a whisper. "I'm beside myself, Annie. I have my kids only until the first." He looked like he was about to cry. "But I am very happy to see you, my *chaver*. I've missed you."

Did he realize she had deliberately been avoiding him?

"What's a *chaver*?"

"A chum, a best friend. What you have been for me this summer." He attempted a grin. "Though you didn't help my diet much." He held up a Humphrey's chocolate chip cookie before popping it in his mouth. "God, I love these. Best cookies in the world, or what."

"Diets-*shmyets*," Annie said, and they both laughed. There was no use being mad at him; he wasn't her husband. And he was right. She didn't know what it felt like to be that lonely, to feel unwanted by your spouse. "Robbie just used the word *schlepp*, incidentally."

Freddy grinned and she could tell he was relieved, that he sensed she'd forgiven him. He leaned over to whisper in her ear. "I was worried I was an idiot to have told you. Thank God you have the patience to understand, didn't write me off. And please let me apologize for saying those unkind things to you. I don't really think you're a ditz. Not one hundred percent sure about the blinders, though." He popped in another cookie, still grinning. "You know something, Annie? You're wonderful."

"What are we reading today?" Lily asked. "Oh no, Beatrice. Your *hair*."

Freddy straightened up in his chair. "For the life of me, I cannot get the three sections of the braid to stay together the way you showed me. *The Lion, the Witch and the Wardrobe.* So what do you say, guys? A quick dip? Oy, it's humid. Want to go in, Lily?"

"I better stay and work on Beatrice's hair."

"A lot of whitecaps today," Annie said, smearing sunscreen on Meg's back. "Do you want to go in, Robbie? You'll be sure to stay close to Freddy?"

"I'm probably the only person on this beach older than twelve who hasn't read this before," Freddy said, handing the Narnia book to Annie and heaving himself up. "I checked it out this morning. Our friend the librarian recommended it." He folded his glasses into their case and slid them into the pocket of the

Black Dog bag. "But you keep going and I'll catch up later."

The four males bounded into the water, and Annie started reading out loud from their place in *The Lion, the Witch and the Wardrobe*. Two paragraphs in, just as Lucy was first venturing through the wardrobe, the wind whipped up and sand sprayed into their faces. Annie put down the book to study the water.

Lily stopped brushing Beatrice's hair and stared at the ocean, also listening. "The waves sound like a wall," she said.

Lily was right; the waves weren't normal.

"I've changed my mind," Annie said. "I'm going to tell them to get out. It's altogether too rough, too crowded." She stood up. "Lily, I want you to take the little girls up to the reading rock right now, and do not let them out of your sight. Take the hairbrush— you and Meg can work out the knots in Beatrice's hair from up there. I don't like the boys being in the water today."

Annie darted to shore. In the water, there were so many new, unfamiliar faces bobbing up and down beyond the break, and so many whitecaps all of a sudden, that it took a while to spot Freddy and the three boys treading water beside him. There was something different about Freddy: he looked tired.

Annie glanced behind to make sure the girls had reached their rock, and noticed that the dark storm clouds had morphed into a massive gathering behind them to the northwest, over Squibnocket. Anvil clouds, these were called, because they came out of nowhere offshore and hammered you.

They needed to get off the beach.

She looked back out to sea and suddenly saw a single, gigantic wave, the hugest she had ever seen on the Vineyard, looming toward them—as gigantic as the ones she and Gordon used to watch surfers chase after in Bali. It looked like a monster, its breaking crest a shark's mouth of white teeth.

It was a colossal wall of water and was headed toward them from a different direction, separate from the other waves. Even over the ocean's roar, Annie could hear everyone screaming—like when a packed roller coaster plummets headfirst. But she could see that not all of the swimmers saw it coming, and she began frantically waving her arms and shouting to everyone, pointing, all the while keeping her eyes fixed on Robbie and the Rosenthals.

A mother next to Annie, dipping her baby's bare feet in the foam, scooped her in her arms and tore up the beach with the baby swinging backward from her hip, crying. Two teenagers throwing a Frisbee let it fall and dashed after her. There was no outrunning this wave for anyone in the water, though: they would either have to dunk underneath it and pray, or somehow attempt to swim it in. Annie, helpless, kept waving her arms and staring, petrified.

Gavin had jumped down from his chair and was blowing his whistle, with two lifeguards Annie didn't recognize. *"Look out! Rogue wave!"*

But only people on the shore could hear them.

Annie watched the wave consume Robbie and everyone else. Together, the swimmers disappeared in a furious, white roil of foam precisely as an electric bolt of lightning zigzagged out of the clouds into the sea west of the horizon, far off Squibnocket Point.

The lifeguards again blew their whistles and screeched for everyone to get out of the water and off the beach.

The enormous rogue wave kept advancing toward Annie, and she saw people caught in all different depths of it—arms, legs thrashing. Although it started to diminish as it advanced up the shoreline, the face of it was at least six feet high. She could not see the boys. The water forced her to start jogging backward, but it was pushing at her with so much power that she had to turn and sprint forward up the beach so it wouldn't knock her down. The wave met the slope of the sand and became fast-flowing water, as if a levy had just given way, and didn't begin to recede until it was halfway to the dunes.

Soaked up to her waist, Annie scanned the sea for the boys and jogged back toward the ocean through knee-deep water. She glanced behind again and saw the girls safely on the high reading rock, Lily and Meg cross-legged behind Beatrice, obliviously brushing out her curls and singing.

People, screaming, were crazily gathering up children and sprinting up the beach in their bathing suits to the parking lot, leaving their drenched towels and bags behind.

Annie kept jogging with the receding water, toward the waves. Swimmers were swarming past her, shouting and trying to find each other in the chaos; some crawled out on their knees, hurt, smashed the wrong way; many were bleeding, their bodies torn and scraped from getting dragged across the slew of stones before the shore.

Another bolt of lightning crackled into the ocean and Gavin blew his whistle in her ear. *"Everybody off the beach!"*

Where were the boys? More swimmers staggered out and it was like the scene in *Jaws* when someone shouts "Shark!" and the whole beach becomes hysterical. The two other lifeguards were farther down the sand, shepherding people to the parking lot and taking stock of injuries. Their shrill whistles sounded like ambulance sirens.

Trying not to panic, squinting, Annie was finally able to make out Robbie and Ben riding in a normal-size wave and Freddy still out there, turning around and looking side to side, treading water.

But where was Tommy? She couldn't find him in the white froth and rising swells, and in a second, it seemed, the clouds had amassed into a cold, ominous black fog that blocked out the sun.

A mother with a crying little boy, his arm hanging askew, rushed up to Gavin.

"I've radioed for ambulances, but you need to take him to the hospital!" Gavin shouted, just as a lone teenage girl, sobbing, nearly fell on top of him, her face all ripped and bloody.

"Annie, everybody out? Only Freddy still in there?" Gavin hollered over the girl, tearing off his tee shirt to wipe blood from her face. But before Annie could shout back, he was surrounded by more people and swept up in the sand.

Waiting, still scanning for Tommy, Annie felt a few fat raindrops splash on her arms. A second later it began pouring, just as Robbie and Ben, holding hands to support each other, at last clambered over the pebbles, both shaking uncontrollably.

"Where are the girls, Mommy?" Robbie gasped, looking backward to the water. *"Where are the girls?"*

Annie pointed to the reading rock, and then wrapped her arms tightly around both boys.

Robbie exhaled with relief and began crying. "That was a rogue wave, Mommy! My counselor told me about them! Freddy told us to hold hands and hold our breath and wait beneath it!"

The boys, breathing so hard that they were barely able to talk, gripped each side of her.

Annie, hugging them both, forced her voice to sound calm. "Did you see Tommy?"

"Dad—had him. They—were holding—hands!" Ben panted, and he began to sob.

"Do you see Tommy anywhere now?"

Another split of lightning crackled out at sea.

The three of them raced back and forth along the shore to look, but no one was in the water except Freddy, and there were no children in sight at all. Everyone had run up the beach already, and Tommy wouldn't have done that. He would have found Annie.

He must still be out there.

Annie held both boys by the shoulders. She saw Gavin fifty yards away, still surrounded by people. "I am going in after Tommy, and you need to tell that to Gavin. Then I want you to get the three girls from the reading rock," she commanded, pointing through the rain. "Bring them inside Freddy's car right now, as fast as you can. Leave all the stuff. But first, find Gavin. *Run!*"

Robbie stared at her and did not move.

"Trust me, Robbie! Find Gavin! Stay together! *Go!*"

The boys, holding hands and looking terrified, took off.

She could see Freddy, still treading water, looking in every direction except hers.

"*I don't have Tommy!*" she shrieked, waving her arms frantically at him across the dark pouring rain and crashing waves. But he kept looking side to side, and Annie, her body braced with panic, realized he couldn't see anything because he wasn't wearing his glasses.

Another jolt of lightning zapped behind Freddy, closer this time, and he started swimming into shore. He must be assuming Tommy had made it in.

Annie waded over the millions of washed-up pebbles and peered across the water. It was difficult to make out anything in the slanting rain and the dark. She was the only one standing in the water and could faintly sense the lifeguards on the sand blowing their whistles and waving their arms and people dashing around, when she finally glimpsed what had to be Tommy, floating out and alone to the east, a tiny white speck on the vast green sea.

Lightning zapped again.

Between Tommy and where she stood was a mountain range of ocean waves.

Annie looked back again to Gavin. The boys were part of a throng of people surrounding him now. The other lifeguards had disappeared. Freddy was headed in to the west, to their right, the opposite direction of where Tommy was being carried.

Annie peeled off her wet cover-up and let it drop. She dove in diagonally east, to the left.

She kicked hard into the crest of the first menacing wave and let it pass over her. Up for air, she took a breath and swam into the next one, kicking furiously and pulling through it toward the next.

Seven, eight, nine huge waves rumbled toward her.

She had to close her eyes as she muscled through the waves, but the second she'd emerge into the froth, she somehow managed to locate Tommy—minuscule, floating, his skinny arms outstretched to buoy himself up. She couldn't lose sight of him.

The teeming rain was cold and pelted her face. Lightning flashed again in the distance. It was impossible to tell what was rain or what was salt water; to hear what was wind or what was the ocean or what was thunder.

Finally through the last, enormous wave, Annie swam overhand, her head up and eyes focused. No words were in her mind, and she wasn't aware of her fast breathing or water sloshing into her mouth or the gunmetal color of the sea or the boiling swells she swam through once she passed the break.

Tommy didn't see her because he was looking away instead of toward shore, probably to steel himself against any more rogue waves. She didn't bother trying to yell over the roar. The current was pulling him east and also out. She had to outswim the tide.

He turned his head and she thought he saw her, but a swell suddenly blocked their view and she lost him altogether.

Terrified that he was sinking, Annie reached her arms forward as far as she could and swam harder. She had to keep turning her head to the side to breathe, but salt water surged into her mouth anyway and she started choking. She forced herself to swallow and focused on keeping her mouth closed, her neck and head up, her eyes on the place where he had been. She could not see him.

The wind sounded alive—an all-encompassing, boundless, relentless roar.

She swam strong in his direction, and just as the whole sky became a smoky black wall of thunderheads, Tommy bobbed back up. A deafening, primeval thunder boom reverberated to the bottom of the sea.

He saw her.

Another lightning bolt.

Annie swam overhand farther, fast and sure, her heart pounding. But then, a few yards before him, a weird thing happened. She switched to a smooth breaststroke and managed to take command of her voice. The last thing she wanted was for him to panic and grab onto her. Hadn't Robbie recently regaled her with one of his camp counselor's tales of a double drowning?

The lifeguards must be on their way. She could do this a little while longer.

"Hold on, Tommy!" she shouted.

He wasn't able to talk and she was afraid it was because he had swallowed so much water, but it was because his teeth were chattering like a Halloween skeleton's.

"Keep your eyes on me! Do not grab my neck!"

He nodded, his skinny legs somehow still cycling beneath the surface, his arms circling outstretched.

A wave folded them toward each other, and she pulled him against her. It was very hard to stay up without the use of her arms, but somehow her legs kicked harder.

"Lie flat and I will pull you!"

He leaned backward so she could reach her arm across his chest. The swells were high even out here, and she let them be buoyed for a few seconds while she caught her breath.

"I'm going to bring you in! I will not let anything happen to you!" she shouted again. "Try to keep your mouth closed! You're okay, Tommy!"

The storm had churned everything up and they were being swirled around amid huge whitecaps, but the prevailing wind on Martha's Vineyard is southwest and that, plus this blessedly buoyant salt water, would help them swim back. Freddy would have seen Gavin and he would be on his way out with the kayak. They were going to be fine—as long as they didn't get struck by lightning.

Annie tightened her right arm around Tommy's small chest and started side-stroking him in. But ... they didn't move forward at all. It was just like before, at Long Point. She kicked harder, but they drifted east, seaward, and all at once, as before, the water got very cold.

She had just swum them into a rip current.

They must be in one of those chance underground troughs, and there was nothing to do but float along and, once again, wait it out. Annie wanted to resist, to swim against the tide, but she forced herself to resist the impulse. She had to make herself resist the resisting, to surrender and float, to trust that they would pass out of this, just as she had before.

The ocean really had not felt especially cold before now. They could handle this for a minute.

Another crack of lightning zapped the water. Annie's eyes were burning from the assault of rain and she looked for the rescue kayak, but nothing was coming.

She felt so remarkably tiny, so insignificant. Like a speck in the universe—isn't that what Freddy had said? Yet ... there was no way she and Tommy were alone: the lifeguards must be on their way. They just needed to trust, to wait. This current would lose its grip on them soon. But even if it didn't, there was no way she would let them get sucked under.

Anyhow, if for some reason help didn't come, she was pretty sure she could swim them back.

Another zap of lightning, another boom of thunder.

Tommy's huge eyes rolled toward the lightning.

"It won't get us, don't worry!"

They floated a little farther east, and there was another zap. She squinted again and could make out that they were past the nude beach, fast approaching the sandy expanse by the pond. She finally discerned Freddy, blurry and far away, running along the beach with two lifeguards—Gavin and someone else. Gavin was carrying a kayak.

"Gavin is coming, Tommy!"

Something in the water shifted—it suddenly felt warmer. They had drifted out of the rip. Pulling Tommy, Annie began swimming at a right angle to the flow, parallel to the beach. This time they advanced toward shore. She was confident she could make it in from here, but would let the kayak catch up.

"We're almost home, Tommy! *Kick!*"

Gavin was paddling toward them and she could see the other lifeguard standing on the shore with Freddy, his arm blocking him, holding him back.

In a moment Gavin was upon them. "You okay?" he shouted, tossing her two round life preservers. "Hold onto my paddle and put these on!"

He leaned over and hauled Tommy up by his arm and reeled him lengthwise onto the narrow boat.

Cords that connected to both life preservers were tied to Gavin's lifejacket. "Gotta get in quick. Let's go!"

He spun the kayak around, and Annie, wearing the life preserver, swam behind in the pouring rain. The muscles in Gavin's back were so exaggerated that he looked like one of those rowers in the old paintings in the Edgartown Museum, of men battling enormous swells to pull a harpooned whale to their ship.

Gavin was trying to angle them back toward Lucy Vincent, but it was too hard and he had to go in the direction of the current. He tried to paddle them straight ahead, but the water sloshed in every direction, and it seemed that every time he would start to go forward up a wave, they'd be pitched back down.

Annie clenched her mouth shut, but ocean water poured up her nose. She was getting tossed back and forth behind him and had to keep kicking as hard as she could to keep herself above water. A lightning bolt splintered and filled the sky, and at last they got to the break.

Through the dark and rain she could see Freddy and the other lifeguard, waiting. Waves were whipping around them, but somehow, standing with their legs apart, they both held their ground. This lifeguard must have insisted that Freddy not go in lest he collapse or get struck by lightning, and Freddy's eyes were streaming with frustration. He looked like a trapped animal scared out of his mind.

Annie righted herself, extending her toes to see if she could stand, but she couldn't. She kicked a little harder and the kayak glided over another wave, and at last she could feel the ground beneath her. Never in her life had she felt more grateful for the pebbles, for the solid earth beneath her feet.

They were far down on the open expanse of beach by the pond, and would have a slow march back.

Freddy lifted Tommy off the kayak. He hoisted him up long against the front of his body, but it was awkward with the life preserver and Tommy's legs dangled down in front. Freddy heaved his own legs forward and plowed through the stormy water like Moshup himself.

Once they reached the packed sand, Freddy fell to his knees and ripped the preserver off Tommy. Annie watched him wrap his arms around him and bury his face into his back, hugging him hard.

"We gotta go, Freddy," Gavin said, and without a word, Freddy boosted Tommy back up and carried him on his hip like a toddler.

Her life preserver still connected to Gavin's, Annie's legs buckled and she crawled out of the water on her knees, just as she had at Long Point. Again, she had to propel herself forward with her arms to stay ahead—not only of the waves crashing behind her, but also of the *swooosh* of water that wanted to pull her back. The rescue cord snaked slack around her in the froth.

Lightning again, just offshore now, and Gavin came back beside her.

"We have to get off the beach, Annie!"

He guided her up, his arm tight around her. She could not stop her knees from shaking, but somehow with his help she was able to get onto the dry sand. The life preserver was slowing her down so she lifted it off, but she was afraid not to be connected to Gavin anymore. Her legs felt like pilings of solid lead.

Freddy refused to put Tommy down even though he claimed he was fine, so the other lifeguard began pushing them from behind, both hands on Freddy's back. Tommy, giving in and shivering, rested his head against his father's mammoth chest. His top teeth had chattered right through his bottom lip. It was bleeding and, along with his ears, fingers, and toes, had turned blue.

They slogged through the dark and the wind and the pelting rain until at last they reached the main beach and everyone's towels and chairs and bags, left there soaking.

It seemed to Annie as if several hours had passed since she'd left her children on the sand. She felt totally removed, as if she had just swum off the world, and was unprepared for the sheer bedlam that greeted them when they at last made it to the Lucy Vincent parking lot. They had, in fact, only been in the water for a few minutes. A zigzag of cars was trying to funnel its way through to South Road around a tall ambulance, siren wailing and red light spinning, fighting toward them like a salmon spawning upstream.

The ambulance slammed on its brakes in front of Freddy's Suburban, and two EMTs leapt out and rushed at them. Annie was freezing cold and couldn't stop shivering, but her legs had recovered enough for her to try to bolt toward the car and her kids.

"Get in the ambulance!" Gavin commanded, steering her by the shoulders. "I'll cover the kids."

Freddy refused to hand Tommy over, so in a cluster they stumbled, crouching, into the back. The heat inside the ambulance was blasting and it felt claustrophobic, suffocating after being outside, and Freddy's size made it feel even more crowded.

He kept saying "Oh, my God, oh, my God," and kissing Tommy's face and arms.

"We're going to wrap you up tight like a burrito," Tommy's EMT said, swaddling him in two blankets and then in an aluminum one, the kind the beach patrol had wrapped Annie in at Long Point, the kind Gordon wore after his marathons.

"Sounds good," said Tommy, grinning through his chattering teeth.

Out of nowhere, Annie's EMT produced a pair of scissors and, without hesitating, slit through the top of her old two-piece. She was horrified because Freddy was staring straight at her from the bench opposite, until she remembered he couldn't see much without his glasses—and anyway, the EMT was blocking his view.

The EMT stuffed heat packs under her armpits and between her thighs, told her to squeeze her legs together. Then he quickly wrapped her in two heated, heavenly cotton blankets, and wrapped another aluminum blanket on top, over those.

Annie tried to tell the EMT that she needed to get to her children in the car next to them, but he ordered her not to talk and slid a thermometer under her tongue. He examined her eyes with a tiny flashlight and checked her pulse and blood pressure and, when he was finished with all that, handed her a steaming cup of tea with glucose added to it. He waited for her to drink it down and told her how amazing she was to have performed such a textbook rescue, and how lucky it was that the South Shore water wasn't that cold now that it was almost August.

Tommy's EMT said he wanted to warm up Tommy a little more, and wanted them to wait. Annie's EMT didn't want to let her outside while there was still lightning, but she was able to persuade him since the two vehicles were essentially touching. He let her keep the big aluminum blanket and make a run for it.

Robbie was watching out the window, and swung open the back door. Lily and Meg tumbled over the back seat to get to her, and Annie hugged her three children harder than she ever had. She was filled with a sense of gratitude more powerful even than she'd felt the first time she'd held each of them as newborns, or at Long Point, and buried her face in the tops of their beautiful heads. She couldn't get enough of them.

She wouldn't let go, and eventually opened her arms wider to include Ben and Beatrice. She didn't know whether her skin was durable enough to contain the joy she felt, and thought she might explode out of it.

They sat, rocking like this on and around her lap, and she told them everything that had happened.

"It's what I figured," Robbie pronounced. "We should start the car, Mommy. You need to stay warm, and we need to get the car ready for Tommy. A nice lady loaned Ben and me her dry towels."

"You must have been so scared," Annie said.

They all nodded, some of them still crying.

"I knew you knew what you were doing out there, Mommy," Robbie said, talking very fast. "I told Gavin you were going in after Tommy and he got the kayak. But it was up the beach and there was only one lifeguard to help him, because so many people got hurt in the wave."

"I told Robbie a lot of times," Lily said. "Mommy always comes back."

"Yeah," Robbie said. "She did."

"I knew you had your wampum bracelet, Mommy."

"That's another silly legend, Lily," said Robbie. "There's no such thing as magic."

Meg popped out her thumb. "Magic works."

"Maybe there is magic on Martha's Vineyard," Lily said, diplomatically.

Ben and Beatrice looked toward Robbie for validation, since he was the authority on all things.

"I think they might be right," he said at last.

Ben handed Annie a sweatshirt. "My dad always keeps one for each of us in the car now."

Annie kissed them all again and, turning her back to the kids, pulled it on over her bare breasts and wrapped herself back up in the aluminum. She wondered, for a split second, whether her skin might at last be rid of the smell of skunk.

Freddy, holding Tommy, was banging on the back door. They piled in too, and Ben and Beatrice smothered them before everyone else joined in, and there was plenty of hugging and kissing in the Suburban all around. It was still pouring rain, and with the heat on and the motor running, it was a nice place to be, although it didn't take long to become intensely steamy.

"Can we open the window a crack?" Annie asked. "I can't breathe in here."

They all jumped as another bolt of lightning split across the sky.

"Not yet, Mommy," Robbie said. "Not until the lightning passes."

Tommy was fine, apparently unaware of how much danger he had really been in. He seemed embarrassed about all the fuss, particularly mortified about the attention from the EMT. The first thing he said was, "The doctor in there cut off my bathing suit."

Ben handed him another sweatshirt and a dry pair of shorts.

"Thank goodness," Tommy said, and they all laughed. "How long did I tread water for, Annie?"

"A long time."

Another roll of thunder boomed, and Annie wasn't sure whether it was their happiness or the thunder that was causing Freddy's Suburban to quiver so much.

"Do you think I can tell my swimming teacher when we get

back to New York, and he'll let me skip to the next level?"

"Absolutely," Annie said, kissing him again.

"Did you know this is actually the safest place we could be right now?" Robbie asked, his words still coming fast. "Did you hear that thunder? I just counted to six, so basically it's a mile away from us. For every five seconds you can count between the time you see lightning and hear the thunder, it's one mile."

Annie and Freddy exchanged glances over the six bobbling heads.

"You were safest when you were swimming, did you know that, Mommy? Better to be in the ocean than in a swimming pool, or in a bathtub with the window open. Salt water is good—it interrupts the electricity, something like that. Otherwise the fish would keep getting electrocuted. It's probably more dangerous for you to talk to Daddy on the phone during a lightning storm than to be swimming in the ocean, Mommy, isn't that amazing?"

He paused for breath.

"How on earth do you know all this?" Annie asked.

"I keep telling you! My *counselor*. That guy's a genius."

Pretty soon the kids climbed to the way back to play a clapping game, and Freddy and Annie sat talking in the middle.

"I don't know how I lost him," Freddy said. "That huge wave came, I was holding him tight with both hands, he was right next to me, we came out of the wave, there was so much spray, then I lost him. I couldn't see him, couldn't see anything. Lauren is going to crucify me, Annie. In one year, I've wrecked everything. Destroyed my family, the only thing that means anything to me."

Annie took his hand. "No one was prepared for that wave, Freddy," she said. "That's why they call it a *rogue* wave—it's not normal. We don't have waves like that here. There was nothing you could have done."

"I should never have allowed such a little kid out there."

"He's been managing all summer just fine," Annie said. "Everything is okay, it's all right, it's over. You're just going to have to figure out how to forgive yourself, that's all. And I think Lauren will forgive you, too … I bet you'll even be friends again one day." She kept stroking his back, trying to soothe him. "Nobody's perfect, Freddy. You just keep being your best self, and she won't be able to resist your friendship."

"You have so much *rachmonus*," Freddy said, tears starting to spill down his cheeks again. "Compassion."

"God, we're lucky," Annie said. "We are so, so lucky."

He kept thanking her, over and over. "What if you hadn't been there? What if you hadn't gone in?" Then, he remembered. "Oh, Annie," he moaned, pressing his head against the back of the leather car seat and wincing, still crying. "You have that *thing*, that thing about waves."

Annie took his hand. "You want to know something weird?" She was warm now, but kept the aluminum wrapped around her legs. "When I got caught in that riptide last month at Long Point, I heard Chase's voice in my mind. That's why I didn't give up. This time I didn't hear anything other than the wind and the waves, but I just knew I could do it. I had this feeling that everything was going to be okay. Maybe that's why I wasn't afraid."

"You don't need Chase anymore, that's why," Freddy said, his voice shaking. "You have all the power and strength you need within yourself."

And with that, he collapsed into Annie's lap, and his crying turned into vehement sobbing. The kids glanced over the back seat at him briefly before going back to their game, and Annie silently held his massive body in her arms. He was, she knew, crying about everything—Tommy, Lauren, what he'd done to his marriage, the loss of his father. She kept patting his back as she tried to comfort him, her dear friend, her *chaver*.

After a while, he sat up again and wiped his cheeks with the backs of his fists. "First thing I do when I get home is go on a diet," he said. "Join a gym. Get into shape."

He blew his nose in a kind of loud honk, then jutted forth his nose, sniffing. Up and down, he sniffed the stale air around the three rows of the car before at last settling on Annie's wet, stringy hair. "Does anybody else in here smell skunk?"

Everybody burst out laughing.

They sat there for a while longer until, as abruptly as the off-shore storm had swept in, the blustery clouds swept out. The parking lot, in an instant, reversed back in time from twilight to late afternoon.

They opened the car windows. It was as humid outside as in, but the air felt glorious. Everyone became disentangled.

"Where are my glasses? I can't see a thing. I was petrified out there without my glasses," Freddy said, starting to sound like himself again.

"Here, Dad, sorry," Ben said. "Annie told us to run straight to the car, but I grabbed our bag anyway. I knew you'd need them to drive."

"You know, Freddy, you could fix your eyes," Robbie offered. "There's this new thing, I think it's called Lasik, or laser something, eye surgery. Then you could see when you swim."

"Let me guess," said Freddy. "Your counselor had that?"

They clamored out and Freddy stood tall, once more like Moshup. He reached his arms to the sky.

"What's the area code for Heaven? I want to call my father and tell him we're all right."

That's when Annie, standing above him on the running board of his car, began to cry.

"He already knows, Freddy," she managed to say. "Everyone already knows."

And at that moment they all looked up to see, rising out of the ocean over the scrub brush and the dunes, the magnificent arc of a rainbow.

30

Recovering, Reframing

Friday morning was cold and overcast, and Annie declared a day off from camp. She still couldn't get enough of her children, and kept spontaneously hugging and squeezing them. No one complained.

Emmie made banana pancakes and, as they sat around the long table sopping up extra Vermont maple syrup, Primo knocked on the door with a hot, extra-large Hawaiian pizza he had made especially for them. Annie had never tasted a more delicious breakfast.

They piled together on her bed, reading *Harry Potter* again. Tashmoo wanted to join them and placed his front paws on the quilt, hoping to inch his way up when no one was looking, but there Annie drew the line.

Jazzy rode her bike over, her backpack full of ingredients to make chicken soup. As Annie hugged her, she said she'd never heard any sound more comforting than her affable Boston accent.

Emmie kept repeating how heroic they'd all been, insisting Annie and the kids spend the whole day in bed, because he was worried about a syndrome he'd recently read about called post-traumatic stress disorder. They needed to be on the lookout for it, he said.

Freddy called to thank her, again going on and on about her courage, and mentioned that he and his kids were also taking the day off. Someone from Morrice Florist brought over a big bouquet of pink roses with a note in Tommy's careful printing that said, *Thank you to the bravest mom I know. Love, Tommy.*

Annie tucked the note in her drawer. They must have driven all the way down to Vineyard Haven to order the flowers.

Lindsay had heard, somehow, and arrived to hear the whole story, but first she took Tashmoo for a walk in the woods. Annie didn't feel particularly traumatized by the rescue, but she couldn't stop asking herself, *What if I hadn't gotten to him in time?* She mentioned this to Lindsay, who said it was important she reframe the story as quickly as possible and focus on the fact that she *did* get to him in time. Lindsay had a way of clarifying everything, of seeing silver linings.

Heather and Apple brought over warm cookies on their way to yoga; they told her she was a celebrity and that everyone was talking about her. Caleb and Jane brought a bouquet of sunflowers from their garden. John Alley and his wife dropped by with a basket of picture-perfect tomatoes from their garden, too.

Gavin stopped by after lunch and they relived the whole thing, wave by wave. Afterward, he asked if he could help her by taking Tashmoo for a while, and whistled for him to follow him out of the house. Annie watched, dumbfounded, as her trusted protector and confidant leapt up, trotted down the path without a backward glance, and jumped into the front seat of Gavin's truck.

Was there no one truly steadfast? Did all faithfulness have a limit? Was every behavior dictated by the situation? One morning Annie happened to forget to walk him, and he simply ditched her for someone else? Lily suggested they find out what sort of dog treats Gavin had, and that they buy the same kind.

Juliet called from Kennebunk, and Robbie took over reading out loud to the girls so Annie could speak to her on the deck. Emmie, of course, had already told her and Lonny all about it, so after Juliet congratulated her ("Although why did you go to the beach in the first place, if the weather looked so iffy?"), she brought up something else entirely. Annie had to go inside and find a pen and paper to write down telephone numbers and addresses, including email addresses, after which Juliet told her the time had come: she absolutely must buy her own personal computer as soon as they returned to Sylvan Fell.

When Annie latched the telephone back on the wall, she felt a sense of calm, quiet excitement permeate her whole being, a sense of purpose similar to what she'd felt the first time she'd held each one of her babies. No confusion, no difficulty thinking this through: she knew what she was going to do.

The phone rang again, and it was a reporter from the *Vineyard Gazette* wanting to interview her. There hadn't been a rogue wave of that magnitude on Martha's Vineyard in anyone's recent memory.

Honestly, it was getting embarrassing.

Friday evening, a tree that had been struck by lightning during the storm on Thursday fell across Middle Road, taking out the telephone wires and causing all of Chilmark and West Tisbury to lose service. Annie didn't realize this until she went to bed, wondering why Gordon hadn't called for his usual goodnight chat, and she actually picked up the receiver to see if there was a dial tone. Too tired to track down her cell phone, she decided to hunt for it tomorrow morning, his Saturday night, and call him then—even though it would be very expensive. She would tell him the story … or maybe she wouldn't. Maybe she'd relived it enough and would tell him next week, after he got here.

Annie could not wait to see Gordon. She wished she could skip over the days until August first, make it come sooner. She worried she hadn't empathized with him enough while he'd been away, vowed to take better care of him. What he had endured in Hong Kong this month was horrific. She felt a strange sensation in the center of her body—in her soul, almost. At first she thought it might be residual ocean water from all that she'd swallowed and inhaled, but then she recognized it for what it was: bonafide yearning for her husband. She missed listening to him breathe while they slept wrapped up in each other, missed not knowing where one of them began and the other ended, missed her spot in the middle of his breastbone. It was time for him to come home.

But the next morning, when she did try calling from her cell phone, she was met with a fast busy signal every time she dialed. Something was wrong with the international data plan—had she forgotten to pay it? Gordon later called her cell phone, but apparently the wind wasn't blowing the right way and it never rang, even though she had it in the pocket of her shorts. Annie didn't even notice that he had left a message—it seemed to appear magically—until that afternoon, and when she finally listened to it, found his words strangely unsatisfying. He didn't say much, and his tone was oddly, uncharacteristically breezy. As she put down the phone she felt overwhelmed, awed at how far apart they were.

Late Saturday afternoon, Annie managed to gather enough energy to take Lily down to Edgartown to find a dress for the St. Clair garden soirée.

At a shop on Main Street, they found a sleeveless lavender linen with a simple boat neck. The petite woman who owned the shop was very patient, clicking around in her high heels and bringing Annie different sizes, then helping her match some new flat, strappy sandals. Annie mentioned that she was worried she still smelled like skunk, and the woman clicked behind the counter to let her sample a few perfumes, commenting that this wasn't the first time she'd been asked to find a "skunk-busting scent." She also gave her some mascara and eye-shadow samples, and some foundation for the sunburn on her nose.

As they drove back up-Island, Annie wondered if maybe that had been Noah Trout's ex-girlfriend. It had to be, she decided. How strange: she was a husband stealer as well as an uncommonly helpful and generous shopkeeper.

Annie was getting desperate to speak to Gordon. Telephone

service was restored Saturday night and she again called his cell phone, but this time it went immediately to voicemail. She tracked down the number of his service apartment in Hong Kong, but there it just rang and rang. She called his secretary, Kalisa, who kindly answered her cell phone at eleven p.m. and said that, as far as she knew, everything was fine in Hong Kong.

Annie lay awake in bed for hours, trying to read but mostly trying to figure out how not to worry or, even worse, drive herself crazy, like Othello, with irrational jealousy.

31

The Garden Party

———

Sunday afternoon, Emmie took the kids to Oak Bluffs for another ride on the Flying Horses Carousel, and Annie made them a Szechuan chicken recipe to eat later for dinner. Gordon still hadn't called, but Kalisa once more assured her that they would have heard if anything was amiss.

Annie took her time getting ready for the party, washing and drying her hair, carefully putting on the new eye makeup the Edgartown shopkeeper had given her. She was pleased with her new dress: she felt pretty. She also felt surprisingly calm. For some reason, she wasn't at all nervous about seeing Chase at the party. She decided to wear the drop pearl earrings Gordon had given her for her birthday, which she'd had no occasion to wear yet this summer, and spritzed on the new perfume sample, praying its skunk-busting power would last the duration of the party. The stormy ocean water, unfortunately, hadn't helped one bit.

At four-thirty, the sun peeked its way through the clouds and Annie drove almost to the top of Indian Hill Road, past Arrow Head Farm's big barn and meandering stone walls and pastures. She followed a line of cars down a steep dirt road through the woods, toward Lambert's Cove. Chase must have cut through this way to the sail shack with the redhead that day, which is why she hadn't seen his Wrangler in the town beach parking lot.

Oh, who cares?

The St. Clair driveway was nearly a mile down. It was rough going, and she splashed through one deep puddle after another while trying to maintain a polite distance behind the car ahead.

A small hand-painted sign, the St. Clair name scarcely visible, was nailed to a tree. Annie joined the row of cars parked in the meadow above the house and, in her new sandals, tiptoed across the wet grass—chartreuse, again—toward the lower lawn. A foghorn sounded low across the water.

The clouds had finally blown out to sea, as Piper requested they do every year, and the sky was now a glassy pale blue. The garden party was held facing west on the water, on the other side of the big farmhouse, so guests could watch the evening sun drop into the Atlantic Ocean, just to the left of Cuttyhunk. It felt at once weird and familiar for Annie to be here again: the gray shingles with white trim, the two brick chimneys, the same American flag billowing atop the flagpole, the palettes of flower beds.

She felt she was in another Impressionist painting, and she paused at the top of the lawn to admire the picture: pink-linen tables overflowing with platters of food, glasses, and liquor; long-legged college-age servers in white and black already circulating hors d'oeuvres; pretty, graceful women in pastel dresses like hers; tanned men wearing khakis and button-down-collar shirts, with Skip St. Clair and some of the older men in navy blue blazers. The emerald lawn, lined with bushes bursting with roses in every shade of red and yellow, seemed to spread into Vineyard Sound. The Elizabeth Islands appeared to be just a stone's throw away.

Piper St. Clair fluttered up to her in a periwinkle Lilly Pulitzer dress.

"*Bonsoir*, Annie," she sang, winking. "You look lovely, dear. Heard how you rescued that little boy. Sounds harrowing! Your old friend Brooke is dying to see you, by the way, not sure where she made off to. A few new people this summer—you'll excuse me, won't you? You know where the bar is, dear, and don't forget to admire your roses!"

Annie adjusted her sunglasses and who should be standing in

front of the bar, but Freddy.

"Annie!" His voice boomed across the lawn like Thursday's thunder. He hugged her hard, and she could tell he was still shaky. She wondered if he had slept at all, or whether his mind kept replaying the storm. "I had no idea you'd be here!"

"Likewise," she said, hugging him back. "Thank you for the flowers."

Freddy held onto her and whispered, in that incongruous pianissimo voice he managed to conjure, "I've never felt more gratitude in my life, Annie, thank you. So courageous. I'll never, ever get over this. Tommy's moved on already, he's cool, but me, oh my God, Annie …"

He released her and began to describe how furious Lauren had been on the telephone, but Annie politely cut him off. People were streaming around them to get to the bar. "Let's talk about it later," she said, her hand still on his arm.

How could Freddy blame Lauren? If something like this had happened on Gordon's watch, Annie would be beside herself. She would be on the next airplane.

"By the way, Freddy, you clean up awfully nice," Annie said. She'd never seen him wearing long pants before. And it was lucky he hadn't gotten around to losing any weight: it looked handsome on him. "I'm so surprised to see you—I had no idea you were friends with the St. Clairs. Do you realize this is Chase's—?"

"I don't know anybody here," he interrupted, not making the connection. "I came with Deborah. You know each other, right?"

"No. We haven't been introduced," said the short woman who'd been standing next to him, not bothering to shake Annie's hand. Annie recognized her curly dark hair and Chanel sunglasses from one of the beach circles; she usually wore a Yankees cap. Since when was Freddy friends with her?

A college-age server with a flawless complexion offered them a tray of miniature hotdogs wrapped in strips of Pillsbury dough,

Piper's famous "pigs-in-a-blanket."

"Oh, why not," Freddy said, helping himself to a couple. "This was supposed to be my summer to lose weight—did you know that, Deborah? I was intending to give up bread. But instead I spent it learning great children's literature, thanks to Annie here." He raised a now-empty toothpick to Annie in a kind of toast. "I am, however, going on a major health kick, starting next week. Have an appointment in New York with a Lasik eye guy, too."

Deborah took a step closer to him.

"Did you know Annie rescued my son in the waves on Thursday? She was spectacular."

"No," said Deborah. "Didn't hear about it."

"You didn't hear about the rogue wave? The sudden lightning? They had to evacuate the beach."

Deborah shook her head again.

"Right," Freddy said, clearing his throat. "I'm supposed to be getting gin and tonics for us. I'll get you one, too, Annie." He lodged his body down the table, using his shoulder to get the bartender's attention.

"I met Brooke St. Clair playing tennis," Deborah said. "She invited me. This is her parents' place. Isn't it unbelievable? I've seen you at the Center and also at Lucy Vincent, with Fred. Didn't expect you to be here. Hope you don't mind I invited him." She chortled a little. "I don't know how you do it, with three kids on your own. I have two and I'm going crazy."

"Oh, well—"

"I got divorced three years ago and I'll tell you what, it doesn't get any easier. Are you divorced yet, or just separated?"

"What?" Annie said, staring at her. "Excuse me? I'm married!"

"You are? No way," Deborah mused, looking truly amazed. "We were all sure you were divorced. Separated, at least."

Freddy extended his arm backward to thrust a drink at Annie, then turned like a gentleman to present Deborah with hers. They were on a date, after all.

"The most fantastic thing just happened, Annie!" Freddy exclaimed. "I met a friend of yours at the bar. I had no idea this was his house." He gestured with his head. "Oy, what a small world."

A beautiful little girl straddled snug on his waist, his feet planted squarely on the ground, Chase stood regarding her, his lips flattened in an amused half-smile. He was looking past the person he was having a conversation with toward Annie.

"Small island, more like," Annie said.

"What a golden couple you must have been," Freddy said, looking from one to the other and wiping the sides of his mouth. "I'm nostalgic, and I didn't even know you then."

Annie excused herself, and she and Chase kissed each other's cheeks in the traditional East Coast way. His lips felt soft on her skin.

"Mom said she'd invited you. Thanks very much for coming, Annie. I'm really, really happy to see you. May I present … my daughter, Miss Hope St. Clair."

Hope, consistent with the Impressionist painting Annie felt she was in, looked like one of Renoir's pastel, rosy girls. Her blond baby curls had been swept into a pale blue ribbon that trailed down her long, apricot-colored dress, matching a satin sash tied in a big bow. Chase's collared shirt was precisely the same shade.

Unconsciously, Annie touched the little girl's elbow, almost to see if she were real—but instead of smiling back, she shied away and nestled into her father's shoulder. She stretched her hand up to stroke his lovely hair.

Annie felt a catch in her throat.

"Surprised to see me as a dad in action, huh?" He would be forever able to read her mind. "To see me acting like a grown-up?"

Annie nodded and took a sip of her drink. Oh, for heaven's sake. Why was she so overcome at seeing Chase with his exquisite daughter? She didn't want any tears to wreck her face, make her new mascara run down her cheeks.

"I'm glad to see you so in touch with your emotions, Annie."

Exceedingly grateful that the glare off the water provided an excuse for sunglasses, Annie focused on the ice cubes in her drink. Chase waited for her to regain her composure but, afraid her voice would crack, she merely gestured her glass in admiration at his coordinating shirt and Hope's sash.

"I know. Élise insists our family's outfits always blend together. Pretty embarrassing, but I have other fish to fry with her right now."

Annie managed to find her voice. "Did she deliberately dress you to match this afternoon's sky?" She giggled. "Sorry, Chase. You both look wonderful. Hope looks just like you. She's such a ... *cherub*."

"Phew," he said. "I was counting on her to butter you up." His face eased into a grin. "If you really want to know, I dressed her like this myself, to help my cause. So ... you've forgiven me, Annie? Was worried you might still be mad." He nodded his head toward the sail shack.

"That was none of my business," Annie said. "And thank you very much for your note."

"Did you like it? The Bard sure comes in handy when a guy needs a little help," Chase said, exhaling a visible sigh of relief. "I've been worried."

"You want to know something else Shakespeare said?" Annie took a long sip. *"All's well that ends well."* They both laughed; Hope, still stroking her father's hair, giggled too.

"Anyway," Annie continued, "I decided you were right. About everything. We needed to have it, and now we can move on. And now, well, we'll always have Paris."

Chase placed his drink on the pink linen of a high, round bar table. "Nah, Banana. Paris was never our place. Europe wasn't."

Annie studied the clouds, strewn over the Elizabeths like a

windblown pasture. She had loved every second of their summer graduation trip eighteen summers ago, and knew he'd loved it just as much. "It's a metaphor," she said.

"Sakes alive—it is?" He gave her a what-do-you-take-me-for look, and Hope giggled again. "You English majors think you have a corner on everything literary, but you're not the only ones who know stuff." He bounced his daughter on his hip. "So. Heard you were pretty heroic the other day over at Lucy. Sounded rough. I'm proud of you."

Annie lifted her sunglasses up to the top of her head and wiped the corners of her eyes. "Nothing like another near-death experience to put one's life in perspective."

"Is that how you got those gashes on your arms?"

"What? Oh. I forgot about these. They're from swimming with my dog."

"Jesus. Been quite a summer for you in the water, Annie. Do me a favor and stay on the sand for a while." He shook his head. "Overheard a guy at the farmers' market yesterday saying that kid would have drowned if not for you. Scared?"

She took a deep breath. "The thing is, no. I really wasn't. I knew I had to get him, so I did. Afterward, I was a bit surprised at myself, maybe, but not at the time."

"I bet you were pretty happy when your toes touched," he said, surveying the crush of guests on his family's lawn.

His cornflower-blue eyes, and Hope's, were casting those tiny, mystical sunbeams, the way Lily's and Tashmoo's did. It must be Martha's Vineyard.

"I meant to ask you, Chase … mind if I have another one of your business cards?"

"Ha," he said, maneuvering Hope to his other hip so he could get his wallet. "I *knew* you tossed the other one. Here you go. We can email. Have lunch when you come to Manhattan." He grinned. "*Only* lunch. Don't get any ideas."

Annie's eyes rested on his forearms and moved slowly up to his shoulders. She would have to be very, very careful. But as long as she didn't invite him over for drinks any time soon, she could probably handle it.

"I'll let you know," she said, her eyes again meeting his. "As a matter of fact, I may have to go to New York on business trips once in a while." It was getting a little breezy, and she smoothed back her hair. "My cousin Juliet has a contact at a small publishing house in Washington and apparently they're hiring, and Friday afternoon I spoke to someone there about a part-time job as—guess what? *A children's book editor.* Juliet had already sent them my résumé. I have a telephone interview next week."

Chase took a step back and bowed to her, lifting his glass and grinning. "That's awesome, Annie, perfect. Congratulations. Sounds like a no-brainer for you."

"Well, we'll see. It would be a big change, not being home full-time."

"You'll be grand."

"Just two days a week to start. Might give me the best of both worlds."

"I know it will. What did Gar—" he cleared his throat. "*Gordon* say?"

"Haven't had a chance to tell him yet. But it means we can't move again."

"Fair enough."

"Think I can do it?"

"Absolutely, you can do it. Didn't you just prove to yourself, rescuing that kid, that you can do anything? Quit worrying so much." He beamed at her for a while before leaning in toward her. "And now, ta da, I have some breaking news for *you*. Élise and I are going to try marriage counseling."

"You?" She cleared something stuck in her throat. "But I didn't think you believed in counseling."

Chase laughed. "I don't know if I do or not. It was Mom's idea—I guess she's onto me. Wants me to come clean. Live a richer, more authentic life. Time to grow up, she said. It would, actually, be nice to work some things out. Do I sound like one of your hokey California friends?" He scanned the lawn again. "A couple weeks ago, my mother told me she had a long affair with a painter from Marblehead. Sounded to me like a sordid John Updike kind of tale."

"Piper?"

"Surprising, isn't it? You just never know about people."

"You can say that again."

"You've helped me this summer, Annie, I don't mind telling you. Helped me get my soul back." He switched Hope to his other hip and, once more changing the subject, nodded toward a very cool-looking man wearing light linen khakis and a long, button-down white tunic. Chase made a face at the man's sunglasses, which somehow stayed propped straight across the middle of his forehead. "See that Hollywood type over there, in front of the rose bushes? I'm pretty sure he's sleeping with Élise."

At that moment, Hope impulsively grabbed Chase's sunglasses from the top of his head. They hung off crooked before falling backwards onto the lawn, just as Annie lurched forward because she saw yet another woman whom she thought for a second was Aunt Faye.

"You okay, Annie? Speak of the devil. Cripes. *Heeeeere* we go," Chase said, flustered, catching his breath and bending down awkwardly around the tall bar table to pick up his glasses, just as a tall woman joined them. "Annie," he said, clearing his throat and righting himself, "I would like you to meet my wife, Élise St. Clair."

Her name went perfectly together with his.

"I've heard so much about you," Élise murmured, reaching out a slender arm. "Thank you for coming." Naturally she would have a sexy French accent, but Annie still wasn't prepared for it.

A French nanny, dressed in a black dress and frilly white apron (how come she didn't get to wear matching blue?), instantly appeared and whisked Hope out of Chase's arms.

There was something liquid about Élise, who was as luminously striking as a movie star. About the same height as Chase in her own flat, strappy sandals, she wore a white dress with, what else, pale blue detail. She exuded inimitable confidence, that Parisian elegance that American women simply cannot mimic—with the possible exception, of course, of Jackie Kennedy. Élise's dark hair was wavy and cut short to frame her face, so perfectly tanned; no sunburn on the tip of her flawless nose. Her high cheekbones glowed, rubbed with some creamy kind of bronzer. She had a very long throat.

"How do you do," Annie said, sounding surprisingly self-assured herself.

Élise smiled curiously at Annie. She had inviting brown eyes that looked playful, mischievous almost, and spoke for a while about something Annie didn't hear, something to do with swimming, because she was so mesmerized by her extraordinary mouth. Lipsticked in a peach that matched something—oh, Hope's dress—Élise's plump lips, the only plump thing about her, every few words or so would somehow pucker into a little *pfff* sound.

A voice inside Annie commanded her to close her own mouth, which she sensed was gaping. She felt frumpy, having felt tall and slim standing next to Deborah just two minutes before, but she didn't care. It was lovely to stand there and admire Élise.

"Is Antoinette here as well?" Annie asked, still sounding surprisingly natural. "Are the twins identical?"

Élise's laugh reminded Annie of Katharine Hepburn's in *Philadelphia Story* when she's deliberately putting on airs—only, Élise wasn't being deliberate.

"No," she said. "Antoinette is still inside, but she should make her debut very soon. She's dark, like me." Her eyes ran up and down Annie in an impolite way that would have horrified Adair. "Our daughters are very happy to meet their papa's sporty, former girlfriend, as am I." She made her enchanting *pfff* sound with her enchantingly plump lips.

"Charming," said Chase. "Let's see how fast we can make Annie run away."

Annie felt her face getting hot, and worried she might perspire so much she would stain her new lavender linen—or, worse, start to smell like skunk. She glimpsed Piper watching them out of the corner of her eye, and sensed her concern. "Ah, well," she said. "That was a long time ago."

"Do you have any children?" Élise asked. Unbidden, Chase swapped out Annie's half-full gin and tonic with a fresh one, remembering that she liked extra lime.

Élise seemed genuinely interested in what Annie had to say, and they chatted for a while. At the other end of the bar, Annie could see Freddy pontificating about something and Deborah smiling up at him as if he were the most fascinating man in the world.

"I think it is so interesting you have a *nine*-year-old," Élise said, sipping a glass of chablis. "Did you already have a career?"

"I had a job with a magazine in Shanghai, but my career sort of petered out after our second child was born. Although I am thinking about—"

Chase inadvertently slurped as he tilted his glass to drain his vodka tonic. Élise shot him a what-on-earth-am-I-going-to-do-with-you look and he chuckled, rocking back on his heels to watch them.

"But you have no *career*, and not lately." Élise smoothed away a wisp of hair before it reached her glossy, peachy lips. Her French-manicured thumb and forefinger became distracted by the silk of her throat and began idly twirling her summery sapphire earring.

"I guess I mostly just wanted to have a family," Annie said, trying to focus on her words. "My husband, his name is Gordon, and I both did. I suppose I meant to go back to work sooner, but—well, I couldn't really imagine leaving our kids when they were so little."

Élise made her *pfff* sound.

"We've also moved countries a lot," Annie continued. "And … well, it's been a great, lucky adventure, to be honest. Amazing. Actually … it's been wonderful."

Élise stared at her, genuinely puzzled. "I *cher*ished my thirties," she said. "I had the twins at forty. I can't im*a*gine giving up those years for children, giving up my *body*. Do you work now?"

"Yes I do, and no I don't, but, as a matter of fact, I am considering—" Annie wasn't sure whether it was the conversation or the *pfff*'s, but for some reason she started to laugh.

"I've been investing in television films," Élise interrupted, scanning the guests and, fortunately, ignoring Annie. "It's been quite easy to work from the Island. I can't im*a*gine spending my whole day with children, like you. I am not trained as a nanny!" *Pfff.* "How am I supposed to know what to do, how to manage them?" Another *pfff.* "What if I get cranky? After about two hours I need some alone time, some 'me' time, as you Americans say."

Not all of us say that but, now that you mention it, Annie almost said, it's about time for *me* to take off. If she hurried, she could make it home for some of that Szechuan chicken and in time to read to the kids before they went to bed. She was overwhelmed with missing them, all of a sudden.

Élise made Annie feel—and all the women here look—very short, and Annie wondered why the Edgartown shopkeeper's incessant clicking hadn't made her think to ask for some high heels, too. Although high heels would have sunk into the lawn.

Élise was so glamorously trendy and adult. Everyone was always telling Annie she looked the same as she did in college, like the girl next door. Was that, in fact, a compliment? Could she, actually, have missed a stage of development? Wasn't it better to keep progressing, advancing through life?

Not that she could ever look as elegant and sophisticated as Élise, not in a million years. Her mysterious aura must be what kept Chase so captivated.

Oh, well. After that new haircut she was planning on getting, she was going to go on a shopping spree. She would find a reliable babysitter in Sylvan Fell, thanks to this new job she was going to get, and she'd leave the kids safely with her and go up to New York City to visit her old roommate Louise and buy a new wardrobe.

Élise turned to speak to someone more fabulous, and Annie decided to stay longer, after all. She chatted with Chase's sister, Brooke, picking up right where they'd left off eighteen years ago and making a date to play tennis on Wednesday morning, and she said hello to several other people she'd known for years through both the St. Clairs and Aunt Faye. She had a very nice time.

The French nanny reappeared briefly with both Antoinette and Hope in hand, and then brought them back into the house. Annie followed them: she wanted to see if Élise's daughters were born knowing how to make that little *pfff* sound, or whether it was a learned behavior.

She tiptoed into the wide kitchen, the screen door slamming behind her. She was again overcome, this time by the familiar fresh-mown-hay smell of the St. Clair house. The kitchen counters were laid out with a few more silver trays of hors d'oeuvres, and a few more good-looking caterers were bustling around. Annie waved to them, gesturing to the bathroom. She couldn't see or hear the twins and, embarrassed at barging in, was about to turn around, when she decided to peek at the old dollhouse.

There it was: still in the corner of the airy living room, standing before the white curtains that were still blowing in the breeze.

The dollhouse, built for Piper when she was a little girl, was perfect. It was an old-fashioned, four-story Victorian sliced in two, with gables on the roof, gray shingles on the sides, and real glass in the windows. One side was open so you could play with the tiny dolls, all in Victorian dress, and rearrange the intricately designed furniture and miniscule sofa pillows to your heart's content. The front parlor had three-inch draperies, and the bedrooms had bureaus with minute drawers that opened. The keys of the little piano went up and down. There were wallpapered rooms and passageways and fine carpeted staircases between floors.

Chase's father, Skip St. Clair, was suddenly standing next to her.

"Hello, Annie," he said, shaking her hand. "Still admiring the old dollhouse, eh?"

She felt herself blushing; he'd always made her a little nervous. "The twins must be enjoying it."

"Brooke's kids do," he replied. "I'm afraid it's too quaint and dull around here for Élise. Where are you living now?"

They chatted idly while Annie organized some of the teeny pieces of furniture. She couldn't resist tucking in the Chippendale dining chairs and smoothing the bed quilts, setting out the miniscule china teapot and matching cups and saucers. She wished she could play with the dolls for a while, make the mother slip up the back staircase and lie down on one of the miniature canopy beds.

"Such a charming dollhouse," Annie said. "I've missed it."

"Well," he said, "sorry to have to break it to you, my dear, but you married the wrong guy if you wanted the dollhouse."

Annie studied the tranquil rooms, replicas of a still life. Each room looked like a nineteenth-century painting you might see at the Museum of Fine Arts. When she and Chase used to lounge around here on rainy days, if Chase happened to be playing backgammon with someone else or napping, she used to rearrange the little dolls and furniture, control them with no living interruptions.

"I still love the dollhouse, but with all due respect, Mr. St. Clair," she said, turning to him, "I didn't marry the wrong guy at all. I married the right guy."

Mr. St. Clair chuckled. "Mighty glad to hear it, Annie, mighty glad to hear it. And happy to have you back on the Vineyard, where you belong." He straightened the cuffs of his white sleeves from under his blazer, and extended his arm. "Shall we? Incidentally, Annie, if you don't mind my saying so, that perfume you're wearing smells terrific."

On the lawn, Freddy appeared at her shoulder. "Deborah said that Brooke told her Élise never touches those twins. Poor little things."

"Who doesn't touch them?" Annie asked innocently. "É-*loof*, you mean?"

Freddy, in his inimitable way, guffawed.

"She's dazzling, though, isn't she?" Annie said, giggling. "Especially if you don't listen to what she's saying. Seems like she should be entitled to a bye from all domestic work."

Freddy was still guffawing. "You're worth a thousand of her, Annie." He glanced over his shoulder and lowered his voice to a whisper. "So tell me, my *chaver*. What do you think of Deborah? Too short for me?"

The sun was blazing atop the water, casting that golden light that made everyone's skin look especially enchanting. People kept their sunglasses on and had to stand with their backs to the water.

It occurred to Annie that part of these many last years of longing for Chase was actually a longing for the Vineyard—for this moment, for this amber light. She had made the Vineyard her own this summer, and now she had it back. It wasn't that she wanted the St. Clairs' life of money and privilege, exactly; she didn't need to be fancy. But she did envy his deep family roots here by the ocean. She envied his close family, and all these old summer friends. So what if she and Gordon would never be able to afford a lawn that sprawled into the Sound? Her Martha's Vineyard could be every bit as grand—for her and Gordon, and for their children. They belonged here as much as anyone else.

And really, was her family so bad? Her mother and father were persistent, that's for sure. Wouldn't let her run away again. Annie resolved to work harder to accept them, to stop wasting time resenting that they weren't the family she wished she had. They, to their credit, seemed to have accepted *her*—not insisting she be a debutante, and all that. Maybe they'd like her even more now, when they discovered she was no longer a high-and-mighty perfectionist.

Get to know your family.

Annie went over to the buffet table to make herself a plate of special Vineyard cheeses, and Chase was at her elbow.

"Having fun yet?" He raised his glass toward Élise, now engrossed in conversation with the cool guy in the tunic. "Yup. I'm right."

"I'm sorry, Chase."

"Everything is so fucked up."

"Prob'ly time for summer to end," Annie said. "Things will settle down once you get back to New York."

"Or they'll get worse." Chase was slurring his words now, staring at Élise. "Marriage sure is a damned lot bigger than the sum of its parts, isn't it? But, I guess … well, it usually does prevail. Somehow."

He looked miserable. He was, clearly, very much in love with his wife. "I'll just have to wait for this asshole to move on, or for her to get tired of him," he said, sliding his hair out of his eyes. "Wonder if she'll be honest with the marriage counselor and confess."

Annie was quiet.

"I know what you're thinking. Or whether I will be."

Keeping her expression neutral, she drank in the sun, burning low in the sky. A few more days, and Gordon would be here.

"She's exciting, I'll say that for her," Chase continued. "Sometimes I wish she weren't so goddamned gorgeous."

He looked out over Lambert's Cove and across the expanse of lawn, his eyes pausing at the top of the hill before they wandered back to Annie. His shoulders rose and fell as he took a slow, deep breath. "*This* was our place, Annie. Martha's Vineyard. Not Europe. Not even Brown, so much." He lifted a hand, and placed it gently on her cheek. "The Vineyard was our Paris. And our summers here, as I told you on Middle Road, will always be a special memory for me. But now, well ... maybe you and I can have the best of everything. We can be friends." His eyes lingered on her face and he smiled softly at her. "We'll always be in each other's skin, Banana."

Annie lifted her own hand and held it over his.

"Thank you," she whispered. "I would like to be friends, Chase, I really would. But ... maybe next summer."

"I get it," he said, slowly withdrawing his hand from under hers. "I understand." He cleared his throat. "Anyway, we can work all that out later. Because for now—" he nodded toward the top of the hill. "Looks to me like someone's up there waiting for you."

At the edge of the meadow, looking pale and thin and a little awkward in his wrinkled khakis, was Gordon.

Annie shoved her drink into Chase's hand and raced up the hill, not caring that she wasn't French or elegant and feeling enormously grateful for her flat heels. The sun was so dazzling that Gordon couldn't make her out until she was practically on top of him, whereupon he opened his arms wide and they collapsed into each other. They hugged and kissed for quite a while, blissfully unaware that everyone on the lawn below was watching.

32

Heading Home

———

Swimming west along the shore, Annie swerved into the cut at Chilmark Pond and, above the water now, sped across to the little jetty near Doctor's Creek. Robbie appeared alongside her and they circled each other, playing, before Meg jumped onto his back and Lily onto hers, two cowgirls. The four of them darted through the creek and across the pond, leaping over Lucy Vincent Beach and turning right to skim across the Atlantic. They saw Aunt Faye and Jared swing dancing in the beach grass, and then the Rosenthals, waving to them from their usual place on the sand. They could hear Emmie playing on his saxophone, but there were also trumpets and trombones, and a male voice crooning. They veered around Squibnocket Point toward Aquinnah, the music beckoning, and glanced up from the water to see Gordon, calling to them. Bells began pealing from the cliffs. Annie held Meg tightly on her back and nodded to Robbie and Lily, and they all soared out of the water just as he swooped down to meet them ...

The telephone rang again and Gordon switched off the portable CD player.

"I dreamt that Robbie and I were dolphins," Annie said, skipping around the packed duffel bags outside their bedroom. The green morning light of summer was beginning to give way to the copper of autumn. "You were an eagle. Kids up yet?"

"Sound asleep in their beds," Gordon said, mixing some eggs for French toast. "That was the Steamship Authority. We just cleared the waitlist and can take the earliest boat tomorrow."

He handed her coffee in what used to be Aunt Faye's favorite mug.

"Such a lovely dream," Annie repeated. "I hope I get to have it again some time. I feel so in love with you, Gordon."

He leaned down to kiss her.

"You still give me shivers," she said, her arms around his neck.

"Glad to hear it."

They kissed some more.

"Wait—didn't the phone ring twice? Who was it the first time?"

Gordon didn't say anything. Annie waited.

"Actually," he said slowly, "it was Pretti."

"Pretti?"

"She's moving tomorrow, back to India. She just wanted to tell me, to say goodbye."

"How did she get this number?"

"I don't know; maybe Kalisa gave it to her. Today is a work day, in the real world."

"Kalisa?"

"Maybe she found it on the Internet."

"The Internet! Our little house?"

Gordon's eyes weren't crinkling up the way they usually did.

"Well, what else did she say?"

"Nothing. I wished her and her kids good luck in India. She'll be okay there; she's made peace with her family. I'm sure I'll never hear from her again."

For a second, Annie felt the wind knocked out of her, as if she had just been punched in the stomach. Her whole body tensed up, bracing, steeling itself instinctively for an impending blow.

She went out to the deck, but her cardinal was nowhere to be seen. She made her way across the field and automatically picked up a few forgotten balls and toys, tossing them back toward the house as she went. She stumbled on something and spilled her hot coffee onto her wrist, then slammed the mug onto the grass. The handle broke off and bounced a few feet away.

Tashmoo instantly appeared at her side.

"Don't tell me I'm going to have another thing to grieve," Annie said, her chest clamping up and her eyes welling with tears.

Was this possible? It was too ironic. She finally was Gordon's— one hundred percent, as Freddy would say. She was over Chase at last and, for the first time, truly "all in" her marriage. It would be too tragic, too unfair, too *sad* if Gordon chose this summer, of all their summers married, to fall in love with someone else.

But maybe that was magical thinking from the old Annie, the one who believed in fairy tales. Her falling one hundred percent in love and her husband's possibly having an affair in Hong Kong were, in reality, totally separate things with no bearing on each other.

Would Gordon really have touched a woman whose husband had just been killed? Would Pretti have allowed it? Would he sabotage their marriage like that?

"Why aren't I enough?" Annie asked Tashmoo, who had picked up the broken mug and stood gazing up at her, holding it in his mouth, waiting patiently.

If Gordon loved her as much as he repeatedly said, and showed that he did, wouldn't he have been able to resist someone else? Had he forgotten that he was married? He had always seemed like such a faithful person.

Whatever—she was probably being ridiculous, probably imagining the worst. But on the off chance anything *had* happened, it was now a world away and it was over. Past. She wasn't going to belittle their marriage by asking for details. Gordon was here now, and he had come home early. That's what mattered. And yet …

They couldn't simply stash their summer's secrets into the shed along with the beach chairs. Secrets weren't good for marriages. She needed to confess, and she also needed to know.

She would wait until they got back to Sylvan Fell, and ask him then. She would explain what had happened with Chase. She would get a babysitter so they could go to a restaurant—no, not a restaurant, that would be too public—what if she cried? A picnic would be better. She would figure out a quiet, secluded park, and they would talk it all over.

Or … was it sometimes wiser to *keep* secrets, if the pain of the truth would be too debilitating? If he confessed something, could she live with it? Could he? *To thine own self be true.*

Would she ever again get to feel as in love as she had when she woke up this morning?

Annie took the mug from Tashmoo and picked up the handle, which had broken in two when it bounced on the grass and was now missing a little chip. She hunted around for it before giving up and going into the house. It would fit together well enough. Aunt Faye had left some ceramic glue on Jared's workbench.

Their last two weeks on the Vineyard, before this, had been idyllic.

The kids wanted to be with Gordon and didn't want to go to the Center once the Rosenthals left, so they stopped going and instead spent whole days exploring new places as a family. They went on bike rides and hikes, ate fried clams and ice cream; they took the *On Time* ferry to Chappaquiddick and swam in the mild water off the beach there. She and Robbie even helped John Alley sort the mail one morning.

They spent a lot of time on the back deck doing art projects and finger painting, and Annie and Lily left the coloring books inside and instead filled blank pages with Meg's type of swirly Jackson Pollock designs.

Annie took everyone to the West Tisbury Cemetery to plant more perennials on Aunt Faye's grave, and she told them about Juliet's astonishment at Priscilla's name being on the stone. She neglected to mention Chase's help that day (luckily Meg didn't mention him, either), because at that point Annie still hadn't decided whether Gordon needed to know about Chase. It had been part of her growing up, and it was done now.

Besides, Annie worried that if Gordon did know, he might not be too excited about the prospect of them all being friends one day.

During these two weeks in August, Gordon acted differently from the way he had in June: he wasn't as jumpy, and he was more fun. He'd also just been promoted for doing such a bang-up job in Hong Kong, and his boss, Zhen, told him he wouldn't have to travel as much anymore. They'd drunk champagne to celebrate, and after that Gordon stopped futzing around the house and started behaving as if he were actually on vacation. In fact, the chrome handle to the kids' bathroom faucet fell off and he simply ignored it until, eventually, Annie got the toolbox and an Allen wrench and tightened it herself.

"You probably won't be as impressed with me and my repairs, now that you know how easy it is to do a lot of this stuff," Gordon said, when he saw her with the wrench. "But it makes me happy to see you so independent, sweetheart."

Lindsay had gone with Noah to Cataumet, on the Cape, because he had won a big landscaping job there and they were staying in the property's guesthouse for August, so Annie no longer got up early to walk Tashmoo on Lambert's Cove. Instead, Gordon took him for runs up and down the hills of Chilmark in the mornings, though never very far. He'd decided to quit marathons, at least until the kids were grown up.

"Hanging out with Pretti all month, something clicked in me," he told her. "I'm sorry I've had to leave you alone so much of the time—both for our sake as a couple and for you as a mom. I don't know how you've managed so well. From now on I want to be more helpful, more available. I've missed too much."

Tashmoo loved Gordon from the start, but he would always be Annie's dog.

"He's not much of a watchdog, is he?" Gordon had commented, after first arriving from Hong Kong that Sunday afternoon. "He greeted me at the door like his long-lost best friend, even though we'd never met."

Annie knew Tashmoo simply felt the same way she did: that they could all relax, now that their family was back together and intact. And while he may have welcomed Gordon instantly, aside from their morning jogs, he always stayed right by Annie's side.

On the beach in the afternoons, Annie read grown-up novels that had just come out: *Cold Mountain*, *The Perfect Storm* (distressing, of course, but she could handle it), *The God of Small Things*. Gordon took Robbie alone to Brickman's to buy them each a glove, and they played catch every day. He taught Meg and Lily how to throw, too.

Gordon also napped a lot. Annie had never seen him so tired, and it made her like him better. He seemed more vulnerable, less perfect. She really didn't miss his former Energizer-bunny, Road-Runner fervor.

They made love every night and he held her like a vice in his sleep, clasping her so tightly that she had to wake him up when she wanted to roll over. Or sometimes they would collapse into bed after playing with the children all day in the sea air and melt together when the rustle of the birds would wake them up at dawn.

Each morning the red cardinal greeted them cheerily, fluttering at the bird feeder or parading up and down the railing on the deck.

"I think this bird thinks it's a person," Gordon said after a couple of days, and Annie grinned. She knew he'd catch on sooner or later. "Would you believe I'd never seen a cardinal until I moved to Boston? We don't have them in California." He'd been reading Aunt Faye's Peterson's *Field Guide to Birds*. "Such a beautiful songbird. It's always the male here on the deck. I wonder where his mate is?"

"I'm sure someplace near, safe and sound," Annie said.

"What will happen when we leave? Do you think it's become too dependent on the bird feeder?"

"She'll be fine," Annie said, deliberately choosing her gender. "She'll be absolutely fine."

While Gordon didn't get to meet Lindsay, he did get to know Freddy during the few days they had left, and they liked each other very much.

It had been sad to say goodbye to the Rosenthals. Freddy insisted on having them, plus Emmie and Jazzy, over for a great striped-bass dinner cooked by Rosa, who cupped Annie's face in her hands and kissed her cheeks several times to thank her for rescuing Tommy.

Ben, Tommy, and Beatrice serenaded them on their violins with a rendition of "Twinkle, Twinkle, Little Star," and Annie resolved to save money, from the new job she was going to get, to buy a piano for their house in Sylvan Fell and get her own kids lessons.

They all made definite plans to meet on the Vineyard in October for Columbus Day Weekend, and when the Tuckers drove to the Steamship Authority ferry dock in Vineyard Haven the next morning to hug their new friends goodbye, everyone cried.

The Tuckers watched Freddy's Suburban disappear inside the ferry and waited on the pier until the Rosenthals reappeared, waving to them from the rail on the upper deck, and they all waved and waved until the ferry chugged out into the Sound and they couldn't make each other out anymore … whereupon Gordon suggested they go to breakfast at the Artcliff Diner on the Beach Road.

Emmie left a week later for Maine to spend time with Juliet and Lonny in Kennebunk, before he had to start school. He'd decided to switch his major from economics to music, and Freddy promised to find him the best tenor saxophone on the Eastern Seaboard. Again at the boat, Annie felt sad. She hugged Emmie and told him she was forever grateful for his help that summer and that, in many ways, she felt she'd picked up where she'd left off with her older cousin Emmett, before he'd died in that long-ago car crash. Getting to know her young cousin had been a wonderful gift.

Annie couldn't wait to host Emmie, Caroline, Juliet, and Lonny in Sylvan Fell for Thanksgiving, along with her parents, and had already copied down Aunt Faye's creamed pearl onion recipe from her old tattered *Joy of Cooking*. Annie had also invited Juliet's parents, Aunt Connie and Uncle Dwight, and they had all been very touched by her invitation; Juliet and Aunt Connie both said they wouldn't miss it for the world. Annie, waiting for the right moment, planned to ask her mother whether she'd mind too terribly if she invited Percy's first wife, Kathleen, and her new doctor boyfriend to join them this year, as well.

The garden party hadn't been as awkward as it might have been. Gordon had arrived after twenty-four hours of traveling to find Tashmoo in an otherwise empty house, seen Emmie's careful directions on the fridge, run after his taxi, and asked the driver to bring him straight over to Indian Hill so he could surprise Annie. He hadn't known whether the kids would be with her or not, but he was desperate to see them all.

Gordon and Annie had descended from their passionate embrace on the hill to meet Freddy, who plowed over to shake Gordon's hand. "I would like to thank you for your wife," Freddy began, and told him all about the rescue and the storm. He had embellished it so much now—*thirty-foot waves!*—that even Deborah, plainly overjoyed to meet Annie's husband, congratulated her.

"Annie was sensational, Gordon," Freddy had exalted. "So courageous. And careful. She knew she could do it, as long as she acted fast and didn't let things get too out of control. Didn't get sucked in by the rip. Such a *mitzvah*." He seemed to have forgotten that he was holding a glass, and was gesturing so enthusiastically he spilled some of his gin and tonic on Deborah.

"You are the luckiest guy I know, Gordon," Freddy went on, truly at his most effusive. "Annie was somewhat unsure of herself this summer, a little reckless at first. Caused her to be maybe, whaddaya say, re*bell*ious. Can't help it—she's a free spirit. Doesn't do well when she's constrained." He began wiping off Deborah's white blouse with a red lobster cocktail napkin until she swiped it out of his hand. "She just needed a wake-up call to remind her how good she's got it."

Freddy was about to plotz, he was so happy, and Annie felt her smile beaming as broadly as Tommy's.

"I feel as if I've just walked in at the end of a great adventure movie," Gordon said, looking a little bewildered.

Freddy nodded and continued to effuse. "The thing about Annie is, she's a very fortunate person—like you, Gordon. And while she doesn't take it for *granted* exactly, I think she expects it a little. You've got to keep an eye on her."

"I'll try," Gordon said, beginning to relax. "But I think she makes her own luck."

"I'm not counting on anything anymore," Annie interrupted.

Maybe there was no such thing as a fairy tale, as Princess Diana seemed determined to teach everyone. But some lives can come pretty close, and hers and Gordon's did. She would be more careful.

Gordon was impressed with Freddy's story, but he didn't seem particularly surprised, and Annie realized why: he didn't know how shell-shocked she'd been about swimming in big waves since

Long Point, because she'd never fully explained just how terrified she had been, or how close it was. She'd played it down. The Annie he knew would absolutely, with no doubt or hesitation, swim in after a drowning little boy. Gordon had missed the scene where she'd almost drowned, herself.

Annie steered Gordon away from Freddy the first chance she got. She wanted to know how his flights had been, how he'd left things in Hong Kong. She was overwhelmed that he'd come home early and tracked her down here. No wonder he hadn't answered his phone! He'd been on airplanes on his way to surprise her; he hadn't been able to call midway from Tokyo because, the cellular technology being different there, his phone didn't work and he'd had too short a layover to find a telephone booth.

"How is Pretti managing?" she asked.

Gordon was fiddling with the collar of the wrinkled shirt he'd been wearing for two days; he seemed to sense that he didn't look like everyone else at this party. "Oh, she'll be all right," he said. "Moving back to India. I doubt we'll ever see each other again." He lowered his voice to a whisper and searched her face. "I missed you like crazy, Annie. You know you're my one and only love."

Before she had time to consider whether this was an odd response, Chase came over to introduce himself, slapping his hand into Gordon's in an exaggerated, old-boy way. He had had too much to drink by then and, unfortunately, wasn't at his best. "None too steady on his feet" is how Annie's father would have described him.

Would Chase drink so much if he had married her instead of Élise?

Gordon, plainly aware that he was taller than Chase, nonetheless stood up straighter than usual, puffing out his chest as he threw back his shoulders—a posture that Annie didn't think was particularly tactful. They had barely made any small talk before Piper rushed over, both to bail out Chase and to greet Gordon properly.

She made a big to-do of the fact that he had just flown halfway around the world.

Élise was so busy networking that no one dared, or maybe cared, to introduce her, and it was Piper who gave the Tuckers a gracious excuse to leave, promising Gordon he could make his proper debut next summer and ushering them up the field toward their car.

A few days after the party and Gordon's return, Annie had her editing-job interview sitting on the back deck, her cardinal listening in. The position sounded interesting and flexible, and the person who would be her boss sounded optimistic. They set up a time to meet for when she got back to Washington.

Annie felt very grateful to Juliet and couldn't believe her luck—yet her hands felt clammy and her throat closed up as soon as she got off the telephone. The red cardinal seemed to be radiating encouragement, but she still wasn't sure she'd be able to do it, and sat quietly at the round teak table while Gordon and the kids played in the field, focusing very hard on her breathing.

Two hours later, Gordon received a call about that private-sector job in San Francisco he'd first heard about last spring. They wanted to know whether he could fly out to meet some people.

Annie left her laundry folding in their bedroom, took him by the hand, and steered him over to the long dining table. They sat down next to each other on the old meetinghouse pew.

"How flattering," she said. "Congratulations. But last week you got promoted, Gordon. The kids have excellent teachers this year; I'm really thrilled about the possibility of this job; I signed up for that masters swimming class and for that mini-triathlon in Annapolis. I'm looking forward to settling into our new house, pulling it together. You planted all those roses for us! I was even thinking about maybe taking up gardening again. Gloria Bradshaw next door found Robbie a Chinese tutor—and me a yoga class!" Annie couldn't control her voice, couldn't stop her words from rushing, compressing. "It's time to settle down, sweetheart. And I forgot to tell you—Gloria wrote that the azalea bush you moved last spring is thriving now!" She leaned forward. "We haven't even given Sylvan Fell a chance, Gordon. It's near *Washington, DC,* for heaven's sake, the epicenter of development agencies. I've invited my whole family for Thanksgiving!" She stopped to gasp for air. "Please, *please,* Gordon. We don't have time to move. The kids and I want to stay put."

Gordon was silent. For a long time he stared at her, his mouth open. He slumped down in his chair and put his face in his hands. She had never said no to him before. He breathed in and out slowly, as if he were counting to ten. "I can't believe I'm hearing this," he said, at last, into his hands. "I thought you *wanted* to move back to San Francisco. I thought you'd be happy."

"It doesn't make sense to move every time a better job comes along. I don't understand why you're always so restless, Gordon. Maybe you could try casting a wider net in Washington if you want to switch careers."

He stared at her again, dumbfounded. "We're talking about *San Francisco* here, Annie."

"And we'll have a great visit there for a few days, before we spend Christmas with your family in Sacramento, before we go to New Zealand to see mine."

"It would be our last move."

Annie laughed. "Sorry, sweetheart, but I don't believe you. Besides," she said, skimming her fingertips along the polished surface of the old table, "before you got this call, you were really excited about your promotion at the Foundation."

"I was. Am. But this could be a lot more money."

"We have enough money. Starting over again is not worth it. The grass is always greener with you, Gordon. I'm not kidding: it's time to stop. We've moved enough."

Gordon was silent for a few more minutes, digesting this change in her. He paced around for a while. Eventually, he said he was going to jog over to the West Tisbury Library to use their computer and log onto the Internet, and that he'd be back in time for lunch.

After roast turkey sandwiches on the deck, no special orders or combinations, Gordon told Annie he'd received an email from an old college professor inviting him to be a lecturer at Georgetown, teaching a course on the current state of development in China and Southeast Asia. The professor he would be replacing had been called up to the Clinton administration.

"I always knew you'd be a professor," Annie remarked, leaning across the pasta salad to smooth his silvery hair. "And—wow. Three new job offers between us, all in one day."

Gordon grinned. "I wrote back that I had to discuss it with you, but that I could meet with him on campus next week. So much for San Francisco."

The kids ran down to play with Tashmoo in the sprinkler on the lawn. Annie and Gordon stood up and leaned their elbows on the deck railing to watch their children, both marveling at how much they'd grown since June. Meg climbed into the hammock, and Robbie held it steady while Tashmoo jumped in beside her.

"Well," Gordon said, after a few minutes, "if we're going to stay in Maryland, let's at least get going on the remodel." He kissed her, his mouth tasting salty and delicious.

"Sorry," she said, pulling sideways away from him. "No, thanks. Remodels are too stressful. So what if our house isn't the fanciest one we've ever lived in? It's ours, and everything works well enough. We can fix it up later. Right now, I want to enjoy the kids and focus on this new job I'm hopefully going to get, and focus on you. That's all I can handle. The last thing I need is the upheaval of construction and then the pressure of keeping up with a spanking-new house. Let the kids paint on the walls if they want."

"You can't be serious. With everything so outdated in that place?" His eyes crinkled up in an unpleasant way, and his face contorted into disbelief. "We already got the *home*owner's loan, Annie. We can actually afford it."

"Save the money for college."

He tried to put his arm around her, but she arched away farther.

"You really don't want to move back to California, sweetheart?" he asked. "Your old friends? That salubrious air you used to talk about? No winter?"

"There is probably no city more beautiful than San Francisco, I agree," Annie said slowly, her eyes focused on the grass below. "But it's not ours. It's not our *place* anymore. Middle Road is, and now Sylvan Fell can be, too."

"I always thought the *world* was our place, Annie. Not just one particular spot."

Annie smiled while she considered this. "I love that you feel that way, Gordon, I really do." She turned to look at him. "But it's too overwhelming for me right now. The kids, and you and I, I think, need some roots—at least for a while. To get established."

Rather than look back at her, he stared at the hydrangea and rhododendron bushes. Slowly, he nodded.

"We live near *Washington*, Gordon, as international a city as there is," Annie repeated. "There's an endless amount for us to do there. It's time for us to make our own family home. So—I'm sorry, Gordon. But no more moving. I need you to commit to Sylvan Fell."

Gordon continued to contemplate the field. The cardinal fluttered down to the railing. Annie stood beside her husband, not saying a word. It wasn't her job to fill up every empty space.

It took a while, but Gordon's face and shoulders finally relaxed. "Okay, okay," he said evenly. He turned toward her and drew her in, and this time she didn't resist. "So that's that, I guess." He exhaled slowly. "I commit."

Annie grinned. "Thank you," she said, nestling her head on his chest and hugging him back. "I thought you would. I commit, too."

They decided to take a picnic supper to Lambert's Cove the night before their departure on the ferry, so the kids could hike out to see Split Rock. Annie had double-checked the date earlier in the week with Aunt Faye's nautical chart to make sure it would be low tide and easy for them to wade out. As she packed up the house that day, after Pretti's telephone call, she forced herself not to worry about what may or may not have happened in Hong Kong with Gordon. She had no evidence—she was probably imagining it—things would get straightened out once they returned to Sylvan Fell.

They ate lobster rolls and Chinese chicken salad on the sand below the path, and swam in the glow of the late afternoon. Languid islands of clouds floated across the Atlantic sky, each shaded in parts as if on a topographic map. The days were getting shorter now and the air was starting to smell different, like crisp McIntosh apples.

When the sun began to blaze atop the Elizabeth Islands, they set out down the beach.

It was wonderful, being a family. Annie carried Meg piggyback while Robbie, Lily, and Gordon played a running game of catch, and Tashmoo, at full tilt, ran back and forth between them.

They followed the footprints of that day's beachcombers along the water's edge. At low tide the beach was wide, and it was fun to navigate around the small boulders and swaths of stones while listening to the calls of the seagulls over the water and the whippoorwills above the dunes, to the shore birds settling for the night and the quiet lap of the waves. The clouds, stacked in vibrant shades of tangerine, pink, and yellow, bled into each other before mixing into different, startling combinations. The horizon seemed to change with every bend in the shore, steadily exploding into ever more brilliant color.

As they passed beneath Makonikey Head, they watched an osprey, carrying a fish in its talons, skid into an elaborate nest she'd built for her chicks on a high platform someone had installed. They could see her three fledglings with their tiny mouths agape, their urgent chirps either saying "me first" or "thank you."

In the distance, the Steamship ferry *Islander* was crossing Vineyard Sound.

As if on cue, their red cardinal appeared along the long stretch of sand before Split Rock and kept up beside them, flying from rock to brush to sand.

"That's strange," Gordon said. "Cardinals are woodland birds. They aren't supposed to come down to the beach."

"But this bird is Aunt Faye," Lily said, jogging beside it.

"Aunt Faye? I explained this, remember? The female cardinal is brown, not red."

"Mommy says not to overthink it," Robbie remarked, and Annie and the girls laughed.

The cardinal flew beside them for the remainder of their walk, occasionally soaring up for a minute but mostly darting about their shoulders, keeping them company.

When they at last reached Split Rock, Annie explained about wishing on a pebble and told them how Lindsay had confided that Aunt Faye had placed many of these stones for each one of them.

"We need to thank her for the wishes," Meg said.

"And for letting us come here," Lily added.

"This rock has a great, mysterious history," Annie told them. "It had to travel a long way to make it this far—who knows what it had to endure. Aren't we privileged that it decided to settle on Martha's Vineyard?"

"The rock got here first," Robbie pointed out. "We're lucky

we found *it*."

The cardinal alighted high on the rock, beating its red wings and watching them. Tashmoo led the way toward his friend, wading in first.

"This is amazing," Gordon murmured.

There was no wind that night, and the late-summer water was warm. This time of year they wouldn't be able to see the sun setting through the crack the way Lindsay had described, but it didn't matter.

The sky blazed scarlet, and Lily was the first to place her pebble. "Come see if there's magic in here, Robbie," she called.

Robbie had been asking a lot of questions about the rock and what a glacial erratic was, and he rolled his eyes—but not as far as he sometimes did. He waded out and placed his hands on either side of the fissure, leaning above his little sister. He rested his ear against the rock.

After what seemed a long time listening, he said, with utmost earnestness, "Yes, Lily. This rock is definitely magical ... I can hear it. You're right."

Annie and the girls laughed again.

"The big crack expanded as water got in there, froze in the winter, and melted again in the summer," Annie said. "It's almost as if it has a human heart."

She and Meg, placing their stones, paused to admire the water, swirling as usual in gentle eddies around their ankles.

"See how perfect it is, even though it's all cracked and splotchy? The imperfection is what makes it so magnificent," Annie said. "It's not a fixed, motionless painting. It's real, like us."

On the golden sand, Gordon was watching her. It was taking him a while to get used to this new Annie, and he was the last to wade out.

Finally, carefully wedging his pebble into one of the cracks, Gordon said, "I love this place—and I can feel it, too. There really is some magic here." Then he bent his head and made a long wish.

Standing in the water, the family stood arm in arm in a little arc around Split Rock and their beautiful red cardinal: Lily, Robbie, Gordon, Annie holding Meg, and Tashmoo beside her. Together they gazed across Vineyard Sound to the Elizabeth Islands and watched the sun sink slowly into the ocean. The sky began putting away its palette of pinks and oranges, replacing them with subtle purples and blues.

That's when the cardinal took off, swooping slowly above their heads, wide around the rock and back to shore. They watched her turn and pause, wings flapping gently over the sand, lingering to regard them one last time. Slowly she fluttered up, clearing the brush and dunes, and, under easy sail, vanished into the woods.

Tashmoo's golden eyes held steady as he watched his friend go, and he let out a withering yelp. His long tail dipped between his legs into the water, and then he looked up at Annie.

They stood in the silver stillness like that until it was time to go home, heading back through the long violet light to school and new jobs tomorrow. Naturally, they spotted heart-shaped rocks all over the place.

THE END

ACKNOWLEDGMENTS

That I was able to finish writing this story and actually get to see it become a beautifully designed and bound book will always be, for me, something of a miracle. It was true serendipity and divine intervention that Regula Conzett of Zurich, Switzerland, absconded with an early draft from our kitchen table in California and then somehow persuaded her husband, Jürg Conzett, to publish it. Without their conviction that *Split Rock* needed to be read, I might have died of old age before this book ever made it into anyone's hands. I will never be able to thank them enough.

My love and gratitude go to many people, but particularly to Dianthe and Bob Eisendrath, of Middle Road and Belmont, Mass., for bringing me to Martha's Vineyard in 1978 as a babysitter for their young sons, Noah and Matthew, and for keeping me part of their family. And while I never could have completed this project without the support of my friends and extended family, I am especially grateful to year-round Vineyard resident Ally Reed, for her cheerful patience every time I made us stop to take notes on a bike ride or beach walk, and for running out to check things all over the Island when I texted her questions from afar. I am also grateful to my sister-in-law, Virginia Hipple, who constantly teaches me the meaning of family, and whose shepherding of her book group to the actual Split Rock was blessed with heart-shaped stones, whimsy, and magic; to Susan Vivian Mangold, for telling me about her red cardinal, reading two entire manuscript drafts, and lovingly sharing the joy of my writing and publishing experience; to Tricia Mansur, for keeping me upbeat whenever I started to doubt myself or let the haters get to me; and to Cathie

Carroll, my childhood best friend, whose only comment, as she dropped everything to read the manuscript, was, "Took ya long enough."

I am indebted to all Martha's Vineyard personalities, but especially to John Alley and Primo Lombardi; to the Chilmark EMTs for explaining rescue and recovery techniques; and to the bewitching Island itself—which, as I suppose is obvious from this love letter of a book, has my reverence and everlasting awe.

My appreciation goes forever to my brave, brilliant mother, the late Margaret Reid Hodder, for being proud of me; and to my kind, spirited great-aunt, the late Virginia Clark Hodder Martin Sherrill—the inspiration for Aunt Faye, and also for me. I miss them both every day.

For their steadfast love and for teaching me how to listen, I must thank my two faithful yellow Labrador retrievers: the late, most loyal Sweet Baby James, and the magnificent, noble Tash.

But most of all, I want to thank my family: my husband of more than thirty-two years, Ed, and our extraordinary children, William, Julia, and Katharine—the undisguised inspirations for the fictional Robbie, Lily, and Meg. Shakespeare, as usual, sums up my feelings best:

> *My bounty is as boundless as the sea,*
> *My love as deep; the more I give to thee*
> *The more I have, for both are infinite.*

My inexpressible gratitude goes to my son, William, for answering my formatting-related texts while in class, for his boundless knowledge and perspicacious reader's eye, for finding me the perfect editor and not letting me settle with the wrong agent, and for pointing out, as the very first person to finish reading the very first draft, where the story was supposed to end (which was not where I had it). I am, as well, exceedingly grateful that he found Maren, a daughter-in-law lovelier than I could ever have dared hope for or imagined. I am inexpressibly grateful to my daughter Julia, for insisting I take myself seriously as a writer after so many years as a stay-at-home mom, for putting her own work aside to help me meet deadlines, for painstakingly editing numerous manuscripts and discussing, thousands of times, characters and plot—and without whom, quite simply, my dream of publishing *Split Rock* never would have become a reality. And, for the treasure chest, my inexpressible gratitude goes to my daughter Katharine, for her contagious, inimitable joyful spirit; for bringing me lunch and making us all supper and running interference over two summers so I could finish the first draft, and then the rewrite, in the West Tisbury Library; for her unwavering belief in me and for her uncanny perception, always seeing things no one else ever sees. And lastly, for his abundant love and indulgence in all things, for relocating me to Toronto during two spectacularly snowy winters where I was finally able to write with no distractions, for never minding when I forgot to organize dinner and for always embracing my imagination, for bringing me coffee in the mornings and for patiently listening to chapters and helping me get them right, I thank my wonderful husband, Ed.

It is easier for me to bake a cake to show my love than to talk about it, and the great composer Anton Bruckner, another late bloomer like me, captured my feelings best: *"I cannot find the words to thank you as I would wish, but if there were an organ here, I could show you."*

ABOUT THE AUTHOR

A New Englander transplanted around the world, Holly Hodder Eger has written travel articles and personal commentaries that have appeared in national and local publications. She began *Split Rock* as a short story when her youngest child was in nursery school, put it aside while raising her family and taking care of her ailing parents, picked it up again several years later—and got to see it published the same month her oldest was married and her youngest graduated from college. She and her husband now live on Martha's Vineyard and in Northern California, where she is at work on a new book. *Split Rock* is her first novel.

Made in the USA
Middletown, DE
23 July 2021